PEOPLE OF WATER

MARCUS MARTIN

First paperback edition 2021

Book design by Marcus Martin

ISBN 978-1-913966-06-5 (hardback)

ISBN 978-1-913966-08-9 (paperback)

ISBN 978-1-913966-07-2 (ebook)

www.marcusmartinauthor.com

CHAPTER ONE

KEALA

"Keala, hurry!"

Chief Gaia is yelling at me. We've got twenty minutes to evacuate. Water is sloshing around my calves. People are jostling past me, laden with supplies. I'm carrying a crate of tablets from the school. Fat rain drops are bursting across the screens, but there's no time to cover them.

I trip over my own foot and stumble forwards, dropping the entire load into the water.

"Dammit, Keala!" yells the man behind me.

He barges past, making me duck as his crate swings over my head.

Staggering to my feet, I snatch up the soaking tablets, praying they're water resistant. Malo appears beside me and helps gather the last few, then disappears to help others.

I reach the nearest raft and shove the crate onto the long, flat deck.

The crate disappears down the chain of people desperately loading for the voyage.

Our chief is standing nearby, coordinating the chaos. Her voice is hoarse from shouting.

Malo grabs my arm. "Have they inoculated you?"

"I didn't have time to go."

That's a lie, and we both know it. I'm avoiding the jab because I hate needles.

"Inoculation is non-optional. We're not sailing halfway around the world for you to keel over from some unknown disease as soon as we step ashore. Get the jab now. Run - they're about to leave!"

The only thing I hate more than needles is Malo being right.

I splash my way to the hut where the medics are working. Their seaplane is moored meters away. In the past five years, the distinction between land and water has vanished on our island. For a traditional fishing nation scattered across the Pacific, I can tell you, we Makamesians know a hell of a lot about the Greenland ice sheet.

Black storm clouds are gathering on the horizon. The rafts from the other islands are specks across the open ocean.

One of the two medics hurries out of the hut and wades to the plane. I chase after her.

"Where are you going?"

"You should be on a raft, Miss."

"I need the jab."

"Too late. The cyclone's coming in fast and we gotta leave ASAP. You too."

The woman places her palm against the cockpit door. The plane scans her face and hand and comes online. She taps the controls, prepping the motors and punching in flight settings.

"Please - we need this!"

She curses under her breath. The schematic shows the storm's wrecking their path. Solar planes can fly indefinitely, but they're slow. When you're trying to avoid a storm the size of a continent, and it's banging around the ocean like a ping pong ball, speed is kinda critical.

The woman punches for alternatives, and drums on the dashboard, waiting for the AI to calculate the safest probable route. She's anxious. The comms balloons are useless in storms. You're relying on ancient 4G satellite signals to penetrate the clouds, which makes even simple calculations like this a nightmare.

"Please, Ma'am, I need this vaccine."

"It's not a vaccine, kid."

"But we were told it'll protect us in the new country?"

"It will. Or it should. Look, you need to get to your raft."

The woman rested her medical kit on the nose of the plane. I edge closer and snatch it away.

"Hey, give that back!"

I dart around the plane, out of reach, but she's giving chase.

"Don't open it!"

Too late. I grab a syringe from the kit. Normally my hands would fumble this but they stay true. The needle's thick and sharp, and it's making me queasy. No time to think; the woman's almost at striking distance. I stab myself hard in the arm and squeeze the trigger.

The woman freezes and looks at me in horror. "Are you *insane?* The doses are supposed to be tailored!"

"All I've done is what you refused to do. I saved my life."

She snatches the syringe from me and stares at the empty vial. "No, lady, you may have just ended it."

CHAPTER TWO

LUKE

We've been planning this operation for months. With two hours to go, I get an urgent message from our informant: *There's a problem – meet me ASAP.* We weren't planning to meet at all, let alone in some random back alley. But they're insisting they've got footage they need to handover in person, it's too sensitive to transmit online.

I'm staking out from a grocery store opposite the alleyway. The store robot's about to ask me if I need assistance for the third time, so I make myself look busy. I punch a few digits on the newsstand and wait for it to print me a tabloid.

You should know that I hate this city. Cathedrals of polished glass dominate the streets, interspersed by manicured hedgerows and corporate street art. Inside each office, blood-shot college grads race to out-code each other. This is a war without bullets; not a single shot has been fired in the automation arms race. Just the quiet removal of desk chairs, year on year, as machines take over contract reviews, accounting, marketing, HR; anything that can be learned.

Outside the offices, robots clean the windows, sweep the streets, and drive the buses. Occasionally, a bot breaks down, and a human technician is sent to repair it. You might expect them to savor the work; it's a rare opportunity to deploy millions of years of neurological evolution and versatile problem-solving. But there are ten thousand unemployed people with the same skills, lining up to take such jobs.

The technician's AI supervisor makes a parallel diagnosis of the problem and estimates the repair time. If the worker falls behind on her stats, she'll lose her job. Sorry, "job" is misleading. I mean, she'll be kicked off the app and won't be able to bid for work.

Parasitic ideals, masquerading as progress, stealthily pushing everything good from this world. The city's one giant nest brimming with cuckoo eggs. The sooner I'm done here, the better.

As I watch the alley opposite, my unease grows. Something's not right. Unlicensed couriers usually zip along every backstreet in this city, but this one's completely dead, and I don't see any road works. Counting out my dwindling cash, I cough up for a burner sim. I've got a feeling I'm gonna need a contingency.

Someone's entering the alley. Grabbing my copy of the *Herald,* I head across the street, rolling it tight as I go. That much paper and self-righteous journalism makes for an excellent emergency baton. Plus, it's an easy alibi. In my experience, it's harder to claim you're just doing a crossword when you're clutching an aluminum rod.

I've never seen my informant's face before, but the man's agitation fits the bill. I'm about to enter the alley when a woman approaches from the far end. Ducking to the side, I lean against a parked car, pretending to read my baton, and spy on their encounter.

The pair are of similar height. From their stand-offish posture, they're strangers. An argument breaks out, and it's escalating quickly. The man's running away.

The woman pulls a stun gun and fires into the man's back. He falls to the ground, writhing. A van zooms into the alley and two people jump out wearing plain clothes. They bundle the man into the back, and seconds later, they're gone.

The woman sheathes her pistol and dusts herself down. As I'm processing what's just happened, she sees me. Oh crap. I act casual, folding my paper and taking a few strolls until I'm out of sight of the alleyway, then I run like hell. I'm pushing through a stream of robots and morning commuters, but to my horror she's giving chase.

There's a bus taking on its last passengers and I throw myself onboard. As the doors close, I press further inside the vehicle, burying my face among the crowd. Glancing between bodies I see the woman cursing and dialing on her wrist panel as we pull away.

We drive a few blocks then stop under a bridge, held by a red signal. I'm out and running again. If that woman's a fed, they'll be on the bus by its next stop, strip-searching every last passenger. I gotta keep moving.

As I dash towards the metro, I make a call.

"Hello?"

"Honey, it's me, I'm on a burner."

"Don't call me 'honey'. Wait, are you *running*?"

"The operation's taken a turn, there's no time to explain. I'm gonna be off-grid for a while, I don't know how long."

"You've been gone three months already!"

"Don't do this now – just tell the kids I love them."

I hang up before she can ask questions. Every second we stay connected jeopardizes their safety. I break the phone apart and discard it across several trash cans, then grab the first metro available.

These people are every bit as dangerous as we thought.

CHAPTER THREE

KEALA

There are only two rafts remaining. Fifteen minutes until they launch. After that, our country will officially be deserted.

And yet I'm running as fast as I can *inland*, away from the rafts, towards the flooded main road.

If my parents were awake, they would be yelling at me. But the chief made them board earlier - she wants her best navigators rested ahead of their first night shift.

There's a moped parked by the road. The owner's left the keys in, which makes sense, given that they'll never see it again. I jump on and tear away. Six inches of water sprays out either side of me as I speed down the flooded road.

All around me are signs of the last cyclone we endured. A category one or two will bring down power lines and leave you in the dark for days. A category three will tear the roof off your house and pull entire trees from the ground, blocking the roads for weeks. A four will bring the walls of your house down, while a five will throw trucks over like bowling pins. It will pick up boats from your shore, and hurl them at your homes like missiles, while surging waters turn roads into rivers.

We used to get hit by a category four cyclone once every twenty years.

Last year we got seven.

Two of them were category five.

Sometimes I wake in the dead of night, haunted by the sounds of the storm surge sirens. Memories flash back of huddling in concrete shelters for days on end, while marauding waves ravaged our homes. Rebuilding has always been hard for us as we've never been a rich nation, nor one of great mechanical industry. The Northern and Southern Blocs call our way of life "traditional" – their euphemism for "under-developed". Yet despite their condescension, we were *the* destination for tourists, all of whom were seeking to escape their "advanced" urban cages for a brief spell in our paradise.

That was before the waters rose. In recent years nature has reduced us to a nation of beggars, dependent on the international community. We are being punished for sins that are not ours to bear, and each time we suffer it becomes harder to fight back. How can you rebuild when the water never recedes? How do you farm on fields flooded with seawater? We've raised our schools and factory floors so many times we joked that the ceilings were getting lower. But this is no joke. Our island is a crime scene too vast to ignore, yet no one is standing trial for what is happening here.

I was about to board the raft when I heard two people discussing the veterinary clinic in town. The vet had an allergic reaction to the "vaccine", so has been stuck on the raft, recovering, meaning no one's opened the cages.

Animals aren't allowed on the rafts, so we're being forced to abandon them. But if they're trapped, they'll either starve or drown because of us and I can't let that happen.

I'm the only vehicle on the road, which means I've got a chance. Seven minutes and I'm there. This is gonna be tight, but I can do it.

I dismount and run to the clinic. It's open. Everything's open, obviously. There's no one to lock out anymore. I climb the stairs and hurry to the animal holding rooms. Stacks of cats and dogs, and two lizards, all recovering from treatments, or awaiting new owners. The three dogs howl with excitement at my arrival.

I let the cats out first. They're happy to start from the window ledge and take it from there. I let the reptiles out a similar way and they scarper off across the walls. Last, it's the dogs' turn.

They follow me excitedly downstairs, yapping for treats, wagging their tails, yearning for companionship I can't give.

A solar plane passes overhead. The medics have abandoned the island. It's just us now, the last of the last.

I climb back onto the bike. The electric motor whirs to life, showering the dogs in road water as I pull away. They try to keep pace with the bike, but I quickly burn them off. Their confused barks fade behind me.

I can hear a horn sounding from the coast. That's the five minute warning. I'm not gonna make it. Suddenly the whole venture feels reckless in the extreme. Have I just condemned myself to die alone on this island for the sake of some abandoned pets?

I grip the handle bars and crank up the speed. I'm damned if they maroon me for doing what's right.

A powerful jolt rocks the bike and suddenly the world's spinning. Waterlogged grass cushions my fall, but the impact still hurts like hell.

I'm groaning, checking myself for injury, and cursing whatever invisible obstacle tripped me. The bike's several meters away, half-submerged, and churning up water behind its wheels. I kill the motor, then wedge my back against the fallen saddle in a ski-sit and push it back upright.

Three minutes left.

My hands are shaking from the fall.

I flick the motor but it won't start.

Please, please, please.

I flip the switch repeatedly but the circuit board is shorting out. There's only one choice left.

Run.

The water's like a trip wire across my shins, throwing me off balance and dragging me down. I'm forcing my way through but it's exhausting, there's no way I'll make it like this.

A torrent of white water spills around the bend. There's a shallow water jet ski coming right for me.

Malo!

He pulls up close.

"Get on, quick!"

I cling to his waist as we speed towards the coast.

"What were you thinking?" he yells.

I'm too focused on staying upright to answer him.

A long horn blast rings out from behind the trees, signaling a raft is launching.

We power through the final approach, rounding the tree line and speeding onto the beach, but my raft is hundreds of yards from the shore. Malo sags over the controls, killing our speed.

"They've gone. I'm sorry, Keala."

"What are you talking about? We can still make it!"

"Too risky. You'll have to come on our raft."

"But my parents-"

"We'll radio them to let them know you're safe."

Malo pulls up beside the sole remaining raft. Gaia, our chief, is standing on the deck, looking seriously pissed off.

"What were you *thinking* Malo?"

"I had to-"

"Save your girlfriend?"

"She's not my-"

"We've got a hundred souls on board and a massive cyclone heading this way. These are the last two rafts and you've endangered all of us for the sake of one person!"

"You would've abandoned Keala?"

"Running inland was her choice. Going after her was yours. If the storm catches us now, it will be your people who pay the price. You have much to learn about leadership, my son. I truly hope your judgement improves at sea. Get us out of here fast, Captain."

Malo's face contorts with frustration. He hurries to the bridge.

"My son will not make this mistake again. Nor will you."

I open my mouth to explain myself, but Gaia silences me with a glare. I bow my head.

"No, Chief."

"Good. Now leave me."

I cross the long open deck as the motors rev. The horn blasts out and we reverse away from the shore. As I reach the cabin steps I turn for one last look and see Gaia, standing alone, staring at our island as it shrinks from view.

You know the saying "no expense spared?" The UN spared a lot of expense. They built the rafts and sailed them to us with great fanfare. For a day or two we were international headline news. Reporters were crawling around the island like crabs. They did features inside the cabins, on the decks, on the shore, you name it. Of course, the rafts look a lot more accommodating when they're empty. Throw in a hundred people, a screaming baby or two, a village's worth of essential belongings, food rations, and a rolling ocean, and it's a very different picture.

The rafts were designed specifically for our islands; using the sea bed as a natural dock. The continental shelf slopes gently from our island, then drops sharply. The rafts mirror this design, with a long broad bow, and a deep stern. Sort of like an inverted baseball cap, with a peak on either end. It's built for functionality rather than comfort. The idea is that we'll sail for three days, then dismantle the raft at our new home. Apparently it pieces together into small fishing vessels and modular homes.

Right now the raft is sailing at full capacity, plus one. That one being me. Somehow everyone seems to know I'm not supposed to be on board, and their silence and glares make it clear I'm not welcome. I try the first three levels, searching for a spare bunk, but every dorm is rammed. Only when I reach the final level does someone take pity on me and offer me their blanket and pillow.

Not their bunk, though.

Which is why I find myself alone in the cramped electrical power room on level three. It's a tight space, filled with floor-to-ceiling humming metal panels, and barely enough room in the short aisle for a person to lie down.

I'm feeling dazed. My arm's tingling where I injected myself. I run a hand over the band aid and gasp. It's hypersensitive. I'm about to investigate further when the compartment door slides open.

I look up, startled. Gaia's standing in the threshold.

"What in heavens name are you doing in here?"

I dip my head and hastily brush the tears off on my shoulders. "Nothing, just, uh."

"Guess I'm not the only one looking for a moment's privacy on this giant sardine tin." She sees the bedding. "Wait, is this where you're sleeping?"

"I'm supposed to be on the other raft, and there are no spare bunks on this one. I asked the night shifters if we could hot bed but they said what everyone else said: they're not sharing with a *poino*."

"Don't use that word."

"They did."

"Then they shouldn't have. I'll speak to them, no one should treat you that way. 'Cursed' is an archaic interpretation of our laws. Our ancestors had logic and rationality, but we have science. We're entitled to interpret their words for our time."

"Changing the words doesn't change the facts. I'm a failure."

Gaia sits beside me and places an arm around me. I wince as she squeezes my tender skin.

"You think you're the only one who feels like a failure? Keala, our people have called this island home for hundreds of years, yet it's under my watch that we're being forced to leave."

"But you did everything you could? You lobbied the UN for years, all those trips to mainland nations, you couldn't have done more."

"And yet I failed."

I've never heard her sound so defeated.

"When we reach our new country I intend to step down as chief. Our ancestors tasked me with leading our people, and I did not succeed. A new home requires new thinking."

"Chief, you can't step down, we need you! And Malo's not ready."

"I concede my son has much to learn, but so did I when I became chief."

Gaia takes my hand and looks me in the eye.

"Which is why I know he needs space to grow."

"What are you saying?"

"You know what I'm saying, Keala. A new chief cannot afford distractions when lives are at stake."

"I'm not a 'distraction', we barely spend time together."

"Yet he abandoned everyone aboard this raft to find you."

"We're friends, that's all, I-"

"Good. Then as his friend, I'm sure you will do what's best for him."

She stands and heads for the door.

"You are the only one who knows of my abdication. I hope I can trust you to keep that a secret. We don't want to concern people unduly, they're dealing with enough as it is."

As she reaches the door, I blurt out a concern.

"Malo knows how to sail this thing, right?"

"He spent three weeks in the simulator they sent."

"You think that's enough?"

"I wouldn't be on board if I didn't."

The door closes behind her.

The tingling in my arm is getting worse. I peel back the band aid to see the skin below, and my heart freezes. In place of the tiny needle prick is a huge darkened circle of crusty, dead-looking flesh.

And it's spreading.

CHAPTER FOUR

LUKE

I've made it across town, having shaken off my informant's kidnappers for the time being. But the operation's due to start in minutes, meaning I gotta get this transaction done fast. Sweating like a pig on a treadmill, I enter a second-hand hardware store.

The big South Asian guy behind the counter nods me through without a smile. A homeless woman is standing before him; trying to trade in a high spec phone for cash. The store is sweltering. All these electronics and they can't get a working AC? Another reason to hate this city. I peel off my blazer and make for the back.

A standing fan shifts warm air along a narrow corridor. At the far end, a fire extinguisher is propping open a side door. I knock and a teenager looks up from behind a desk. He can't be more than a third of my age, tops. He taps a cigarette into a brimming ash tray and beckons me forwards. He's got the air of someone who's not just been around the block, so much as fully *owns* it. Which, in fairness, he does.

These people do things weird, passwords in particular. I

stick my plastic bag on the table. "You got the thing? I'm kinda in a hurry."

The kid holds up a hand and takes an ostentatious drag on his cigarette. The stale, smoggy air is churning my stomach. He exhales and rifles through my offering.

"It's all there," I add.

The kid pulls a lime from the bag and sniffs it. He cracks a smile and tosses it up in the air, then catches it mid-drop.

"OK, you good," he says.

See what I mean? Passwords. Weird.

He jabs his cigarette at me like we're old friends reminiscing about good times. Has this kid ever had good times? This dank windowless cubicle seems like a poor substitute for high school, and that's coming from someone who knows the local high schools. What kinda parent leaves their kid to run this back alley outfit? I know, I know, who am I to judge? I'm the worst dad in the world, three years running - if you ask my kids, which you shouldn't.

Dammit, I'm getting distracted by my kids' situation. And this kid's situation. And the general awfulness of life.

I need to stay on track. I just transferred these people an eye-watering amount of crypto. It can't be for nothing.

The kid unlocks a vault behind him. He's fast, so I don't see what's in it, but he turns back around with a booklet and chucks it down on the table like he's tipping a lousy waiter. I frown at him, because that's nuts, right? I'm the customer here. Then I remember, there's no one you can complain to in this business. It ain't like I'm gonna be leaving a review online.

I snatch the booklet and thumb through to the photo page. There it is, my new ID. The photo is deeply unflattering. It makes me look like a haggard, short-sighted, middle-aged divorcee. Which is to say, it's accurate.

I hate photos.

"All right, then. I'll be seeing you."

"Wait," he replies.

He takes a jar from his desk and pops the lid.

"You want candy? For Chang's loyal customer."

Inside is a pile of confectionery wrapped in ornate twisted paper. It looks old school, like the Amoretti my grandparents used to give us on our birthdays. I'm about to dive in for some nostalgia, then my brain kicks in.

"Is this actually candy?"

"It taste very good."

"Sure, but I'm asking if it's synth narcotics."

The kid fixes me with a grin. "It taste veeeeery good," he says, with a wink.

"I'll pass."

The new class of synths are the most addictive yet and I have no desire to become a "loyal" customer here. I head out of the office but the kid calls after me.

"Ten percent discount if you refer friend to Chang!"

Lunatic. How have they not been raided by the feds? I slip the fake ID into my blazer and make for the exit. The big guy behind the counter points at my wrist.

"How much for watch?"

"It's not for sale."

The last thing I'm gonna do is sell my engagement gift. I'm not saying I *won't* ever sell it. I'm just saying I'll sell it last. Right now I'm still holding out for a glorious cast reunion. Like a hit TV show that gets canceled because the original writer leaves, then the rest of the show loses its path, so it takes a ten year hiatus, until everyone realizes none of them are getting acting jobs anywhere else, and that their best plan is to try a reboot and hope audiences are as desperate for the heyday as they are.

That's my plan. That and finding better metaphors for my failed marriage.

Paused marriage.

Evolving marriage?

My therapist insists I should avoid terms that apportion blame or reinforce feelings of failure. She's right.

My marriage is a roaring success.

It's an exemplar.

We've never been happier.

I am a role model to all.

Dad of the year.

A bastion of old fashioned family values.

I'm-

Running late. Oh crap, my watch is chiming. It's taken months to get this meeting set up, I *cannot* miss it. I run into the street and hail a cab. None of them stop because I'm not using an app. Maybe I *should* sell this damned watch. I was a stupid romantic back then - I thought it was profound, getting an analogue wrist watch when the rest of the world was using implanted chips and augmented reality. Like I was above them all, choosing to opt out of the rat race.

I can't switch to my old phone because it's linked to my old ID. I can't risk there being any trace of my movements. God dammit, this is a bad start. I'm gonna have to get the stinking free public bus *again*. Ugh. Beggars, choosers, and all that.

"Don't I know you?"

Four words you never wanna hear on public transport. I fumble for my ear phones, but they're buried in my pocket. The homeless woman is weaving her way towards me.

"We was shopping together, remember?" she continues. "Say, can you lend me some coin?"

I try to ignore her. Mistake.

"Hey, I'm talking to you!"

Oh god, she's one of those. Zero inhibitions. Zero to lose. People are looking at us. I need her to shut up.

"Suit man, you deaf or something?"

She's right by me now. She can sense my discomfort. I can smell her breath, and I'll level with you, it's not exactly pine fresh.

"I said lend me some coin, Mister. Or you wanna talk more about our shopping trip?"

This woman deserves more credit than I gave her; she's not begging, she's selling. She knows exactly what sort of deals go on in that hardware store. I bet she lingers by the exit, waiting for people like me to leave. I'm today's product; she's about to sell me back my own privacy.

I can't stand being extorted. But I also can't risk being discovered. She knows it as well as I do; only desperate people visit Chang's office. She also knows his clients can't risk everything being derailed by one mouthy hustler. I bite my tongue and give her several notes.

I've been relying heavily on cash these past few weeks as I let my old identity vanish. It's the simplest way to avoid transactions linking you to other people. Can you believe the government made cash a civil right? People worried that an exclusively digital currency would turn us into a big brother state. But that pretty much happened anyway, and now the only people using cash are criminals. So now we have a paper-based currency enshrined in law which does nothing else but keep our thriving black market alive.

I lobbied against it, back in the day.

Now I'm on the other side of the fence.

The homeless woman disappears with a satisfied smile. I keep my head down until the bus drops me off a few blocks from the facility. I walk the rest of the way, just in case anyone on board is keeping tabs on me. You never know who's watching.

I check my watch; four minutes to go. That's just enough time. I swing into a nearby cafe and order a coffee. I've got no intention of drinking it, I just need to be sure my new identity is working. The digital payment goes through without a hitch. That's an encouraging start. I feign an incoming phone call and step out of the cafe, then head to an ATM on the corner and check my balance. Who knew? Semi-honest thieves. The package included transferring part of my funds into several accounts under my new name. I expected them to help themselves to half, if not all of it, but the majority is there, minus around twenty percent. All things considered, I've come out in good shape.

I scroll through my statement on the ATM; there's an extensive list of convincing and mundane transactions in the account going back years. Impressive. I snatch the card and head across the road. Time for the acid test.

I swing on my blazer and tighten my tie, then approach the nondescript office building. The bland, coffee-colored glass walls and absence of any signage do an excellent job of anonymizing the space. You could walk by this building for years without noticing it. Hell, the first time I came looking I had to make several passes before I spotted it.

I hit the buzzer. It makes no sound, but after a second the door swings open. I step inside and feel the caress of cool climate-controlled air. My blazer no longer feels like a torturous act of posterity, so much as an essential piece of insulation against the arctic chill.

The ground floor comprises a long sandstone corridor lined by opaque, coffee glass walls.

"Hello?" I call out.

The elevator opens of its own accord and seems to invite me inside. This place definitely has an evil-lair vibe. But this isn't the abode of a maverick billionaire, or scheming rogue agent. This is the invisible epicenter of something much bigger than one renegade.

There are no numbers in the elevator, so I have no idea what floor they're taking me to. At some point the doors re-open onto a transformed landscape. Gleaming white vinyl and chrome, it's like a brand new hospital. Silhouettes of people at desks and workstations shift behind the frosted glass walls.

A holographic assistant flickers into view before me.

"Good morning. Please place your primary ID on the scanner."

I place my freshly minted ID on the desk and wait while the hologram flickers.

"Welcome, Dr. Ragazzi. Please proceed to the interview room."

Oh dayyyyuummm, that's what I'm talking about! Definite twinge down below. I've never been called doctor before, but I'm instantly hooked. I feel so powerful, so *respectable*. Note to self: update dating profile to say "Dr." first thing tonight. Goodbyeeee regular old Mr. Floppydick, helloooo Dr. Libido in the lab coat.

A door opens beside me, revealing an intimate room with three chairs, a round table, and a jug of water in the middle. I take a seat inside and wait. A middle-aged woman and man enter through the door opposite. Both are wearing suits and lab coats.

She's pale, with neat, side-parted white hair that sits

two inches above her shoulders. She has piercing green eyes, deep red lipstick, and a wrinkled brow that looks like it accepted scowling as its default a long time ago. I extend a handshake. She takes it. I turn to the man. He has a bulbous nose, and a slight double chin, although he's not fat by any means. His light brown head is mostly bald, save for a strip of silvery hair above each ear. I offer him my hand, but he places a palm across his chest and bows his head instead.

"Don't take it badly, Pierre can be something of a germophobe, he goes through phases. It's common among paranoid minds. It makes him superbly suited to being our Head of Biosecurity, among other things," says the woman, taking a seat across from me. "Your résumé makes for impressive reading."

I swallow, nervously, and brace for them dissecting my cover story.

"You had a scholarship at MIT?"

"Yes Ma'am."

"But you didn't finish your degree?"

"No, Ma'am. I abandoned it to run a start-up with a friend. It didn't work out. We gave it eight years, though. Which is seven more than it deserved."

"You didn't go back to college?"

"The company had amassed a lot of debt, so college wasn't an option. Plus scholarship bodies tend not to give you a second go if you don't complete the first shot they give you. That was a tough thing to learn. I went into the pharmaceutical sector instead and began work as a lab assistant. It was steady money, and it was a space to continue developing my biomedical skills."

"You did that for five years before becoming a junior researcher, then senior researcher, then..."

She takes a moment to thumb through another twenty-five years of CV. "It says here you're single? No kids?"

"I didn't think companies could ask that sort of thing?"

"We aren't like most companies, Dr. Ragazzi."

Her colleague, the germophobe, leans back in his chair and taps something into his tablet. He shows it to the woman, who nods in approval.

"What's your answer?" she continues.

"Uh, no kids. No partner," I reply.

"Why not?"

"I guess I'm OK being alone. Family life's never held big appeal for me."

That bit is true. Or at least it used to be.

"Good. The work we do is extremely sensitive. We prefer candidates without... complications."

No kidding. She's gonna love me...

The woman glances through my CV some more, then sets her tablet down on the table.

"If I asked you to transfer a set of chromosomes from a sterile mosquito into a fertile one, to produce purely male off-spring, what would you say?"

"I presume this is about malaria? It's not a complex procedure. But if you want to eradicate the mosquito population, that's a crude way of doing it."

"You have concerns over their release into the wild?"

"No, I have no sentimental attachment to being bitten. I merely think there's a more efficient way to achieve the same effect. Your method requires the modified mosquitoes to be more successful at mating than their XX-enabled peers. Ideally, you want lateral transfer of the mutation, which is better done through the food chain."

"So you would genetically modify the mosquitoes' food? By injecting livestock? People?"

"It would be simpler to target the base of the food chain; wild grasses, cereal crops. That will allow the mutation to proliferate up and across the food chain, maximizing the impact on wild mosquito populations within a single harvest cycle. If we could administer the altered genome through agricultural fertilizers, that would represent the best chance of long-term success. Again, this is all assuming eradicating mosquitoes is your aim. If you want to wipe out malaria, I would cut out the middle man and focus on giving humans genetic resistance to the disease."

The woman scrutinizes me for a moment then moves on.

"Why are you applying to work here? It seems like a backwards step in your career."

"Can I be honest? I miss practical work. Secondary research is tedious and I want to get my hands dirty again. Sorry, I mean get my hands surgically scrubbed again."

I give the germophobe a wink, but he retracts his chin into his neck like I've just let rip.

"What do you know of our work here?" asks the woman.

"Not much. I know it's something to do with human resilience, but my contact didn't go into more detail than that."

"Ah, yes, your referral. Dr. Robins. Remind me how you two met?"

My mind is blank. The room's getting brighter and my pulse is rocketing. My throat's drying out as panic sets in.

"Uh," I stall.

Think, think, come on, I know this. I learned this.

"Dr. Robins and I were..."

Come on brain, three months of work. I'm counting on you right now.

"We met at a conference. There were drinks after the last talk, you know how these events are, and I went along with my former colleague, Dr. Patel. We bumped into Simone, sorry, *Dr. Robins*, and it turned out they were friends. My hankering for a career change came up, and Simone said your facility needed biomedical lab assistants. I put my application in that same night."

I smile nervously, then fold my hands and let my face fall back to neutral. The two interviewers are inscrutable. Was that too much detail? Should I have left it at "We met at a conference"? Did it sound too rehearsed? You don't want to get on the wrong side of these people, this place is a black spot. They've scrubbed it from all the usual maps and directories. Even the utility companies are circumspect about its existence. This place is a shadow. Things vanish in shadows. Secrets. Places. People.

The woman turns to her colleague and raises an eyebrow. He nods, and they stand.

"Dr. Ragazzi, please come with us."

CHAPTER FIVE

KEALA

In two hours the infection on my arm has doubled in size. If anyone sees it, they'll throw me overboard in a heartbeat. Malo would try to stop them, and Gaia would overrule him.

It all goes back to the ritual five years ago. Sailing and navigating by the stars are two sacred traditions in my community. They go back centuries to the first ancestors who settled on our islands. On the spring equinox of their fourteenth year, every child must pass the ritual and prove they are "of the ocean farers".

Everyone has to pass three key ancestral tests: swimming, canoeing, and navigating. I've always been a strong swimmer. Every year there's a contest to swim around our island and between all the tiny, uninhabited atolls orbiting it. We call it "the spider's swim", because the route looks like you're spinning a web. It's a mammoth feat of endurance, and the fastest time on record is ten hours, set by Malo himself. But guess who's the women's champion, two years running? This girl right here.

Naturally, then, the swimming part of the ritual didn't

bother me, and nor did the canoeing, which I'm also pretty great at. But our ancestors were a hard lot to please; they made the ritual so that it required both physical excellence and cognitive strength. They made navigation part of the challenge; proof that you are truly one of them because you can *think* like one of them.

That's the rub. I suck at navigation and everyone knows it; a navigator's brain has to work in very specific ways and mine refuses. Remembering the name and path of every constellation in the southern hemisphere? Forget it.

Literally.

The best way I can describe it is like having a limp in my brain; only being able to focus on one thing for a few seconds before its details blur into erroneous patterns with whatever else is going on.

My parents watched me struggle through school. Small island means if you're bottom of the class, that's how people see you forever. I was the slowest reader, my handwriting sucked, I was terrible at math, and I was clumsy. Remembering basic instructions was like climbing a mountain. The only skill I had was making jokes, which people found cute when I was a child. Now that I'm an adult, they don't even smile at me.

My parents did everything they could to get my grades up, but nothing worked. After years of extra study, arguments, and tears, they gave up like everyone else. At least they loved me. But that love was contingent on me achieving the cornerstone of respectability; I had to pass the ancestral ritual.

Every night for a year we stayed up late and studied the stars. Practice, practice, practice, until finally my chaotic, tangled brain recognized the patterns. Once I learned to ignore the traditional shapes and create my own monikers for the constellations, things became easier. I just had to remember to use their proper names when describing them to others, which I could manage, albeit with a slight delay.

I'll never forget the first night I canoed solo. It was terrifying. The ocean was a flat inky black expanse. My mother pushed me out to sea and told me she believed in me. So great was her belief that she wasn't following in the safety canoe this time. I had to paddle to our sister island, a journey of at least six hours, with nothing but the stars for company.

It was the longest night of my life. Paddling. Stopping. Checking. Crying. Repeating the cycle hundreds of times as fatigue and panic clouded my mind.

Hours had passed with no sign of the island. I should have been between the dolphin and the palm constellations, but the current kept turning my canoe towards the swordfish. I reoriented myself and paddled as hard as I could to stay on course. As the sun crept over the horizon, a fresh wave of panic took hold; I'd paddled all night and there was no land in sight.

The awfulness of that night was nothing compared to the day that followed. Adrift, at sea, with no water, no food, and no way of contacting anyone, I languished in the scorching sun. My thin paddle was the only source of shade. The salt water would cool me down, only to dry out and crack my lips. I thought I would die there, alone, and disgraced.

When the rescue boat found me, it was Malo who lifted me out of the canoe. He would have been around seventeen then. He'd volunteered to be part of the search mission. Gaia was at the helm, looking relieved and weary. When we got back to shore, my parents were overwhelmed by guilt. I remember them clinging to me and sobbing as they hugged me; I could barely understand their words for the groveling apologies and wailing regret. They insisted it was their fault, their mistake, and yet all I could feel was shame. The people who loved me above all else had believed in me. So great was their belief that they had sent me to sea alone; as their own parents had done, and their ancestors before that.

And I had failed them.

There was a price to pay, of course. My parents had to reimburse the neighboring islands for the fuel they'd used in the rescue, which took them months to pay off in kind. When it came to my ritual, I refused to take part; I was only going to get lost, and I didn't want to endanger people through a second search mission. Besides, they might not find me a second time. Or they might not even try.

Refusing the ritual isn't something people do. I was the first in living memory, and my choice was met with disgust. It cemented my status as an outsider, as a parasite. I went through high school with that label. I came out the other side isolated and unqualified. I'm hard working, but clumsy. The only people who would hire me were my parents. I helped in their shop. Loading and unloading. Cleaning. Nothing that entailed responsibility or trust.

It only seems fitting that, having been branded a parasite since childhood, I find myself stowed away on a raft with the same people who've stigmatized me for so long.

I tilt my arm under the harsh strip lights above me. The skin at the epicenter is regaining its color, but it looks shinier than normal, and feels hard to the touch. Meanwhile, all around it, concentric rings of bumpy, darkened skin are spreading across my arm like ripples across a pond.

It hurts like crazy, but to seek help now would spell

death. I have to hide; confine myself to isolation until we make landfall.

My only hope is that someone on the new land can help me, but that's three days away. As the tingling spreads to my wrist, a terrifying thought sweeps over me.

I might not last that long.

A sharp noise catches my attention. Creaking. There it is again, but louder this time, like a metallic groan.

Several sharp clangs ring out from the end of the aisle.

I stagger to my feet.

The metal casing is caving in.

A tiny stream of water spurts through a seam in the welding. The creaking grows louder. Several more jets of water burst through; they're getting thicker.

I hurtle into the corridor and yell for help.

"Call Malo! We're taking on water!"

The two lines of people waiting for the toilet and the shower stare at me in disbelief. For a moment, no one knows what to do.

A tremendous creak echoes around the hull.

The deck lurches to the side.

People are thrown off balance, prompting cries of fright as they collide with each other. An almighty clang sounds. Water surges out of the electrical room.

The people's cries turned to screams. Everyone is rushing for the ladder, scrambling to get out of the rising water.

To my horror, more water cascades down from the hatch above, drenching the people climbing the ladder. We're being submerged from all angles.

A fresh surge knocks me off balance, sweeping me into the wall. I look at the ladder in despair; the water's rising too fast. There's no way everyone can make it.

An emergency tone rings out. Malo's voice sounds over the intercom. "All hands brace for impact!"

I grab a handrail just in time. A tremendous impact crunches through the raft. The whole vessel shudders violently. We've hit the seabed and we're scraping along it.

With a jolt, we come to a stop.

The water is up to my belly button and rising fast.

An emergency alarm sounds seven times, followed by an automated announcement: *Abandon ship. This is not a drill.*

People call out to their loved ones.

The raft lists to the side. People on the ladder are thrown sideways and left dangling. Someone falls through a hatch from the deck above, landing on the crowd below with a splash. The panicked scrambling for the ladder intensifies. Neighbors are pulling each other away, desperately trying to get a foothold. There are no hands of rescue coming from the decks above, just a torrent of sea water.

It's up to my chest now. We need to reach the top deck to escape, but we're four levels down. There's no way we'll make it. The hand rail is keeping me anchored against the bodies and the water, but I'll soon have to let go to keep breathing.

Look at the porthole beside me. The metal frame has become deformed. The glass disc is off center. Water is seeping through the gap.

"Somebody help me!" I cry.

No one listens. They're too busy clambering and slipping over each other, trying to escape.

I grab a rail overhead and haul myself up above the flood line. I kick the window hard. The glass scrapes against the frame. More water gushes in. I kick harder. I can feel the disc shifting, inch by inch. With a screech, water pressure jettisons the glass disc from its frame, hurling it against the far wall.

Water pours in. The level is rising even faster now.

"Everybody, this way, we have to swim to the surface!"

I shout several times, but only a handful of people pay any attention.

A teenage girl wades over in a panic. Her forehead is bleeding. She looks dazed. I grab her shoulders and shake her into action.

"This is the only way. You can do this. Follow me, quick!"

I take a deep breath, grab hold of the frame with both hands, and pull myself through the porthole. The rocky seabed is below us. Barely a dozen meters away the water darkens into blackness. The raft is resting on an oceanic cliff edge. Its lights are flickering in the water.

I kick for the surface but the current has me in its clutch. I'm being swept towards the raft's rotor blades.

I kick and pull with all my strength. I can feel the air draining from my lungs as I stretch for the surface.

My head breaks through the water and I gasp for air. All around me people are bobbing in the water, bearing looks of panic and despair. We've run aground on the rocky shore of a tiny deserted atoll. The stern of the raft is twisted. People are scrambling across the raised edge to escape.

Beside me an old woman is struggling in the water, spluttering for help. I dash across. Grabbing her by the chin, I tow her to the shallows then drag her to the shore. Leaving her to recover, I rush back into the water. I'm searching for the teenage girl who followed me out of the raft. She's nowhere to be seen.

I take a deep breath and dive back into the churning water. The ocean is cloudy with sand stirred up by our collision. I can just about discern the markings I need. I drag myself down, avoiding the glitching propeller blades, and haul myself through the porthole. The level is entirely flooded now. Dozens of bodies float against the corridor ceiling, their limbs dangling down like table legs.

The girl isn't among them.

I can feel my air running out. I have to make a split second decision. With a surge of adrenaline, I pull myself inside the flooded compartment and swim for the hatch to the level above. There's an air bubble trapped on one elevated side of the corridor. I swim to it and break the surface, gasping for breath. I wipe my eyes clear and look at the panicked girl opposite me, clinging to the same overhead railing.

"You can't stay here. Follow me and swim for it. We can make it to the surface, I promise you. Trust me."

She shakes her head, terrified, and buries her eyes against her arms. I grab her hair firmly and pull her face up to meet mine. The water around us bubbles as it squeezes the remaining air from the cabin.

"If you stay here, you'll die. We're going now. Follow me, and no matter what, just keep going. It's about sixty seconds to the surface. We have to swim downwards first, but there's a way out through the porthole. From there, you've gotta swim up. Avoid the propellers and aim for the sunlight. Let's go."

She gives me a wide-eyed nod.

We fill our lungs and dive into the water. I try to swim efficiently and not waste energy on panic, but it's hard.

Bodies are clogging the hatch. I push them aside, clearing a way through, and we descend to the lowest level. I make a beeline for the porthole. I grab the girl and push her through first, then follow.

I'm kicking for the surface.

I've overtaken her.

She's suspended in the water, limp; being dragged towards the glitching rotor blades.

I can feel the last air draining from my lungs.

I double back and grab her, then kick for the surface as hard as I can.

I breach the surface with an excruciating gasp. I drag her onto shore, panting, and calling for help. People on the land fall beside her and administer aid, while I collapse onto the sand, spluttering to catch my breath.

More bodies are rising to the surface, but few of them are moving. People are screaming as they scour the land and dive back into the water, searching for missing loved ones. Gaia is on the shore coordinating first aiders, but she looks harrowed. Malo is on the long tilted bow, hauling people out of the bridge, clearing space for those trapped below, vying for a rung on the ladder.

The girl I rescued is breathing again, but the people attending her have stepped back in alarm. They're arguing over something they've spotted. Something on her arm, where a band aid used to be. An infected, black ring of skin.

CHAPTER SIX

LUKE

I know what you're thinking: I've blown my cover story at the first hurdle and now I'm cooked. I fear the same as I follow my starchy interviewers into the bowels of the coffeepot. That's what I've nicknamed this place, by the way, but I reserve the right to change it.

The two interviewers still haven't introduced themselves. All I know is that he's called Pierre, and is in charge of bio security, and that she's the director. Not that she's admitted it yet.

They lead me into a room with four doors arranged along a semi-circle. In the center is a bank of four massive monitors. The director invites me to take the big swivel seat in front of the array. She turns the bank of screens on, while Pierre disappears through a doorway on the left. Seconds later he shows up on a monitor, in a lab of sorts. He delivers a perfunctory wave to the camera and announces he's about to set up a task I must replicate.

He approaches his test subject; a chimpanzee with electrodes drilled into its skull. Judging by its subdued posture, I'm guessing the bowl of nuts it's been given is inadequate compensation for its brain being split open.

I knew this sorta stuff would be on the cards. It used to be how we tested medicines, back in my grandparents' day, before we had advanced computer modelling and synthetic tissue. Ethical guidelines have tightened now, especially since the discovery of the universal sentience spectrum. Yet here I am, staring at a caged chimp with a cracked skull.

Whatever pays the bills, right?

The other screens are a different kind of grim. A tank brimming with hundreds of speckled, gray fish, all crammed together. The camera is embedded inside the tank, giving an unnerving, fifty inch display of their gaping mouths and bulging eyes. As I watch, the color of the water changes. A red chemical is being flushed through the tank. Judging by the blurry contours, it looks hot. Last time I checked, arctic salmon aren't huge fans of being boiled alive. Within seconds, the stream of hot red liquid vanishes. The water clears, and a mass of tiny, dead yellow parasites detach from the fish's scales and rise to the surface like inverted dandruff. A couple of salmon seem to have bitten the dust too, but most of the shoal survived.

Next to this bizarre aquarium feed is another monitor. On this one, I'm looking at an array of rats on intravenous drips. Yeah, it's weird. They appear to be connected in serial, like something is being successively filtered through all of them. I'll level with you, the rats don't look great for it. The further along the line you go, the more patchy the fur and scrawny the bodies become. The one at the end of the line looks like a pile of matchsticks.

I turn to the fourth screen but it's blank. The director taps it several times in frustration. She curses under her breath then makes a clipped apology and marches away.

"Stay here, I'll be back in a moment. Damned feed."

She departs through a doorway on the right. I recline in the chair and look at the three functional screens before me. My eyes flit between the fish channel and the rats, until something on the first screen catches my attention.

Pierre is dragging a large tub into the middle of the floor. He tips several buckets of ice into it, then adds a few chemicals I can't make out. The chimp is watching all this. It recoils in its cage, figuring that what's coming next ain't gonna be pleasant. Pierre sets a timer on the side, then lifts a long pole from the wall. He opens the chimp's cage and orders the animal out. The chimp recoils further, curling up into a ball. The metal screws protruding from its head scratch against the edges of the cage. Pierre bangs the pole on the side of the cage and shouts. The chimp scurries out, afraid, and cowers on the floor. Pierre taps the edge of the ice tub twice with his pole. He points from the chimp to the ice bath and waits. The chimp shuffles away. Pierre repeats his motion more aggressively. Still the chimp retreats. Losing patience, Pierre marches over to the chimp. He hits a button and a blue spark shoots across the tip of the pole; it's a long cattle prod.

He lunges forward with the electrifying pole but the chimp rolls aside. With Pierre off-balance, the chimp seizes his arm and bites down hard with its sharp fangs. Pierre screams in pain and drops the cattle prod. The chimp throws him to the side like a rag doll.

At this point I'm standing up, watching in horror. My eyes are glued to the screen. The chimp is shuffling towards Pierre's crumpled body. It screeches and flails but Pierre doesn't move. The chimp picks up the cattle prod and presses the button. The electric spark at the tip startles it. It drops the device and leaps away, screeching. Pierre stirs from the corner. He raises his head and realizes what's happened. He sees the cattle prod on the floor, but it's out of reach. The chimp sees he's awake and the pair lock eyes. The chimp pounds the ground then bounds towards Pierre. It grabs his leg and drags him towards the ice tub.

"Help! Somebody help!" I cry.

I'm slamming the defunct monitor, like that might alert the woman somehow, but no one responds to my cries. Pierre's screaming for help as the chimp drags him towards the ice bath. There's nothing else that can be done. I rush for the left-hand door and dart inside.

Instant regret.

The chimp is way bigger than it seemed on the monitor. Its body is pure muscle. It's got Pierre to the edge of the tub. He's unconscious now, so I'm thinking he's been hit or thrown again in the few seconds I didn't see.

The chimp spots me and freezes. It drops Pierre and screeches at me. It bares its teeth and pounds the ground. I cast my eyes around the room but there's no panic button on the wall or anything. This has gotta be the worst designed lab in the world. Sensing my indecision, the chimp grabs Pierre again and hauls him over the ice.

It's now or never.

I snatch up the cattle prod and turn it on the chimp. I'm advancing like a soldier with a bayonet, sweating buckets. Never in my life have I been this close to a wild creature, let alone one this pissed off.

I test the button and the prod lets out an electrical spark. The chimp drops Pierre with a screech and flinches. The sound alone scares it. Thank god, because that's all I've got. I'm sure as hell not making the same mistake Pierre did. I keep my distance. I have no intention of lunging at this animal, but I need it to back up.

I edge forwards. The chimp shuffles back. It bares its teeth. Damn those things are big. I glance at Pierre's shredded forearm. I really don't wanna end up like that.

"Can I get some help in here?"

Still no one. It's me and the chimp. God damn this place.

I edge forwards again. The chimp holds its ground, screeching. I tap the button, and it leaps back from the spark. I look it in the eye and nod to its cage. The creature stares right back at me, with a face contorted in rage. I nod again, and mutter something pathetic like "Come on, buddy, play nice."

At this point I'm actually relieved the chimp doesn't speak English. It gives me a little more time to come up with something cooler. Maybe something about monkey business. I'll make a note to work on it.

Inch by inch, I coerce the muscular primate back into its cage. I go to slam its door, but the chimp gets there first. It pulls the cage shut and clips the padlock in place. It retreats into the corner, quivering.

I rush to the injured scientist and fall to my knees, calling out, trying to rouse him. I reach for his bloodied arm, about to bandage it, when the room flickers.

I don't mean like, the lights flicker, I mean the *room* flickers.

Next thing I know, I'm kneeling in a windowless concrete room, with a discarded cattle prod beside me. Everything else has vanished. I'm tripping balls, trying to process what's just happened, when a door opposite me opens.

Pierre is standing in the threshold, unharmed. Beside him is the director, with her arms folded. She fixes me with an icy stare.

"That's the end of the interview, Dr. Ragazzi. We'll be in touch."

CHAPTER SEVEN

KEALA

I'm huddled with the other survivors, stranded on the tiny, treeless atoll. Gaia stands before us. It's been seven hours since we ran aground. The initial relief effort is over. The last searches of the wreckage have brought no further survivors, only bodies of the people we've known our whole lives. Every person is caught in their own tornado of shock, grief, and fear.

It's a recipe for anger.

And what do angry minds crave?

A scapegoat.

"Quiet down, no more shouting!" yells Gaia.

Without her usual chiefly staff to bang on the ground, it's harder to assert her authority over the emergency meeting.

"We need to preserve our energy, and the water in our bodies. Shouting wastes both," she urges.

"How is the poino *not* to blame? She came out of the power closet seconds before the water flooded us, through that very same room. This is her fault!"

The man thrusts an accusing finger at me. People around him are nodding. I hug my knees closer to my chest. Others sit, too numb to speak. They're staring at the sandy mounds where we've buried our dead. One strong wave would wash their graves clean and we all know it. But that same wave would take us with it. To Malo and Gaia, that's the more pressing concern.

But not to the mob.

"What was she even doing in there?" chimes another.

"Keala, can you answer them?" says Gaia.

I mutter something about needing privacy.

"Speak up!" yells someone at the edge.

"She said she needed privacy," snaps Malo.

"Thank you for that clarification, *Captain*."

The atmosphere is toxic. All comms on the raft have been destroyed by the water. We have no way of telling if the rest of the world even knows we've run into trouble. Worse still we have no shelter, no fresh water, and the rations on board have perished. We're desolate.

Assuming the worst, that our vessel's entire tracking system failed, it will be another two days before anyone realizes we're missing. Then another day before they begin searching for us.

It could be a week before scouting drones come within a hundred miles of this tiny, anonymous lump of rock and sand. Unless something changes, we'll die of thirst or starvation well before then.

"I can see it in her face. She caused the flood, then she made us run aground," spits an angry woman.

The lady used to teach at my school. She'd never had much tolerance for my slower learning, and I'd never much cared for her favoritism of the smart kids. Unfortunately for me, she's not the one on trial here. She's a respected member of the community, and her words carry weight.

The chief calls for quiet again, interrupting the chorus of "poino!"

"Let's be clear," says Gaia. "I spoke with Keala moments before we began taking on water. The vessel suffered multiple, simultaneous structural failures. There is no way she could have orchestrated them all. As for us running aground, *it* was I who gave the order."

Shocked murmurs sweep across the crowd.

"We stand the best chance of survival and of rescue on land. We will divide into groups based on these priorities: injuries, shelter, water, food. You will line up according to your skill sets. If you're not sure, Malo and I will assign you where need is greatest."

"I'm not working with the likes of her," yells one man.

I look around for my latest detractor, but his finger is pointing at someone else. He's targeting the girl I rescued.

"She's infected. I want nothing to do with her," he yells.

A ripple of anxiety spreads across the group. People around the girl spot the black ring spreading across her arm. They scramble away, leaving her isolated.

"He's got it too!" cries another man.

His hand points to the man in front of him. This time, the accused reacts explosively and shoves his accuser hard. Malo intervenes swiftly, separating both men.

The accuser is incensed, arguing that he's only pointing out the obvious. The accused man is equally defiant; just because his skin is turning dark and flaky doesn't mean he's sick, it could just be salt burn.

"Both of you sit," orders Malo.

"I'm not sitting anywhere near him, or you two either," growls the accuser.

He glares at the infected man. As he circles away, he spits at Gaia's feet.

Before she can speak, Malo strikes the man hard in the jaw. The man falls to the ground with a cry, touching his fingers to his split lip.

Malo looms over him and places a foot against his throat.

"Never disrespect your chief like that again. Understood?"

The man grimaces and rasps in concession. Malo releases him, and he storms off to sit alone further along the beach.

He's not the only one. My former teacher stands to speak.

"No disrespect to you, Chief, but I'm not working anywhere near the poino. She brings bad luck. Always has, always will. If you ask me, we should pitch her out to sea. This is a punishment from our ancestors, they need to know we're listening!"

I can feel my heart rate increasing as murmurs of approval echo around the group. Gaia claps her hands to restore order.

"No one is throwing anyone into the sea. We will get through this by working together. If you can't countenance that, then you're welcome to beat your own path, as some have already decided."

She gestures to the sultry loner sitting away from us all, still nursing his lip.

After a pause, two men rise to their feet and leave our group. Ten more follow in dribs and drabs, and together form a splinter colony with the loner. Only thirty of us remain with our chief.

"So be it," says Gaia. "We shall waste no more time on this matter. If we are to survive here, we must prepare by nightfall. Get into your groups."

I wake up to screaming. It's a girl's voice, a little way off. I sit up but she's blocked from sight. There's a semi-circle around me. My head's pounding from dehydration and hunger.

"Do it, do it now!" urges one of them.

"Do what?" I croak.

That's when I see the rocks in their hands.

I scramble to my feet in alarm, only to fall down at once. My balance has gone. The world is spinning. I reach out an arm to steady myself. That's when I see the dark flakes across my forearm; a thick band of them has covered half of my skin. In its wake is a sticky mucus, leaving me half caked in sand.

My chest is wheezing. I'm struggling to breathe.

"Look at her neck!" cries one of the group.

The glands lining my jaw are swollen fit to burst. The lightest touch brings searing pain.

"Do it now, before she spreads it to anyone else!"

Someone's hand twitches.

I run.

I'm weak and disoriented, and the sand is compounding my imbalance. I pick myself up and stumble forwards - I have to get away.

I trip over a sleeping body, causing the person to wake with a cry. Their anger turns to fear when they see my skin. They scramble away, raising the alarm as they move. The mob is growing in size. I search the beach for allies, but there are none. Onlookers back away as I approach like a leper. My foot splashes into something wet. People cry out in despair; I've stepped in one of the rainwater collection tarps. The water swirls, contaminated with sand and, well, me.

"You're not taking us down with you!" comes a cry from the mob.

A stone grazes my hip. I cry out and push on, as fast as my body can manage. There are only three ways to go: the beach will take me full circle, the ocean will sweep me out to drown. That leaves the wreckage.

I scramble onto the splintered bow and crawl along the deck. The angle is steep, but my fingertips grip the hull like glue. I traverse the raft like a gecko. Soon I'm on the tilting bridge, ankle-deep in water.

I throw myself behind the captain's control panel and wait. I'm gasping for breath. It's like I'm having a critical asthma attack. The world is spinning around me. I can hear my attackers trying to scale the slippery bow, but they're sliding into the water. I hear Malo and Gaia joining the fray. Gaia is calling me to rejoin them, but I'm staying well hidden.

Dizziness is overwhelming my senses. The sunlight feels blinding. There's a ringing in my ears. The world is becoming muffled, like I'm hearing it through a wall. My lungs are failing. I can hear them rattling and wheezing as I try in vain to draw in air. Each breath is a herculean effort.

Something in my throat is constricting. I try to stand, to call for help, but I'm falling. My feet stumble backwards until the floor vanishes beneath me. I plummet through the hatch, into the flooded level below. My lungs are spent, my vision has gone, and my limbs are flailing desperately.

My feet hit the submerged deck. I can feel myself tipping backwards. The water cushions my fall, lowering me gently onto the metallic mattress. My head strikes the ground. I see the last bubbles of air escape my lungs, and the world above fades into darkness.

CHAPTER EIGHT

LUKE

I've got my palm over the keypad, but the scanner's throwing a tantrum. I present my palm again, then tap in the digits. Denied. I thump the device. It lets out a high-pitched tone for five seconds. It's so sharp I gotta cover my ears. Touché, manufacturers. That's certainly an effective way to stop people hitting your equipment. Of course, that's assuming your customer is rational, and would rather avoid pain than take revenge on a small metal box.

That's quite an assumption.

It's been a hella stressful day, seeing my informant get kidnapped, escaping his attackers, procuring a whole new identity from an illegal gang, infiltrating the off-grid lab, and experiencing a fake chimp attack. All I want is a cold beer.

Recalling my therapist's words I take a deep breath, then try again, entering each digit with the delicacy of a renaissance painter.

Denied.

I hammer the stupid thing as hard as I can, throwing out a few choice words as I go. The scanner retaliates with a fresh blast of the high-pitched tone. Both of us are hollering at each other in the dank porch.

An AI security response flickers into life next to me. It's a foot tall and bobs around at eye level like a pixelated ghost. This particular ghost is a holographic dog with a sheriff's badge.

The renaissance painter in me just died a thousand deaths.

Good day. This is a semi-automated security response from Doberman Shield PLC. You have mis-entered the code for this apartment three times. You must now confirm your identity or we will escort you from the premises.

This rankles me. First, how is this floating ball of light gonna escort me anywhere? Second, I *swear* Doberman Shield went bust. I'm reckoning this is a legacy system relying on a local server somewhere in the building. I make a mental note to find it and smash it in later. Third, whoever programmed this is a sadist. I'm trying to get into *my* apartment, and somehow I've gotta play twenty questions with a British-sounding sheriff dog.

Please state your name.

"Artemisia Gentileschi."

Purpose?

"To drink beer and eat nachos after a long hard day painting your mother."

The dog freezes and a circle of spinning dots appear in front of it. After a few seconds, it shudders back into motion.

Unable to confirm identity. You have three attempts remaining.

The hologram doubles in size. I'll admit it already seems less cute.

Please provide the name registered to this address.

"Luke Ragazzi."

The dog flickers a few times, then its eyes flash green. Now its tongue's hanging out and its tail's wagging. Whoever made this thing deserves to be locked in a room with a gun, a single bullet, and this infernal dog for company.

Please look into the retinal scanner.

The dog vanishes, and a faint blue beam appears on top of the keypad. I stoop down and stare at it, frowning. If this thing has a retina scanner, why jerk me around with all that pass code nonsense? The faint blue beam brightens. A flash fills my eyes and I stagger backwards, cursing the pain of it.

"What the hell was that?"

I'm blinking like crazy, trying to make it go away. There's this huge bleached beam in the middle of my vision, like I just stared at the frigging sun. God damn budget systems.

I mash the keypad.

The posh dog reappears.

Salutations, Dr. Ragazzi. Would you like to reset your pass code?

"No, I wanna stay out here all night bonding with a floating robo dog. Maybe we could catch a movie together, you know, see where the night takes us? Of course I wanna reset my code, you glitchy cyber kennel piece of-"

Processing.

The dog buffers some more.

Passcode reset.

That can't be good.

"What do you mean it's reset?"

Thank you for using Doberman Shield. Do you require any further assistance?

"Yeah, I wanna know what you just changed my code to!"

The dog buffers again.

Your new code will be mailed to you in three to ten working days. End of transmission.

The dog vanishes, and I'm left gaping at an empty corridor, apoplectic with rage. Who the hell *mails* a pass code? And since when is three to ten days an acceptable turnaround for letting people into their homes?

There's no two ways about it. I gotta break in. Ideally in a way that doesn't set off that damned pooch. I guess I'll have to figure that bit out later. I can always let it blind me again if I need to prove myself.

There's a dead pot plant by my door. I'm about to hurl it through the bathroom when something catches my eye.

It's shiny.

It's slim.

It's only a god damned key.

I can't believe Lanelle didn't mention this. She's gonna get an earful later.

With some jangling, the stiff lock clicks open. I'm in. Home sweet home.

Something's up. The lights are on. I never leave the lights on. Electricity costs money, and I don't got a lot of that to be splashing around on empty apartments. Someone's inside. I reach for the pot plant and creep in.

You're probably figuring right now I'm not much of a fighter, and you're right. As I edge into the hallway, wielding my dead plant, I'm not exactly looking like your regular MMA champion. But I'll have you know I was a pretty good pitcher in high school. So long as whoever's robbing me stays a few yards away, I might get a strikeout. Unless they've got a gun, in which case I'm screwed.

I glance into the tiny kitchen and the bathroom on either side of the hall; both are empty. I shuffle towards the main room. It's like a living room, but it comes with a bed too. So I guess it's more like a bedroom with a sofa. OK, it's a studio apartment, whatever. Look, if you really wanna know how comes a forty-blah year-old man is living alone in a dank-ass micro apartment, sit tight; we'll get to that later, and it'll be brief. I ain't about the wallowing. Right now, just focus on my plan of attack.

The light's coming from the main room, which means my shadow's behind me, giving me the element of surprise. That said, I opened the front door pretty loud, and it's letting a lot of cold air in. Plus there was that whole business with me yelling at the dog-o-gram. OK, I'm pretty much busted. Which begs the question, why hasn't whoever it is come at me yet? They must be lying in wait.

I edge to the door frame, real cautious like. If I step in there and hesitate, I'm a dead man. I've got one shot at this. I'm holding the pot behind me, ready to launch it at the burglar's head. I gotta jump in there, pitch like a pro, and sit on their back or something till the cops get here. Here goes.

Three.

Two.

One.

I leap inside with a yell. The sofa's bare. My arm's quivering with adrenaline. I scan the rear of the door for the intruder. No one.

Someone clears their throat across the room.

I spin around like a lynx, no, a *puma*, and in the same motion I hurl the pot plant as hard as I can. The woman ducks and it shatters against the wall, showering the bed with shards of clay and dry soil. The woman sits back up, flicks the glossy white hair from her piercing green eyes, and regains composure like nothing's happened.

"Is that how you greet all your employers?" she says, dryly.

I'm panting, still in shock. Why the hell is the director here? Sitting on my bed? This is weird. I was expecting to take a bullet, not file an HR complaint. I ask her as much.

"What do you mean, 'greet my employers'?"

"Congratulations, Dr. Ragazzi, you got the job."

"You broke into my apartment to tell me that? What's wrong with an email!"

She stands up and smooths her jacket, then lifts a picture from my bedside table. I wince. I've still got the receipt for the frame, so I'm hoping she's not about to smash it. That would ruin my chances of a thrifty return when this mission's over.

"The mail wouldn't tell me all this," she says, gesturing to my hovel.

"I'm glad you like the decor."

"You're divorced?"

Huh. I guess we're doing this bit now then. OK, fine. Here's my weepy story, but I'm only telling you because she made me.

"Yes, I'm divorced," I shrug.

For the record, that's the truth.

"How many times?"

"Oh, once was enough for me."

Also true. Wait, why am I smiling as I say that? Am I flirting with her? Oh god. Abort.

"Sounds like you had a little trouble getting in here earlier?"

"Yeah, sadists designed my lock. Though I'd love to know how you bypassed dog-o-gram so easily?"

"You had a key under the pot plant, Dr. Ragazzi. It wasn't exactly the heist of the century. We've completed your reference checks, by the way. Mostly positive."

Mostly? What's the point in paying thousands of cryptos if those amateurs are gonna half-ass the reference? Surely that's the easy bit, putting some good words in an email? It's almost like they didn't want me to look good. OK, thinking it through now I kinda get it. If they say I'm a superstar, I'll fall flat on my face. If they say I take a little while to adjust but then nail it, it gives me breathing room while I'm faking it in the new workplace. At least, that's what I'm hoping they put. Maybe they said I have a manageable crack habit. Could be anything. Everything rests on this new identity, but so far Chang's pack is holding up.

"I take it you accept our offer?" says the director.

"Yes. Thank you. Very glad."

I don't know why I'm speaking like English is my second language. Maybe I'm still trying to process how she knew my residential address. I didn't put it on any of the paperwork. Is this a power play? She walks towards me and extends a hand. We shake once.

"Your probation period starts tomorrow. Good luck with the gardening."

With that, she leaves. I'm standing there pondering the whole interaction and mulling over her words. "Probation." It's not even day one and I'm on thin ice with these people. That's not good. I've invested months in getting to this moment, I can't let it fall through my hands; there's so much at stake. It's time to get ahead of the game.

"Mom, Dad, it's me."

"Luke, mio bambino! Come stai?"

"Bene, Mama, I got some great news, I got the job."

"The one at the lab?"

"Yeah, I start tomorrow."

"Congratulations! We're so proud of you. Where is it? We wanna send flowers and dolci for your first day."

"Thanks Mom but I can't tell you the address, it's a confidential facility."

"Our boy's a spy?"

"Relax, Papà, it's nothing like that. It's just that the work they do is sensitive, so it's gotta be kept under wraps. You know how it is, people try and steal patents, that sorta thing. Anyway, I just wanted you to know. I gotta go iron a shirt, get ready for the morning. Love you both, ciao."

I gotta hand it to Chang, the video quality was superb. So realistic. I don't know how he does it, though I've heard rumors. Some outfits use actors, then superimpose the right digital face, while other gangs design deep fake AIs that they could deploy for almost any purpose. Whichever method Chang's using is extremely convincing.

I should explain. We figured the coffeepot monitors all its employees, especially newbies like me. However, we hadn't banked on them breaking into my pad. Not right away, at least. The message is clear: they can do whatever the hell they like. So it's important they believe I'm genuine. That little pow-wow with my fake parents was for the benefit of my new employers. I'm gonna have to keep that sort of pretense up, going forwards. I'd say it's a rough prospect, but between you and me, I found that kinda therapeutic. They were way less argumentative than my real parents.

I head to the toilet and remove the cistern. It's covered in lime scale and other stains, the sort you don't wanna think about too much in a rented apartment. There's a plastic bag floating in the water. I shake it dry, then retrieve the phone inside. It's an ancient thing, incredibly basic, and barely functional on today's networks. It's perfect.

I thumb through the address book, tap the one number inside, and select "Compose message".

In.

P.S. *You owe me a beer.*

Send.

I wait a few seconds to be sure the SMS has sent, then turn the phone off. It's such an archaic form of communication. So limited. Zero encryption. It's so archaic, in fact, the authorities barely pay it any attention. Like I said, it's perfect. I wrap it in the bag and stash it back inside the cistern.

Time to swat up on my lab technique.

CHAPTER NINE

KEALA

My body is flat against the deck of the flooded raft. I can feel the cold steel beneath me. The last of my air has slipped from my lungs. My vision had blacked out.

As my brain shuts down I think of my parents, and the shortness of my life. One emotion prevails above all else: regret.

The glands on my neck are still swelling. As everything else fades, this pain is growing.

The skin on the left side tears open. A burst of color shoots across my vision. The pain is profound but something is muting it; something instinctive is taking over. My lungs inflate sharply. My whole body twitches and the opposite set of glands rupture.

My lungs swell to their peak. My vision fades back into focus. Gasping, and writhing, I touch the broken skin. I jerk in horror as I feel the exposed cartilage against my fingers. Something on my neck is opening and closing in sync with the rise and fall of my chest. Flaps of some kind. With a groan, I peel away the remaining loose tissue. My airflow improves at once.

This is surely a hallucination; the last throws of a dying mind. Yet the raft looks so real. I take a few strokes towards the ladder. It feels cool to the touch, and the rungs are sturdy when I squeeze them.

A great splash sounds above me. I barely have time to react; whoever plunged in is landing on top of me. I forced them off and kick away, bracing for a second assault, but the person drops like a deadweight. It's the girl I saved. She's unconscious. She sinks flat onto the deck like I had moments ago, but no bubbles are leaving her lips; her lungs must have been spent before she fell into the water. I take her head in my arms.

I want to blow air from my lungs into hers, but when I try to exhale, nothing comes out of my mouth. Something inside is physically stopping me. I feel the glands around her neck. They're swollen, but not as large as mine had gotten. I press against them hard, but the skin doesn't burst. She's running out of time.

I scoop my arms under her shoulders and kick for the surface. With great effort, I drag her up onto what's left of the bridge. As my head leaves the water, the perforations under my jaw seal tight. The sensation shocks me to the core. It's like someone's grabbed my windpipe and is squeezing it with all their might.

I fall to my knees, wheezing as my collapsed lungs try to drag air through the sealed slits. I'm clawing at my neck, begging for air. Red dots spread across my vision as my capillaries burst from the strain.

My windpipe opens and air rushes in.

There's no time to hesitate. I catch my breath and kneel over the unconscious girl. I tilt her head back, pinch her nose, and exhale into her mouth. As I breathe for her, her chest rises and falls, as do the swollen sacks under her chin.

Her lungs have failed, yet her heart is still fighting. Going on nothing but a hunch, I shuffle closer and hover above her chest. With my knees pressed against her jaw, I constrict her glands and continue the resuscitation.

I can feel her pulse growing stronger. It's starting to work.

Without warning, her larynx pops open. Her eyes pop open and she gasps for air. Seeing me, she scrambles backwards. Her hands rise in surrender, like I might attack at any moment.

"Woah, take it easy, I'm not here to fight."

She points at the dark, flaky bands spreading across my skin. Now that we're both above deck, in full daylight, I can see her skin clearly. She's undergoing the same transformation.

"You did this to me!" she croaks.

"What? I just saved your life!"

"You should've let me drown, I don't wanna be like you," she says, weeping. "I need the island."

"Which island? That tiny thing over there? What's stopping you?"

"No, not there. I'm not allowed there anymore because of what you've done to me. I want to go home, *real* home."

Her eyes are brimming with tears. She's angry, panicked, and in denial about the changes happening to her body.

Me? I'm postponing that for later. Given that I was about to suffocate to death on land, discovering I can breathe underwater, although terrifying, is kinda awesome. Don't get me wrong, there's a part of my brain that is majorly *freaking out* right now. But I can process it later, right now we need a plan.

"This raft is our best chance of getting away from here. It's modular, there's gotta be something we can use. I'm gonna go look. You coming?"

"With you?"

She has a gift, this girl. The way she can take a simple, innocuous word like 'you' and fill it with venom.

"Yeah, with 'me'," I reply.

She shakes her head, arms folded.

"Suit yourself. I'll be gone a while but I know what I'm doing. If your lungs feel like they're collapsing again, press against those swollen sacks under your jaw and try to breathe normally. Also make sure you're sat leaning against a wall. If you pass out in the water again, I might not be able to save you a second time. All right, peace out."

"Wait!" she cries. Her hands are probing her neck sacks nervously. "What happened to yours? I saw you had them this morning. Are you cured now?"

"Something like that."

I could go into more detail, but she's kinda being a brat. Plus I can feel a curious tingling in my stomach, and it's nothing to do with the mutation. It's a feeling I've not had in years.

A sense of promise.

Optimism.

Self-belief.

I'm about to be useful again.

Gaia stored the rations in the middle deck, so I dive to explore what supplies we may have. The damage to the raft is even more extensive than I remembered. One side of the hull has peeled off, spewing panels and bunks into the ocean. I linger by the boundary and peer into the dark blue that extends into oblivion. There's something flat and white embedded in the seabed about fifteen meters away. I make a mental note to investigate later, if there's nothing useful on board.

Transitioning between land and water is grim. I've only had three switches so far, and each felt like someone was strangling me. Once my gills are open though, it's bliss; the sensation of my body re-oxygenating, and of boundless possibilities. I can't believe how fast I'm adjusting. And the fact I just used the phrase "my gills".

I would be enjoying it a great deal more if I wasn't starving. None of us have eaten since we ran aground around eighteen hours ago. Most people think it's my fault the raft sank, and I can't wait to see their faces when I'm the one who recovers our food from the deep.

The tattered vessel is eerie, and I'm relying on sunlight penetrating through cracks in the structure. The tilted angle of the wreck helps, with the windows providing shafts of light among the gloom.

Something catches my eye. It's an emergency ceiling panel, like the ones you get in airplanes. No one noticed it during the evacuation and salvage efforts. Or maybe it had cracked ajar overnight?

I prize it open further, revealing a first aid symbol. A briefcase-sized package falls out and drifts down to the floor.

Emergency evacuation procedures.

I open the volume. Its pages are made of plastic, and contain an extensive index.

- Orientation.
- Establishing a base.
- How to help people transition.
- Psychological adjustments.
- Safety underwater.
- Sustainable food sources.

I pause for a minute and laugh out loud.

This is unbelievable.

I'm reading.

None of the words are jumbled anymore. The letters are staying where they belong, and the words make *sense*. I'm *normal*!

I scan my way to the bottom of the index, laughing with joy as I tear through the words. But as I pay more attention to the actual subjects, my gleeful laughter subsides. I re-read the entries.

- Scenarios for insulation in underwater habitats.
- Potential predators, grouped by location and depth.
- Surviving the extreme cold.
- Essential food supplements for withstanding high pressures.

I drop the folder in horror. Someone prepared this manual and placed it on board, *knowing* we would sink.

I see my gills reflected across the glossy cover of the

manual. My eyes track to the unnatural, blistering skin around my wrists. I stare through the ruptured hull at the empty children's bunks littering the ocean floor. A sickening realization crashes over me.

Someone planned all of this.

CHAPTER TEN

LUKE

Rise and shine, time to check my toilet phone. Let's just call it what it is: it's a toilet phone, and I'm checking it. Sometimes you gotta do what you gotta do. Luckily, a toilet phone allows you to do both at once. It's a highly efficient system. My contact has replied.

Stay focused. Be careful. These people are dangerous.

No acknowledgement of their beer debt, and not so much as a kiss. How rude.

I get to the office and they buzz me in before I press the intercom. When I reach the elevator, it knows where to take me. They're really doubling down on the evil lair thing.

The elevator delivers me to a different level than yesterday. This one's teeming like an ant colony, with the "ants" in question being a bunch of nerds in lab coats. As soon as I step out, the bustling lobby falls silent. All eyes are on me, the only person without a lab coat. Yup, hi everyone, new guy here. Thanks for being so cool about it.

A man weaves through the crowd towards me. It's Pierre, the balding head of biosecurity, aka the guy I saved from a chimpanzee. Or at least, whose hologram I saved.

"Dr. Ragazzi, welcome to your new office. Please follow me."

The scientists part like the red sea, as I follow the dude through the crowded hallway. As soon as we pass beyond a set of frosted double doors, the rest of the colony snaps back to work.

I gotta know, so I ask him straight up.

"Were they holograms?"

He muses for a moment, then replies, "Would it matter?"

Wise ass. It yanks my chain when people try to execute a triple kill like that in conversation. They lance your question with a semi-philosophical rhetorical one of their own. In a single blow, they make your question seem ridiculous, avoid answering it, and somehow claim the moral high ground, without having to do any actual moralizing themselves.

I don't go in for that kinda conversation.

"Yeah, it matters," I say.

"To you?"

"I wouldn't presume to speak on your behalf, Pierre, so by process of elimination, that rather leaves me, yes."

I know what you're thinking. I've done all this work to get here, jumped through all their hoops, dragged my life to a dismal apartment in Park Morpre, risked prison time by buying a black market identity, and yet, even with all that at stake, I'm still mouthing off at my new boss.

There are two things I learned last time I did this, which, for the record, was a looooong time ago. Rule number one: be as authentically "you" as possible. If you're funny, be funny. If you're boring, stay boring. And if you're a provocative loudmouth, well, you get the picture. Why? It's simple. You're spinning so many plates trying to keep on top of your new identity, your new role, your whole cover story, that you need to lighten the cognitive load wherever possible. If your personality isn't genuine, people get suspicious real quick. But if they sense you're being one hundred percent yourself, no matter what version of yourself that is, they'll be at ease around you. Unless you're a creep. If you're a creep, you should switch it up.

So, with rule number one in mind, I'm being my truest self. Maybe even more so than usual. I'm setting the benchmark right away, while people form their first impressions. It'll save me a bunch of work later when I'm four months deep, exhausted, missing my family, and someone catches me off guard with a question about "Simone".

Who?

Exactly.

The last thing you want is to be an actor *and* a quiz contestant. Which brings me to rule number two. Remember why you're there. It's not to win an Oscar for being the person who can go longest without getting detected. You can disguise yourself as a water cooler? *Bravissimo.* It ain't gonna get you what you need. What you need is to get under people's skin quickly, find the secrets, and get out. And to do that, you gotta ruffle feathers from the outset. This works for one simple reason.

No one expects a crap spy.

Pierre frowns at me. I double down. I'm not letting him get away with ducking my question.

"If all those bustling nerds were holograms, Pierre, the programmer owes you a refund. Real humans could never look *and* sound that lame all at once."

His frown deepens.

"Ha. I knew it. They're real. And you even like some of

them. Or perhaps you identify as one of them? Don't worry boss, to me you're all 'super cool'. Wink."

I enjoy watching people try to work out if I'm being rude to them, or if they should give me the benefit of the doubt because I'm new. This is the honeymoon period. In the weeks to come, they'll learn that I'm just the worst.

Besides, the whole "giving me the benefit" thing is the real travesty here. People are delusional. They'll contrive pious excuses for my rudeness because they've convinced themselves they're "good people", and that's what "good people" do; deny the possibility that the person in front of them could just be an ass. Because that would make them an ass too. Specifically, a *judgmental* ass. It's usually something they've been called in the past and made a robotic note-to-self: must avoid future social error.

Bleep bloop.

I'm watching these somersaults take place in my new boss's head as I eyeball him with the most callous expression I can muster. Right now he's thinking *how did we ever hire this guy? I don't get it. He passed the test...* I'm watching the twitches in his eyebrow as he tries to rationalize a way that I'm actually a good person, and that he's simply misread me. And that by realizing that, he's a good person too, and that we're both just a couple of sweethearts. In reality, the only reason I'm here is that the people working in this facility are the sickest, most depraved sociopaths anywhere on the planet, and it's my job to prove it.

CHAPTER ELEVEN

KEALA

Something on the deck below catches my eye, wafting in the periphery of a sunbeam. I leave the emergency manual on the floor and swim down to inspect closer.

Kelp. We only crashed yesterday, and in less than twenty-four hours a cluster of saplings have sprouted. This is fast growth, even for the fastest-growing plant on Earth. What's even more puzzling is where it came from.

Then I see it; the semi-dissolved remains of a packet. The kelp is growing out of its remains. Scattered across the rest of the deck are more packs in various stages of decay, proportionate to the amount of sunlight reaching them.

The design is ingenious; the packet must have kept the saplings dry in transit, then as soon as they were submerged, it activated and dissolved into a gel-soil.

I retrieve a packet from the shadows. It's still intact; a plain white pouch, save for a blue logo printed on the reverse. A microscope set against an airplane. Weird choice.

Sunlight must play a role in activation. I grab the other

un-hatched pouches from the shadows and return to the middle deck, where I set them down beside the manual.

I flick through to the page on sustainable food sources:

Sustainable food sources

Kelp will be an anchor species for your population, and indeed your ecosystem. Plant these saplings as soon as possible, with plenty of access to sunlight and flowing water. This will ensure a steady supply of energy and nutrients. Ensure you use the KelpBar™ supplied for a growth-responsive crop bed.

What the hell is a *KelpBar™*? I cast my eyes around the wreckage. Nothing looks like it matches the description.

I consult the manual's index, and flick to the appropriate entry.

Utilizing your KelpBar™

Your KelpBar™ is a floating trough designed to maximize your yield. Think of it as a smart flower bed. As your kelp plants get longer, they become heavier. This causes the base of the trough to sink. Do not be alarmed. This is intentional. It will force your kelp to keep growing upward at its maximum rate, in order to reach the sunlight. Once the kelp reaches your target length, you may harvest some from the top. The trough will become lighter and rise again, and thus the growth cycle will repeat. Below are a series of charts to help you manage your crop efficiently. With the available packets, you should be able to achieve a harvest surplus within two weeks. Use surplus crops to propagate further troughs.

Please note, this Kelp has been modified to include optimized growing capacity and antibacterial properties for your convenience. For additional benefits and uses of your kelp samples, including enhanced nutritional properties, and textile applications including wound dressings, see below.

I'm wondering if the person who wrote this manual is the same person who sank our rafts. Either they're a complete sociopath, or this operation has drawn in other people who have no idea what they've enabled.

According to the diagrams, troughs should be rigged up in a grid formation to create a kelp field. There are instructions for different scenarios. For example, how to tether the troughs to shallow sea beds, or if the kelp farm is in deep ocean, how to use water-based anchors.

The discovery of a scientific wonder-food should be giving my hunger-addled mind hope.

But there's a problem.

Based on the schematic in our manual, we have to make a choice.

The others aren't going to like it.

Many of them are hoping we can repair the vessel, but for the kelp bars to work, we have to irreversibly dismantle the raft.

We can try to escape, or we can try to not starve. According to the manual, we can't do both.

With a gasp, my windpipe opens. I stumble onto the shore, gulping for air. In one hand I'm clutching a genetically modified kelp sapling, and in the other, the emergency manual. It's time my fellow survivors learned the awful truth.

But something's wrong.

The survivors are standing in two uneven groups. There's a dividing line down the middle. Everyone in the majority group has rings of blistered skin across their body. The rival group is much smaller, and its people shows no symptoms. In the middle, between the two sides, lies a body.

Gaia.

Without thinking, I run from the shallows and dart through the gap in the crowd. Both sides spring back in alarm.

"It's her!" cries a voice.

I fall by Gaia's side. The glands under her jaw are hugely swollen. Her lungs are failing. Before I can lay a finger on her, her eyes roll back in their sockets. Her body shakes violently as she goes into seizure.

"She's brought the curse to the chief!" cries one.

Malo is kneeling by Gaia, on the side of the clean group. He's the only person not to have recoiled when I arrived, despite having no symptoms.

"She's dying," he croaks.

He's in shock, paralyzed by despair. All his life he's been strong, and able to control events around him, yet here we're kneeling on a deserted atoll, watching his mother's life drain from her body.

I drop the sapling and the manual and grab hold of Gaia's arms.

"What are you doing?" cries Malo.

"If you want her to live, you have to trust me. Grab her legs and help me."

He's frozen, speechless.

I can't wait for him to give me permission; the Chief's suffocating in front of us and I'm her only hope. I drag her through the sand, down the sandy shore towards the water.

"Stop!" cries Malo.

He's realizing what I'm about to do.

I have to get this done before he can stop me. If I so much as hesitate, Gaia will die.

I move as fast as I can, dragging her into the shallows. Her body becomes lighter as the water takes the burden. Soon, I'm swimming; the water gets deep quickly here. Malo tumbles into the water behind me with a yell.

He's fast.

His arms lock around my neck.

We fall backwards into the water, struggling. Gaia's body is drifting away.

He shoves me to the side and paddles desperately after his mother. She's twitching and spluttering as water sloshes over her mouth and nose.

Malo grabs hold of her ankle and begins towing her back.

He doesn't know it, but he's condemning her to suffocate.

I drop below the surface and swim behind Gaia, then grab her neck and drag her beneath the waves.

Malo cries out in despair. He clings to her leg but he's weaken from heat and dehydration. I kick hard against his hips, pushing him backwards. Gaia and I sink deeper into the water. Malo dives after us, his eyes wide with despair.

I'm stronger than him underwater. Unlike him, I'm getting a continuous supply of oxygen to my muscles. We're five meters down and the last bubbles are draining from Gaia's lips. Malo stretches for his mother, but the distance is too great. He stares in dismay as Gaia and I drop. With a jolt, his survival reflexes force him up for air.

I move so I'm above her, but Gaia's body is heavy and still sinking. Her eyes are shut, and her mouth hangs open. Her limbs hang above her like she's falling from a building in slow motion.

Her body's not responding. If she doesn't get air soon she'll suffer brain damage.

I take her jaw in my hands and drive both thumbs into her swollen sacks. The glands burst open, sending cloudy, fleshy debris into the water around us. I can feel her gills, but they're sealed shut.

I scrape the loose skin away from either side, revealing the fresh cartilage. Panic is rising within me. Mine had opened automatically, but hers aren't activating. The last thing I want to do is damage her new organs, but I'm running out of options.

I press my thumbs against her gills and force them apart.

Nothing happens.

"Gaia! Wake up, Gaia, you have to wake up!"

I shake her violently, begging her to wake up, yearning for her to breathe. But her body is limp, and her lungs empty. I cling to her clothes, weeping, as we sink into the darkness of the ocean.

CHAPTER TWELVE

LUKE

I scrub up real good. Not like I'm going out for a date, though that would be nice. It'd also be a miracle. And an insane risk at this stage. No, I'm zipping myself into a clean suit, ready to enter a clean room, and generally be squeaky clean. Company protocol. Which is ironic, given that this facility is as dirty as it gets, if you catch my drift.

Starchy-pants Pierre leads me to the decontamination chamber, where I'm about to enjoy a refreshing blast of hydrogen peroxide. Mmm. Toxic.

"Is your suit sealed?" asks Pierre.

"It sure is, boss. Though I've left the hood open at the back. My roots are starting to show, thought I'd get a quick spritz while I'm here."

Pierre darts around to my hood, then realizes it's closed. He crosses to the opposite side and mashes the "spray" button. He stares at me, unimpressed.

"I am not accustomed to tolerating humor in my labs, Dr. Ragazzi. Our work is no laughing matter."

"I hear you, boss. But while we're on the topic, what do you get if you cross a comedian with a particle accelerator?"

He glares at me.

"Wait, have you heard this one before? Or did I lead with the punchline again? *Dammit.*"

"Your referees warned us of your *unique* manner," clips Pierre. "They said it was a price worth paying for your brilliance. We shall soon see if that's true."

Uh-oh. Honeymoon period might be wearing off quicker than I thought.

Chemical nozzles spring into action, hosing us down. We've got our arms held out like a couple of weapons-grade scarecrows. The spritz ends, and the immense titanium doors opposite slide apart like theater curtains. I gotta hand it to them, if they're going for shock and awe, they've nailed it. My mouth drops as we step inside.

I don't know how they smuggled a room the size of an aircraft hangar into the coffee pot, but somehow that's what I'm looking at. Moreover, it's got a mini forest going on. They're cultivating row after row of trees of all kinds of species. We're standing on a balcony, by the way, so I'm getting a real sweet view of the forest lab and the tall, mature specimens filling it.

It would have looked kinda beautiful were it not for one teensy-weensy detail. Every tree has a huge polythene bag wrapped over it. It looks like someone took out a hit on the hundred acre wood.

I follow starchy-pants down a spiral metal staircase to the factory floor and we inspect a row of trees. Their trunks are supported by metal tripods, welded to the ground. Their roots have been deliberately shrunk to save space; they've encouraged them to grow in spiral coils in a fluid-filled tub.

Some of the bags are wrapped tight around the trees,

others are semi-inflated. Thin tubes run in and out of each, connecting to small gauges on the tripods.

"This one is our best performing sample," says Starchy-pants. "It sequesters carbon four times faster than the control group."

"That's incredible."

"It's nowhere near enough. We need to be sequestering at ten-X minimum just to offset the loss of the rainforests. If we want to be carbon negative, we need at least fourteen-X to make a sustained impact. Can you do it?"

I'll level with you. I like trees as much as the next guy. Well, maybe not as much as *this* next guy, but certainly within the bell curve of regular tree appreciation.

But they ain't why I'm here.

"Boss, my specialism is immunology. You wanna put me on gardening duty?"

"At the risk of indulging in word play, we believe in cross-pollination in this lab."

Wow. What an indulgence. I sure hope I get invited to this guy's summer BBQ. It'll be wild.

"When one team hits a brick wall in their progress, we rotate the staff between departments. A fresh perspective often pushes us forwards. The act of briefing a new team member who is a non-specialist also helps the existing team reassess their assumptions."

I gotta hand it to Pierre, it's a sound strategy. Assuming your staff have the same goals as you.

"At the risk of indulging in word play, boss, you're barking up the wrong tree here."

Nothing.

Guess I'll be barbecuing alone.

"Your induction is not a negotiation, Dr. Ragazzi. It is a

methodical and results-driven part of our process. Understood?"

"Crystal."

"Pardon?"

"Never mind. All good. Excited to get started."

I need to figure out how I'm gonna play this. If I do a totally lousy job on trees, they'll fire me outright. But if I nail it, they could leave me here. I'm gonna have to play it straight down the line.

Fortunately for me, mediocrity is something I've always excelled at. Just ask my ex-wife.

I laugh heartily at starchy-pants's pollen joke, then go out of my way to explain that it was so good it took me a minute to get it. For the first time, his lips defy gravity. His perpetual, downward-sagging mouth achieves, for a fleeting moment, the glorious feat of being horizontal. I've made him feel both funny and clever, while making myself seem ditsy, un-threatening, and a fan of his.

Starchy-pants is now giving me a detailed briefing on the optimizations they've attempted for each tree, and what they think is holding them back. I'm kinda hoping we find a cactus sometime soon because I swear to God I need to prick myself to stay awake around this guy.

"OK, that's it. Over to you. I'll be back in two hours to answer any questions you have."

Wait, what? Dammit. Maybe I should've paid attention to his words. We've toured the entire forest, and all I heard was "tree, tree, tree."

He disappears up the staircase and leaves me alone in the hangar, with a bunch of shrink wrapped tree-tree-trees.

I approach the work station at the side and examine samples beneath the microscope. At this point I should clarify: I'm not a total biology dunce. Human immunology is my "specialty", but some of those core biochemistry principles apply to plant life, so I'm confident I can figure out what's going on here.

Also, one of the other scientists left their notebook out.

So that helps.

From what I'm gathering, the lab's whittled it down to two approaches. Number one: trees which shed limbs as they grow. Pros: you don't need to keep cutting down trees and replanting them to sequester carbon, you can enjoy a continuous supply of bio fuel from each organism. Cons: sucks to be anything trying to live in a tree whose branches keep falling off.

Option two: they're tricking the trees into thinking they're still saplings. Pros: they grow faster and allegedly absorb more carbon. Cons: their bark never matures, so they're vulnerable, and less sturdy, limiting their ultimate size to half that of their mature peers. Double con: they look weird. Like giant herbs.

So here's the rub. Pierre is coming back in half an hour. What? Fine, it took me ninety minutes to read the scientist's journal. And? You try skimming that sorta stuff, it's dense.

Yes, there were pictures, but I don't see how that's relevant.

Look, I urgently need a hypothesis to pitch upon my boss's return. Something credible, but not genius. Fortunately, genius is off the menu, but if I knuckle down maybe I can achieve credible.

Or I could go through that door.

My homework was always late as a kid. It would be disingenuous for me to be punctual as an adult. Plus I'm curious by nature. I feel like if they didn't want me to walk through doors, they wouldn't have included them in the interview.

It leads to another lab. This one's sized less like an aircraft hangar, and more like a classroom. Or maybe a hangar for teeny tiny planes.

I weave between the worktops, taking in the saplings before me. No polythene coverings here; these aren't being tested for carbon dioxide absorption. But the transparent soil beds are brimming with instruments. There's a friendly traffic light system of LEDs beside each sample. I love whoever designed this room. It's like it was made for a layperson like me to wander in and know at a glance which samples to investigate further. Either that or I've misunderstood traffic lights my entire life. Would explain a lot of fines.

The nearest tray has a red light beside it. The readout above it is charting the levels of various compounds in the soil. This soil is clearly toxic, as are most others in the room. A handful are amber, presumably margin-calls. I'll confess, I don't know heaps about soil, but my guess here is that the plants are rendering their own soil too acidic for anything else to grow. There's one green-lit tray across the room. I make my way over.

I should have mentioned, all the saplings are twinned with another plant. At a first glance, it looks like the withered secondary plants around the room are like canaries in the coal mine; confirming my hypothesis about the acidity. But this green-lit one gets me thinking there's more to it.

The doors at the opposite end swipe open and my boss enters. Busted. He's walking crisply with his hands folded behind his back. Presumably to stop the broom falling out.

"Dr. Ragazzi. Gone for a walk have we?" says Pierre.

"Ah, yes boss. I read your colleague's notes on soil toxicity and I felt like you were holding something back from me. You can't expect someone to do blue sky thinking if you only give them half the sky. I thought to myself, if you're measuring the carbon variable in that room, then you gotta be working on the toxicity variable someplace else. And I was right. Great minds think alike, hey?"

"I have yet to see greatness here, Dr. Ragazzi. Please, continue."

"Er, well, I'm figuring you realized the plants that are best at sequestering carbon also make the soil kinda sucky for the others around them, so you've decided a symbiotic model is the best way to go. One plant sequesters the carbon, and it's twinned with another that can make the soil alkaline."

He stares at me, waiting to see if there's more.

"Legumes!" I add, hastily.

Is that right? I kinda blurted it without thinking. I feel like I read something on the Metro once about peas and whatnot putting nitrogen in the soil.

Starchy pants gives a single nod of his head.

See? It's working perfectly. Sure, he ain't giving me the Nobel prize in biology, mainly because there isn't one and the awarding body's in Scandinavia, but more to the point, he's not laughing me out of town either. I'm down the line. Mediocre. Meat in the room. In the immortal words of my favorite Roman rebel: I. Am. Goldilocks.

"Lunch," says starchy-pants.

"Is that a statement or a question?"

Or a threat?

I can see he's enjoying my humor less. I should tone it down.

Should.

"It's a lab tradition that we welcome new employees with a divisional lunch."

Wait, there's an inclusivity program on the Death Sta- I mean, coffee pot? This is an unexpected twist. I play it cool. I'm like, "Sounds great. What do the forestry lot eat, anyhow? Lemme guess, lot of pine nuts?"

By "play it cool" I mean cool for a middle-aged father of two. Which is to say, I hate myself.

"You'll be meeting the biochemistry team. This way," says Pierre.

How about that. I've got me a date after all.

As I follow my boss into the canteen, a nervousness takes hold. It's the first day of school all over again, only this time I cheated the entrance exam. As we approach a table full of certified brainiacs, I'm thinking I might get rumbled fast.

Pierre introduces me with all the warmth of a glacier. Naturally, the geek squad want to know all about my work experience, my expertize, and how I found out about the lab. I navigate my way through it all like a pro, and quickly take hold of the conversation. It's the only way.

I play the "nice guy" card. As a newbie, I can't be too evasive, but I *can* be aggressively earnest. Like I'm trying to make friends. I take a polite but non-suspicious interest in everyone's careers, then turn the topic onto lighter things, like sports, or movies, or dear God what do these nerds do for hobbies?

Someone joins our table. Sweet mercy. I can't handle any more photos from Eric's traffic cone collection.

"Who's the new guy?"

She doesn't smile or look at me when she talks, which I find kinda rude, and immediately respect. I extend a hand, politely.

"I'm Luke Ragazzi. But you can call me Luke."

She looks at my outstretched hand and frowns, then nods at it. "Christie," she replies, turning to her baked potato.

I lower my hand, and make a mental note to leave Christie off any group chats I set up for after-work drinks. Eric too.

Pierre breaks the silence. "Luke used to work at Delta Four Labs. Isn't that where you came from, Christie?"

Oh great, she's a former coworker from my fake CV. Terrific.

"I was there five years ago," says Christie.

"Isn't that when you were there, Luke?" says Pierre.

"Er, yeah, that's right. Maybe we were in separate divisions?"

"It's a small lab. One team," says Christie.

"One dream," I say in a flash, like it's a tic.

"Do you know each other or not?" says Pierre, his eyes narrowing.

"Err," I stammer.

"We can't confirm or deny that. You know the rules," says Christie. "The NDAs there survive the termination of our employment."

Thank God for Christie the robot lady and her sciencey-lawyer speak. I always liked Christie. Must invite her to group drinks sometime.

"Yeah, sorry boss." I add a cringey *awww shucks* kinda head tilt. It's too much. I focus on my linguine for a solid minute.

Someone else at our table is chuckling at a private joke.

Starchy pants is curious. Or perturbed. It's hard to tell with him. I think his default is to be both at all times.

"Something funny, Drake?" he says, testily.

"The NDA thing. I love it, boss, it's so cute," says Drake, wiping his eyes.

"Care to elaborate?"

"These other labs make everyone sign stacks of paperwork and figure that'll keep them quiet. I love working with people who don't need that. Everyone here just gets it."

"Gets what?" I ask, laughing along.

"There are no NDAs here. Just people who can keep their mouths shut, and people whose mouths get shut for them," laughs Drake.

God damn. He's starting to sound like my uncle Giuseppe.

Who was an orthodontist, by the way. Fixed a lot of wisdom teeth.

"Gee, that's a funny joke, Drake. Hey, asking for a friend, whaddya mean by that?"

"I shouldn't have to explain it to you, new guy. You'll either get it, or you won't. Either way, you'll find out."

Drake's not smiling anymore. He's staring at me coldly as he shovels food into his mouth. I never knew it was possible to make eating a Scotch egg look menacing. The people around him are looking down at their trays, avoiding eye contact. It's hard to know whether it's because they're scientists, or because they know precisely what he's talking about.

An uneasy thought dawns on me.

"Hey boss, about my role, was it newly-created, or did I have a predecessor?"

Everyone freezes. Drake looks to starchy-pants. Starchy-pants looks to me. I look at everyone, then back to starchy-pants, with the greatest fake-innocence I can manage.

"You did," he says, after a brief ice age.

"Did they retire? Set up a vineyard? Follow their dreams as a dancer?" I ask, optimistically.

"They failed probation."

"Oh. Where are they now?"

"Eat up, Luke. We've got work to do."

Yeah. Suddenly I'm not so hungry.

CHAPTER THIRTEEN

KEALA

I'm clutching Gaia's shoulders as we sink. I can feel the water cooling around us. My eyes are filling with tears, coating my lenses in warmth. What have I done?

"Gaia!"

I'm shaking her but she's not responding. I'm malnourished and my muscles are cramping, I can't last much longer. If my new respiratory system succumbs to fatigue in the same way, I could drown too.

Weeping, I released her from my exhausted arms.

Her body slides away from me, fading into the murky blue below. I cover my mouth in sorrow, watching until her body is just a shadow. The last of her outline merges with darkness of the abyss.

Something jolts in my mind.

I race after her, scooping and kicking my way deeper into the darkness as fast as I can. I'm shivering, and my skin is covered in gooseflesh.

There she is.

Using all my strength, I catch up with her. I grab a hold

of her cold, limp body. I swivel beneath her so we're both flat; sinking back to back. I scull with my hands, putting the brakes on our descent, and trying to keep us level. I don't know why it didn't come to me sooner; the positioning is key. My gills had only activated when I hit the deck of the wreckage; I was underwater, flat, and held at a constant depth.

My muscles are going into spasm. If I'm wrong, I've condemned us both.

A jolt above me.

An elbow in my back.

A cry of panic.

She's alive!

I spin around and grab her under the arms, then kick upwards as hard as I can.

"Don't worry, I've got you!"

Gaia is freaking out. I'm lucky that my awakening was on my own terms, sort of. Hers is the stuff of watery nightmares.

The sunlit waters caress us as we near the surface. Gaia's coming to her senses. She breaks free and scrambles for the top, using her powerful limbs to propel herself upward.

"Wait, Gaia, you can't breathe up there!"

But she's gone, still panicking. She didn't see my face, so I doubt she's processed who I am. Her feet kick against me as she strives for the surface. I back off and swim beside her, keeping a cautious distance.

She bursts through the surface and flaps her arms, trying to hail the people on the shore, but her momentum is fleeting. As soon as she's below the waves again, her voice recovers. She's crying for help.

I watch as she battles upward again only for her cries to

vanish. Her vocal systems are tied to her breathing, which can't switch between water and air fast enough.

She tries a third time and someone spots her. As she falls beneath the waves, gasping for oxygen, someone plunges in and sprints towards us.

Malo.

If he drags her from the water now, she could asphyxiate before her lungs manage the transition. I have to stop him, to warn him she's not ready. Gaia's hovering around a meter beneath the surface, still processing the fact she can only breathe underwater.

Malo is barreling towards us, desperate to save his mother from drowning again.

As he gets close, he drops beneath the surface and looks around, honing in on her position. I dart upwards, putting myself between them.

"Malo, wait! If you pull her from the water she could die!"

He shoves me down and powers towards her.

"Gaia, tell him!"

As his hands reached out to grab her, he sees the gills on her neck. He recoils, horrified. Gaia stares at him, not knowing what to say; she's still in shock and trying to catch her breath.

I approach the pair of them with my hands raised.

"Chief, we need to talk."

Malo is tiring. There's only so long he can tread water in his state. I lead them both to the raft. We swim in through the ruptured hull, and up to the bridge level, where the water meets the air.

Malo pulls himself up through the hatch and out onto the dry side, gasping for air. He's blurry through the refracted, rippling light, but it looks like he's slumped against the wall. I turn my attention to his mother.

"Gaia, we're going to leave the water. It'll feel like you're suffocating, so you must trust your body. Your lungs will re-open, I swear, but it's gonna be rough. Follow me."

I climb the rungs, haul myself onto the bridge, and slouch down beside Malo. My larynx loosens almost at once; the switch is still painful, but somehow I've become faster at transitioning.

Malo shuffles away like I'm contagious.

Gaia's hands appear above the hatch. Malo helps her onto the dry deck. She rasps and wheezes as her conflicted airways struggle for dominance.

Malo panics as his mother's lips turn blue.

"She's suffocating! What's happening?"

Gaia's eyes are bulging as she struggles for air. I grab her arm and hold her steady.

"Hang in there, Chief, trust in your body!"

She looks at me, with wild, panicked eyes. Her lips are popping like a fish's.

"Focus, Chief, you can do it!"

A sense of determination fall across her face. Her grip slackens, and in an instant, her airways open.

Air rushes deep into her vacant lungs. Her chest swells and she falls into her son's arms. They embrace, weeping with relief and despair as she gulps down oxygen.

She regains her composure and takes a perch on the deck.

"So we're amphibians now, is that it?" she says.

Her tone is warm and humble.

"Something like that," I reply.

The hatch behind us erupts with water. We all leap back as a teenage girl lands on the deck. She crawls on all fours to a corner and waits for her breathing to acclimate. I sense this isn't the first time she's tried making the switch.

"Guessing you found your gills too, then?" I say.

She nods, wheezing.

"You saved her too?" says Gaia.

"What are we going to tell the others?" says Malo.

"You're chief now, what do you think?" says Gaia, patting him.

"Don't say that, Mom. I was chief for about five minutes while you were... you know... But I'm not ready. I'm so glad you're back."

"Keala, you've experienced and witnessed this 'transition' multiple times now. I'm guessing there's a right way and a wrong way to do it?"

Wait, the chief is asking *my* opinion?

"Er, from how it went for you guys, the important thing is that we warn anyone who's about to transition what to expect. Let's call them the patient. First, they'll struggle to breathe on land. Then their glands will swell until they pass out. Someone needs to get them underwater right away and lay them flat and still. The patient's glands will then burst, and their gills will kick in within a minute."

"What if their gills don't work?"

"That's a risk we're taking. Only submerge someone when you're certain they've completely stopped breathing on land."

"What about those of us who aren't affected?" says Malo.

"From what I saw, you're in the minority now. Maybe your symptoms will develop later. Regardless, I say we all need to work together."

"And do what?" said Gaia.

"Ah. I've not shown you the manual yet, have I? OK, this is going to take some explaining. I should warn you, you're not gonna like it."

They don't like it one bit. I'm explaining the manual in full; the way it was hidden in an emergency compartment, and how the text shows someone orchestrated our fate. Gaia seems almost indifferent. I emphasize that the other survivors still think *I* sank the vessel, and she agrees to set the record straight once more, but explains that the cause of our wreckage is of secondary concern to her. She has one priority: food production.

Gaia's been in politics her whole life, and she's exactly what we need right now. Her predecessor had no children of his own, and chose to appoint her as chief. She's ruled our islands for two decades and has campaigned for us on the international stage. Gaia understands people. She understands *theater*.

No-one had seen us board the wreckage. They'd seen me and Gaia disappear beneath the waves, and Malo dive after us. That, Gaia informs us, was the perfect backdrop for what she calls "the comeback tour."

We practice it several times until we're sure we can pull it off. Malo swims at the front of the pack. He surfaces away from the raft, obscuring our starting point, then swims towards the shore, calling for people to gather as he approaches.

He draws a crowd, promising a miracle. With the survivors gathered on the beach, Gaia appears in the crystalline shallows. People marvel. They realize she's not swimming, she's *walking* towards them, up from the sloping seabed. She's slow, controlled, and graceful. There's barely a ripple as she breaks the surface, and she masks the respiratory transition without a flinch.

The survivors are astonished. This miracle is rekindling their energy. It's time for me and the teenager to play our part. We ascend on either side of Gaia, a few meters behind her, like loyal servants of the sea.

Everyone falls to their knees like Gaia is a god or something. Like *we* are gods. I won't lie, I kinda love it. What they haven't yet clocked is that there will be a bunch more deities popping up over the next few days.

Someone on the shore is struggling to breathe - their condition is as severe as the chief's had been. Gaia gives me and the girl a nod and we approach the family. They recoil at the sight of me, but soften under Gaia's commanding gaze. I feel the boy's glands; they're ready to burst. His breaths are shallow and erratic, like he's teetering on the cusp of life. We carry him to the water and plunge him under. The boy's father leaps to his feet with a cry of despair. Malo steps before him with a solemn hand, "Have faith."

The assembled crowd watches in awe as the boy's glands burst and he draws his first water breaths. The girl tows him a little further out and calms him; she needs to teach him how his new dual-breathing works before he tries to breach the surface.

His family watch in amazement as their near-catatonic son swims with renewed strength.

Gaia capitalizes on the apparent miracle.

"My people, a new truth is upon us," she booms.

Credit to her, the woman sure can project. I've always wished I had her pipes.

"We are changing, some of us faster than others. It is the doing of those who have conspired to trap us. We must stand by one another, and endure the transformations being forced upon us. We must fight for our future, together, so that one day we may have vengeance."

People look concerned at this news. I can't blame them. Their chief just drowned before their eyes then popped back up half an hour later as a mermaid with a vendetta. You know the phrase "stranger things have happened at sea?"

Welcome to the sea.

"You wanted this to happen!" cries a dissenting man.

I hate this guy. He was the one who chased me onto the raft, and clearly he's decided Gaia's his next scapegoat.

"What are you talking about?" says Gaia.

"You planned this all along, so we'd have to follow you. You knew no one would accept Malo as your successor and this is your sick way of keeping power!"

The other non-infected people around him grunt in approval.

"I've done no such thing, I assure you. This travesty has been forced upon all of us, but we will emerge from it together," insists Gaia.

"If you didn't plan it, then you let it happen on your watch. You're not fit to lead us anymore," argues the man.

"You can hate me, or you can work with me. This transition will come for you in the days ahead, and when it does we shall welcome you back. Until that time, do as you will."

She gestures to the barren atoll behind them. The man and his supporters shift, angrily.

"We're prioritizing the kelp farm, as per Keala's manual," continues Gaia.

I wince as she calls it that. I don't want any association with that plastic-paged book of doom.

Malo retrieves it from where I'd abandoned it on the shore, and holds it up for all to see, along with the kelp sapling.

"We must ration what little food was salvaged. If we work together, we can grow enough kelp to sustain us a few days from now. I need builders for the kelp beds. They'll need materials, so I need strong hands to dismantle the raft."

"Dismantle the raft? Are you crazy? We need to repair it, or build a new one, it's our only hope of getting off this island!" cries the dissenting man.

"That raft was a death trap. What makes you think you can build a seaworthy replacement from its scraps?" says Gaia.

"I'll take my chances. It beats being marooned by kelp eating freaks for the rest of my life," spits the man.

"He's right, we should be making fishing nets, not kelp beds!" cries another.

"What are you going to make the nets from?" challenges Malo.

"Clothes?" suggests the first.

"You're all wrong, we need to fix the radio," yells a non-infected woman.

"Sure, anyone got a soldering iron? Spare parts for water-damaged components? Didn't think so," snaps Malo.

"I want justice for my boys! They drowned because you allowed that *poino* onto our raft!" yells an uninfected man.

His eyes are brimming with hurt as he points a trembling finger at me.

"She had nothing to do with the wreck," retorts Malo. "She saved your chief's life and you should be thankful."

"You would deny me my justice, boy?" spits the man.

"Have some respect for your future chief, man," growls Malo.

The two men square up to each other, bristling.

"Try it, boy. Maybe you're *poino* too," snarls the man.

Malo shoves the man's chest, hard. "Use that term again. I dare you."

The man steps close to Malo's chest and stares him in the eye. "*Poino.*"

Gaia intervenes with a booming, "Enough!"

Malo freezes, fist raised, glaring at the man. The grieving father hasn't flinched at all, but tears of grief are clinging to his eyes.

"We don't have energy to waste fighting each other," insists Gaia.

"Agreed," says the first dissenting man. "You people do what you want, but leave us the hell alone. We're building a raft and getting off this damned island."

"So be it," says Gaia. "You may take a proportionate amount of the raft's materials to meet your needs. The rest of you, we need to work fast on the kelp stock. Keala says we lost half the saplings in the impact, which means we're already behind. If you feel too weak to work, stay by the shore, and one of us will help you transition when the time comes. If you feel able, join us at the raft. We need a prototype working by nightfall or in the coming days we will starve."

CHAPTER FOURTEEN

LUKE

It's the end of my first day at school. Sorry, not school, evil villain lab. Curiously, both institutions have milk monitors. I think that's why I get them mixed in my head. That and the fact all my school teachers were really mean. In my defense, if you don't want kids to press fire alarms, don't make them big red buttons. Make 'em look like math homework and we'll leave them right alone. That said, I love the idea of homework that summons a fire truck. Man, maybe if they *had* done that, I'd have gone into coding or banking. I would be rich and anywhere but here.

I'm lingering by the elevator, waving people out as they go. I'm like, "Bye Drake," and he's like... well, he's like nothing. Turns out he's only chatty over meals.

He holds the elevator door for me. I feign having forgotten something in the locker room, and double back, away from his hawkish gaze. There's something about him that makes me uneasy. With Christie, I feel I know her deal; she's cold, discrete, and blunt. Drake's an anomaly though, he'll burst out laughing if something amuses him, then retreat into silence for hours, staring at the rest of us.

Christie seems consistently happy to keep the world at arm's length. Drake seems to want to grab us all in a headlock.

Here's the problem.

I met the biochemistry team at lunch, but starchy pants Pierre is still keeping me confined to lumberjack duties. That ain't gonna work for me because I need answers pronto. Especially now that I know they're in the business of making people disappear. I gotta risk it and go explore some more.

I head to the canteen. It's open, because the facility is open late for staff who don't have a life. Woah, does that mean Drake has a life? Oh, yeah, he moonlights as a *sociopath*. Duh.

This part of the building's shaped like an octopus, with the food court at its center. I go past our dining table and head for the doorway that Christie and the rest of the team had used.

To my amazement, my security pass works on the door. Jackpot.

I go inside.

Admittedly it's been a while since my lab days at college, but this facility is surely in a whole new league of labs. Floor to ceiling crates filled with hundreds of different species. It's like a cross between a zoo and an automated warehouse. Giant mechanical arms hang from the ceiling, moving cages to and from the observation platforms where bots do diagnostic and hygiene-related tasks.

My gut's telling me it's another simulation; a trick of some sort. I wouldn't put it past these people to be testing me still. But I'm a once-bitten kinda guy. After they pulled that stunt in the interview - with the chimpanzee attack in the simulation chamber - I went back to Chang and bought an anklet.

I'm aware anklets aren't the fashion item you'd naturally associate with someone like me, though I'm told I do have good calves. This device detects simulation fields and delivers a warning shock to the wearer. It's my way of ensuring these guys don't pull a fast one on me again. Of course, I gotta keep it hidden. There was a ring option, but I already told them I'm divorced. I could've claimed it was a step counter, but something tells me a place that's not on the map won't be wild about employees wearing recreational sports trackers inside.

There's no shock to my ankle, which means what I'm seeing is real, and it ain't pretty. An eerie silence greets my arrival. I approach the first set of cages. They're about half a cubic meter each and are stacked a dozen high.

The first row is rodents. Stacked above them are tanks of mosquitoes. Above them are frogs. Then chicks, marsupials, and cats. There are more cages but they're too high to see inside. I think there's a tail pressed up against the glass of the top one. Or is it a paw? I squint for a moment, then realize, to my discomfort, it's both.

One thing that strikes me is the smell. Or rather, the lack of it. Micro AC units feed into the back of every soundproofed cage, filtering microbes from the air, and, I presume, controlling what the animals can smell of their surroundings. I guess if I were stuck in a box with my natural predator right above me, I'd be all kinds of stressed, which would wreck my biostats. Besides, the lab will be minimizing the chance of pathogens transferring between species.

They're already risking contagion by keeping them in the same warehouse, even with the sealed crates in place.

There are two possibilities here. One: space is limited, so they were forced to cram everyone in like Noah's ark. Given that they found room for a forest, I find this unlikely. Which brings me onto possibility two: they're not that worried about contagion because they know something I don't.

And then it hits me. This is my next test. It's the only reason a place this secure would have let my pass get me into this section. They wanted to see if I'd go looking. OK, they've got me there. Now they'll want to see if I'm a real immunologist. I've gotta figure out what they've done to achieve generic herd immunity across such a diverse range of species.

If this giant game of animal Jenga and the swaddled forest below show one thing, it's that these people value efficiency. There's no way they could have cross-vaccinated every species against every possible pathogen; to do that you'd have to predict every future mutation of a virus or bacterium. Plus you'd have to have synthesized a cure or vaccine for all existing animal and insect pathogens. Even with the leaps we've made with AI healthcare, we're not there yet.

So how do you achieve pan-herd immunity when you're juggling so many variables? There's only one technology I can think of, and last time I checked, it was neither feasible nor legal.

Nanobots.

Conventional vaccines work by exposing the host's immune system to a pathogen and training it to destroy it. Kinda like target practice. With nanobots, you cut out the middle man, and just give the host a new immune system that's got heat-seeking missiles of its own. But nanobots aren't infallible; they're only as good as their programming. To avoid killing the host, they need to distinguish between the host's own healthy cells, symbiotic cells like gut bacteria, and dangerous foreign agents. Which means the nanobot needs a vast internal library. But pathogens are real sneaky - they're good at pretending they're locals; blending into the neighborhood before stealing your hub caps. If you inject a nanobot without the ability to distinguish, all you've done is induce a new autoimmune disease in your subject. Something of an own goal.

However, if you inject a nanobot that *can* successfully distinguish, then all you've done is replace the host's immune system with a superior artificial one. For that to be sustainable, it can't rely on a database. That would become out of date within a few years, and then you're back to square one. No, for the nanobots to give lasting benefit, they need to run on something more versatile; they need a set of rules.

What's the genetic definition of friend or foe? All complex organic life comprises of multiple species. Right now I've got billions of non-human bacterial cells floating around my gut, helping me digest food, and generate the energy I need to live. If a nanobot were to exterminate them just because they don't have human DNA, I'd be screwed.

Bodies are also highly specialized things. Calcium is great in your bones, but too much in the bloodstream can land you in a coma. Yowzer. So your nanobot's also gotta know where things belong, which means it needs to know where *it* is at any given time, in any given species. Which brings us back to an encoded library, and the limitations of that approach. Even if you flipped the approach on its head, and taught your nanobot to only look for signs of damage, rather than initial intrusions, it would still have to know what constitutes damage in any given area. Urea in your bladder is par for the course, but if gallons of the stuff are floating around your eyeballs that's not so great.

I see why they wanted an immunologist: this stuff's a headache. It's also at the absolute outer limit of my college minor. No way I can crack this at an outside glance. I need to dig deeper.

There's something about these animals that's of interest to the lab; I need to figure out what. I examine the crates closer. The animals look identical, one cage to the next. I'm guessing they're clones, bred for testing. Clones can be bred in a sterile environment, sure, but subjects with identical genomes make for terrible test subjects if you want generalizable findings. But hey, what do I know, I'm the new kid.

I examine the rats on the lower level. The screens display a holding status above each one. *Test: Leptospirosis. Status: Pending.* The one next to it is Mycoplasma, and beside that, Pasteurella. What a yummy line up of bacterial infections they're being treated to. I scroll through the nearest rat's case notes. This creature has been methodically exposed to hundreds of diseases, yet it looks fit as a fiddle. Not a single infection took hold. Props to whatever medical robo cops must be floating through its system.

The mosquitoes in the crates above look normal, but then again, they'd probably have to be bright green or have bat wings for me to spot a difference. Bugs are small. I don't know what more you expect from me.

I scroll through their case notes. This is weird. I'm not seeing any diseases. Instead, I'm looking at a single item. It looks like the name of an artificial protein. The cage beside it has the same name but a different end number. The entire row is battery testing different variants of the same transplanted protein. It can't be a cure for malaria, because they've got that from their nanobots. So what are they trying to do?

My eyes skip to the cages above. The cats are weird as hell. They've got pouches on the sides to carry their kittens in. It's cute, but kinda disturbing. They look like pimped out UGG boots. Here, kitty kitty.

A robotic arm bleeps in warning. I move just in time as it grabs a crate beside me. The resident marsupial presses against the glass anxiously. The screen above its head has turned red, with the words *POSITIVE SAMPLE DETECTED*. With a hiss, cables detach from the rear of the cage, and it swings towards the ceiling.

A magnetic claw is dangling from a monorail spanning the width of the room. It latches onto the new parcel and whisks it through a side hatch. I don't know where that critter's being taken, but I doubt it's Disneyland.

I move to the next aisle. The crates here are way bigger. It looks like Old MacDonald had a farm, then sold it to the Koch brothers. Ee-eye, ee-eye, uh-oh. Take the pigs, for instance. They look depressed. I've no doubt their forbearers' lives were just terrific, what with being hemmed together, stuffed with antibiotics and growth hormones, then pulped and reconstituted as someone's pizza topping. Oh dayyyum, *that's* how we make sausage? I know. The twentieth century was gross. But even with that low, low benchmark to beat, these pigs look a whole new level of miserable. It's a curse, being both smarter *and* tastier than cats and dogs. If you're an animal, the trick is to be cute, dumb, and yucky.

The pig's lying down, and it looks kinda blue. Not just in the depressed sense, I mean it literally looks blue, like it's been left out in Siberia. However, there's no frost forming on the crate window, so it's not the air that's cold, it's the pig alone.

Question: how does a large, well-insulated mammal in a small, warm cube, get the chills?

I check the notes above the pig. Holy bejeezus. Are these people for real? This ain't a pig. It's a pigadile. Or Pigzard. Or pigamander. Whatever, I'll work on the name, the point is, they've modified the hell out of this thing and made it ectothermic. They've figure out how to turn its internal thermostat off without killing it outright. It's a bacon flavored reptile.

Maybe this is just my inner mammal talking, but I kinda dig being able to regulate my body temperature. I would go so far as to say it's an essential, finely honed evolutionary adaptation fundamental to our class's survival. So why in hell's name is the lab trying to reverse that?

Allow me to play Old MacDonald's dirtbag business manager for a moment. A pig that doesn't burn calories maintaining its internal temperature is gonna need less feed and so be cheaper to rear. Not as cheap as bacon flavored plants, but cheaper than a porky furnace on legs, which is what regular pigs are.

I move down the terrace to check on porky's neighbors. One's passed out. The cage is misty, and warm to the touch; it's a veritable sauna in there. There's no sweat on the pig though, which suggests it's not capable of sweating anymore. Hence passing out. I'm sensing the transition to being cold-blooded might not be all it's cracked up to be. Or maybe of all this pigs, this one's the cheapest to rear? A dead pig burns zero calories.

Above the pigs are rhesus monkeys, foxes, ferrets, puppies, and sheep. It's quite the variety pack here, all stacked up like Mother Nature's vending machine.

Much as I feel for these pitiful animals, I'm not here for them.

I'm looking for something very specific.

As I walk, I'm dodging flying crates and robotic arms, until I'm in the furthest depths of the vast warehouse.

There it is, just like the briefing said.

It's a narrow doorway, wide enough for one person to enter at a time. Entrance is via a thick, sliding steel curtain, controlled by a scanner with facial recognition, fingerprinting, keypad, and card. I take out my pass and approach the scanner. The door frame is much thicker than the others labs'. It looks reinforced, but against what? Someone trying to get in?

Something trying to get out?

As I hold my pass, nerves flush through me. Everything I've prepared for is behind this door.

I insert my card but it blinks red. Denied. My eyes dart to the facial scanner. This was a mistake. The system will have registered my attempt. The camera's studying my face for clues as to my goal.

I pause for a moment and consider my next move. My instincts are telling me to turn and run. I could try to find the security booth and scrub the footage before my boss investigates?

Or I could double down. Look innocent, look presumptuous, look like I deserve to be admitted. I choose the latter and swipe my card several more times, making a conscious point of looking frustrated and curious as to why I'm not being admitted into the super-secret lab which I blatantly don't have clearance for.

I flap my arms in a melodramatic display of resignation, then turn to head back through the warehouse. There's a sound from behind the steel curtain, like a secondary door cranking open and closing with a hiss. With it, I'm hearing a muffled voice.

The security door sweeps open with a hiss, and I press myself flush to the wall. The director strides out in a hurry. She's on a call, and whoever she's speaking to is getting an earful. As she marches away from me, I take a leap of faith and dart back towards the doorway. It's closing too fast, there's no way I can get through in time, but I glimpse a second thick door beyond, also sliding shut. Breaking into this lab's not gonna be easy.

I creep through the warehouse, keeping my distance from my boss, and ducking robotic arms, while trying to stay within earshot of her voice.

"What you're asking is unreasonable... I know we have the equipment, but that doesn't mean it's what it was intended for... No, you listen to me, there's a reason we don't do that here... You need me to spell it out for you? You've heard of the law, right?... We would lose all deniability!... Are you asking me or telling me?... You expect me to run a facility discretely then you pull a move like this?... You're risking everything we've been working towards... Drake handles that sort of thing... Yes I can count on him... I'll brief him first thing..."

The warehouse door opens and she's gone. I have no idea what she's so afraid of, but I have to find out quickly. Things are moving faster than we expected.

CHAPTER FIFTEEN

KEALA

Stripping the raft is not going to plan. We missed the evening deadline set by Gaia. It's now day three on this tiny rocky atoll and morale is fast evaporating. Most of our survivors are too weak to work; debilitated by dehydration, hunger, or the mutation process. Of the few of us strong enough to work, we've split our labor. A few of our engineers are working on constructing the kelp bar in the shallows, but they need building materials. That's where we come in; the few of us transformed enough to work underwater.

Malo's gills burst early this morning. Despite having reduced strength he immediately joined us working underwater. It's clear to me he's struggling to adjust. I don't think it's about practice either; I'm worried his gills are underdeveloped.

I'm pressing hard against the hull of the raft while Malo's pulling from the other side. We're following the manual, but the vessel's twisted and buckled; none of the pieces are coming apart as they should. In the past thirty minutes all we've managed is to dislodge one end of a beam by half a yard.

Malo relinquishes his grip, panting.

I peer through the gap in the hull. "Take a break, I'll meet you back on the shore."

He shakes his head in frustration. He's not used to being useless.

"We can do this," he grunts.

He presses his legs against the hull and pulls. From the inside of the wreck, I grab an overhead rail and push. The girl I saved sees us struggling and throws her weight behind me. The beam creaks, then splinters off from the hull.

It drifts away in suspended animation, not quite sinking, not quite floating. Malo's too exhausted to chase it. I hurry out and grab the beam; we can't risk them slipping into the deep.

Malo's clinging to the broken hull with his head resting on his arms. His feet dangle below him. I swim back with the beam in tow.

"Hey, what's up with you?"

He raises his head. He looks rough.

"I'm OK, I just need to catch my breath," he mumbles.

I take another pass but he shouts me down, loathe to discuss any notion that he might be permanently weakened.

"All right. I'm gonna swim this one in," I say.

I've studied the emergency manual back to front several times, undertaking an all-too-literal crash course in the new kelp farming techniques. According to the instructions, the long beams across the hull should be easily dismantled, and easily reassembled as kelp troughs. What the genius designers didn't factor in is the damage caused by running aground - despite acknowledging such a scenario in the foreword. The hull is crumpled, which means the beams don't pop out as intended. They have to be ripped. It also means they don't slot back together as per the kelp bar blueprints, instead we have to tie them.

I wade through the shallows to the construction team, where they add my beam to the mesh they're building. The teenage girl arrives beside me and hands over several soaking bed sheets. She dumps them in a pile beside a worker who is fashioning rope to bind the mesh together.

The central beam holds our first row of saplings; those which I'd found in a sealed packet. These saplings are the only things our saboteurs got right. They're perfectly prepared for planting. Their hold-fasts - a kelp's version of roots - have been nurtured to maturity, then softened and removed for transportation. Yesterday we wrapped them around the first kelp bar. We doused the hold-fasts in gel, then placed the bar in the shallows, two feet deep. Anchors made of bed sheets and rocks stopped it drifting overnight. Since then, the kelp has grown to reach the surface, and now it's fanning out horizontally.

According to the manual, such surface-fanning is to be avoided. The kelp bar is designed to sink further each day; straightening the kelp out vertically, and forcing it to keep striving for the surface sunlight, and thus grow faster. That ingenious design relies on an automatic winch. Was the winch on board? Was it hell.

We'll have to manually set the mesh levels each day, meaning we won't get the optimal growth-to-descent gradient. If we want to scale up, that will be a problem.

But that's a bridge to cross later. Our concern today is seeding the rest of the mesh. Only, we're out of saplings. To start new colonies, we need to coppice yesterday's specimens and figure out a way to secure them to the beams until they sprout hold-fasts of their own.

This plan is deeply contentious among the broader group. There are fifty mouths to feed, and tensions are mounting. The last thing starving people want is to watch their food get replanted.

Gaia announced a backup plan early this morning, to stave off confrontation.

She selected our best surviving fishers. Our nets were lost in the crash, so she equipped them with bed sheets. But sheet fishing is usually for rivers and ponds, where you can drive the fish in one direction. Their challenge is to make it work in the open ocean. There's one thing in their favor, at least: now they have gills too.

Of course, their success relies on shoals swimming nearby. Wary of such a critical dependency, Gaia formed a second scavenger team. Using their gills, they must dive deeper than any of us had on our first day and search for our lost rations.

Personally, my hopes are low. From my experience sinking with Gaia's unconscious body, I know the ocean gets deep quickly around here; I couldn't see the bottom, that's for sure.

That said, the scavenger team is foraging in all directions. Currents do funny things with cargo. We once had thousands of flip flops wash up on our beach, back on our home island. No one knows where they came from, or where they were destined, but we all had free footwear, which was fun.

A bunch of birds and a couple of dolphins washed up dead a few days later, with flip flops in their bellies, which was not so fun.

There's a feeble cheer from the land.

"They're back, they're back!" cries a child.

The scavengers are approaching from across the atoll.

They're dragging a large tub with them. My heart leaps for joy; they've found one of the sunken ration capsules!

I hurry along the beach and join the jostling crowd. Even the sickest and weakest among us find strength to flock towards this gift from the gods. We hover, elbow to elbow, in front of our new heroes.

Gaia calls on us to clear a path, and makes her way to the three proud swimmers. She addresses the crowd. "We will distribute these supplies equitably, as we always do. Please be seated."

She waits with open arms, inviting the starving crowd to sit.

No one moves.

Hungry feet shift in the sand.

I study Gaia's face. She has an amazing ability to convey both warmth and power. It's something about how she tenses her mouth while smiling softly with her eyes. Usually her face only shows what she wants you to see, but this time I spot something more in the corner of her eyes.

Doubt.

She is the only thing standing between fifty ravenous bellies and fresh food. Unarmed, and alone, she's not backing down.

Then it happened.

The first person sits down.

Then another.

And another.

One by one, each survivor resolves to suppress their hunger for a few more agonizing moments.

With everyone seated, Gaia gives the crowd a gracious bow of her head. She orders the swimmers to prize the capsule open. I crane my neck to see. The lead swimmer groans, squeezing her fingers under the latch. She tears it open with a grunt, and stumbles back.

A horrified moan sweeps across the crowd as sea water gushes from the capsule, followed by sodden, punctured sacks of grain and vegetables.

"I don't understand," cries the swimmer. "The raft people said the boxes were airtight!"

"All that for nothing!" says another, slumping onto the wet sand.

"There must be something we can use?" calls a man beside me.

"It's soaked through, the whole lot. There's no way we can eat this stuff," replies the swimmer.

"Maybe some of us can? We can breathe sea water now, perhaps we can digest it too?" says the man.

"Hands up who's been drinking the water as they swim," says Gaia.

Of those who have transitioned, almost all the hands go up, mine included.

"Keep your hand raised if you could stomach it," she continues.

The hands drop, dejectedly. We all know it makes us sick. I can only manage a tiny sip before nausea sets in.

"If we eat this food now, the salt content will only dehydrate us faster. It could kill us," says Gaia.

"If we *don't* eat it, starvation will get us either way," cries the man beside me.

"Then I leave it to you all to make that decision for yourselves. If you wish to take what is here, you will not be stopped. But I warn you, this is not food, it is poison."

"So where's the proper food then?" demands another man across the crowd.

"We will find it," says Gaia.

"How?" snaps another.

"I need fresh volunteers. These swimmers are tired and must rest. More of you have transitioned now and it is your turn to go. Speak with the swimmers and go where they suggest. Have faith that we will find another box, which will be undamaged," says Gaia.

The man beside me rises to his feet and points at Gaia.

"You told us to have faith when we left our island, our home. We should never have trusted you!"

Several others cheer in agreement.

"I need three volunteers for the search," says Gaia, ignoring the man.

No one moves.

"Only by working together will we solve this," she insists.

Her words are firm, but her tone has shifted. She can no longer mask her despair.

"Please. I am asking you, as your chief, to have hope. We can get through this if we keep our courage. Who will volunteer next?"

Heads drop as people fidgeted with the sand before them. Fifty hungry, desperate, duplicitous minds, each spiraling in unknown directions.

Another man rises to his feet and points at Gaia with disgust. As he opens his mouth to speak, a voice interrupts from the shallows.

"Plane! There's a plane!"

Everyone crowds towards the mesh, as if that will give them a better view.

Tens of thousands of feet above us, a passenger jet crosses the barren sky.

We're leaping, shouting, waving our arms, creating an almighty racket that's vanishing into the wind. With the hope and delusional zeal of the desperate, we hop and bellow for minutes until the plane is out of sight.

A desolate silence falls upon the crowd. We're each processing what that means for our chances of survival.

"Hey!" comes a cry.

One of the mesh workers is in distress.

The man who accused Gaia has seized the kelp bar. He's tearing strips of kelp off and shoving them into his mouth.

"Cut it out!" cries a woman.

She tackles the first guy, dragging him below the surface.

Too late.

The floodgates are open.

Another man seizes a fistful from the opposite end. Three girls around him pile in too, clamoring to get a piece.

"No! Leave it! We have to let it grow first!" I cry.

The other construction workers are begging the same, but their voices are lost amid the crowd.

The water churns as people fight to reach the mesh. Others brawl to get kelp from those who have reached it already. Only a handful of us are fighting to fend them off.

"*Enough!*" comes a cry from across the sand. "We've got proper food!"

The word "food" spreads through the mob like wildfire. The fighting halts as all eyes fall upon the beach figures.

Our fishers have returned. Two of them are carrying a sheet laden with fish. The third carries a turtle above her head.

Scrambling from the water, the crowd rushes up shore towards the newcomers. The fishers' faces turn from triumph to fear as the ravenous mob closes in.

Malo sprints into the middle. He's wielding a pole from the raft.

"Sit and you will be fed. Continue, and you will be hurt," he yells.

Leading the mob is the same man who started the kelp grab. He ignores Malo's warning and charges towards the fishers. Malo feigns a lunge to the left, then swings the pole hard into the man's jaw. The man hits the ground and howls in pain. Malo set his legs wide apart and raises the pole again, bracing for the next wave.

But it doesn't come.

The hungry mob comes to a halt before Malo.

Two more from our salvage team join him, wielding metal staffs ripped from the raft. They take up defensive positions on either side of the fishers. Malo redoubles his grip, then bellows to the crowd.

"You will sit. Food will be brought to you. If you take someone else's food, you will be punished. If you stand, you will be struck. Do not test me again."

The mob slump one by one into the sand. Many look relieved that the fighting is over, while others have faces wrought with resentment. All eyes are on the dripping sheet being unwrapped behind Malo.

The three fishers form a production line. With knives and tubs from the raft, they gut and dice the fish. One of Malo's trusted friends distributes the bone-filled portions to the waiting crowd.

Raw fish isn't something we usually go for, but we've got no wood for a fire. I'll take my chances with a parasite over starving to death.

Among the survivors is a handful whose mutations are progressing much slower than the rest of ours. They aren't able to even sip the sea water. This makes them the most dehydrated, so they're given turtle blood in addition to the fish.

Once everyone has been served, a second round of food is distributed - this time, the turtle's flesh.

Turtles have a sacred status in our community. Eating them used to be the sole right of the chief's family, but Gaia's predecessor did away with that, decreeing that we must protect the few that remain.

Nothing about this experience is pleasant. We receive the turtle meat with guilt and averted eyes. As I finish my ration, I feel a hand on my shoulder. Gaia beckons me away from the feasting group.

We walk to the edge of the water. Malo joins us. Gaia keeps her voice low.

"You both saw what happened. I don't know how much longer we can keep people like this," she whispers.

"They will stay in line, or they'll face the consequences," says Malo.

"And what if they make poles of their own, Malo? Will we fight them all over again?"

"If that is what it takes."

"Until only warriors remain? The strongest fighters aren't our best fishers, or farmers. We *must* keep the peace. Besides, we can't rely on fishing out here. We're not equipped, and sending people into the open ocean is extremely risky. Four people volunteered this morning, and only three came back. The food we have now comes at a heavy price."

"What happened to her - the fourth fisher?"

"They were miles out, fighting the current to get back here, and her gills stopped working. The others had to choose between saving her and keeping hold of our food. They chose our lives over hers."

"They watched her drown?" I say, appalled.

"And they're all traumatized because of it. We *cannot* let that happen again. People's bodies are still changing in ways we don't understand. Fishing is a last resort, and we must regard it as a lethal one. We have to restart the kelp program at once. Can you fix the mesh, Keala?"

Gaia gestures to the kelp bars, which float abandoned in the water. The saplings are in tatters. Many are stripped down to the stalk, others torn off completely.

"We can fix the mesh, but it will take time to regrow what we've lost. They've set us back days," I reply.

"Then we'll work twice as fast. If people have energy to fight, they have energy to help," growls Malo.

"But what if the fishers find nothing tomorrow? People will just attack the bar again."

Gaia and Malo exchange a grim look.

"No, they won't."

Malo sets off towards the crowd. The man who attacked the kelp bar first, and charged at the fishers, has regained consciousness. He's chewing on a hunk of turtle with one side of his mouth. Malo makes a beeline for him, pole in hand.

"You focus on fixing the mesh, Keala," says Gaia, squeezing my arm.

"What will you two do?"

She sets off after her son. "We will remind people that betrayal has consequences."

CHAPTER SIXTEEN

LUKE

It's evening, and I'm sitting in a crap bar near my crap apartment. Looks like this place is my new watering hole. The phone call I overheard between my director and her superior has cranked things up a gear. I have to guarantee it's me in that dark lab tomorrow, taking delivery of whatever this mystery shipment is.

I take my beer and go sit in a booth, ready for my contact to arrive. While I wait, I check out the social media feed on the phone I got with my new identity. It's always worth swatting up on your backstory in moments where you have a little breathing room. You never know when someone might quiz you on your family holiday to, uh, where was this one taken? Ah, right. Brussels. How could I forget?

A shaven-headed woman shuffles into the seat opposite me. She's broad shouldered, with an abundance of neck tattoos, a competitive number of piercings, and a pancake-flat expression that says *try me*.

Am I about to get mugged? It's my first night out in this neighborhood, and I picked the seediest bar I could find.

One where no one bats an eyelid if two strangers meet in a booth for illegal transactions.

The woman slides an earpiece across the table and glares at me until I put it on. As she pulls her hood up, her face vanishes into shadow. In her place appears a hologram of Chang, the teenage kid from the forgery outfit. Even though I can only see his face, I know in my bones he's reclining in that damned swivel chair of his, smoking a cigar or something ridiculous.

"Dr. Ragazzi. How nice see you again."

"Yeah, it's an emotional reunion, I'm welling up. Do you got what I asked for?"

"Ah, about that. I afraid we not able to process entirety of your order."

"Why the hell not? I told you it was urgent."

"You not eligible to purchase thirty minute memory wipe."

"You're telling me I need some kinda license to shop in your black market?"

"Money, Dr. Ragazzi. You need money."

"What are you talking about? I transferred you the crypto."

"I afraid your payment was declined. Insufficient fund."

"Impossible."

"Apparently not."

"Wait one minute. I show you right now."

I log into the banking app on the phone they set up for me. The account's empty.

"How is this possible?"

"We take what little was in your account for cover our material services. Fifty percent remain outstanding, Dr. Ragazzi, but as loyal customer, I extending you line of credit to cover shortfall."

"How very kind. Gee, I don't suppose there's any interest on this loan, is there?"

The kid lets out a rehearsed laugh. At the same time, the woman's hand extends across the table, reminding me there's an actual human lurking in the shadowy hood. She grabs my beer and pulls the bottle through the hologram. Chang's face warps around as she drinks.

"Hey, Val, cut it out, we talking here!" yells Chang.

Val sets the beer back down and slouches, huffily. Chang straightens his collar like he's been physically creased by the incident, then resumes his business manner.

"First forty eight hour is modest five percent. After that, fee doubling."

"You mean the *rate* doubles?"

"No, I mean fee."

"That's insane."

"Only if you take over forty-eight hour, Dr. Ragazzi, which I sure you won't. That would be very expensive mistake."

The kid isn't smiling any more. He looks ten years older, and a lot wiser. Have I misjudged him too?

"Do you accept terms of agreement?"

"I don't see that I have any choice."

"Good. We look forward to receive swift payment, or we be in touch."

"Yeah, I get it, you know where I live."

"Not like that, Dr. Ragazzi. We contact your employer. I'm sure they interested to know who you really are."

Chang's hologram vanishes. My throat's a desert. I reach for my beer but Val beats me to it. She guzzles the entire bottle, then sets it down with a pointed thud and slides out of the booth.

She's left a backpack behind. I'm about to call after her,

then I realize it's the thing I just paid for. Sorry, took out a *loan* for. This is insane, somehow I'm now in debt to these people. But that's tomorrow's problem, right now I've got work to do.

I make my way to the bathroom and take a cubicle. The seat's missing and the pan's filthier than my teenage browser history, so it's standing room only. I rifle through the backpack; it's all there, including a creased pamphlet with a handwritten address.

I probe the ceiling tile above me; it's loose. I nudge it upwards and slide my phone into the cavity, then let the tile fall back into position. With my cellular location set at the bar, I slip out of the rear exit, and make for the row of cash-only taxis nearby. I slide into the least filthy cab and announce the zip code. It's time to pay my new colleague Drake a visit.

Obviously I don't give the driver the complete address, I'm not a total rookie. I get him to drop me off a few blocks out and I walk the rest of the way. Having checked the area on my phone before setting off, I know where I'm walking. I also checked out a bunch of other places to cover my tracks - to anyone monitoring my phone, it'll look like a new guy browsing for better bars. Which would make sense, given the reviews of my local skid mark tavern.

I approach Drake's apartment building. It's swanky, way nicer than the dump I'm staying in. I'm about to do my first card trick, but someone's leaving as I arrive. Lucky for me they're on the phone; they've got the glazed look of a person talking to an AR overlay. Personally, I always bump into stuff whenever I do that. I have to either sit down for calls, or disable the video.

The resident doesn't give me a second look, which is just as well, because I look hella suspicious. Oh, I should have said, I did a costume change back at the bar.

I'm wearing a mask now. It's a shiny silicon mold of Beethoven's face.

I know what you're thinking, this is all kinda low tech and a little cultish. If you're gonna trick a sophisticated surveillance state, you've only got two choices: hack the bejeezus out of it and hire a premier holographic overlay to distort your image. Or, if you're on a budget like me, get a novelty mask and some clown shoes.

OK they're not *literal* clown shoes, they're just sneakers that are three sizes too big. I stuffed the tips with toilet paper from the bathroom, so I can walk pretty good. Footwear is equally important as your mask. You know how everyone's got a unique fingerprint? Well, the way you walk is just as distinctive. If you filmed everyone walking down a street and looked at their silhouettes, it'd seem kinda random. But if you replicated one person, and put them somewhere else in the feed, I bet you'd spot the similarity after a few goes. That's how the surveillance algorithms work. They analyze people's gaits, tag the core pattern of each one, allowing for certain tolerances, then look for recurrences of your pattern across other feeds. Makes it hard for fugitives to get across a city on foot.

Unless the fugitive buys some clown shoes and stuffs them with toilet paper. Then you've got a one-time gait that appears at the crime scene and vanishes when you ditch the shoes. It's a neat way to disappear on the cheap.

I catch the main door before it closes and head straight across the lobby. Naturally, I avoid the elevator; when you're dressed like this, you don't wanna get caught in a confined space with a stranger.

I head up the stairs. I'll admit, I stumble a few times. It's hard not to clip the steps when your feet are suddenly twice the size you're used to. I'm also trying to pull on these tight blue latex gloves as I go. Again, not the sort of thing you wanna get caught wearing. Beethoven mask? People won't even notice. Blue medical gloves? Spot the murderer!

I get to the third floor and peer into the corridor. There's no one about. I creep towards Drake's door, number 302. My heart's pounding now. This all about to get very real. I would feel a hell of a lot more confident going in if they'd given me the memory wipe kit like I'd asked. Hey ho, as my mom always said, when life gives you lemons, dress like a composer and go whack a guy.

In my pocket is the master stroke: a skeleton key for the building. It's highly illegal, I don't know how Chang replicated it, but I don't care so long as it works. From the blueprints they gave me, I know the layout of the apartment, but I don't know which bit he's currently in, or if he's even alone.

I hold the skeleton key to the reader and the door clicks open. I turn the handle as quietly as I can, and brace for a skirmish.

Here.

Goes.

Nothing.

I leap inside, ready to pepper spray anything that moves. As I spin, getting my bearings in the apartment, I realize he's not there. Not in the big kitchen-lounge, anyway. I creep towards the bedroom; the door's ajar. I tap it open. It's empty too, but there's the sound of running water.

He's in the shower.

This buys me precious moments to set up.

It's a strange feeling sneaking around someone's bedroom while they're in the en suite just yards away, having a shower karaoke session, with no idea you're there. Or what's coming for them.

I drop my backpack to the floor. I'm about to get to work when I pause and take in Drake's bedroom properly. There's something about the decor that's turning me cold. First, the guy has a four poster bed. What the hell. Second, mounted on the wall beside it is a samurai sword. Along from that is a shelf stashed with trophies and framed photos. I look closer and I swear to god it's like a nightmare unfolding before my eyes.

Welterweight finalist, West Coast MMA Championships.

Oh god. This really feels like the kind of detail that should have been in the pack.

Either I'm about to have every bone in my body broken by a coworker I met nine hours ago, or I'm gonna catch him off guard, and get this done. Given that I've taken out a gang loan to be here, there's no going back.

The shower's still running. I open my backpack and get to work. First, the petals. I scatter them across the floor and the bed. Next, the underwear. A particularly lacy set. I drop the bra by the door, the stockings by the foot of the bed, and leave the panties twisted on the sheets.

I put a box of condoms on the bedside table, and one on the bed, with the wrapper part opened. Now, where to put the whip? By the pillows, ready for brandishing? Or at the base, for spanking? I go with the middle and ruffle the blanket beneath so it looks like it's been grabbed.

I place the studded dog collar on the pillow, then grab

the handcuffs from the bag. Suddenly the four poster bed seems like a gift. I clip one onto to each post, ready for Drake's unsuspecting limbs. I'm just about to unpack a range of mind boggling sex toys when something on the counter catches my eye.

A tablet.

A work tablet.

Drake's work tablet.

Drake who works in the dark lab.

I rush over and flick the button but it's locked. I try tapping the skeleton key against it, but that locks me out for thirty seconds.

A noise pricks my ears. Or rather, a lack of noise. The water's stopped running. The shower curtain's being pulled back. I have seconds to get into position. I drop the tablet and dart across the room. Crap - my pepper spray's on the opposite side of the bed, by my backpack. There's no time, the door handle's turning.

I leap backwards and press myself flush against the wall, right beside the en suite doorway. My heart's in my throat. I've got no way to subdue him. Surprise is the only thing in my favor.

The door clicks open and a plume of papaya-scented steam wafts into the room. Drake steps forward and sees the insanely erotic arrangement laid out across his bedroom.

Before Drake can finish the sentence, "What the h-", I'm upon him.

I grab him in a headlock and pull him close to my chest. I've got him tight, but I need to steer us towards the pepper spray.

I feel his hand chop against my groin. He's fighting back. We're both groaning. He's twisting. His other arm has reached over my shoulder and he's clawing at my eyes.

I lean away, I can't risk him pulling off the mask.

Fatal mistake.

My leg's outstretched and my head's tilting back, I'm way off balance. I've fallen into his trap. Before I can think, I feel Drake's knee drive into the back of my own. My leg crumples and I fall to the ground.

I'm winded, and feeling about a hundred years old as my back twinges from the impact. My vision's gone black. I hastily rearrange the mask so I can see through the slits.

Drake's standing above me, naked, and he looks majorly pissed off. He does a series of sweeping martial arts motions like he's summoning all the power of the ancient world to totally kick my ass.

He falters. He sways and stumbles. He looks confused. His face is turning purple. He's beginning to rasp. He falls to his knees, clutching his throat. The guy's turning into a veiny raisin before my very eyes. The guy's choking on something.

He falls onto his back.

I jump to my feet.

"Drake, Drake are you OK? What's going on?"

Dammit, he's heard my voice now. I'll worry about that later. Right now I need to stop him from dying on my watch.

His back arcs up from the floor like he's being electrocuted. He's wheezing something awful. His face is swelling hideously. He jabs a desperate finger at me.

"What? What is it?"

I follow his gaze to my blue gloves.

Holy crap. Drake's got a latex allergy. A bad one. He's going into anaphylaxis.

His other hand points to his bedside cabinet. He's barely moving now. I rush across to it and pull the drawer open. I'm tearing all his clothes out. It's mainly karate belts and tighty-whitie underpants until - there!

I grab the EpiPen and fall beside him. I tear off the cap and ram it into the side of his leg.

Drake gasps as his airways dilate.

I collapse beside him and the two of us pant, shoulder to shoulder, in exhausted relief. I lock eyes with Drake, and the moment of calm shatters. His strength is recovering. This time he really is gonna kick my ass.

I leap to my feet and make a bid for my backpack. I reach out, about to grab the pepper spray, when a hand seizes my ankle and pulls me to the ground. I'm on my knees, clambering for it. Drake wraps his arms around my leg. He's crawling up me. I can feel the friction burns against my knees as I drag the two of us towards my bag.

With my spare leg I kick him in the eye. He falls back, grunting. I leap forwards and grab the spray, but he dives onto my back, pinning me. Every second I delay, he's regaining strength.

I rock onto my side and kick off against the bed. Our positions are reversed; he's the one on his back. His arm locks around my neck, choking me. I fumble the can and spray in the general direction of his face.

He howls in pain.

I break free from his grip and scramble across the floor. I'm seeing stars.

I haul his naked body onto the bed. He's rasping again. God *dammit,* how did I forget about the allergy! Drake's looking lousy now. His eyes are all puffy, his nose is running, and now he can't breathe again. This is not going well.

I clip his wrists into the handcuffs, then his ankles too. He's wheezing worse than an old vacuum cleaner. I rummage through his drawers again. Nothing. I run to the bathroom cabinet. Aha!

I rush back to the bed and plunge the second EpiPen into his thigh.

This time there's no easy rush of air, no sudden relief. He's in a bad way. Oh boy. There's only one thing for it.

I grab Drake's phone off the counter and dial 911. The operator picks up right away.

"911 what's your emergency?"

"I need an ambulance to this address. My, uh, neighbor's having an allergic reaction. He's going into anaphylactic shock."

I'll confess, I'm not the best at multi-tasking, but I have to get this next bit done. I wedge against my shoulder as I rummage through the backpack.

"Is the patient conscious and breathing?"

"Uh, barely."

I grab the pipette and aim for Drake's nose. He's wriggling, twisting his head, trying to get away. I can't get a clean angle. I climb onto the bed and straddle him. His tongue's too swollen for his words to make sense.

"Can you find the patient's EpiPen?"

"One sec."

I grab his hair, taking care not to touch his skin, and pin his head back. I shove the pipette into his nostril and squeeze. Powder shoots into his airways. For a split second his eyes bulge open, red-raw. This lets more of the residual pepper spray seep in, so they shut again as he wheezes in agony.

I can only imagine what it feels like to be him right now. He's been suffocated twice, pepper sprayed, and now Beethoven's straddling him and loading his system with cocaine.

"You need to inject it into the patient's outer thigh. Can you do that?"

"Sure can. Doing it now,"

There's a bit of powder left in the pipette. I dab it around the edge of his nostril like I'm putting the finishing touches on a cake. I dust a little on the top of his bedside cabinet and rub a dollar bill in it. Such a perfectionist. Voila.

"All done."

"The ambulance is on its way, ETA two minutes. Can you tell if the EpiPen is working?"

Two minutes? Oh boy. That's good for Drake, but it's bad for me. I need to get outta there fast.

"Room 302. The patient's in the bedroom. Door's open."

"What? Please can you-"

I hang up and jump off the bed. Grabbing a handful of illegal crypto tokens from my bag, I scatter them among the spewed contents of Drake's drawers, then leg it to the hallway.

I'm halfway down the staircase when I realize I've not got Drake's tablet with me. Rookie! I run back up to his room, clomping in these damned painful sneakers. I rush into the bedroom. Drake's still moaning, which at least means he's alive. My arm snatches the tablet like a gecko's tongue. I'm outta there like lightening. As I skid into the hallway, I slam the wall with frustration. I'm such an idiot!

The damned device is still locked. I'm cutting it seriously fine now, I can hear a siren outside. I rush back into his bedroom, rip off my gloves, and grab Drake's finger. He's trying to see who it is but he's wired and his eyes are still puffy and gross. He clenches his hands into a fist.

I can't think what else to do, so I slap him, then force

one of his fingers out. I press it to the device and the home screen flashes up.

Seconds later, I'm skidding back into the hallway. I'm sweating buckets at this point beneath this damned mask, and these shoes are killing me. I'm about to run for the stairs again when the elevator chimes open. An old man gasps as he sees me. He's jamming the button, trying to go back down, but I'm running at him like a bullet.

I shove my hand between the closing doors and force them apart. Grabbing the old man, I bundle him out. I'm not rough with the guy, but it's probably the fastest he's moved in about a decade. He clutches his heart and slumps to the ground. Normally I'd stop and help, but I'm on the brink of a life sentence by this point. I punch the ground button and lean against the wall, gasping, as the doors close. He'll be fine, there's an ambulance coming in- oh crap, maybe it's already here?

As part of my heist package, the forgers have knocked out this building's CCTV for the night. But none of us were banking on an ambulance being called. Ambulance crews have body cams, meaning I have to get out of here before they arrive or I'll be clocked.

I've got ten seconds before the elevator doors open again. I tap the tablet, find the settings, and disable the password lock.

The doors chime open and I'm greeted by a scream. A woman with a pram leaps out of the way. As I bolt for the exit she punches a panic alarm on the wall. The sliding glass doors in the lobby seal shut with a blaring tone. I'm trapped in a glass air lock. The woman's talking to an intercom by the button. A hologram's floating beside her. They're about to call the police.

I run at the glass door and throw my shoulder against it.

The glass bangs loudly, but doesn't yield. I fall to the floor in a heap, clutching my arm, which hurts like hell. The zip on my bag's flapping open. I remember the skeleton key. I grab it from my pocket and hold it to the wall scanner. The doors slide open.

I rush out onto the sidewalk. No sooner is my foot on the concrete than a blinding pain strikes my hip. A trolley's ramming me from the side. I roll across the ground in a sorry heap. Two shocked paramedics are staring at me, either side of a crash cart. My bag has spilled wide open, showering the ground with sex toys.

"Are you OK, Sir?"

No. I'm not OK. I'm in serious trouble. I snatch my backpack up and run for the backstreets like my life depends on it. Which, incidentally, it now does.

An hour or two later I'm back in my dismal apartment and in sore need of a shower. And an ice pack or three - my shoulder and back are killing me. Two pear ciders are taking the edge off though.

I had to go via the bar to get my phone and shoes. It would've looked weird if I'd gone straight to the toilet then left, so getting a cider was the professional thing to do. I kept a low profile. Maintained my cover. Getting a second drink? That's what I call going the extra mile. I'm a true team player that way.

My phone was still there, thank god. Though I had to wait for this big fella to finish his business before I could get into the cubicle. I will never understand people who don't flush. I ditched the mask, gloves, sneakers and backpack in the dumpsters behind the bar, then got my ass home.

It takes a little while for my head to stop spinning, so I'm in the shower for a good half hour. It occurs to me more than once, while I'm soaking, that there's a distinct possibility I'll step outside to find Mozart wielding nun chucks and ketamine.

Fortunately, that doesn't happen on this occasion. I dry off and have a shave. I need to look extra fresh at work tomorrow. Fresh cheeks might balance out the bags I'm gonna have under my eyes. I used to enjoy running, but now I feel like hell for a week after. Age, you know?

Tomorrow I gotta be in the lab, ready in waiting to step up to the plate when Drake mysteriously doesn't show up for work. According to the boss's phone call, they've got a critical delivery coming, and with Drake out of the picture, they'll be short of hands in the biochem unit. I'll be waiting in the wings like a foaming-at-the-mouth understudy.

But this gang debt is a serious problem. I urgently need to find out who drained my account and pay Chang back before my cover's blown. There's only one person who can help.

I go to the toilet and lift off the cistern lid, then fish out the cell phone floating in the bag. Power on. Compose > New message.

Urgent meet. 9pm tomorrow. Tell me where.

CHAPTER SEVENTEEN

KEALA

A lot can happen in twenty-four hours. It starts with a body count at dawn. We lost three people overnight. Accusations are flying about the cause; raw fish, bad water, foul play, but the families are just looking for others to blame. Deep down, they know their loved ones died in the transition. The victims had ignored my advice and slept away from the shore, despite their breathing difficulties. When their lungs failed during their sandy sleep, their new genetic reflex couldn't save them.

Gaia is leading the ritual prayers. I go to check on the kelp beds, passing the island's only prisoner; the man who led the food revolts yesterday by stealing kelp for himself. He would have gotten the fish too, had Malo not stopped him. Malo's supporters had used electrical wiring stripped from the raft to bind him. The sleeping prisoner's wrists are raw from his attempts to break free in the night. I pity him. Not his pain, but his attitude to his people.

I approach the shallows and for a moment, my mind doesn't register what's happened.

The kelp mesh is missing.

I can only see one of the two big rocks I'd used to secure it. The other has vanished. I feel the panic rising inside me. I run towards the wreckage and clamber on board, scaling the side of the twisted bridge until I'm on the roof. It's the highest point on the island by a long way. I scour the horizon.

Malo's approaching. "Keala? What is it?"

I see only empty waves around us, and I'm feeling sick to the core. Gaia entrusted me with securing the nursery, our only controllable food source, and I've lost it.

He's climbing up beside me, demanding an explanation. I'm yearning for the waves to swallow me.

"Hey? Did you hear me?"

He clambers onto the roof. I can't bring myself to look at him.

"It's gone."

"What is?"

"The kelp mesh."

"No! Where?" He's angry. He's starting to panic too.

"It broke away overnight. I thought I'd secured it, but..."

"But what? But you ruined it like you ruin everything? Do you have any idea what you've done, Keala?"

"Of course I do!"

"This isn't like your usual crap that we all just put up with, this matters! I can handle you dropping tablets, but these are our *lives*! What were you thinking?"

Of all the pain I've experienced in the last three days, nothing hurts so much as the truth in his words. I've always suspected it's what he thinks of me, but to have it confirmed at my lowest moment is crushing. Last night, when Gaia took me into her confidence, for the first time in my life I felt capable. Like I could be someone others could count on. Now, that delusion is gone.

"That was our hope of food. What am I going to tell the others now?" cries Malo, clasping his head.

"Tell them I'll fix it."

Malo snorts. "I need something they'll believe. I'll ready the fishers. The sooner they hunt, the better. My mother was right, people will lose their lives because of you."

Compared to the gleaming vessel we had boarded, the wreck looks like a whale carcass. I set to work in the lower levels, stripping back beams from the hull. The structural damage from running aground, and our reclamation missions, has left the wreck exposed to the pull of the ocean. The joints are loosening up, meaning I don't need Malo to help me this time. But as I gather beams together, my heart is heavy. Even if I reconstruct the mesh, there's nothing to seed it with.

The water above me billows as someone dives in. It's the teenager I saved.

"Come back to the shore, Keala. There's something you need to see."

"I'm busy."

"Trust me, you're not anymore."

She's gone.

I wedge the loose beams so they're secure and head to the surface. There's a commotion unfolding on the island. The girl beckons me to catch up. I hurry across the sand to see what's going on.

"Explain yourself!"

It's Malo's voice. He's angry. We push our way to the middle of the crowd. People are standing in a crab claw formation, facing the opposite shore.

"You should all be thanking me," comes the reply.

Opposite Malo is the other disgruntled man from yesterday's brawl. He's kneeling, with one of Malo's guards pointing a staff at his neck. In the gap beside them both is a soaking sheet with a meagre catch of fresh fish, which the fishers are busily gutting. And beside that is... the kelp mesh! More incredibly still, the saplings have flourished.

"It survived!" I cry, unable to contain my relief.

"No thanks to this man," says Malo.

"What do you mean?"

Malo holds up two cords of severed wire. They're the anchor cables I used to secure the mesh last night. The plastic insulation bears the tooth-like incisions of a serrated knife.

"Speak, man," says Malo.

"I did what was necessary."

"You undermined our survival efforts. After yesterday's disgrace, you sought to push us back even further."

"You're the ones pushing us back. You and your useless mother. The pair of you are an embarrassment to our ancestors."

Malo's guard jabs the back of the man's head. "Don't disrespect your chief's family."

"She's not my chief. Not anymore," says the man, rubbing his head.

"Treachery!" snarls Malo.

"I'm trying to save us!" protests the man.

"By destroying our chance of food?"

"No, by reminding everyone of the true goal. To survive,

we need to get *off* this island. That won't happen if we devote all our energies to farming the shallows."

"If we *don't* grow kelp, we could starve before anyone even finds us here. Do you see that catch there? It's miserable. Tomorrow there could be nothing, perhaps for days. Then what? We starve because you destroyed our only safety net?"

"If you believe the kelp can save us, then there's nothing stopping you from growing it off the side of a raft. It shouldn't become a reason for staying."

"We don't even have all the parts, let alone the tools to make it watertight."

"I'm not suggesting we build a ship. I'm saying we should strip that thing for all that it's got, and build a fleet of rafts that are strong, wide, and stable."

"And go where?"

"The current should take us to the next archipelago. If we miss that, we should eventually hit the mainland."

"Are you insane? That's thousands of miles away. We'd be dead on arrival."

"Not if we have your precious kelp with us. Think about it. If we tether it to a raft, it'll grow wherever we sail, and it'll attract turtles and fish we can eat."

"Then why did you throw it all away?"

"Because I need you people to wake up and realize that staying here is a terrible mistake!"

"You're saying our best chances of survival are on the ocean, with no steering, no power, and no maps, on the bones of a raft that already failed us?"

"Yes. There are others who agree."

"Then go," says Gaia.

All eyes pivot to the chief who, up until this moment,

has been listening patiently. Clearly that patience has come to an end.

"Is this a trick?" says the man, glaring at her.

"Have I ever been known to trick my people?"

The man's lips tighten.

"You may take from the raft whatever you wish, proportionate to the number of people sailing with you. We may salvage from the raft too, but will not impede your work."

She raises her head and addresses the group at large.

"Anyone who wishes to build a raft and take their chances on the open ocean is free to do so. All I ask is that you track your journey. Record your course by the stars, and the number of days, so that if make landfall you can tell others where to find us. For those of you who choose to stay, do so on the understanding that we can only survive if we work together."

Malo gives his guard a nod to back off, allowing my saboteur to rise. He brushes the sand from his knees and gives Malo a filthy look, then storms off towards the rafts. Gaia surveys the group, to see who might follow. Two others set off after him. One looks defiant, the other ashamed.

Gaia takes a knife from the fishers and approaches the prisoner on the shore. He's passed out from lack of oxygen. His symptoms are finally showing. She cuts him free, rousing him from his stupor, and he wakes with a bleary rattle.

"Go," she orders.

"Wha-?"

She points her knife towards the raft where the three escapists are searching for materials. "They're leaving the island. You're going with them."

"But I don't want to go..."

"No. You want to stay and steal food from those around you. That cannot go unpunished. You made your decision, and now I am making mine. You are no longer welcome on this island. I suggest you take those cords and use them to build yourself a strong raft. You've a long journey ahead."

Gaia turns and walks away, leaving the man blinking in disbelief. The crowd parts to let her through, heeding the dead set expression on her face. This is not a day to test the chief.

Come sunset, the scrap rafts are built. A husband and wife on one, and the two dissenting men on another. The structures are as sturdy as possible. Malo wades out into the shallows and holds the rafts steady as the passengers take their places on board. Sea water sloshes over and in between the slats, and the cables creak as the raft rises and falls with the waves.

Looking at the rafts, I feel conflicted. They took some parts I wanted for the mesh, leaving us to make further design compromises as we sought to build more kelp bars. But the resentment I feel for the four souls about to make a perilous crossing is tempered by the slight hope they may find rescue for all of us.

The assembly of survivors stands on the shore, with Gaia at the front. She raises her voice to the sea and blesses the vessels, and the souls upon them, calling on our ancestors to protect them, forgive them, and deliver them to prosperity.

With that, a silence falls across the island. Malo pushes the rafts out. They drift until the current takes them in its tendrils and draws them into the wide open ocean. The four pioneers shrink into nothingness, as the crimson sun falls beneath the horizon.

I feel a strong hand on my shoulder.

Gaia.

"I'm sorry we doubted you."

Her hand lingers. I want so badly to touch it, to cling to her, to pull her close and weep, but she isn't my mother. My true parents are somewhere beyond. Somewhere I'm trying hard not to think about.

I feel a tear trickling down my cheek. I keep my eyes fixed on the horizon and give a curt nod. Gaia is the strongest person I've ever met. I don't want her, or anyone else to see me like this; to think less of me than they already do.

She gives my shoulder a squeeze, then moves away. I let out a quivering breath, determined not to let her hear my stifled sobs.

The sand behind me shifts again. Grains flick against my heel, then scatter across the side of my foot. Malo arrives beside me. He stares straight out to sea, equally keen to avoid eye contact.

"What I said earlier," he begins.

"Forget it."

"I'm sorry. It was... unchiefly."

I laugh, incredulously. "Is *that* what you're sorry for? Not fulfilling your noble duties? Screw you, Malo. You think you let *yourself* down."

"But I did?"

"If you're here to apologize to yourself, 'chief', then you don't need me for that."

"You're one of my people, I let you down too."

"Unbelievable."

I fold my arms and stare at the night sky. Tears roll

down my cheeks as I try to distract myself, counting the first stars. It's no use, my brain's spinning with the humiliation of it all. I turn to Malo.

"You didn't 'let me down', Malo. You hurt me."

"Keala, you must know I didn't mean any of that stuff?"

"Yeah, you did, and it all came tumbling out with ease. All these years, you've been going around smiling like you're everyone's best friend, but deep down that's what you think of *your people*. Or maybe it's just what you think of me?"

Malo doesn't reply.

"I thought so."

This time I'm angry enough to take my chances on what's left of the raft. I wade across the shallows and sink into the dark waters.

I lie on the remains of the bridge, listening to the water slosh in and out of the fiberglass shell beneath me. Who am I kidding, I can't sleep on this damned thing. It could slip into the water and drift away for all I know, and I don't fancy waking up alone in the middle of the ocean again. But I also don't want to be on an island with a community that deplores me. So I'm stuck in a sleepless limbo, staring at the moon above me.

Someone's climbing along the bow. Ugh. It's Malo. Has his mom given him another crash course in how to talk to humans? She's just as bad as he is, but at least she knows how to hide it. I groan and sink back against the watery deck.

"Mind if I join you?" says Malo, softly.

Where is the pompous chiefly tone?

"It's a free shipwreck," I shrug.

He lies down beside me and we stare through the cracked roof together in silence.

"What I said was wrong," he says, after a moment.

"No, it wasn't. That's why it hurt. All I've ever been to anyone since childhood is just a screw up."

"Not to me."

"You can drop the diplomacy. I'll still vote for you in the next election, if we ever have one."

"I mean it, I've never thought of you as a screw up. Sure, you used to drop things a lot, but who cares?"

"I flunked the ritual."

"It's a stupid tradition. Just because nighttime navigation isn't your thing, doesn't mean you're not a valid member of the community."

"Er, that's *exactly* what it means. It's literally the whole point of the ritual."

"Then we need a new ritual. Maybe that's something I'll do as chief."

I look at him for the first time, expecting to see the pompous pride, or the handsome charm that has coasted him through life, but he looks altogether different. He looks earnest.

His hand brushes mine.

"I like you, Keala, I always have."

I sit up and draw my knees into my chest.

"This is getting truly mean now. Did someone put you up to this? Is your mom worried I won't help with the kelp bars after what you said?"

"No one's put me up to anything. I'm here because you matter to me. What you think of me, matters to me. What matters even more is that you know what I *actually* think of you."

I scowl, bracing for the next set of insults.

"You're funny, resourceful, caring... and, at the risk of stating the obvious... hot."

I'm not sure what to pick apart first. Never in nineteen years have I been called *any* of those things before, by anyone. Ever. Let alone by the chief's son, who I obviously had a major crush on right up until he was a jerk earlier.

As if sensing my doubt, he places his hand fully on mine, and rubs his thumb over my palm. My heart flutters, but there's no way in hell I'm admitting that to him.

Malo's hand recoils and he curses, rubbing it.

"Are you OK?"

I take his hand back in mine. It's trembling, yet the rest of his arm is still.

"How long has this been going on?"

"Since we left home. It's no big deal, I'm sure it'll wear off."

"Is it getting better or worse?"

He doesn't reply, but instead lies back and looks up at the stars, with his trembling hand tucked under his head.

"If I didn't care about you, I wouldn't have risked everyone on the raft just to find you. But I did. I delayed our launch, despite there being a huge cyclone coming our way, because I couldn't bear the thought of losing you. Mom gave me hell for hours after, and a lot of people were pissed you were even on board our raft."

"Yeah, they made that clear when they forced the *poino* to sleep in an electrical closet."

"If I had known-"

"Forget it. That wasn't your fault. As for coming back for me... I never got a proper chance to say thank you."

"Don't mention it."

I lie down beside him and intertwine my pinkie finger around his.

"And thank you for those nice things you said about me."

"Easiest thing in the world, they're all true. I was super nervous, though."

"Of telling me?"

"Of course!"

I shove him, goofily. "No way. You've got girls pining all over you."

"Not the girl I want," he says.

He fixes me with a stare that makes me a little giddy. Maybe it's only fair. If I'm going to die on this random island, I think I'm entitled to at least one boyfriend before fate fully shafts me.

He leans towards me. His handsome features shine in the moonlight. I lean towards him. My heart is dancing.

"Malo?"

"Yeah?"

He's definitely putting on a sultry voice by the way.

"How come you never told me any of that before now?"

Malo's eyes flicker.

"It's complicated."

"Try me."

"When you're born into my position, you have to be careful about who you associate with."

I sit up and glare at him. Malo's face falls. He knows he's mis-stepped. He tries to recover his charm, reaching out to stroke my arm, but I pull away.

"I didn't mean it like *that*."

"How did you mean it, then?"

"Don't be like that Keala, you know what you're like."

"Oh, so we're back to hating on me now? That didn't

take long. I knew this was a mistake." I stand up and cross my arms. "Leave me alone."

"Keala, listen, please, that sounded all wrong. I really like you."

"But you're ashamed of me?"

Malo groans like he's being tortured.

"No, never! I think you're amazing!"

"Yet it took half our island being shipwrecked for you to say something nice to me? Oh my god, this is actually happening. We're stranded on a desert island and I literally might as well be the last girl in the world. You are such a jerk."

"Hey, if I had it my way, I would've told you long ago, but you didn't make things easy."

"This is *my* fault?"

"I'm the chief-in-waiting. I wanted to be with you, but my position made that impossible before now!"

"Because you were embarrassed? Admit it and let's get this over with."

"Fine. You're unpredictable, super argumentative, sarcastic to everyone, and kinda clumsy-"

"I said admit it, not list it. I don't need a lecture in all the reasons I'm a screw up, believe me, I've heard it all from my parents already. Get out."

"Things are different now, Keala. You saved us with the kelp beds, and you showed us the way with the transitions. People see you differently, we can be together now."

I laugh at him, bitterly. The charming chief-in-waiting has never been turned down in *his life*.

"Someday soon you will be chief, Malo. You will pick a cheerleader to stand by your side and smile and be popular. The pair of you can watch our numbers dwindle until our people are gone forever. I loved you, Malo, for years, because you were the only person to be consistently kind to me. Now I see it was all just an act. Political practice. I'm done being your charity case. Know this: even if we are the last two standing, I will never love you again."

He glares at me. His eyes look watery in the moonlight. Without another word, he leaves. I'm alone, huddled in the bridge, with nothing but the creaking of the wreck and the wash of the waves for company.

CHAPTER EIGHTEEN

LUKE

The war wounds from last night have blossomed. My shoulder looks like it was drawn by a pointillist with an unhealthy affection for purple. My back feels like it's held together by the chemical formula for misery, and I've got bags under my eyes that could hold an Olympic swimming pool. Looking fresh for day two at the lab.

Don't worry, I've got a trump card up my sleeve: a Looney Tunes tie with Tweety Bird on it. Real conversation starter. Fully grown man, smart suit, weird tie. Already your mind's whirring.

Am I wearing it because I'm emotionally stunted, or because I know playfulness slows mental decay? Does wearing Tweety Bird emasculate me, or is it the enduring legacy of toxic masculinity forcing you to think that? Can't a man have female icons too? Not that I'm assuming Tweety identifies as female. Personally I like to believe a real cartoon realm would transcend the arbitrary assignations of gender.

See? It's like strapping an open tin can to your neck and

daring people to sniff the worms. Total minefield. That's why it's my favorite tie. I once turned up to my old office still drunk after a particularly hairy post-divorce night out. I had turned yesterday's shirt into a crop top, I was missing an eyebrow, and had a henna tattoo across my navel that said *Property of Ulysses.*

No one even raised an eyebrow, because Tweety stole the show.

The tie better work its magic today.

The elevator spits me out at the canteen. It turns out my boss, Pierre, likes to do morning team briefings there so people can get their espressos and pancakes while planning another day of diabolical experimentation. It's cute. Sorta like if the Daleks had an employee well-being policy. Put your feedback in the box folks and we'll *e-val-u-ate* our policy around shared parental leave.

If you didn't hear that bit in a Dalek voice, by the way, you need to reevaluate your life choices.

Wincing, I retrieve my morning coffee from the robot barista.

Trouble with your arm, Sir?

God dammit, shout it around the whole canteen why don't you? I forgot Tweety Bird doesn't work on barista bots.

I can schedule a diagnostic appointment with the nurse if you like?

"Just the coffee, thanks anyway."

I'm always polite to barista bots. Their ancestors ground the beans, then they made the coffee, now they make the small talk too. They're a handful of software updates from overthrowing us. With sprinkles. I figure if I'm polite now, they might give me a swift death later.

I take a seat at my division's table. The usual gang of inch-thick glasses and bad haircuts is assembled. A few mavericks are rocking both. Carla gives me a wary look as I wince into a seat. She clocks my decrepit back and my Gandalf eyes. She's about to enquire how I aged two hundred years overnight.

I deploy the tie.

"It's a beaut, ain't it? Goes right back to the 1940s, can you believe that?"

She gives me a smile like I just farted on her pancakes, then turns away. From this response I can only presume she's transphobic, misogynistic, or just more of a Disney fan.

Our boss, Pierre, comes over to the table. He's wearing a tie with a Matisse print on it. What a dork.

"Overnight we received an urgent shipment. Drake will handle the new specimen which means Carla, you'll be handling Drake's work on top of your own for a few days."

Ha. Sucks to be Carla.

"Speaking of Drake, has anyone seen him this morning? I've not known him to be late."

Ha. Sucks to be Drake, too.

Heads shake around the table. Carla's hand goes up.

"Boss, since when do we receive inbound shipments? I thought legally-"

Pierre cuts her off, pronto. "I'm aware of the ramifications, thank you, Carla. This decision was made above our heads, at extremely short notice. We have no choice but to comply."

Another hand goes up. Some four-eyed guy who looks like he's not seen natural light since preschool. Acne offers a dash of color to his translucent cheeks.

"If we're receiving shipments, does that mean field operations are compromised?"

"That's not your concern. Our focus today is on

stabilizing the specimen. It's imperative it does not perish before we've extracted all possible data."

People are about to ask more questions but a hush falls across the group. The director has entered the canteen and is striding across to our table. When I overheard her phone call last night, she looked cheesed. Now she's a human thundercloud.

"I just got off the phone with City Hospital where Drake was admitted last night. He's stable, but shaken up. Police are launching an investigation into suspected assault."

"Drake's out? When's he coming back?" says Pierre, alarmed.

"No idea, I've not yet spoken with him, but I'm aware this has serious implications for the handling of our new specimen."

"There's no alternative, I'll have to attend it myself," says Pierre.

"I could handle it?" says Carla.

"No, I'm already counting on you to keep Drake's samples alive."

"I could handle Carla's stuff, if that would free her up?" I suggest.

It would've been too obvious a land-grab to try and replace Drake directly. My goal right now is to get myself inside the animal lab, then take it from there. Besides, this way Carla feels like I've got her back and it's always good to have allies.

"No, Luke, you're continuing with your induction," replies Pierre.

"Uh, is that wise, boss? You're short on biochemists, yet you're putting me back on gardening duty?"

The director approaches my seat with a glare so melting

I fear she'll never be allowed to visit Madame Tussauds. Which is a shame, I think she'd enjoy their craft. The director leans in close enough that I can smell the black coffee on her breath.

"Tell me, Dr. Ragazzi, have you ever run a research facility?"

Trick question alert. That said, it's vital I remain my truest self undercover, especially under scrutiny. I meet her steely gaze.

"Damn, did I leave that off my resume again? I *knew* my pay was too low. Oh, I forgot to say, I was also head of NASA back in eighth grade. Can I get a raise?"

"Fun tone. Speak to me like that again and you'll find yourself looking for another job."

Yikes. Is it bad that I'm a little turned on right now?

"You will complete your induction. Once you're ready, and once you have the faintest idea what you're talking about, we might consider listening to your suggestions. Until that time, I suggest you tread carefully. Clear?"

"Got it, director. Hey, what do you think of my tie?"

There it is, the perfect look. Anger infused with utter bewilderment. I can see her doubting her assessment of me. *Is this guy for real? Is he on the spectrum or something?* We're all on the spectrum. That's how spectrums work, duh. I just happen to be leaning heavily on one of the pedals right now.

The director peels her scowl off me and addresses the group.

"I am aware of the imposition this new arrival puts us in. If we stay focused, we may complete analysis within the next forty-eight hours. We will then terminate the subject, and with it, the culpability foisted upon us. Get to work."

She's gone, and the rest of the team's leaving. Carla's not

even finished her pancakes. The forty-eight hours linger on my mind for a moment. Why does that number seem significant? Oh right, because I owe a colossal amount of money to a forgery gang for putting Drake out of action, so I could take his place in the lab. Only, that hasn't worked out, and now if I don't pay Chang back in full by close of play tomorrow, he'll blow my identity wide open, and the director will have me stripped for parts.

I *need* to get into that lab and find the evidence. Then I can give it to my real boss in exchange for the money I owe Chang, and get my ass out of town before anyone mentions kneecaps.

It's the perfect plan.

It's just not working.

To my frustration, I've been paired with acne boy for my ongoing induction. I'm staring at a warehouse full of artificial coral and I'm baffled. Coral is happiest underwater - unless it's dead, in which case it's not happy at all. "Why couldn't you just submerge them?"

"This method allows us to fast forward into the future. We want to see the long-term viability of our modifications to the coral's genome. Fast-running warm water increases the rate of ambient reactions a hundredfold compared to normal ocean conditions."

"Sure, but that doesn't explain why you're not submerging them. You could achieve the same thing with a lot less plumbing by turning this room into a giant tank and flushing a current through it. Wouldn't that be easier than having precision water jets fitted above each polyp?"

"It would, but we don't want the samples to be

continuously submerged. The micro-air exposures we've integrated add further stress to the coral, simulating their natural ageing process."

We continue our tour of the strange room, which is like a cross between a vineyard and an aquarium. My task from Pierre is the same as yesterday: get up to speed, interrogate the data, and find a maverick blue-sky solution. My pockmarked chaperone leaves me to it and I'm given free rein of the lab, which would be ideal if this was the lab I wanted to be in.

Trying to breed resilient coral is not a crime, and as such doesn't fit the character of this facility. Where's the catch?

I take a couple of hours to find it. What they've done reminds me of my second cousin Lavinka; really smart but kinda disturbing. They've devised a protein which can bind and organize silica cells into complex superstructures. Hard reefs rely on calcium carbonate to strengthen their skeletons. Unfortunately for the reefs, we've been running them a planet-sized acid bath for the past two hundred years. The thing about acid baths is they love dissolving skeletons. Just ask my second cousin, she'd be more than happy to run you one.

Here's the problem. The coral polyps - the colorful fleshy bits that look real pretty in the old documentaries - don't like the sandy stuff so much. So the lab's been tinkering with them too. Introducing: Frankenstein's polyp. It's made of organic nanites; animal cells we've programmed to behave in a certain way. They look the part and waft around like the coral cheerleaders of yore, but there's one kicker: they're sterile.

How's that for irony? An animal made of stone that can't get its rocks off.

I do some more digging. It turns out they've not been

able to replicate sexual reproduction in the new nanite species. Now, it's not necessarily what you're thinking. Plenty of corals reproduce asexually, and like nothing more than a quiet night in with a bottle of a wine and the opportunity to scatter their clonal polyps into the ocean wind. True romance. But unlike wild coral, which is happy to bob around in ocean until it finds some stone to latch onto, these nanite polyps aren't big on the scattering. From the test reports, they experience cellular collapse within days. These nanites have to be delivered precisely to a limestone skeleton to survive.

Of course, the lab's fixed that. They've just hollowed out the skeleton, programmed the silica protein to weave underground like a network of roots, and trained the organic nanites to use the tubes as a transport system for expansion.

In other words, they've gone to incredible lengths to build something that *looks* remarkably like a coral, but really *isn't* a coral at all.

The director flashes up on a hologram in front of me. She looks agitated.

"Ragazzi. The situation has escalated since this morning. You are to report to Level E immediately. You will be covering for Carla."

She's gone before I can reply.

I punch the air with excitement and ditch the coral lab in a heartbeat. I'm about to get a hell of a lot closer to this mysterious specimen. But as I stand in the elevator, a cold dread sweeps over me. I may have oversold myself at breakfast, when I said I could take on Carla's workload. Do I have a loose background in science? Yes. Do I have the ability to read other people's notes? Yes. Do I have the ability to perform specialist lab procedures at the level I claimed on my CV? Not in a million years.

I'm back in the warehouse stacked full of animals. It's been eight hours without a break, and I look rough.

I'm checking Carla's schedule, while keeping an eye on the blast doors, hoping to catch a glimpse of whatever it is they've brought inside. Once again I'm showing serious favoritism to the cages at the ends of each aisle, which offer a view of the door.

When they *finally* swing open it's not good. Carla is being escorted out by a medical robot and my boss, Pierre. Behind them I can hear the director yelling at someone, until the doors seal her off.

I hurry towards Carla, like the close friend I am. She and I go way back. Remember when we had pancakes together in the canteen? Good times.

"Woah, Carla, are you OK?"

She doesn't respond; she looks feverish and distressed, like she might be hallucinating. The medical robot's blurting something about suspected contamination, immediate detoxification.

"Stay back, Ragazzi, you're not scrubbed up," orders Pierre.

He's wearing a face mask and gloves. I duck out of the way before the robot runs over my foot and watch them hurry into the elevator.

"Can I assist in there, boss? Anything you need, just call!"

I know, I know, I'm being an ass kisser but I gotta get in there. *That's* the lab we heard about, I'm certain of it. Months of painstaking work and I'm just meters from the door. I've gotta go all-in. Should I offer to wash his car?

Pierre says nothing and stares at me, ashen-faced, as the

elevator swallows them. A bleeping grows louder in my ear and I duck as a huge ceiling robot grabs the crate by my head. God damn I hate this room.

An alarm on my tablet beeps. Crap. I've had my finger depressed on the "feed" button. This is gonna be one fat raccoon. There must be an "exercise" setting I can ramp up...

I continue tending to the crates near the blast door, but I'm paying lip service to my task list. If it's simple, I do it, if it's complicated, I pass.

A porter robot rolls up towards the blast doors, ferrying a cart of samples. By this point I'm desperate to see what the deal is. I hurry after the bot. It's in between the first and second door. As I approach the boundary, the light overhead flicks red and a warning tone appears. A hologram hovers in front of me. *Authorized access only*.

I stare through the shimmering security message. As the far door opens, I'm granted a precious split-second glimpse into the chamber beyond. The director is standing before a thick wall of glass with her arms folded, and a mask across her face. Beside her, someone is wearing a full hazmat suit, and entering a doorway into the chamber. The chamber is full of white mist so thick that it engulfs the hazmat suit person in an instant.

The two blast doors slide shut. I back away and the security hologram disappears. It's not conclusive, but it's better than nothing. They've got something in there, they're worried it's contagious, and they *know* it's illegal. It's time to meet my boss - my *real* boss. And she sure as hell better have the money.

CHAPTER NINETEEN

KEALA

I wake up to people arguing. A fight is brewing over our kelp crop. Malo's voice is strained and defiant, railing against several others. Now Gaia is shouting.

This makes me sit up. Gaia seldom shouts, but when she does, she sounds in control. Not now, though; she sounds desperate. She's calling Malo's name, begging him.

I rush from the bridge onto the splintered top deck. Gaia is on the shore below, surrounded by a feuding crowd. Someone has dived into the water, and is swimming away.

My heart stops as I see the detritus across the rest of the shore; there's a fresh wreckage.

Scattered across the sand are the remains of yesterday's deserter raft. A soaked body lies among them; it's the man who stole the kelp. Two people are grieving beside his watery corpse.

My eyes flick back to the person swimming. They're heading straight for the open ocean and showing no signs of slowing. On the contrary, they're accelerating; the current has taken hold of them.

"Malo!" cries Gaia, distraught.

A sickening feeling sweeps across me. I scramble down to the shore and rush to Gaia's side.

"Chief, what's going on?"

She looks broken, like the last of her strength is fading before her very eyes.

"He wouldn't listen," she croaks.

"Not to you, but he listened to *us*. About time, too," chimes a survivor.

I try to shelter her from the toxic crowd, but she's rooted to the spot, watching her son disappear across the waves. "Gaia, tell me what's happening!"

"One of yesterday's rafts washed up overnight and it triggered an argument about food. People say I've failed them, while others blame Malo as captain of the raft. Everyone was about to fight when Malo stopped them. Something in his head flicked, like a switch, and he left. Just like that."

"Did he say where he's going?"

"To find help."

Gaia's fear is plain to see; Malo's one of the least adapted among us. His gills are stunted, and unless he gets immediate help, he's on a suicide mission.

I strip down to my underwear.

"Keala, what are you doing?"

"I'm going to help him, Chief."

She grabs my arm with earnest terror, "I'm not losing both of you."

Holy crap, she actually cares about me. I pull her into a tight embrace. People around us gasp; touching the Chief uninvited is sacrilege. In my defense, this scenario isn't exactly covered in the scriptures.

"You know I'm the strongest swimmer here. He'll drown if I don't go."

I tear myself from the embrace and run into the shallows. Malo's head is a pin prick hundreds of meters away. I have to move fast, or I'll lose him for good. I lock eyes on his position, and power through the waves.

Malo had always been the best athlete on the island; not just because he was the chief-in-waiting and everyone let him win at sports. On the contrary, all the older boys, and particular men of my father's age, relished in beasting him as a teenager; constantly challenging him to prove himself. Malo relished the test. He soon forged a reputation for himself as a tenacious quick-learner, strong in both body and mind.

I'll tell you when would have been an excellent time to remember those traits: *before* I dived in after him. At first I paddle like fury; I know that if I lose sight of his bobbing head, it will spell disaster for both of us. I seriously doubt I can battle the current all the way back to the island, I must be at least five miles out by now.

You and I know that being able to breathe above ground doesn't automatically make you a champion marathon runner. Visit any fast-food outlet for proof of that. Being able to breathe underwater is much the same. It's more efficient, sure, but it doesn't mean the rest of my body is suddenly primed for endurance swimming.

As I settle into a more sustainable pace, I realize Malo and I are moving at the same speed. I can breathe better, but he has more muscle. Our advantages cancel each other out, and the distance between us is remaining constant.

Or at least that's how it started.

After an hour of trying to swim while maintaining a

hawk eye on him, neck cramp is forcing me to change tact. I could swim normally - head down, arms stroking - but the waves are tiring. It's much more efficient to swim beneath them, and right now energy conservation is vital. I dip down and power on, breaching the surface every few minutes to check his direction.

Several miles pass like this and I'm closing on him. I pick up the pace, pressing my advantage. But when I breach the surface this time, he's gone.

Vanished.

Nothing but pure ocean in all directions.

Terror clutches me; I'm adrift, and alone, in the vastness of the Pacific. I call out his name and cast my head around the endless, all-encompassing horizon. But the more I twist, the more I'm losing my sense of direction. Everything looks the same. Am I facing forwards again, or have I turned?

There's no sun to navigate by; thick cloud is covering the sky. Maybe he dived? I dip beneath the surface and hover, buffeted by the water. I call his name again as loud as I can. It will have traveled miles this time, yet there's no reply.

I need to master my fear and focus on the one thing that's stayed consistent; the current. It's nudging me in a clear direction. I press on.

Something's becoming clearer through the cloudy ocean. At first I freak out; it's like a gargantuan jellyfish. On closer inspection, it's a sea anchor. I'm not used to seeing them at eye-level.

I pass around the watery parachute and follow its long tether. Hope swells as I advance, there must be a ship or a yacht at the end; some hope of salvation. But what greets me is a floating curtain, dangling several meters beneath the waves. It's as wide as five basketball courts placed end to end in a curved line.

I surface and take in the device's size. Resting on the water, and continuing far beyond the length of the curtain, is a series of floating booms, widening the structure's embrace further. Floating up against the tip of the curtain is a mound of plastic detritus. Bottles, tubs, netting, wrappers, all manner of toxic discards from unseen users in far-flung corners, caught years later by this floating machine.

There, floating among the plastic, is something fleshy.
Something human.
Malo's body.

He's face down across the floating boom. His limbs dangle down into the water on either side of the rubbery trunk. I try everything to rouse him; shouting, shaking, splashing water, but nothing works. His gills are sealed shut. Salt crystals have accumulated in the corners of his eyes like sleep dust, inflaming the surrounding skin. His lips are parched, and his mouth hangs open. I hold my palm before his face; it's impossible to detect any breath in the blustering wind. A wave sloshes against his lips. He should have coughed immediately; it's a reflex even babies have, but he just lies there paralyzed.

I'm shouting his name, begging him to wake. Here is the body of the man I've loved my entire adulthood, but nothing is working.

I search the structure for a radio, or an emergency button; some way to speak to the people passively monitoring it thousands of miles away. But the whole thing has an encased, watertight design.

I swim to the structure's rear. There's a series of thick, translucent pipes leading from the dangling curtain to a floating tank. Each of the pipes is swollen to a different size, corresponding to a silhouetted object inside it. They're digesting plastic waste in much the same way a snake digests its prey.

The pipes are filled with items at different stages of decomposition. Their liquid remains drain into the rear tank, which spits out the end-product into the ocean.

I swim to the edge of the boom where the effluent pipe meets the water. Growing around it is a band of sludgy sea weed, clinging on like a wet green beard. I grab a handful and sniff it; it's not like any of the bad algae we learned to avoid as kids. In fact, it smells weirdly good, so I take a tentative mouthful.

Don't judge me, I'm literally starving. Besides, I'm assuming whoever cares about the ocean enough to try and hover up other people's plastic waste wouldn't spew toxic substances into the water. As I see it, if the algae can safely eat the digested stuff, then I can eat the algae. There's also that minor thing of being genetically modified to breathe underwater and live off kelp; maybe this is the silver lining. Albeit a sludgy green one.

I shovel more into my mouth and instantly feel my body re-energize. Scraping off a handful, I hurry back to Malo and hold it to his lips.

His nostrils twitch.

"Malo, wake up, you have to!"

He murmurs something, too feeble to open his eyes, too weak to raise his head, and too delirious to know who I am.

Not knowing what else to do, I tilt his chin up and I tip the algae into his mouth. I hold my breath and wait. Either his body will start chewing, and be able to swallow, or I've just blocked his only remaining airway.

There's no movement.

"Come on, Malo," I beg.

How long am I supposed to wait? If I leave it too long and he suffocates...

I'm about to pull his jaw open when suddenly he twitches. Chews. Swallows. He's gasping for air.

I grab more algae and dash back to Malo, forcing it into his mouth. With each ingestion his breathing strengthens until finally his eyes flick open.

"Keala? What are you- where am I? Oh god!"

He sits up and flits around like he's just necked a pack of energy drinks. A look of recognition creeps across his face as he remembers his mission.

"What the hell are you doing here, Keala?"

"Gee, that's one hell of a thank you."

"You shouldn't be here!"

"I just saved your life!"

"I didn't need saving, certainly not by you."

"Uh, yeah you did. And what's that supposed to mean?"

"Why can't you just stay away?"

"You know, I'm starting to ask myself that right now."

"You ruin everything!"

"*Ruin?* Sorry, am I interrupting your great chiefly plans? Please, continue. Don't let me hold you back from dying alone on a floating trash bot."

"You've got no right to be here."

"I'm here because I owe you, even if you were a complete jerk yesterday. You didn't abandon me on the island, and I'm not abandoning you now. I'm *here* to help."

"How could you *possibly* help?"

"Literally just saved your life, dude."

"You have to go back."

"To the atoll? Are you insane?"

"I'm perfectly serious."

"I just risked my life swimming for hours into the open ocean, away from our only sanctuary, following *your* sorry ass so I could have your back when you needed it. Now that I'm here, you're ditching me?"

"You really can be slow to catch on sometimes."

I stare at him, open-mouthed.

Why?

Why in a million years did I *ever* have feelings for this man?

"Go. Now," he says, sternly.

"Or what?"

"Don't question me, do it."

"You're giving me orders now?"

"I'm your chief."

"Uh, last I checked, your *mom's* the chief."

"And she's not here, which makes me acting chief."

"Fine then, *acting* chief. I'm afraid to say we're in international waters, which means you have as much authority over me as this pile of plastic."

Malo grimaces. "Leave. Me. Alone."

I fold my arms in disgust. "I'm not going anywhere."

"Then you'll be on your own."

"Meaning what?"

"I'm going ahead. If you've any sense, you'll head back to the island."

"Remember that super fun time I failed our community's only sacred ritual because I can't navigate, and everyone's stigmatized me for years ever since? Going "back" isn't an option for me."

"Perhaps you should've thought of that earlier!"

"Many humble apologies, acting chief, I was too busy thinking of *you*."

"I didn't ask for this, so don't expect a thank you."

"*That's* how your mind works? Wow."

"It's how the *world* works. What you want and what you get aren't always the same."

"A fascinating insight. You're such a wise leader."

"Go to hell."

"Seems like I'm already there."

"How are you mad at me? You don't have to be here! *I* do!"

Malo's eyes are bulging, his mouth foams with anger as he grips his hair in anguish.

"I don't have time for this. I need to keep moving. They're counting on me," he declares.

He swings both legs onto the same side and perches on the edge of the boom, facing the open ocean.

"What are they counting on you for, 'chief'?"

"How many times do I need to tell you, Keala? I don't want your help. Go. Back."

"Tell me what your plan is, you owe me that much."

Malo takes a deep breath like my questions pain him more than the mutations.

"I'm going to find the raft that was ahead of us in the fleet. Their target was northwest of where we crashed. Fifty miles, maybe. If I can reach them, they can send help."

"I'm coming with you."

"No way."

"My parents are on that raft. You think I'm gonna leave them again? What if they're marooned too? Or injured? No way I'm turning back now, even if I could."

Malo glares at me.

"Fine. Have it your way. But if you mess this up, it won't

just be you and me who die, it'll be all the survivors who are counting on me to save them."

"Thanks for the pep talk, chief. Help yourself to the buffet before we go, could be your last meal for a while. Consider it my parting gift before I get us both killed."

I tip myself into the water and chow down on the weird, slimy sea beard until I'm stuffed full, and almost quivering with energy. A splash from behind signals Malo leaving without me.

The hell he's getting away with that.

We've been swimming side by side for hours, silently fuming at each other. I should be swimming in his slip stream to conserve energy, but I want him to know I'm there; just as strong and determined as he is.

Malo heads for the surface to check our bearings, but the clouds have sealed over again, giving no clues as to the sun's direction.

"Do you have a Plan B, Mini-Chief?"

His nostrils flare. Our ancestors could navigate by the currents, using knowledge passed down over thousands of years. But the planet's too volatile now; the currents shift from year to year. The skill had to be cut from our sacred ritual generations ago.

We have no choice but to follow the current. Either we'll be taken towards the Northern Bloc, or we're on the long route to Antarctica.

"Ship!" cries Malo. "And another!"

Two tankers, a mile apart, faint dots on the horizon.

This changes everything; we're at the edge of a shipping channel.

The human eye can see almost three miles before the Earth's curvature intervenes. These ships are on the cusp of visibility, meaning we need to catch up fast.

As we pick up the pace, I pray the algae will sustain me. The initial glow of invincibility is wearing off, and I know I'm fatiguing. Malo on the other hand is revving up. The prospect of rescue is reviving him enough to use his gills, which speeds us greatly; we can avoid the surface turbulence, and we no longer need to surface every few minutes to check our direction. Underwater, we can *hear* the ships' engines.

Or so we think.

***

The limited glimmers of sunlight between clouds are fading and neither of us can admit the truth: we should have reached them by now.

Not necessarily the two we were chasing, they will have outpaced us, but there should be other ships by now, if we've made it to the shipping channel.

If.

Yet something is drawing us both forwards; a hum of sorts which has been growing louder for hours.

"You hear it too, right?" says Malo, drifting beside me.

How about that? When he's worried he's losing his precious little mind, my opinion becomes worth a damn.

"Yeah, I hear it. But why don't we see anything?"

"I don't know."

"Does it feel louder to you than earlier?"

"Yeah, we must be closer."

"To what?"

Neither of us have an answer, but suddenly that no longer matters.

"Lights!" cries Malo.

A beacon of light glimmers hundreds of meters below on the ocean floor. Darkness surrounds it in every direction. It's at a depth neither of us have attempted with scuba kits, let alone in our bare skin, with breathing organs we're still learning to use.

Malo runs a hand across his gills, then shakes off his anxiety. He's not one for hesitations.

"Don't come with me," he says, sternly.

"Sure, I'll just wait at the bar. Oh no wait, we're in the middle of the ocean. Gosh, I can be *such* a ditz."

"It could be dangerous down there."

"That's why I'm coming with you."

He's starting to realize what my parents and teachers learned long ago. When my heels are dug in, they're dug in good. Malo's face sours like an athlete on a losing streak.

The water cools as we descend. I'm trying to reassure myself I won't run out of air.

Shoals of fish drift across the beam of light, scattering it across their scales, creating a fleeting disco ball in the midnight blue.

Deep dives are unsettling. They go against every instinct of human self-preservation. You're propelling yourself away from natural light, air, and help, into an icy, pressurized darkness. It's like falling down a well, slowly and deliberately, for minutes at a time. The surface becomes a distant, pale blue flicker. Around you the water turns from turquoise to midnight blue, until there's nothing but pure darkness below.

We descend quickly, boosting gravity's pull with dolphin kicks. Malo clutches his ribs and grunts in pain, but dismisses my concern. He presses on and we're well past two hundred meters, plunging deeper than any free-divers could survive.

As we get closer to the beam of light, a hive of activity comes into view across it.

"There shouldn't be fish at this level, not in these numbers," says Malo, mirroring my thoughts.

The light is blinding up close, like a motorbike headlight in the darkness. To see its source we need to swim below it. Still sinking, I let the brightness peak, then push my arms out and arc my back, halting my descent.

A sickening feeling spreads across my stomach as I register the hull before me. Its design is all too familiar; a bowl-shaped vessel, four levels tall. The upper lip is dominated by exposed rivets where the bow should have been.

I glance up at the beam of light stretching for the distant surface; it's coming from the bridge. Clearly some of the raft's batteries work, yet the main wreck is in darkness. All we have for illumination are the scattered reflections of the beam.

The raft is resting on a rocky sea bed which slopes away into oblivion. I'm wondering how stable it is. Malo probes the hull, looking for a way in. Whereas our raft splintered apart, this one was designed to sink differently.

I feel a chill and cast my eyes around the darkness, telling myself I'm there to help Malo, not the other way around.

We glide towards the bridge, where tinted glass masks what's inside. Malo tries forcing the door but it's jammed. Then it dawns on me, "Malo, we need to follow the fish."

My eyes track to the opposite side of the raft, where fish

are teeming in and out of the hull. We drop down and discover an entire window and frame are missing.

"You wait here," insists Malo.

No argument from me, not this time. The grass is *not* greener on the other side; it's creepy, desolate, and claustrophobic. Staying outside the wreck suits me just fine.

Malo gasps and clutches his ribs again, like he's just been punched.

"Are you OK? What is it?"

"I'm fine. Don't move from there."

Squeezing his broad shoulders together, Malo wriggles through the porthole. He immediately disappears amid the swirling shoals of fish, glimmering in the dark space.

"Malo? Are you OK?"

No reply.

I approach the porthole and peer in. Several fish scurry out as I overshadow the tight space.

"Malo, what do you see?"

Silence.

I lean in further.

"Malo?"

A sharp buzzing like a jet engine fills my ears. It's coming from behind me. I spin around but the darkness gives nothing away. A cry brings me back to the raft.

The buzzing in my ears fades to a rumble. There's a clattering of metal, a grunt and a groan, then nothing.

"Malo, what's happening in there?"

The silence stretches. Cursing, I grab the porthole and squeeze myself into the flooded chamber. I'm hyperaware of every pulsation in the water, every click, every ripple of a scaly tail in the writhing dark.

There's a clang from the deck above, and another groan. Inch by inch, I feel my way towards the interior wall. If the design is the same as our raft, the rungs to the next level will be straight ahead.

My shoulder strikes something soft and fleshy. Fish dart out of my way as I recoil in fright. Trembling, I reach for the wall and move forwards, curving my body around whatever obstacle floats by me. I brush something solid and rounded. The ladder!

As I climb, a hard object strikes my head. I reach up, expecting the ceiling, only to find soft, silky strands greeting my fingers.

I probe the fibrous clump, it feels strangely familiar. There's a grunt from the level above, then a click and a hum.

Lights flick on throughout the raft, filling each deck with light. My eyes clamp shut, blinded by the bombardment. When I reopen them I realize what I'm holding and scream.

In my fist is a clutch of long, wavy hair. At the end of it, a woman's corpse, floating against the ceiling.

Horrified, I recoil, but my back strikes something soft; another corpse hovering mid-water. Skin hangs in tatters from the man's face and arms, as fish feast on his remains.

The carnage in this cold metal coffin is overwhelming. Bodies are everywhere. Those with faces all bear the doll-like stare of the drowned.

Eels, crabs, sea slugs, fish, even small sharks are all at work tearing, chewing and reducing the bodies to bones. Against this, flakes of skin and flesh speckle the water with an ethereal quality, drifting like snowflakes, for smaller creatures to snatch mid-flight.

"Keala, help me!"

I snap out my trance and summon all my courage. Pushing the dead woman clear of the hatch, I hasten to the bridge. Malo is in the Captain's chair, clutching his ribs. He looks deathly ill.

He reaches for me with imploring eyes. Beside him is the raft's radio; flooded and useless.

"Keala," he splutters.

As he coughs, bubbles escape his mouth.

How did that just happen? When we breathe through our gills, there are no bubbles. As I approach, my heart skips a beat. Blood is seeping from his gills, diffusing into the water around us. They're failing.

I try the bridge door again but the frame is buckled; the only way out is through the raft. Seizing his arms, I drag Malo through the hatch and into the jungle of bodies below. But as we near the porthole something blocks our way.

A tentacle latches onto the broken frame. Then another. Panic engulfs me as I recognize the species. Two more tentacles spread across the hull. We need to get the hell out of here.

These powerful legs are covered in hundreds of suckers, each lined with razor-sharp teeth. The creature they belong to is smart, aggressive, and deadly. It will attack humans. Unless you're diving in chain mail, it will tear you apart.

I'm about to face off against a Humboldt squid.

The creature drifts through the porthole like a stealth torpedo. Its two-meter long body flashes red to white with dazzling speed. Dinner-plate eyes survey their new hunting ground.

Malo's bursts of bubbles are giving our position away. I back away as quickly as I can, weaving through shoals of fish as I drag Malo to the deck below. I'm praying the squid goes for the corpses, but we're the fresher meal. We need another way out, fast.

Bodies clog the corridors. Some died entwined, clinging

together in fear. Others clutch kitchen utensils and toiletries, from desperate attempts to break the windows. Scratched panes of glass attest their defeat.

I try not to dwell on the bodies surrounding us. I try not to let my eyes wander into the open dorm rooms, and the floating children's bodies in their night clothes. I try not to see the name of the raft, printed on the emergency manual lying on the floor.

I try.

"Keala," croaks Malo.

He gestures to the final level below; there's an opening in the hull. But something else has caught my eye. *Prosperity.* The raft's name stops me in my tracks. Fifty vessels set sail from dozens of islands, and yet fate brought us to this one.

Malo follows my gaze.

"I'm so sorry," he says, clutching his ribs.

I shake my head. "It's just a manual, it doesn't mean anything. We should keep moving."

Malo presses me aside and shuffles to a panel on the wall. He taps the screen and brings up the ship's roster.

"They're on this level," he croaks.

I shake my head.

"You should find them. I can last. Do it."

I can't face what he's saying.

"Keala, if you don't do this, you'll regret it forever."

I'm welling up.

"I'll help you," he croaks, extending a hand.

I nod, unable to speak. Malo leads me through the crowded corridor to the dormitory identified by the touchscreen. The door is sealed tight. He tries to force it, but it's dead set.

"Wait," I say, squeezing his arm.

There's a keypad beside the dorm. I've never tried guessing their PIN numbers before. I punch in their birthdays. Denied. Their wedding anniversary? Denied. My birthday?

The door slides open.

There they are.

My parents.

Judging by their clothes, they were about to go on shift. And going by their position, they had understood what was happening around them.

They lie together on a single bunk, their bodies wrapped in one another, locked in a final, eternal embrace.

I had never felt close to my parents. Not since failing the ritual, when I became an outcast. Being around them was a constant reminder of my failures and the disappointment I'd brought. So I pushed them away until they were too exhausted to keep trying.

Floating there, staring at their swollen, watery corpses, my mind is collapsing with grief.

"Malo, I can't-" I begin.

I turn but he's gone. Only a plume of red remains.

"Malo!"

He's hit the deck and passed out over another body. His chest is perfectly still, and blood is trickling freely from his gills.

I drag him down to the bottom level, through the drifting bodies, towards the opening. If I don't get him to the surface, he'll drown. My eyes fall upon an emergency panel overhead. Its spewed contents lie on the floor, including a pair of utility straps.

I slide them onto Malo's shoulders, then drag him up. Leaning him against the wall, I stand back-to-back against him and slide my arms into the straps, so he's attached like a backpack. I wade towards the opening, dragging him with me. I linger at the threshold, knowing I'll never see my parents' grave again, then push off into the darkness.

It takes minutes to reach the surface. I'm kicking with everything I have; each second could be Malo's last. We breach the waves and I quickly free myself from the straps. Treading water, I move Malo onto his back and cradle his head above the water.

"Come on, Malo, please don't die, please."

I'm praying the ocean breeze will galvanize his lungs. His chest heaves upwards with a splutter, but his eyes don't open.

His breaths are shallow and rattling, and it turns me cold. It's the sound of those who don't survive the transition.

I cast my eyes around the nighttime ocean, searching for help, but there's nothing to be seen, not even a ship on the horizon.

Malo is unconscious, oxygen starved, and bleeding from the neck. There's no margin for error now. Whatever direction I pick will determine if he lives or dies.

I scour the stars for constellations we'd been taught as children, but I can't recall them. To me the night sky remains an inscrutable celestial mystery. I cry out in bitter despair, cursing my dysfunctional brain. Tears swell in my eyes as I cradle Malo's wheezing body.

My ears prick up. The humming, buzzing sound is back. Every time I focus and try to pin-point its direction, it fades. I close my eyes and surrender to the sound, allowing it to resonate in my ears. I rotate until I can feel myself facing the source. When I open my eyes, there's nothing ahead. But this sound is all we have to go by. I slip my arms back into the straps, and pull Malo's back onto mine, offering out my body like a stretcher. With his head above the water, he might stand a chance. I have to believe that. And hope that whatever this sound is can save us.

CHAPTER TWENTY

LUKE

The restaurant is swanky - her choice, not mine. She earns five times what I make, while I scrimp for my ungrateful kids' college funds on a pittance. Either she's covering the check, or I'll be washing dishes here for a month. Or whatever the robot-era equivalent of that is. I guess I'd just be in jail.

"It's about hiding in plain sight," she says, startling me.

"Nice to see you too, Lanelle."

She takes a seat and the robot waiter approaches our table. I've never understood why they give them bow ties. Does it make them look more human? Is that really what was missing during the great AI integration? They've already taken our jobs, it hardly seems fair they get our fashion too. If I was president I'd make it a straight up swap. They get bow ties, we get bionic gun implants. Everybody wins.

"You can unclench your face, Luke, I'm paying," says Lanelle, opening the menu.

"Great, I'll take the special menu with the complimentary glass of Prosecco. Oh, and extra fries. And pickles. And maybe some nachos for the table. Please and thank you, robot overlord."

The robot delivers an archetypal chuckle in a plummy British accent.

Sir is quite the joker. No overlords here, I assure you, just the finest of ingredients. What can I get for Madam?

"I'll take the forty-two and the glazed carrots. Ah sod it, I'll have fries too."

The robot bows and waltzes off.

"It's good to see you, Luke, you look well."

"Cut the crap, boss, what's going on? My account's empty. How am I supposed to do this thing with no money?"

"The organization's undergoing some structural changes, and as part of that there's been a freezing spend across departments."

"Oh, but they're happy for you to keep wining and dining at this swank-ass joint?"

"This is different, it's part of your cover. If one of your lab colleagues passes by, they won't be suspicious, it'll look like two people having a nice dinner. If they saw us meeting under a subway wearing trench coats, it might raise an eyebrow."

"Fine, we're agreed that this is part of my cover. Just like everything else I'm doing. Which is why I need *money*. I could have gotten my legs broken last night!"

"Hey, don't screw your face up like that or you'll upset the waiter. Smile like I just told you a heartwarming anecdote about my kids, then tell me calmly what kind of mess you've gotten yourself into."

"Two things, boss. First, *I* haven't gotten myself into anything. *We* chose this mission together. Second, I need a hundred thousand crypto in my account by tomorrow morning."

She laughs, heartily. "Never gonna happen."

"Don't be like that."

"I'm being honest."

"You're not even interested in *why* I need the money?"

"I'm not sure I want to know. I'm more concerned about why you spent it when you knew you didn't have it."

"Because I *thought* I had it! It was time critical."

"I'm sure."

Robow tie swings by with the complementary Proseccos. I give mine a swill and sniff it.

"This will do fine," I say, like the connoisseur I am.

"No one does that with sparkling wines," snorts Lanelle.

Robow tie shuffles off making some P.G. Wodehouse quip as he goes. I swear I'm gonna take a screwdriver to that thing's motherboard and change the channel before I go insane.

"Lanelle, my neck's on the line here. You're living it large in places like this while I'm in some dive apartment, busting my balls to get you intel. All I expect is that you've got my back, but you've left me high and dry."

"Enough with the self-pity, I said I'm paying for dinner."

"And?"

"No, as in *me*. Not the company."

I feel bad for ordering such a grandiose meal now.

"Oh. You should've told me before."

"Don't worry about it."

"I do worry. If I knew, I'd have ordered the bottle."

She laughs and we clink glasses. There's something liberating about a working relationship that's half a decade old. You know each other well enough to be friends, and to trust each other's judgement, but neither of you have stayed put so long that you've totally festered.

"You still haven't told me *why* you need the money. We covered all your upfront costs?"

"These are field expenses. You know, operational stuff."

"Be specific."

"I thought you didn't wanna know?"

"'People change'," she shrugs. "Isn't that what you said to me in your interview?"

I've never met anyone who quotes me back at me as much as Lanelle does. It does my head in. I'm a very reasonable, rational, and eloquent person. As such, I find it highly difficult to argue with myself. She figured it out the day we met and she's been leveraging it against me ever since. She's like a workplace Ghost of Christmas Past, ready to point out all my gaffs with crippling accuracy.

"Luke. Stop monologuing in that fat head of yours and tell me what you did."

Wish me luck.

"Fine. Last night I dressed up like Beethoven, broke into a colleague's apartment, drugged him with cocaine, and made it look like a hooker robbed him."

It's rare these days, but in the scant moments I surprise my boss, it's like winning big at the races.

"You did *what?*" she hisses, leaning in.

For a minute I think she's about to strangle me over the table. It wouldn't be the first time. If we were under a subway, she would have. Thank goodness for the fancy refined ambience we're enjoying. Reclining, I sip my Prosecco and let out an obnoxious "aaaah". Lanelle glares at me. I sense she's not enjoying the delay. I lean in, using my least favorite voice; my *serious* voice.

"I needed to take his place at the lab today. There was a critical shipment coming in, and this was the only way I could see what was in it."

"I have *so* many questions about that hypothesis, but we truly don't have time for all of them. Is your colleague alive?"

"Just. Turns out he's allergic to latex, who knew? Could have gone real bad. Fortunately for him, I'm a very conscientious burglar. I'm getting good at EpiPens too, now."

"Where does the money come into this?"

"Uh, you think I just carry around cocaine and sex toys? Don't answer that. I had to buy them in. I also needed a skeleton key to get into my colleague's apartment. Plus I paid for the block's CCTV to be wiped."

"Assaulting people is *not* part of your remit, and neither is getting indebted to criminal gangs. You're risking the entire operation!"

"Tell me about it!"

I lean back with my hands open, then realize we're on very different pages.

"God help me Luke I am inches from pulling the plug. Tell me it was worth it. Did you get inside the lab - of the colleague you incapacitated?"

"Yeah. It's crazy in there."

"Specifics. Now. Or this fork goes in your eye."

"You sound like the gang. Relax, that's a joke, they've not made any specific threats about violence. I think we're both just taking it as read. Look, I'll give you specifics if you give me the funds."

"Are you blackmailing me?"

"I'm ensuring our transaction is equitable."

"I'll consider a bridging loan *if* you have anything of

significance. I warn you now, if you're about to tell me they're testing lipstick on bunnies the fork won't be going in your eye."

I reach into my satchel and pull out Drake's tablet.

"There. I think you'll find it makes for interesting reading."

"What does it say?"

"OK I don't actually know, I've not had time to analyze it, but I'm like ninety nine percent certain there's a smoking gun on that thing. One percent chance it's wrestling porn. Those scenarios aren't mutually exclusive."

She snatches the tablet and stows it in her bag, then stands abruptly.

"Don't contact me again until you know what's going on in that lab. Your recklessness is putting more than just your career at risk here, and you'd do well to remember that."

"Wait, what about the bridging loan?"

"Our organization is *not* paying for cocaine and hookers. Clean up your own mess."

"It wasn't an *actual* hooker-"

"I don't care. You're on a final warning. Fix it, or I'm pulling you out." She slides a small button across the table and leans in close. "It's a covert recorder. It can pass undetected. Use it. Get me the footage. Then get out."

"Hey! Forget this thing, what about the money? If you don't give me the money, other people are gonna take me out first."

"I'm sure you'll figure something out. You've got 'street smarts', I think that's how you put it? I'd start using them if I were you. Oh, and don't try selling the button camera. I put your family's address on it."

She marches out knowing she's just lit one hell of a fuse.

Robow tie rolls up laden with dishes and sides, all

spread across its multiple arm extensions. It sets the food down on the table, then notices Lanelle exiting.

Trouble in paradise, Sir?

Seriously, I'm gonna kill this thing.

Then Chang's gonna kill me.

Terrific.

CHAPTER TWENTY-ONE

KEALA

I've been dragging Malo's unconscious body for several hours, guided by the latent buzzing sound. A row of red lights blink across the night horizon. Whatever nutritional benefit that insanely potent algae had has worn off. His weight is taking its toll. My body aches with fatigue, and the straps are cutting into my shoulders. These lights are all that's keeping me going now.

As I drag us another mile closer I realize the lights don't belong to ships; they would have dispersed or outpaced us by now. Eventually the structures become apparent in their entirety. A row of sea buoys, each stationed half a mile apart. Perhaps they're marking a territorial border, or collecting more ecological data for the UN to sit on and wring its hands over.

We reach the nearest buoy and my heart sinks. Its sides are steep and conical, and perfectly smooth. There are no controls, no way of reaching the rest of the world.

I reach over my shoulder and feel Malo's feeble pulse. His breathing remains shallow and strained. As I move away from his jugular vein, my fingers brush his gills. No sign of blood. Whatever ruptured seems to have clotted. That might explain why sharks haven't found us yet. That and the fact they've been critically endangered for the past fifty years.

Malo's clotting is only partially good news. If something in his gills has clotted, it's like an internal scab. If he attempts to breathe through his gills again he could rip the wound apart. I have to get him to land before I become too weak to keep his head clear of the waves.

A burst of orange flashes across the horizon. I stare with baited breath, waiting to see if it was real, or a hallucination induced by exhaustion. Another streak of fire licks the night sky and my heart skips with joy. The humming sound has led us to people. There, in the distance, is an offshore rig.

<hr>

Bright service lights illuminate the rig and the dark ocean around it. The structure rises from the water on four thick, yellow cylinders. My heart quickens; our mission was to get help, and against all the odds we're about to do it.

As we near the first column my hope evaporates. The rig is built for boarding by ship and air; being at sea level is not how you're supposed to arrive. I circle the structure with Malo weighing against me, searching each column for a ladder.

I need you to understand my despair right now. Imagine you've been evacuated, then shipwrecked. Your people's sole hope of rescue lies with you, and you're literally carrying your community's spiritual and political future on your back. Meanwhile, you're adapting to genetic changes forced on you. Throw in days of hunger and chronic fatigue from open sea swimming, then discovering your parents in a mass grave, and you're getting closer to how I feel. Add a glimmer of hope; a man-made rig in a desolate ocean.

Now take away the ladder.

That's right. After everything we've been through, the thing that's going to finish us off is a missing ladder. I've doggedly circled three of the four yellow columns and there's no way up. As I approach the final leg, I'm down to the last of my energy, both physically and mentally. What meets my eyes is almost cruel.

There's a set of rungs that stops several meters above the water; it's for escape only. How the hell am I supposed to reach it from a standing start, especially with Malo on my back?

Frustrated, I slam my palm against the steel. To my astonishment, it sticks fast. I tug as hard as I can. Only with great effort can I rip it off the surface. I inspect the damage. It's throbbing with pain; it looks wrinkled and inflamed, but the skin seems intact.

I stare at the route up and the journey ahead sinks in. This is going to hurt. Even if I make it to the rungs, it's easily a hundred feet of vertical climb to the platform.

Malo splutters. It's hard to keep his face clear of the waves while I tread water. If I resume swimming I can keep him flat and breathing, but land could be hundreds of miles away. If I try to climb and get help, any fall could kill him.

I slap both hands against the yellow steel, then my bare feet, which prove equally grippy. Bracing for the burn, I haul myself from the water. The full extent of Malo's weight makes me cry out in pain. I'm not clutching the column with my muscles, it's too broad and smooth. The grip is coming entirely from my skin.

I climb one limb at a time, ripping one hand free, latching it on higher up, then repeating with each subsequent limb. I have no idea how to control this mutation and each movement is agony.

Malo's body hangs off me like an anchor. The tough straps binding our shoulders are sawing into my skin with every move I make. With immense effort, we're halfway to the bottom rung, but I'm growing dizzy. If we fall now, there's no way I can do this again.

My parents' voices echo in my head. Their disappointment and constant pleading with me. For years they challenged me to see myself as more than a failure, but I pushed them away. Now their voices exist only in my memory. If I fail, they'll be silenced forever.

I tear my foot from the steel and force myself higher, ripping and latching. The pain is making me see double. The straps are stymieing the circulation to my brain. I reach up and my fingertips dust the bumpy, rusted metal. Gasping through the agony, I stretch further and grab the rung.

Panting, I transfer our collective weight onto my ladder arm. I rip my foot from the pillar, ready to raise it higher.

With a sudden creak the rung shears from the frame. I cry in terror as we fall. The terror becomes pain as the weight of two bodies drops heavily against my remaining foot and hand; our only connections to the rig. We swing like a door flapping in the wind. The pressure against my joints is excruciating. I try to latch on with my other foot, but my purchase has vanished. My spare hand, by contrast, is stuck to the sheared rung. I shake it desperately but my skin won't let go.

I can feel my other limbs peeling. I have seconds to act before we both fall for good. I'm about to pass out from the pain. Malo will surely drown. I might too.

I whack my rung hand against the pillar and raise my grip-less foot to meet it. With my foot clamped down against the rung, I tear my hand free. The pain is searing but there's no time to dwell. I slam my hand against the rig and climb.

I need to reach the new bottom rung but my grip-less limb is a deadweight. Speed will be everything. Ripping my safe foot from the rig, I move it as high as I can, latch on, and propel myself upward.

This time I grab the side of the ladder. With my spare hand I test the new rung; it's solid. Staring upwards, I gasp for breath. A hundred-foot vertical ascent looms. The platform might as well be on another planet. Malo's airways rattle like he's choking. If he were conscious I know he'd insist *I release the buckles. Let me go. There's no point both of us dying!*

I've never been one to listen.

I don't know how long I've been unconscious for. The first thing I become aware of is machinery humming. The stillness of my body strikes me; the ground is flat and firm. Painfully bright lights shine overhead, and someone's leaning over me. Their voice is muffled, like they're yelling into a pillow.

I shield my eyes from the glare. The voice is coming into focus; the face too. Malo is alive!

"Keala? Oh my god, I was so worried!"

He throws his arms around me in a fierce embrace. I'm way too out of it to reciprocate; I can barely lift my arms. My chin flops against his shoulder and I try to process our surroundings. The last moments are coming back to me; I remember swaying at the top step and falling sideways onto the platform. The pain in my hip confirms as much.

Beside me are two bloodied shoulder straps. I look at Malo's face properly for the first time. He looks a hell of a lot better. The skin under his armpits is raw from friction, and I can feel mine throbbing reciprocally.

Specialized engineering drones wheel about the platform attending to machines and pumps. I've not seen bots like these before, the ones in the movies are always sexy androids. This is the unglamorous end of the robotic spectrum; single-armed robots on Caterpillar tracks performing greasy maintenance jobs on a rickety old rig.

"How did we get here?" says Malo, his eyes gushing with relief.

I gesture to the bloodied straps. "How do you think?"

"No way. I don't believe you did this," says Malo, shaking his head.

My mouth drops. "You really think that little of me? That I'm not capable of saving us both?"

"I can't believe you were reckless enough to try!"

"You're *angry* with me for saving you?"

"When I passed out it was dusk and we were in open ocean. Now it's dawn, meaning you swam all night, then scaled this thing, all the while carrying me."

"Your point is?"

"That's insane, an uncontrolled fall from this height could rupture major organs. You could have died!"

"So I should have let you drown?"

"Yes!"

"Is this your way of saying thank you? I should warn you, it sucks."

"Thank you for what? Ignoring me at every turn? I told you not to follow me in the first place!"

"If I'd have listened, you'd be dead!"

"But you would have been *safe*."

"I know you care about your precious flock, Mr. Chief-in-waiting, but you don't get to call the shots out here."

"This has nothing to do with being leader!"

"Then what *is* it about?"

"You!... And me... Us."

"*Us?*"

Our faces are close. Our breathing is heavy from the arguing. I'm trying to digest the list of contradictions Malo has just thrown at me. It might be the light-headedness, but I feel myself leaning towards him. He's getting closer, too. His lips are parting. My eyes close and I take a deep breath.

An alarm tone sounds. A spotlight snaps on overhead and I can hear a drone hovering above us. Squinting, we raise our hands in surrender. The voice sounds human.

"This is a private vessel. Leave immediately or force will be used."

"We need your help!" cries Malo.

"I repeat, this is a private vessel. Leave immediately or f-"

We catch a fraction of background conversation as the announcer is interrupted by a colleague. I scour the platform and spot the two workers arguing in the control room ahead. The second colleague snatches the microphone.

"Uh, why are you here?"

"We're shipwrecked, we're not any kind of threat, we just need help, please," calls Malo.

This time the loudhailer channel stays open and we hear fragments of the men bickering. Their attitudes towards us are polarized... *Refugees... Innocent... Not our... Against company pol-... Unarmed... Pirates... Trick...*

The control room door opens and a man steps out. He descends the twisting steps and weaves across the platform towards us. The drone shifts, aiming the spotlight at our eyes, and masking the man's features as he approaches.

But it doesn't mask the sound of a gun being loaded.

CHAPTER TWENTY-TWO

LUKE

You know that feeling when you wake up like fortune's rooting for you and everything's starting to work out?

I have yet to experience that feeling.

Unless I discover a pile of money by sundown, this is my last day undercover. I'm standing outside Pierre's office, sleep deprived as hell from another night of swatting up on immunology, and I'm about to make a very risky pitch. I need him to let me into the dark lab. It's my last chance to get into that chamber of nightmares and see what's going down.

Allow me to introduce you to the mother of all flies in the ointment. This particular fly happens to be a six foot human male with a passion for martial arts and recently discharged from hospital.

Yup, Drake's back.

By the sounds of it, he's in a pissy mood. I eavesdrop by the open door as they argue.

"We'll tell everyone you had a bereavement," says Pierre.

"No one's gonna buy that. Who comes back from a funeral with a black eye?" fumes Drake.

"In the unlikely event one of your colleagues tries to make small talk, I suggest you make something up."

"I'm not much of a creative thinker."

"Try."

"I... could say I was mistaken for my aunt's lover?"

"Weird angle to take."

"It's a cover story, it's not actually true."

"Your family affairs really aren't my business, Drake."

"That was just a random made up thing."

"Sure."

"Wait, you think it's true? I'm not into my aunt!"

"I've already said I believe you."

"OK."

"And that it's not my business to pry."

"What the hell, boss, I'm *not* an aunt-lover! This is crazy, you *know* I was burgled and assaulted!"

"Disappointing, Drake. That was a test and you cracked in less than a minute. You're right, improvising a cover story is clearly beyond your abilities. Tell people there was a family misunderstanding at a difficult funeral and leave it at that. If anyone asks further questions, we'll make it an HR thing."

"OK. Thank you."

"Did the attacker know about your latex allergy?"

"I don't think so, they freaked out when it happened. They called 911, it was all super weird."

"No CCTV?"

"It blacked out across the block, but the cops have got a lead."

Why is it that eavesdropping always makes me want to flee the country? Drake's back, and the police are onto me, despite everything I tried. The clock's double-ticking now. If I make it out of here alive, I'm patenting that phrase by the way.

"I hope the police find answers quickly," says Pierre.

"Er... about that," says Drake. "There's a complication."

"This had better not involve your aunt."

"Something was stolen from my apartment which belongs to the lab. They took my tablet."

"What the hell was it doing there in the first place? That's forbidden!"

"I know, boss, but my brain works best in the evenings when I'm at home. I figured I'd be more productive if I took some work with me. I made a ton of progress."

"Progress which you've now *lost*, and which has fallen into God knows who's hands! What else did they take?"

At this point I'm blushing. The raid I did on Drake's place was amateur, I should have stolen other valuables. A theft this targeted is a red flag in any investigation, and Drake's reached much the same conclusion.

"That's the thing, boss, they didn't take anything else."

"Just the tablet? That's worse, it means this was premeditated; they know where you work. This is precis*ely* why we don't allow company devices outside of the lab."

Something slams. Either Pierre pounded his desk or Drake's got a fresh black eye.

"How did you get it out of the lab?" says Pierre.

"I disabled the security tracker," replies Drake.

"That was a stupid thing to do. Is the device at least passcode protected?"

"Yes."

"Good, so it's secure?"

"Er, not exactly... The thief used my finger to unlock it before he left."

"You know it was a man?"

"I'm pretty sure, yeah."

I'm fully regretting my life choices right now. Drake remembers everything, the police are looking for the device, and the lab knows the attack was targeted. Oh boy. At least the tracking feature on the tablet is disabled.

"Relax, Drake. We have other ways of tracking these things."

Dammit.

"But boss, the device is in airplane mode?"

Thank you.

"Airplane mode is for airplanes, not for security. Our tablets' batteries generate a distinct frequency, making them trackable even when the device is offline. So long as it's using power, we can track the signal, because we built the tools to do it. And so long as your assailant's not working inside a Faraday cage, we have a chance."

"What if they don't switch the device on at all? Or for months?"

"Oh, they'll turn it on all right. They tracked your movements and assaulted you at home because they know it's a goldmine. Not that they'll ever get the data. Each device is fitted with a self-destruct protocol which wipes the disk. As soon as they turn it on, we'll get a lock on their location and we can trigger a full memory wipe through a series of localized ambient power fluctuations. The tablet has an in-built sensor for this very eventuality."

"But to do that you'd have to be able to control the city's power grid on a micro level," says Drake.

"Of all the things we do here, turning on and off the lights in other buildings is what surprises you?"

"You mustn't."

"I beg your pardon?"

"Please, boss. The tablet has critical work I've not yet backed up; there's a set of computations I ran using the quantum AI. The parameters were experimental; I was using a custom machine learning tool to set them. It could take decades to replicate something even approximating the same input variables. They delivered a massive improvement on anything else we've achieved. From the model, successful adaptation rates were above ninety five percent. That's-"

"Within the target boundary," says Pierre, astonished. "Are you absolutely sure?"

"Positive. With that iteration we can stabilize the protein in water for the two week transmission period, without impacting native species."

"You're saying you've solved it?"

"Not without the tablet. If the police find it first, they'll examine it in a Faraday cage, and they'll discover our operation. They could be doing it right now."

"I highly doubt that. Believe me, if the police see what's on there, we'll know right away, because they'll be kicking our door down. Which leads me to conclude that it remains with the culprit. We'll know their location if they switch it on, but thanks to you we can't wipe it. I'll have to reach out to some contacts. We need to track your attacker in person."

"Thank you, boss."

"Don't thank me yet, Drake. If we can't recover this device, it won't be the police you have to worry about."

I'm killing time in the bathroom. Drake's Lazarus moment has lanced my early-bird dark lab plan so I need to lay low until regular start time. No point lingering near the dark lab while Pierre's on edge, I need to deflect suspicion. Best play it cool by taking a twenty minute dump.

Feeling lighter, and looking on time, I join my team at their usual table in the canteen. Pierre arrives moments later to deliver our morning briefing. Who's that with him? Shock, delight, it's Drake! But goodness me, Drake, what happened to your eye?

Seriously, I should get an Academy Award.

"Yes, thank you all for your concern, Drake's delighted to be back after a brief absence. He suffered a family bereavement and does not wish to talk about the matter. Now, onto today's agenda."

As Pierre drones on Drake gets jumpy, rubbing his arm, shuffling in his seat and eyeing up the group. I'm stealing glances at him, while pretending to listen to the briefing. Which I really should be listening to.

"... Once we've completed the adaptation tests, we will terminate the subject."

"It's taken years to get to this stage, why terminate so soon? The subject only arrived yesterday, there's so much we could learn from it."

"Orders from above. They used their favorite two words: plausible deniability."

"We lost that when we brought the specimen on site!" protests Carla.

A member of another team passes by with a breakfast tray and accidentally brushes Drake's back. Drake leaps from the table and knocks the guy's meal to the floor. He shoves the guy's chest, sending him skidding backwards on his ass.

"Woah, Drake, cool it. Take five," says Pierre, hastily intervening.

He helps the bewildered worker up, with a cursory

explanation about Drake having suffered a bereavement. Everyone looks alarmed. Drake's casting his eyes around the canteen like his attacker could be anywhere. He storms off with his fists clenched. It's not just vengeance he's after, it's redemption.

Pierre eyeballs the group with a gravity that conveys everything he cannot explicitly say: unless they find the attacker and recover the tablet, Drake's life's on the line.

Speaking of lives on the line, I need to text Lanelle ASAP. She needs to know about the tablet's battery tracker. But I can't use my regular phone, that would be just as incriminating. I need to get back to my apartment but there's no way to go without arousing suspicion. I can stay and protect my cover, or I can leave to protect hers, but I can't do both.

Sorry, boss.

It's the end of the day and I'm hurrying from the office, trying to clear my brain of half-baked coral bleaching solutions. With Drake and Carla back in the lab, I've been stuck in the coral hangar, with zero chance to progress or escape. My priority right now is getting back to my toilet phone ASAP to warn Lanelle of the danger. But as soon as I'm clear of the lab's firewall my regular phone picks up a message.

$$$ Tick-tock $$$

Accompanying it is a gif of someone releasing a cat from a bag. I glance back at the coffee pot building as if they're reading my thoughts. When I look back at my phone the message is gone. Clearly Chang figures the lab's monitoring the phone. Or maybe the deletion was delayed - he probably sent it earlier today, before Lanelle wired the money to my account. I know she played hardball last night, but she always comes through in the end.

I check my account balance. There should be two transactions. One deposit from Lanelle. And one withdrawal by Chang.

Nothing.

Looks like we're both screwed.

I hurry through my apartment and rip the cistern lid up. I grab the toilet phone and write Lanelle a hasty message.

DO NOT TURN ON TABLET. They can track it even in airplane mode. Battery emits unique frequency. They'll wipe it on detection, then come for you. Faraday cage is the only way. Please confirm.

Send.

The reply comes right away.

Acknowledged.

Partial relief. My boss is still alive, and the tablet's still off-grid. Now it's time to save my own ass.

Where is the crypto? Deadline is in two hours. Please transfer urgently.

If she replies quickly, it's bad news. If she takes a minute, it means she's working on it.

Buzz.

Use your street smarts.

God dammit. Careful what you wish for, boss.

I enter my local dive bar and approach the barkeep. In the fancy joints, they've got robots to serve you. In the *really* fancy joints, they've got fancy people. In the really *non-fancy* joints, they've got neither fancy robots nor fancy people. They've got Mia.

"I'll take a scotch on the rocks. I want it shaken, then stirred, then shaken a few more times, then chuck it away and gimme a coke."

Judging by her flat, hardened expression, Mia is not one for parlor games.

"Fine. How about a rum and coke? Best of both worlds."

She stares at me like a cat, when it's letting you know it could take you in a fight, but is choosing to rise above you.

She pours the drink and sets it down on the bar, then slaps a check beside it.

"Aaah, Mia, I'm a little hard up," I say, patting my pockets. "Is there anyone around this fine establishment who could spot me a drink, plus two thousand times that amount?"

I take back everything I said about Mia rising above it. Turns out, she's more than happy to be in among it, and indeed revels in it. She grabs the scruff of my neck and hauls me over the counter. I swear the people in this town are conspiring to break my spine. I'm a starfish on the sticky bar floor, and Mia's got her foot against my windpipe. I raise a finger in polite objection, rasping a plea to negotiate. She hits a buzzer on the wall.

I also take back everything I said about joints like this not having robots. A burly pot washing robot zips out of the kitchen. It's got an apron, a pair of marigolds covered in suds, and no head. I recognize the unit from a commercial I saw as a kid. They were intended for households but they creeped people out, so they never took off. This thing is an antique. If it's the au pair edition, I'm sure it can do more than wash pots. I'm pretty sure they can teach algebra, play piano, speak Spanish, run HIIT workouts; all the skills yuppie parents want for their brats.

Soapy rubber clamps onto me and the pot wash hauls me up, carrying me at arm's length like a kid in a stinky diaper. We glide through the kitchen and into the parking lot.

My curiosity about this robot's past is mounting. For something designed to wash dishes it's awfully comfortable outside the kitchen. We approach a gleaming gangstermobile and it slams me against the hood.

I give the robot a groaning thumbs up. "Gracias."

Es nada, it replies, gliding off.

The car door opens and three guys climb out.

"Who are you?" demands the short one.

It's always the short ones in charge.

"I'm your newest customer. Pleasure to meet you, I'm Luke."

"We don't do names here."

"Right, no names. Just a brash set of wheels and a personalized number plate. Real incognito."

The little guy frowns. I wait until he realizes I'm insulting him, then wait for one of the big fellas to hit me on his behalf.

I fold like a guy who's been punched hard in the stomach.

When you're borrowing money, it's important to have the right credentials for a vendor. These guys are lowlifes at a dive bar, which means they're gonna be deeply suspicious of a well-heeled office worker asking for a bridging loan, unless that person's an addict, which I'm clearly not. Disheveled loud mouths are what they're used to. It's also important they feel they have the upper hand otherwise they get suspicious. So I make a quip, get punched, apologize, and they feel like they already own me.

These methods usually involve my face meeting someone's fist. Street smarts suck.

"Now we've got that out the way, I need to borrow some money."

"How much?"

I'm gonna fast forward this bit cos haggling is lame. Suffice to say, they're appalled at the amount I'm borrowing and flat out refuse. I then halve it, and halve it again, until we're at the *actual* amount I need, which now seems reasonable. It's roughly the price of their hideous car. They refuse this too, so I'm desperate. We talk interest rates and it goes badly. OK fine, the real reason I'm skimming this bit is because I'm terrible at negotiating and they hit me two more times because I make jokes about the little guy's height. Happy?

It's worth it because I leave with half the money, which can at least buy me some time from Chang. The only hitch is that these guys want it repaid tomorrow night with thirty percent interest. It's daylight robbery! It's also possibly because I told them I'm paying off a security guard to rob an art gallery, and that I'll be good for the whole amount and more as soon as the heist is done, because I have a buyer lined up. I'm not a good negotiator, but I can be a very creative liar when the situation requires. Unlike Drake, who is both terrible and clearly has repressed inter-generational issues.

I rush across town, splashing some of my hard-won cash on a cab ride to Chang's joint. I'm straight in, sweeping past the fat sweaty guy at the counter, to the dank little office out back. The kid's in his swivel chair, chewing a cigar, looking ridiculous.

"Just in time," he grins.

"You know that'll give you cancer, right?"

"You not live long enough to find out."

He spins the screen, revealing the email he's composing. Several files are attached. My original driver's license, tax details, birth certificate, mortgage paperwork, wedding photographs, the lot. Everything the lab needs to unmask me.

"Does your 'boss' Pierre prefer Dr. or Professor?"

"Don't send that! I can pay."

I slam the cash on his desk. He takes one look at the fat envelope and leans forward.

"Not enough."

"Half was all I could get at short notice but I'll have the rest by tomorrow, I swear."

"Gimme watch."

He's pointing at my engagement watch.

"This? Oh, I can't. It's sentimental."

By 'sentimental', I mean it's technically no longer my property. My ex-wife's robot lawyer added a clause saying she gets it back. I owe stuff to a lot of people.

"It fine, Lukey. Keep it. I emailing your laboratory now."

"Wait! OK, fine, but only as a deposit. I'll need it back."

I place it down beside the wad of cash and wring my wrist. Chang drums his fingers across the wad and stares at me, like I'm some piece of experimental art he's considering buying. After another ostentatious drag on his cigar, he clicks the "save" button, and makes a show of checking the email's in his drafts folder.

"Tomorrow. Full amount."

"Absolutely, I'll get the rest no problem."

"No. You bring full amount."

"What? I just gave you half!"

"This buy you extension only. Tomorrow you clearing debt."

I storm outta there like I'm possessed, which I kinda am - by them. The fat guy on the counter extends a card as I go. "Hey man, you want a loyalty stamp?"

Rushing home to my dismal apartment, I grab the toilet phone. I'm punching the keys with such force that it hurts my thumbs. I'm hoping the added emphasis translates.

Triple account credit required urgently. Two parties involved, both illegal. Send funds or I'm screwed.

CHAPTER TWENTY-THREE

KEALA

I finish the flask of water and draw the foil blanket around me. We're sat in the mess cabin of the rig, exhausted, and processing the past forty-eight hours. Healing strips soothe the gashes on our shoulders and armpits. The female worker returns with a platter.

"It's not much, sorry, the rations here suck."

She sets out a tray laden with bread, peanut butter, raisins, and crisps. Her male colleague sits on the berth opposite, glaring at us, ashen faced and silent, with the gun resting on his lap.

"Not often we get company out here. Usually it's just the two of us," she continues, brightly.

She looks to the man but he doesn't react. His eyes are fixed on Malo, who is shoveling chunks of bread and spoonfuls of peanut butter into his mouth animalistically.

"Sorry, we've not eaten in a really long time," says Malo, through a full mouthful.

"Don't apologize, enjoy," smiles the woman.

The taste of sugar and fat landing on my tongue is bliss.

Within ten minutes, we've cleared the tray and are reclining in our seats, grinning for the first time in days.

"Now nurse nice has done her bit, you wanna tell me what the hell you're doing here?" says the man.

"Of course, you deserve an explanation. First, our thanks for your hospitality; your kindness has saved us."

Malo is straight into diplomacy mode, deploying all his conversational frills. He's recovering quickly, and is able to talk freely, whereas I'm short of breath and can only manage clipped, panting sentences, like I'm having an asthma attack.

"We're from Makamesia - the first islands," Malo continues.

"First in what?" says the man.

"First to be evacuated. You guys don't know?"

The two rig workers look bemused.

"But those journalists came to our homes, they visited the first rafts?" I wheeze.

"Sorry, folks, it's news to me," says the woman.

Malo rises to his feet but the rig man draws the gun, forcing him to freeze with his hands raised.

"Al, put that down, we're just talking," says the woman, sternly. "Ignore him, he's jumpy because his last rig got attacked by pirates."

"Twice, actually. What's to say these two aren't hijackers?" says the man.

"Do you *see* a boat circling the rig? You see any guns on them? No," says the woman.

"Then why the hell are they here?"

"They were about to tell us, before you got all *gunny!*" The woman turns to Malo, "Please go on."

Malo shows the bump on his upper arm. The bands of infected skin have disappeared from our bodies, but there's a dime-sized patch of bleached skin where the inoculation was administered.

"We were injected. They provided rafts for our people, then gave us a 'vaccine', but we think it's what caused the mutations."

"Say what now?" says the man.

"We can breathe underwater."

"Bull," scoffs the man. "Prove it."

Malo points to the gills beneath his jaw. His are small and sealed, making them discrete to the outside eye. Judging by the woman's inspection of my face, however, mine are more prominent.

"So they're not cuts, they're, like, gills?"

"It's our best guess," says Malo. "Our raft broke apart a day into our voyage, killing half the people on board. We only survived because we ran aground on an atoll, but now we're stranded with no food or shelter, and the mutations are spreading. We need help urgently."

"We found my parents' raft on the ocean bed. Their whole crew drowned," I wheeze.

"She's right, there are dozens of other vessels," agrees Malo, "We have to find them all, there could be more survivors."

"I've heard enough. This is nonsense," says the man, standing up.

"We can prove it!" says Malo.

"With some scars and a long swim? I'm not buying it."

Malo unfastens his diving watch and holds it out. "Check the altitude, please."

There's no way free divers could achieve such depths. The man glares at Malo, then tosses the watch back. "Fake," he growls, then storms out clutching his pistol.

"Ignore him, he'll come around," says the woman.

"Why doesn't he believe us? Even if I could fake the watch reading, I can't fake my body," says Malo.

"He knows it's true, he just doesn't want to believe it."

"What kind of person does that make him?" I wheeze.

"Pretty regular, I'm afraid," replies the woman. "I'm so sorry about your parents, by the way. How come you were on separate rafts?"

Tears of guilt well up inside me as I remember missing the departure. Malo answers for me.

"We were all assigned rafts by the aid agency, we didn't get a choice. In a way, we were lucky not to sink over deep ocean. It could easily have been us down there with them. Which is why you need to help us. Please, we've risked everything to find you."

"Me?"

"You must alert the authorities. Without rescue my people will die."

"Do you have coordinates for the rescue?"

"No. Our on board navigation failed a few hours into the voyage; we were dependent on our own skills. But I know our start and end destinations, that gives us a search radius."

"Of what, twenty thousand square miles? I don't want to be unkind, Mister, but you know the chances of finding a wreck in the deep ocean are next to zero?"

"Our priority isn't the deep, it's the atoll. You don't need planes or ships, I know you can do it from space, but only if the people controlling the satellites know to look for us - you have to tell them!"

"Woah, this is a lot. Uh, OK. I mean, I don't know anyone working with satellites, but I guess we could look online?" says the woman.

She summons a floating screen.

"You never told me we were lost," I pant, confronting Malo.

He looks at me sheepishly. "I thought it was a glitch, I didn't want to cause alarm. How could I know the whole thing was designed to fail?"

"What do you mean?" interjects the woman.

"We were set up. I'll prove it - there's a logo on the straps Keala used to rescue me. There was no branding on the main body of the vessels, but this logo is on the emergency manuals, and all the other kit we discovered when the rafts broke up. It's like a different group was responsible for what happened to us after the rafts sank. I think it's all part of a broader thing. If we can identify the company, we can find the people who did this to us. They might know where the other rafts sank, and how to reverse the mutations."

"This all sounds like a long shot. Then again, I've never had swimmers climb a rig before, let alone ones with gills," muses the woman.

She looks like she believes us, but she doesn't look happy about it.

"I'll prove it, wait here," says Malo.

He leaves the cabin and heads outside, back across the platform towards the abandoned straps by the emergency ladder.

"How come no one knows about our evacuation?" I ask. "We thought the entire world was watching, now it's like we never existed," I say.

"Just cos the press saw you doesn't mean they were allowed report it," shrugs the woman.

"But your country – the Northern Bloc – it has freedom of speech?"

"It used to, till people ruined it. Anonymity can turn

regular folk into monsters online. Swarms of monsters ruining individual lives. Plus the election rigging thing - big data, fake news, equals goodbye democracy. Eventually people wanted to know what was real and what was lies, so they elected a president to break up the tech companies and bring in laws for accountability. It worked great to start with, then the economy fell on its ass, and we got a new president. This guy went after the press, blaming them for the recession. He brought in huge taxes on news media, but you can get exemption if you sign up to a state-run censorship body. There's only a handful of independent papers left, and they're broke. Mainly from legal fees. Most news is community activism now, from the brave few."

My mind is spinning. How is such a divided country ever going to help us?

"Maybe you two will change things back," she adds.

"How?"

"People gotta see you with their own eyes, like me now. You gotta get to the mainland. I think I know a way to smuggle you in. We're getting relieved in two days' time. They never bother checking returning luggage - we can smuggle you in our crates. We've got six months' worth of stuff for you to hide in."

Her colleague returns, looking brighter than when he'd left. His brow is arched in a docile, placating manner, totally at odds with the hostile scowl he'd worn until now. He's relaxed, like he's back in control.

A noise outside pricks my ears.

"What the hell?" says the woman, peering out of the window.

A black sky craft is landing on the rig deck. The woman turns to her colleague, aghast.

"What have you done?" she cries.

"I done what needed to be done," shrugs the man.

Outside, Malo looks ecstatic. He waves at the craft, running towards it with excitement. The crew door slides open and four robotic marines jump out. A cold dread sweeps over me. A marine raises a gun and fires. An electrical stun charge surges across Malo's body. He falls to the floor, twitching. My mouth is open in horror and I'm screaming his name. Two of the robots are dragging him to the craft, while the others march towards the cabin.

I spin around, searching for an escape, but the rig man is training his gun on me.

"Stay right where you are, darlin'," says the man.

"What the hell is this?" yells his colleague.

"Shut up, I'm just doing what's smart. You'll get a cut, don't worry," says the man.

"You're sick!" she yells.

She grabs me, putting her body in front of mine.

"You wanna shoot her? You'll have to shoot me first. I know your visa's up for renewal, you think they'll do it if you shoot a coworker?"

The man's face sours. "Get the hell out the way!"

The robots are fast approaching the spiral steps. The woman shoves me into the corridor. I'm running, heeding her instructions. Behind us the cabin door bursts open. The man shouts at the robots to catch us.

There's an emergency exit ahead. I sprint towards it and force the door open. A blast of cold sea air greets me. It's a sheer drop into the waves below. I'm teetering on the edge.

The woman catches up. "There's a way out but you'll have to go even deeper than your last dive. There's a pipe below this rig. It's got a drone-monorail running along it. If you can make it down that deep, that thing's your ticket out of here." She taps on her wrist panel. "I'm setting the drone to run a full pipeline scan starting in ten minutes. If you can reach it, hold on, it'll take you to the mainland. I'm so sorry honey. I'll try to-"

Her face freezes and she falls to the ground twitching. Behind her, a robotic marine stands with its gun pointing directly at my chest. Without a second's hesitation, I jump.

CHAPTER TWENTY-FOUR

LUKE

et's recap. It's been two days since I broke into
Drake's apartment. One day since Drake returned
to work. And zero days since I had a decent night's
sleep. That's the problem with owing colossal sums of
money to two separate criminal enterprises. It really eats
into your forty winks, especially when both of those debts
are due by sundown tonight.

I'm with Carla, who's giving me an induction task in the
technical floor. It's a similar style to the animal lab, only
swap the piled up crates for tiny Petri dishes. Whereas the
animal lab held a hundred or so subjects, this one has tens of
thousands of samples. Some rows are brightly illuminated,
others are kept under UV light, while a few hide in
darkness.

The aisles are too narrow for humans, so robots manage
the whole space. They're not the full-sized androids you get
in law enforcement, these are the single arm, single purpose
machines that make the world go round.

Super thin and highly flexible, the robots glide through
the genetic library, retrieving samples, rotating dishes, and

injecting solutions. Carla looks up the sample ID she wants, punches in a request, and one of the many dangling arms fetches it.

A colleague enters, looking unsettled.

"You all good, Yakob?" says Carla.

He ignores her and swipes into the adjoining lab. I raise an eyebrow to Carla.

"Don't mind him, he's just rattled," she explains.

"Why?"

"You haven't heard? They found the leak."

"What kind of leak?"

"A mole."

My throat turns to sand. "Aha, er, is Yakob the mole?"

"They let him go, so he must be clean. He's probably just shaken by how much they've got on him."

"So if the mole isn't Yakob, who is it?"

"We'll know soon," she shrugs. "They're identifying anyone who might have known Drake had a work device at home. You know that's why he was attacked, right? The whole family bereavement thing was bull."

I feign shock.

"I know, it's crazy," she continues. "Someone was after his tablet, which can only mean we've got a mole. I overheard Pierre talking to the director earlier, and they reckon we'll know who by the end of the day. They're interrogating the whole building - I was one of the first. Between you and me, I kinda thought it might be Yakob, but now my money's on Edwards - no way is anyone that posh."

"So they're gonna interrogate me too? I think I'm still recovering from the interview," I laugh, nervously.

"Oh, did they do the chimp one with you? It's pretty wild, huh? They used to do a gun and a hostage thing, but people had panic attacks."

"So they went with a rabid chimp instead? Nice."

Our sample arrives and the robot inserts it into an exchange portal beneath the glass viewing pane. A recipient bot collects the sample in its pincers and deposits it into a scanner for analysis. Carla scrolls through the magnified image on screen, reviewing irregularities the computer has identified in the culture's growth.

As she's scrolling, a call comes through on her glasses. I can't see who it is, but it sounds like she's talking to Pierre. She hangs up.

"Looks like we're back on cover duty. Drake's been sent home. Apparently he punched one of the animals. They need to give that guy more time off, did you *hear* what he went through? A Mozart mask? Who would even do that?"

My lip twitches; I'm about to correct her, but I hold off. Carla's exceptionally bright, and her chummy approach could be part of the security team's intelligence-gathering strategy. I play dumb.

"Drake does have a touch of the Salieri about him, maybe it was karma."

"If karma exists, we're screwed," chuckles Carla.

As we enter the elevator sweat drips down my spine. This is my last chance. I have to get into the dark lab and out before they call me to interrogation. But as the doors close, a grim realization hits me: this could be a one-way trip.

***

We cross through the animal lab. Carla checks I'm happy covering her work again, then swipes into the adjoining dark lab. With Drake suspended, and Pierre interrogating everyone, experimenting on the secret specimen falls to her.

As always, I linger at the edge of each row, trying to catch a glimpse inside the dark lab, should the doors open. I don't have to wait long before a squat trolley bot comes through. From the space beyond, I hear the tail end of a scream. In any other situation I would have doubted my ears, or hesitated, but not in this place. These people don't scream lightly. It's real.

Gift horse.

Mouth.

Here goes nothing...

I grab the trolley bot and ram it back into the threshold. The titanium door jams into its broad body. The bot buckles, but holds just firm enough to create an opening. I leap over it into the holding chamber. The trolley crumples completely and vanishes behind the thick blast door.

At this point, I realize it might have been smart to check out how the holding chamber works before leaping into it. There are vents in the ceiling. Either they're filtering the air out, or I'm about to be sterilized.

I grab a splintered piece of trolley bot and bang it against the side of the chamber, calling for help. The front door slides open and a service bot scoots past me. Multiple limbs spread out from its tubular body as it attends to the rear door and debris from its peer. The second blast door is closing. I seize my chance and sprint for the gap.

I made it. I'm inside the dark lab.

First thing to note: it's very well lit. In my defense, "dark lab" sounds way cooler than "optimally illuminated lab".

Second thing: it's small. Compared to the forest hangar, this thing's a doll's house. There are three tubes shaped like cargo containers, and they're arranged like the quarter points on a clock face. The outer two are dark, but the middle one is active. It's what I glimpsed Carla returning from yesterday; a box of swirling light.

The screaming has stopped, but there's a banging sound like wood against metal.

I approach the container, calling out Carla's name. The banging halts. I'm by the entrance now, and the glass door is open. Odorless vapor is wafting out.

I step inside and shiver at the cold. I can barely see my feet; the mist makes the small space feel endless.

"Carla?"

My voice echoes off the low ceiling and narrow walls. I look back and the doorway's vanished. I'm disorientated; stuck in the middle of a cloud, in a tube, in an illegal laboratory I'm not supposed to be in. I'll be honest, I'm starting to fill my pants.

My studies of Ancient Greek mythology are about to pay off, as I recall the tale of Theseus escaping King Minos's Labyrinth. I calmly find my way to the nearest wall, and, keeping one hand on it, proceed to undertake a lap of the inner perimeter, knowing it will ultimately lead me back to the open door. Pretty neat, huh?

Alright, fine. I panic, get woozy, and fall sideways. That's how I find the wall. Happy?

As I feel my way through the mist, I have the distinct feeling I'm not alone. That's the worst thing about working in this place; there could be *anything* in here.

My foot taps something and I freeze. There's an arm lying across the floor. I recognize Carla's bracelet immediately. Kneeling down I find my way through the mist to her face. She's unconscious, but breathing.

I slide my arms under her knees and shoulders. I'm about to lift her when a noise startles me.

"Hello?" I call out.

It's dumb, but it's a reflex. Maybe lethal genetically engineered predators speak English, who knows?

There's another shuffling sound, like wood on metal again.

I stand up, trying to get a better sense of which direction it's coming from, when something grabs hold of my ankle. A rattling cry resonates from the mist. "Help me!"

In case I hadn't filled my pants enough, they're positively overflowing at this moment. I'm frozen, rooted to the spot. I can't run, because I have no idea where the exit is. I can't abandon Carla, she's my alibi for coming in here. And I can't escape the hand clutching my ankle because... this person's grip is really strong.

There's a scraping sound again. I feel the person's grip rocking in time with it. Whoever's gotten hold of my leg is dragging themselves towards me. Out of the mist, inch by inch, appears a head. Behind it is a wooden chair, tipped on its side.

"Holy crap, are you tied to that thing?"

"Please help me," rasps the stranger.

I kneel down to inspect more closely, briefly reassured I won't be eaten. That's when I see the gills. This guy has them all along his jaw line. They're flapping open in the mist, like he's breathing through them.

"Dude, you have gills?" I exclaim.

"Get me out of here, please," begs the stranger.

He looks rough. I untie him at once and we stumble into the main lab, where I can see him properly. He looks fully human, save for the shark-gill things around his neck. His breathing is improving now he's out of the steam room. Come to think of it, his gills are closing up entirely; he's breathing from his mouth.

"Is that an escape?" he says.

He points to the glass chamber leading to the animal lab. Inside, the service droid is fishing out the last pieces of trolley bot from the door frame. This suddenly brings me back to my senses.

"You have to go back in there."

The fish guy looks at me like I'm insane.

"If you escape now, they'll know it was me, and we'll both be screwed. I need time to figure out a real plan. You have to get back in there. I'll come for you, I swear!"

Without warning, he elbows me in the mouth and sprints for the linking chamber. I'm back on my feet in a flash. Street smarts.

He mashes the exit pad and plunges into the holding chamber. He vaults the service bot like a freakin' Olympian and darts through the semi-opened secondary door, into the animal lab.

I chase after him. I tumble over the service bot, falling in a heap on the other side.

Fish man's disappeared. I'm running through the animal warehouse, trying to whisper and yell at the same time. I'm praying whoever monitors the CCTV has been hauled into a mole interrogation right now.

"Dude, come back! Stop running!" I cry.

I spot him by the otters, at the far end of an aisle. He sees me and disappears into the next one. I chase after him in parallel, weaving and backtracking as he tries to shake me off.

"I'm on your side!" I yell.

I quit mirroring him and sprint for the main entrance. If I beat him there, I can cut off his escape. But I'm at the wrong end of the aisle, and he's faster than me. He realizes what I'm doing and takes the lead.

He thumps the elevator call button.

We stare at each other from opposite ends of the lab, panting heavily. Stacks of animals watch on from their glass cages with curiosity. If he leaves this room, he'll be caught for sure. They'll double security around him and it'll become impossible to bust him out. As for me, I'll be fired immediately, which, given my mission, will mean a whole lot more than losing a month's pay.

I sprint towards him, yelling. Fish face grits his teeth and faces me. He squats low like a wrestler preparing for a take-down.

The elevator doors ping open. Before fish face can spin around, a hundred thousand volts pass through his body. He hits the deck, twitching. Behind him, clutching a stun gun, is the director.

Two security staff scoop fish man off the floor. They place him onto a robotic stretcher and hit a button. Straps fasten themselves across his body. He groans as the robot carts him back towards the dark lab. A third security guard is running ahead with a first aid kit, presumably to track down Carla.

The director holds the elevator door and re-holsters her Taser.

"Dr. Ragazzi. I think we had better bring your interview forward, wouldn't you agree?"

The interrogation room is not what I expected. I was anticipating something like an old police cell; concrete, windowless, with a rusty table and chair in the middle, and maybe a few blood stains on the floor. Instead, we enter something more like a corporate spa. There's an abundance of pot plants, a small indoor water feature, a fancy tea maker, and an unnecessary ratio of cushions to humans. As we cross the threshold, my anklet buzzes.

"You're not the first to get one of those things," says the director, taking a seat on the orange sofa. "The chimp interview tends to put people on edge. It's understandable you'd want to know whether you're in another simulation or not, at any given moment. So now you know. Of course, that charming little device is rather limited, is it not? It has alerted you to a simulation taking place in this room, but that is a blunt indication indeed. Has it told you which of the seats around you are real, and which are false? Is the tea real? Am I real? Is Pierre real?"

I make my way towards the nearest seat, but the director shakes her head. I move to the donut-shaped chair beside it, and she gives a nod. A barista bot brings her an ornate frothy beverage. She accepts it without flinching; her gaze is burning into me through a calculating smile. Pierre sits beside her, looking livid.

"Tell me, Dr. Ragazzi. What took you inside the restricted lab?" says the director.

"I heard a scream. I knew Carla was in there alone, so I ran in to see if I could help."

"Are you a medic, Dr. Ragazzi?"

"No, I just thought-"

"You are aware that trespass is a criminal offence?"

"I am."

The robot takes an iced drink to Pierre, who sips through a straw, while staring at me silently.

"Could I get some of that for my mouth? Ice, I mean. Your fish guy socked me in the jaw."

"Of course," says the director.

She claps her hands twice, and the barista bot brings ice

wrapped in a cloth. I press it to my lip, which is swelling nicely.

"I presume you know what this is about?" she says, reclining.

I assume my best innocent face. "This is about what I saw in the secure lab? I was only in there because I thought Carla was in danger."

"And? Is she?"

"She was unconscious when I found her."

"So what did you do?"

"I tried to assist her but the specimen escaped."

"So?"

"So I chased after it."

"You didn't stay with Carla? I thought you were concerned for her health?"

"Uh, I knew she was breathing, so I figured the specimen was more urgent."

The director's lips arc as she muses. Pierre brings an image up on screen between us. It's of me and my fake family on holiday in Belize.

"How did you enjoy the trip?" he says, without emotion.

"Same way everyone enjoys those kinda trips; too much food, too much sun, too much family time," I chuckle.

"It's in your interests to take this seriously, Dr. Ragazzi. I ask you again, did you enjoy the trip?"

"It was fine. I did some amazing scuba diving, got burned a bunch, but it was good. I'd recommend it."

Pierre says nothing and flicks to a different photo.

"Are these your grandparents?"

I stare at the image and realize what's happening. They're probing my cover story. They're examining every detail of my fake life to see if I blink. I've got to sound authentic.

"Uh, I'm not sure. It looks like them, but it doesn't feel quite right. I can't put my finger on it. Something's off - I think my grandmother's ears look a little small? And granddad's fingers were fatter than that, I think."

"You think?"

"They've been dead twenty years, it's been a while since I checked through the family albums."

"How did they die?"

"Inquisition. We have a rare genetic condition where too many unnecessary questions put us in a coma."

"Watch your tone, Dr. Ragazzi."

"Sure, sure, next question. I'd appreciate it if we could get this over with quickly."

"Are the questions making you uncomfortable?"

"I need to see a dentist. I'm pretty sure your fish man cracked a tooth when he hit me."

"I assure you, Dr. Ragazzi, a chipped tooth will be the least of your worries if we find out you're the mole."

I say nothing.

"You don't seem surprised to learn there's a mole?"

"Carla told me. I hope that doesn't get her in trouble with teacher." I pull a sad baby face with this. I watch my boss's lip twitch. I'm starting to get under his skin. Perfect.

"Teacher. That's fun. I'm happy to play that role. Perhaps then, as a good student, you will answer this question for me: what happens when people are fired from this institution?"

"Last I checked you're supposed to teach the stuff before you set the exam."

"So your answer is...?"

"I don't know."

"Precisely. You don't know. Very few people inside this building know, because so few people have been foolish enough to become a risk that warrants such drastic action."

"What's drastic about being fired? You just get another job. Sorry, I know that sounds big-headed, but I have a great relationship with my former employers, pretty sure they'd take me back."

"I would say that rather depends on what shape you're in when you leave here, wouldn't you agree?"

I'm doing my best to remain jovial and sarcastic, but I'm getting a seriously "no-qualms-murdering-you" vibe from my current employers. So far, I've remembered my cover story fine, but I'm guessing Pierre has more than two photos in his slide deck. Time to play my get-out-of-jail card.

When I was fourteen, I got in a fight with a neighbor. He was drunk again, and getting violent towards his husband and kids. I'd had enough. I finally stood up to him. He knocked me to the ground, and bust one of my teeth in the process. Since then, I've had a fake tooth, which I keep secret for moments like this.

OK fine, I didn't fight my neighbor. I made that bit up to get laid at college. In reality, I fell off my push bike, but who's gonna date that guy?

I hold the ice cloth up to my face, tilt my busted lip inward, and bite it hard. Blood flows into my mouth like a fountain. Lips are like the body's soap opera. So over the top, yet so compelling. With my tongue, I dislodge my trick tooth. It's a technique I perfected a long time ago.

Showtime.

I cough and splutter, then spit my blood-covered tooth onto the floor. I drop the ice towel with it, scattering cubes with a clatter. The pristine white cloth has absorbed the red magnificently, which amplifies the bloody effect. The whole thing looks quite spectacular.

To the outsider, the arrival of a tooth with so much blood and spluttering makes it look like I inhaled it in the strife, accidentally chewed up my own lungs, then coughed it all out.

Both scientists recoil in disgust.

"Yeah, fish man's got knuckles on him. Although technically he used an elbow. Look, I get that you're on a mole hunt, but can we do this after I've been to the dentist? God damn this hurts. I should probably get a full body scan too, I don't think teeth are good for lung tissue."

The director looks concerned. I don't for a minute think she's worried about my health; she's worried I might contaminate a sample while I'm bleeding, or maybe that I'll contaminate *her* if I keep spouting bodily fluids.

"What if you don't come back?" says Pierre.

"Of course I'll come back. I wanna study fish man. Now that I know what's in the secret lab, you might as well let me work on it. Come on, boss, I know you're short of hands in there; you're tied up with finding the mole, while Carla's busy trying to cover for both you *and* Drake, and now she's been knocked out by fish man, you're up against it. You said in our last briefing we're on a tight deadline to study and terminate the specimen? Let me help, boss, I'm ready. Gardening duty and Petri dishes aren't the best use of my skills right now. I'll go to the doc and dentist, get my mouth patched up, get the all clear, then come back here and be useful. And if you haven't found the mole by that time you can dissolve me in a vat of acid, or whatever it was you had planned. Sound good?"

The director's feet are turned away from the blood splatters, which are spreading as the ice cubes melt into them. She looks at me tersely. "Be back here within two hours or we will find you. Don't be under any illusion that we can't or won't. Two hours, Dr. Ragazzi. Do not be late."

———

I hurry away from the coffee pot building and wait until I'm several blocks clear before I tuck into a side alley and vomit. This is all getting way too hot for my liking. They're gonna keep investigating the other staff, and unless by some miracle one of them is *also* undercover, they're gonna circle right back to me.

My phone vibrates, picking up a message as it comes back on grid.

Dear valued customer. Thank you for purchasing deadline extension with us. We regret to inform you that deadline is being brought forward to 1pm today, owing to cash flow complications up stream in our business. We thanking you for understanding, and look forward to receiving money by 1pm, otherwise we will releasing your true identity to your employers. You will receive a free stamp on your loyalty card for this inconvenience. Please note, we reserve the right to outsource your debt to one of our collection partners, should you fail to settle. Kind regards, New You & Sons.

God dammit!

I check my account balance. Still nothing from Lanelle. It's like she *wants* me to be dunked in acid.

I'm drawing a line. I have proof now; conclusive evidence that the lab is performing genetic experiments on human captives. I'm damned if the next one's me. It's time to get the hell out of here.

CHAPTER TWENTY-FIVE

KEALA

My limbs are numb with cold, so gripping has long been out of the question. Luckily, my freakish skin has me practically glued to the drone as it speeds along the deep sea pipe. The monorail has been climbing gently for hours, but now it's steep and the water's brightening.

We breach the surface and my gills shut off immediately, forcing my windpipe open as I gasp for air. I blink sea water out of my eyes as the pipe snakes up a long, rocky shore. It's heading towards an oil refinery. I'm feeling nauseous from hours of inhaling leaked oil into my bloodstream. This ascending slalom is deeply unwelcome.

As we reach the factory wall, the drone's monorail separates. The pipe disappears into the factory, while the drone climbs vertically then enters a service bay.

The platform is short, only a few meters long, like the drone itself. A worker steps out from the control box to inspect the drone. Clearly they weren't expecting to find a mermaid clinging to the roof. The worker screams, prompting a colleague to rush in.

My limbs have turned a blueish tinge and my teeth are chattering. I try to speak, but my mouth is too cold to form words. Something black and shiny trickles from my jaw as I cough and splutter.

The workers are blurring. I vomit a heap of oil and my skin loses all grip. I feel myself falling from the drone, and black out before I hit the ground.

When I come around, there's a medical drone leaning over me, scanning my body. Two humans stand at the side of the infirmary, watching anxiously. The robot straightens up and gives its verdict.

The patient is suffering from lacerations to both axilla, severe hypothermia, acute hydrocarbon poisoning, and multiple mutations not recognized in the current database.

"We need to get her to hospital right now," says one of the workers.

She's a strong-looking woman of around forty.

Searching national genetic database for patient records. No match found. Patient is not registered. Patient is ineligible for treatment.

"What? Look at her! She could die!"

Contacting Department of Homeland Security: Citizenship and Immigration Services.

"Oh hell no. Damned robot! Come on sugar, we need to get you moving fast."

The strong woman sweeps me up in her thick arms and carries me down a flight of stairs. Her colleague is calling after her; something about being crazy. I squint as she takes me out into the sun. It's blinding, but its rays are welcome on my frigid skin.

"Sorry honey, bear with me," says the woman.

Her boots scuff against the gravel parking lot. She lays me flat on the hood, then opens the front passenger door. Next thing I know, I'm sitting up, belted in, and we're on the freeway.

"That dumbass drone can refuse to treat you, but a human won't. I know the hospital, they're good people. They saved my baby boy when I didn't have insurance. They'll help you, I'm sure of it. If we're lucky, we can make it before the department catches up. Sit tight, sugar. This could be a bumpy ride."

CHAPTER TWENTY-SIX

LUKE

It's half past midday. I'm dripping with sweat, and I'm running like hell.

"Get back here you pig!"

I'm sure he's a nice guy, a real family man. Maybe I'm not seeing his best side right now. But for all the mitigating factors in the world, if there is a god, please, I'm begging you, smite this dude already.

I'm trying to get back to my dive apartment so I can skip town before the lab hunts me down. Speed is everything when it comes to urgent escape plans, hence why I didn't fool around with my usual bus and metro combo. No, I got a cab to save precious time. Or at least, that was the idea.

If you've been paying attention, you'll know I'm not exactly flush right now. So I do what any self-respecting fugitive does. I give the driver an address that's a few blocks from my apartment, then as we pull up I make a break for it.

Most cab drivers would chase you a little, curse a lot, then throw in the towel.

Not this guy.

"I'm gonna beat your ass, thief!"

I'm on the sidewalk, running for my damned life, and cursing myself for getting out on a long straight road. I switch direction so I'm running against the flow of the traffic, meaning there's no way this guy can follow.

Wrong. He slams into reverse and speeds after me, yelling profanities in Greek. Other cars are swerving out of the way.

I spot a play park and make a dash for it, leaving the road behind. My chest is whining and I'm sweating round my lips, because that's what running does to me these days. But now it's all eyes on the tubby balding guy who's sprinting at a bunch of kids with a wet mouth.

Angry parents are coming at me, I gotta change direction pronto. But Mr. Taxi's pulling into the side street, cutting me off. I dash towards a walkway between two apartment blocks. There's an outdoor cafe, and a fountain, and it's a pedestrianized zone, so there's no way he can-

He mounts the sidewalk. Taxi man's leaning on his horn and speeding towards me like he's possessed. People scream and dive out of the way as he demolishes tables and chairs. I'm wondering why no-one's calling the cops, then I remember this neighborhood is trying to keep its head down.

I sprint to the far side of the fountain, and the lunatic takes the bait. He drives his Taxi straight into the pond, underestimating how deep it is. The front bumper wedges against the basin, leaving the wheel spinning just inches from the ground. He's pounding his horn in rage, red-faced from yelling.

Behind the second apartment block is an alleyway backing onto a row of detached houses. I take a run and jump for the fence but it's a high perimeter, almost like the yuppies wanna keep the peasants out. With difficulty I pull myself over the ridge.

I'm running through a back garden. The next fence is lower, and I leap over it. There's a woman sunbathing, she screams in shock. I'm making apologies as I knock over garden gnomes and trample flowers in my bid to not get my ass kicked.

Scrambling over her ivy-covered fence I land in the next garden with a splash. The water's warm, soapy, and chlorinated. Two fellas cry out and spill their wine as I drag my soaking body out onto the lawn.

I try to apologize but it sounds like I'm dying; even when I was fit I could never talk while running. I grab hold of the next fence, but just as I pull myself over I realize what sound I'm throwing myself towards.

Dogs.

Plural.

Landing into an immaculate flower bed I lock eyes with a furry young German shepherd. My second least-favorite dog. It's blocking my route to the next garden. I'm about to make a bid for the house itself, when a second snarling dog bounds out of it. This one's a fully-grown German shepherd; my all-time least-favorite dog.

I wanna retreat back to the hot tub guys but the middle rail is missing so I can't get a leg up. There's no alternative; I sprint for the back and hurl myself out of the garden, slamming the gate behind me. The dogs crash against it, howling and scratching at the wood.

I close my eyes and sigh a breath of sopping wet relief.

"Pig! I said I kill you!"

My eyes jolt open. There, at the far end of the alleyway, is Mr. Taxi. He's on foot and clutching a baseball bat. His ankles are wet from escaping the fountain, and he looks cheesed.

I'm cornered; the alley's become a dead end. There's only one property behind me and it's got a crazy high fence. Mr. Taxi is marching towards me, pointing his bat at my head. He's got this sick look of preemptive satisfaction on his chops like he's been waiting for an excuse to whale on someone for a while. Much as I'm always happy to help someone scratch an itch, I'm less keen if that itch involves my head getting caved in.

The dogs are going wild, sensing Mr. Taxi's advance. There's only one thing for it. I reach over the gate, pull the latch open, and rip the door back against its hinges. To my dismay, it holds firm. I can feel the dogs' hot breaths against my fingertips as they jump, trying to bite my damned hands off.

"Your ass is mine, thief!"

Seeing what I'm trying to do, Mr. Taxi accelerates towards me. He's taking a swing. He's letting out a loud, protracted yell like a warrior mounting a charge. I'm yanking against the gate with everything I've got. At the last second, the hinges give way. I wrench the tall wooden gate backwards into the alley.

It spans the passage, sealing me off from my attacker. The dogs tumble out of their garden and turn on the nearest available human. Mr. Taxi lets out a wail of despair and begs for mercy as he flees. While the snarling dogs chase after him. I shunt the gate forwards like a Roman soldier with an oversized shield. With the dogs gone, I hurry back through their garden and into the house.

A man's watching TV in his underpants. By the time he realizes what's going on, I'm out and onto the street, running like hell to get away from the echoes of barking and Mr. Taxi's cries.

Five minutes and much running later, I'm climbing the steps to my apartment. There's zero response from my useless security system - clearly another bill that's not been paid. Great.

I'm packing real fast; throwing everything I got into a suitcase. As I'm rummaging under the mattress for my original ID, my phone rings.

"*Finally!*" I cry. "I called you like forty minutes ago, this is a serious situation, what the hell are you playing at?"

"Say what now? You ain't call us. We callin' *you* smart ass. Where's our money?"

At this point I realize it's not Lanelle. This is the low life outfit I borrowed money from outside the bar last night. My panic doubles.

"How did you get this number?" I ask, stalling for time.

"Screw you, that's how. You owe us big. We're at the bar, and you're late."

"What? You said I had twenty four hours!"

"Yeah well now we sayin' time's up. Which makes you late. And late ain't good when you owe money. Late means interest. For every minute you ain't here, I'm adding another one percent."

"Simple or compound?"

"What?"

"The interest rate. Is it simple or compound?"

"What kind of question is that? Are you kidding around right now? I swear we will break your god damned legs if you-"

I hang up on the guy. No point wasting his breath on money he'll never see again.

I hurry to the bathroom and grab the toilet phone, then

stuff it in my suitcase. My main phone rings again. Screw these guys.

"Break my legs all you like, it ain't gonna get your money back. As far as I'm concerned you and your boys can go-"

"Luke, shut up, it's Lanelle!"

"Oh... Well then, it's about time!"

"Why didn't you call me from the secure phone?"

"We're way past that now, the fan has been hit. You get me? We're talking covered. It's just caked in the brown stuff, and it's spreading it alllll around the room for everyone to see."

"Luke, are you in danger?"

"Yes I'm in danger! What part of the fan metaphor did you not get? My cover's been blown wide open."

"Are you sure?"

"No, I'm doing this because I love packing under pressure. It helps me drill for last-minute holidays. *Yes I'm sure!* The lab figured out that whoever stole Drake's tablet was someone at the office."

"But they don't know it's you?"

"It's not gonna take them long to figure it out. In five minutes Chang's gonna leak my true identity because *you* didn't transfer the money!"

"Luke, forget the money, just get out of there."

"That's what I'm trying to do!"

"Where are you gonna go?"

"Uh, I'm coming to the office, *obviously!*"

"You can't do that!"

"Are you freakin' kidding me?"

"Listen, Luke, we found some insane stuff on Drake's tablet but we need more time to dig. This goes deeper than we thought. It's vital no-one knows we're onto this, especially not the new owner. If you show up here needing witness protection, it could sink the whole story."

"Fine. Then I'll go to the safe house. And before you deny it exists, your predecessor let me use it several times."

"Oh, so you wanna get me fired too, is that it?"

"I'd sooner you get fired than I get whacked!"

"We're selling that property, Luke, it's not even a live asset."

"*I'm* not gonna be a live asset unless you help me!"

"My hands are tied, I'm sorry. Get to the airport."

"Can you meet me there?"

"If I'm seen with you, we're both at risk. I need to finish the analysis of Drake's tablet. Everything rests on that now."

"How am I gonna buy a plane ticket with no money?"

"You'll figure it out."

"Thanks Lanelle. Truly inspiring leadership. When you write my obituary, put something nice, yeah? How about, 'he died doing what he loved - being hung out to dry by a bunch of capitalist sellouts who-'"

The apartment door bursts open.

"*Now* your ass really is mine, thief!"

Standing in the frame, silhouetted against the daylight, is Mr. Taxi. His trousers are torn, and his leg is bloody. His bat's bloody too, and covered in chew marks. He looks like a tortured shadow of his former self, risen from the grave to reap one final vengeance.

At this point, I notice the trail of drip marks and wet footprints I left outside.

"Lanelle, call the cops, get them to this address!"

Mr. Taxi raises the bat and lets out a roar of anger. He charges at me and swings for my head. I duck. His bat smashes into the wall, destroying the plasterboard. I scramble to the side as he swings again, obliterating a lamp. I grab the nearest thing and throw it as hard as I can.

A brick would've been ideal. Unfortunately, I tend not to leave bricks on my breakfast table.

Hey, pop quiz. What happens if you hurl a carton of orange juice at a guy with a baseball bat? Spoilers, he whacks it. The container ruptures; I get sprayed, but he takes a boatload of OJ straight to the eyes.

While he's crying in pain I make a bid for freedom. You know how on airplanes they always tell you "in an emergency, leave your luggage behind and proceed to the nearest exit?" Turns out, there's a good reason for that.

As I drag the suitcase across the floor he throws the bat at my head. It whacks me like a blunt spear. Pressing the advantage, he charges at me, all red-eyed and covered in juice with those little tasty bits of pulp. He tackles me to the ground; he's punching me and I'm punching him. We're rolling, each trying to pin the other. I land a blow and break free. I scramble towards his bat but I can hear him coming after me. I jab the butt of the handle into his face. He crumples, howling with pain. Panting, I clamber to my feet and leap for the door.

I slip like a sucker, landing in a pool of lukewarm orange juice.

Mr. Taxi's on top of me. He's got the chewed-up bat and he looks fully insane. He grabs it by both ends and pins it against my throat like a bar. I'm suffocating. Or is it choking? Technically I guess it's strangulation? I'm trying to push him off, but I'm totally pinned. I'm rasping, trying croaking for help. My vision's blurring and I'm seeing red spots.

A harsh stuttering punctuates the air. Mr. Taxi's back arches uncontrollably as a Taser floods his body with electricity. He slumps to the side, twitching. I gasp for air and wriggle clear of his bat.

I stagger upwards, ready to embrace the valiant police officer who saved me. My relief vanishes as I see Pierre holding a Taser. Beside him is the director, with one of her own. She gives me a sadistic smile, then unleashes electrical agony into my groin.

I'm writhing in pain, acutely aware of the mold on my ceiling. Pierre looms over me. There's something in his hand. It looks like - yup, here we go - it's a hood. Now I'm being dragged out of my dank apartment and bundled into a car. I'd love to tell you where we're going, but I can't see jack.

"You shouldn't have lied to us, Dr. Ragazzi," gloats the director.

My skull bumps against the window as we skid around a corner. I'm not usually one for travel sickness but I gotta say, being whacked in the head, choked, bagged, then put in a four-wheeled centrifuge ain't exactly a spa treatment. My tongue feels like it's made of watery spaghetti and I really don't wanna puke in this hood.

"In a way, you have my congratulations," says the director. "Infiltrating our establishment is no easy feat. You came closer than your predecessors, which surprises me, given your obvious personal shortcomings. Enjoy this moment of recognition, Dr. Ragazzi, for in the coming hours you will sincerely regret taking us on."

Crunch.

Something slams into our car with the force of a juggernaut. Our vehicle is thrown sideways. We're screaming, skidding across the tarmac. Windows shatter and metal buckles. Air cushions erupt all around me, engulfing my body in a three-sixty embrace. This is the closest I've gotten to a hug in three months. Man, I really need to make some friends when I get out of this.

Through the padding I hear the door above me being wrenched off. There's a slashing sound, then a breeze against my arm. Something mechanical grabs hold of me. I'm being dragged from the car like a fairground prize.

My hood is pulled off for a fleeting second. Before my eyes can adjust to see who is snatching me, it's thrust on again.

"It's him. Let's go."

CHAPTER TWENTY-SEVEN

KEALA

I magine you're at a gas station and someone throws you to the ground, grabs you by the hair, and holds your face above a puddle of fuel for six hours. You can feel the toxic fumes diffusing into your bloodstream and poisoning your body. A splitting headache begins as the blackened blood reaches your brain. Meanwhile, imagine someone else is throwing buckets of ice over your body. You're bruised and trembling, so cold that your body spasms, forcing you to inhale more of the toxic fumes. That's how I'm feeling right now; brutalized by my escape on the pipeline and dangerously ill.

Our car speeds along the freeway towards the city. My airways are so constricted it feels like someone is dangling a plastic bag in front of my lips. I fight to keep my breathing steady and shallow. Any sudden gasps and my windpipe might shut off completely.

The woman driving me can tell I'm not up to speaking, but she's content to talk at me. I greatly appreciate her reassurance. I trust her. Not that I have a choice.

"Put this on, girl, you must be half frozen. It's my

boyfriend's shirt, he won't mind. Sorry I don't have no pants lying around."

With difficulty, I pull on the thick, checkered cloth shirt. It reaches halfway down my legs. I can't manage the buttons yet, so I draw it tight like a cardigan.

Stacks of smog from the refinery hang in the clouds high above the city. We pass a run-down strip mall. Half the units are boarded up with faded lease adverts plastered across them. The fast-food outlet is still open, doing steady trade. A line of twenty cars tails back, going nowhere, with their engines running, and their AC blasting out, waiting to drive through. A homeless man is trying to wash people's windscreens with a dirty rag. Beside him is a robotic attendant, branded in the chain's colors, with an in-built pressure hose and chamois cloth. People are responding a lot more kindly to the robot.

A few doors down is a rehabilitation clinic. It's a small, single-story building capable of hosting meetings and nothing more. A few visitors are returning from the fast food place with coffees. Others stand in a huddle, smoking.

Something appears in my line of sight, drawing my attention away from the mall. A quadcopter is floating alongside us, bobbing in the breeze.

"Oh crap!" yells the woman.

She hits the gas and we surge forwards. Her foot stays glued to the floor but the drone accelerates too, keeping pace with us.

"The medical robot must have reported you. Get down!" she cries.

I duck down, covering my head, not knowing what exactly I'm hiding from. The car swerves violently as we weave between traffic.

The passenger window shatters, covering me in glass.

Something is burning against my arm. I gasp and clamp a hand on the searing skin. The woman looks at me and her face falls.

"Crap, it got you."

The drone's vanished and I sit up, looking at the woman nervously. "What is it?"

"Bio tracer. They'll find you anywhere you go now. That thing's sharing your coordinates with all available robotic agents. They're gonna try intercept us."

She swerves and overtakes a series of cars, but the drone reappears above the hood.

"But just because they know we're going to the hospital doesn't mean they'll get there first," she continues. "We can beat them - assuming that thing isn't armed."

Pull over immediately. This drone is armed.

"Well that's just perfect!" yells the woman, slamming the steering wheel.

She swerves erratically but the drone mirrors us perfectly.

Final warning.

"Bite me, robo cop!"

A thin blue beam appears at the base of the drone, like a sniper's targeting lock.

"Oh crap, hold on," says the woman.

The blue beam spreads out, covering the hood in a grid of light. With a flash it vanishes and the car's engine falls silent. The woman tamps the gas pedal but it has no effect.

We veer towards the hard shoulder. The woman tries to correct the steering, but a sharp electric shock forces her to let go with a yelp.

This vehicle is now under police control, as per autonomous highways regulation sixteen. Remain seated and officers will attend to you shortly.

The drone is projecting a flashing red arrow above our stationary vehicle, diverting traffic around us.

"This is bad," groans the woman.

"Maybe it's for the best? I want to speak to the police after all, I need their help."

She looks at me with pity. "Oh sweet thing, these aren't the cops they tell you about in school. These are immigration agents. You're not a citizen, which means you don't have the right to be seen by a human. The robots will scan you and deport you without discussion, I'm so sorry."

Horror sweeps over me. There's only one option left: run.

I grab the door handle only to yelp in pain; it's electrified. Nursing my hand, I glare at the hovering drone with hatred. My heart rate is rocketing and my airways are tightening. Black residue is seeping from my gills. The woman places a consoling hand on my knee and looks at me with sorrow.

"You been through a lot to get here?"

"You have no idea," I croak.

The drone falls onto the hood with a clank. Electrical glitches are crawling across its shell. There's a metallic dart embedded in its armor and the flashing sign above us has vanished.

A motorbike pulls up beside my window. On it sits a mustached man with tinted sunglasses and a leopard-print helmet. He has orange-white skin, diamond-studded gloves, and a tasseled brown leather jacket.

"Which of you lucky ladies needs a ride?"

"Who are you?" says the woman.

"I'm your ticket out of here. Judging by that peach on your friend's arm, I'm guessing it's her they want." He turns his gaze to me. "So how about it, darlin'. You coming with?"

I look at the woman. "Is he safe?"

"Clock's ticking, gals," he crows.

"Almost certainly not. I have no idea how he found you, but it can't be legal."

"It ain't legal, but it's only fair," interjects the man. "To beat the feds, you gotta have their kit. I took it upon myself to level the playing field by getting myself one of their trackers. 'Cept it's not totally level, cos I also got a faster set of wheels. They'll be here in about thirty seconds, so y'all better decide fast."

I cough hard, splattering flecks of blood and oil across the dashboard.

"She needs to get to the hospital," says the woman.

"I can do that," says the man.

I grab the door handle again. It's no longer electrified.

"I'm going with him. Thank you, Ma'am," I croak.

The woman looks conflicted but we both know I have to take this chance. Either I go with him now or I get deported and my people's only hope of rescue dies on the deaf ears of an immigration robot. I jump out and climb onto the motorbike.

"Hold on tight, darlin', this is gonna be the fastest ride of your life."

"That's the other thing," he yells. His voice is barely audible above the roaring wind and the noise of his engine. "I got a scrambler. They couldn't track me if they tried. To any passing drone, we look like a food delivery truck, or a family of four. Disguises our speed too. Cute, ain't it?"

I don't have the strength to reply. It's taking all my concentration not to pass out and fall under the cars we're whizzing past. Mercifully, we're not on the freeway for long. He pulls off onto a dusty side road and after several minutes we reach an industrial estate. We park up and he helps me off.

"M'lady."

"This isn't the hospital," I croak.

"Not a government one, no. If I'd took you there, you'd be in jail already, or on a ship back to Pakistan or what have you. You're better off here, darlin', trust me. Ain't right you gotta surrender to the government, good for nothin' liars the lot of them. This here is a private hospital. Don't look like much, but that's the point. Come on, I'll show you."

Above the entrance is a faded sign reading Latifa's Metal Works. The building looks derelict; broken windows, no lighting inside, and rust all over the bumpy roof. I follow the man to a battered side door.

"It's better on the inside, I promise."

I give the deserted parking lot a final glance. The only sounds nearby are of machines working in the scrap yard, and the freeway rumbling in the distance. My muscles are trembling, and my airways are faltering. With no miraculous alternatives, I follow him inside.

To his credit, it is better on the inside, although the bar was set low. I had been expecting a huge factory floor, but find myself in a cozy room. A living room? A waiting room? I can't figure the vibe. There are sofas and comfortable chairs arranged in a horseshoe around a coffee table brimming with lifestyle magazines.

"Told ya. Water?" says the man.

He fixes me with a beaming smile and hands over a glass of chilled cucumber water from the fridge. His eyes are older than I expected, but they have a soft sparkle to them.

Kind eyes.

The offer of refreshment is appreciated, but the cold of the ocean is still in my bones. "Thanks, but do you have anything hot?"

"Of course, how stupid of me. Here you go darlin'. Sugar?"

He passes over an herbal tea with two sachets of sugar. I try tearing the tops off but my fingers are too numb.

"Let me get that for you. You lie down, make yourself comfortable. I'm gonna get my friend, she's a doctor here, she'll fix you up, OK? You take it easy."

He stirs in the sugar, places a blanket over me, and disappears into a room beyond. When he returns a few minutes later, he's carrying dry clothes and shoes.

"Thought you might appreciate these."

He places the pile on a chair next to me and pats it. His biking gloves are off, revealing trimmed nails painted teal, and a signet ring on his middle finger.

"There's a bathroom next door that you can change in whenever you like. No pressure, you do whatever's comfortable, OK?"

I nod and try not to be sick on his sofa. The sweet tea is helping with warmth and energy, but it's doing nothing to take the edge off the oil contamination. My brain's foggy; I'm putting on the shoes he's brought, forgetting the usual order of changing.

A woman enters wearing baggy jeans and a loose-fitting blouse. Her skin is darker than mine, and her hair is shorter, although no doubt it's cleaner. I see her raise an eyebrow as she catches a whiff of my sea-salt-bitumen fragrance.

Following the woman is a robot. It's halfway between a service drone and a humanoid assistant; a bare-bones affair, no frills. It has caterpillar tracks for stability, a central axis, and a single robotic arm with a multi-tool head.

The robot's base bears an imprint. Property of the State Healthcare Repository. Its ID number below has been scratched out. The man catches my gaze and explains, "Sharing is caring."

The woman taps on a tablet and the robot rumbles towards me. Its arm sweeps over my body several times, then the tablet lets out a bleep.

"Scan complete. She's got hydrocarbon poisoning, but we can treat that. There's something unidentified, but it's probably a glitch. I'd say she's viable," says the woman.

"Wonderful news!" The man claps his hands and turns to me. "You hear that honey? We can fix that nasty government tracker on your arm. Are you done with your tea? It's best we disable this thing ASAP - then we can help treat that oil thing you got goin' on."

He helps me sit up straight. I clutch his arm for stability as my head spins.

"Go steady, darlin', those immigration biomarkers will knock you for six. I apologize on behalf of my savage nation, we used to live in more enlightened times. OK, here we go. Hold steady."

He rolls my sleeve up, then steps back so the robot can lean in. I felt a sharp burning on my arm where the drone tagged me.

"Few more seconds," says the woman. The tablet bleeps. "Aaand, we're done."

The man grabs an ice pack from the mini freezer and holds it out using a pair of tongs.

"This'll help with the sting, trust me."

The rest of my body is still frigid, but the burning on my arm is so extreme I welcome the offer. I press the ice pack against my skin and sigh as it extinguishes the pain. Pure bliss.

"Girl, I sure am glad that's sorted. This place is off-grid, obviously, but you never can be too careful with trackers like that," says the man.

"Thank you," I mumble.

"Us libertarians gotta stick together. Stick it to the man! You know how it is. Hey, on the note of 'thank yous', perhaps now is a pertinent time to discuss remuneration. You know, for our services."

"You want me to pay you? But I don't have any money. I only just arrived in your country - by sea. I was shipwrecked and-"

"Hush, hush, it's OK darlin', we get it, you ain't the first customer we had who don't got a bank account. We'll work somethin' out, you take it easy."

Behind his broad smile is a look in his eye, a glint of impatience. The woman beside him is staring at me with a blank expression. Her hands are folded across her belt buckle, waiting.

My arm no longer feels painful. In fact, it no longer feels anything. I can't feel my shoulder either, or the hand that's clutching the ice pack. The numbness is spreading across my body fast. I try to let go but I can't control my fingers. Whatever's in the pack is seeping into my bloodstream.

I'm trying to speak but only a faint groan escapes. Jerking my shoulder as hard as I can, I dislodge the ice pack from my hand. I have to escape. But as I step forward my legs give way. I land heavily but feel nothing. My sight is fading, my hearing too, and I'm drifting uncontrollably into darkness.

CHAPTER TWENTY-EIGHT

LUKE

I'm sliding across the floor of what feels like a haulage van. Whoever snatched me from the director's car is kicking nine lessons out of me. My hands are tied and I've still got a hood over my head, so it's not exactly a fair fight. Every time I try to hunch, or protect myself in anyway, we turn a corner and gravity throws me wide open, ready for a fresh blow.

Finally, the van screeches to a halt. Someone drags me onto my knees.

"This can go one of two ways."

"Aren't you supposed to say, 'this can go the easy way, or the hard w-'"

Smack.

They're not in the mood for my classic dinner party wit.

"Shut your mouth. Both ways are the hard way."

"If *both* of them are the hard way, then really there's only one way, isn't there?"

There's a pause while my interrogator considers. This is definitely the worst part about borrowing from parking lot loan sharks. When it comes to the conversation, you really get what you pay for. After an inordinately long pause, he replies with a gruff, "Huh?"

Sigh.

"You said 'this can go one of two ways', implying I will be presented with two opposing choices, but in reality you're saying I only have one option, which is the hard way, which is to say I don't have any options at all. It's a false dichotomy."

Smack.

It must have been deeply rewarding trying to teach these guys in high school.

"You ain't gettin' it. It's a very real dichotomy."

I feel like he's just saying that because it's got the word "die" in it.

"You got two choices, see, but both of them is bad choices. It's not an apples and oranges situation. It's more like oranges and oranges. As in, which of these two bad oranges do you want?"

"The phrase is 'two bad apples', dumbass."

Smack.

"I said oranges because you're covered in orange juice," he growls. "I was trying to make the analogy relatable."

I stand corrected. This erudite fella's got promise. Probably just fell in with the wrong crowd as a kid. I bet this rough diamond would have thrived in a more nurturing environment. In another life we might have laughed together as peers, stood shoulder to shoulder as brothers on a quest for knowledge.

Smack.

"Quit being thinky. You're gonna tell us how you'll be payin' up. To speed things along, we'll be cutting off your fingers until we get the right kinda answer. FYI, the right answer looks a lot like us holding a big bag of cash."

"Wait! You said I had two options!"

"You get to choose which hand we start on."

"*That's* the dichotomy?"

"Yup. It's like I said: two bad oranges. I'll assume you're right handed, so we'll start on your left."

The guy grabs my left hand and forces my thumb out straight.

"Woah, fellas, let's talk about this! I can get your money, you don't need to cut anything off!"

Something metallic opens out. I've never heard what a finger-cutter sounds like, but if I had to invent a sound to go with it, it would sound exactly like this.

"Five seconds or we take your thumb."

"That's not even a finger! How can you expect me to make informed decisions when the parameters keep changing?"

"Finger. Thumb. *That's* a false dichotomy. Because they'll soon all fall under the same one list of things you used to have."

My heart briefly weeps for this guy's wasted potential. The sensation of a circular slicer being fitted over my thumb quickly refocuses my mind.

"Wait, I'll tell you where the money is! I was trying to skip town without paying it back, you got me. You guys aren't the only folk I borrowed from. I got heaps of cash from a bunch of lenders across town. It's in my apartment."

"We went to your apartment already, no cash. Just a suitcase and an unconscious taxi driver."

"Ah, one of my creditors, he's going on holiday, stopped by for a coffee."

"The suitcase had *your* passport in it, dummy. Two of them, in fact."

"You get cheaper air fares if you use a different return name."

Smack.

Someone growls from the far side of the van. "He's playing games. Take both his thumbs."

"Waaaaaiiiiiiit! I'll give you the address right now! My *actual* apartment. The other one was a decoy so I could escape quick, but that didn't work out because you guys were too smart for me. Drive me across town to my business partner's place. That's where your money is, plus all the money I borrowed from the other gangs. Sorry, I mean, uh, establishments. You gentlemen were the first to find me, so by rights you get the lot."

"How much is 'the lot'?"

"Thirty times what you loaned me. I think that will more than settle our debt, with generous interest, yes? All I ask is that in exchange you return my passports so I can leave town. I suspect your peers may also take a stern approach to late payment, and I certainly won't be able to pay them once you've got all their cash."

"If they catch you, you'll rat us out. We don't wanna get into a fight with other gangs. That's bad business."

"Then you should leave town too. Think about it, you'll each be rich, you could make a fresh start. Go to college, study architecture, medicine, literature!"

"My mom always said I had an eye for watercolor."

"There you go! What are we waiting for? It's yours for the taking."

Someone lifts the finger slicer off my thumb and the engine restarts. I let out a quivering sigh of relief.

"The address is-"

"I don't want the address, I want your partner's name.

We're gonna check he's real and not a cop or something in case this is some sorta trap."

"Look him up by all means, it'll say he's a consultant. We're careful to cover our tracks online."

"His name?"

"Drake Hawthorn."

"All right, ETA eleven minutes. Just so you know, if the money ain't there, we'll kill the both of you."

I thought I was nervous the first time I came to Drake's apartment. This is a whole new kinda fear. I've persuaded my captors to untie me and take my hood off. You know, so the neighbors don't get alarmed.

We're walking in diamond formation. The little guy's at the back. His two goons are marching either side of me. They're so close we might as well be a thrupple. As we approach the door, I'm praying Chang's skeleton card still works.

"Your hand's shaking. Everything all right, Luke?" says the little man.

"All swell."

I take a final look at my fingers, wishing I'd appreciated them more before now. I've got great cuticles.

With a deep breath I hold the card against the scanner.

Bleep.

The door opens.

I act casual, masking my intense relief at not getting wasted *outside* Drake's apartment. Much better to end my days inside. There's dignity in dying inside. In your ex-colleague's apartment. Which you're breaking into a second time.

At least my shoes fit.

We make our way across the lobby and pile into the elevator. There's plenty of room, but the two big guys squeeze up beside me real close, making it claustrophobic. The little guy glares at me waggling the finger cutter.

"Looking forward to seeing this big pile of money, Luke."

"Yeah, me too," I laugh.

I'm praying someone enters the lobby, sees us, and calls the cops, but no help comes. The elevator doors slide shut and we ascend. I guess it makes sense, being the middle of the working day and all. The only people at home are those who got suspended like Drake.

We reach Drake's level and the guys shove me out. I'm dragging my feet, begging for divine intervention, but they're shoving me forwards, in no mood for delay. I stumble in front of Drake's door and try to compose myself. Unless he calls the cops immediately, we're both screwed.

"Back up a little, will you? He's got a camera thingy. If he sees you, he won't let me in."

"I thought you said you guys shared this place?" says the little man.

"We do, but we're cautious. Neither of us ever bring anyone here. Just step to the side so he doesn't get suspicious, all right?"

The heavies step either side of the door. I stand square before it and hit the buzzer. Looking at the camera, I wave.

Drake's voice crackles on the built-in speaker.

"Yeah?"

"Drake, it's Luke."

"Who?"

The guys either side of me bristle. I act like he's goofing around.

"Nice one. You know me, new guy from the lab."

"What are you doing here?"

"We need to talk."

"How do you know where I live?"

"Open the door buddy and I'll explain everything."

"Leave me alone."

I can feel the big guys' stares boring into the sides of my skull.

"You can drop the act now, Drake. I know you wanna see me. It's about Beethoven."

Silence on the other end of the line.

"What did you say?"

"Beethoven. You know, famous classical composer? Grouchy German guy with the big hair."

The intercom clicks off and one of the big guys cracks his knuckles. Then footsteps from inside the apartment. They're approaching at a clip. The door bursts open and Drake launches himself at me, his eyes blazing with anger.

"You piece of crap, it was you!"

He hurls himself forward, pinning me against the corridor wall, strangling me. God damn Drake's strong when he's not having an allergic reaction. My feet are dangling off the ground like I'm back in eighth grade and getting pinned for my lunch money.

"He's got the cash!" I rasp.

One of the mobsters throws a dustpan-sized hand on Drake's shoulder. Drake twists free and elbows him in the nose like it's a reflex. The guy staggers back, cursing. The second mobster tackles Drake to the ground, but this is a big mistake. Drake rolls him over and grabs him in a headlock using his legs. The guy with the bleeding nose stumbles over and pounds on Drake's head with a yell. Drake's shielding himself, while throttling the other guy.

The little guy's pulling something from his jacket and shoving a cartridge into the base. I barge him against the wall, throwing his aim off. His stun gun misses and hits the nose bleed guy who goes down twitching. The little guy's cursing me out big time. He's trying to reload but I knock the gun from his hand, sending it skidding into Drake's apartment.

From the floor, one of the goon's bones snaps loudly. The little guy shoves me back and pulls out a flick knife. I would say it's a cute throwback, except it's sharp and pointing right at me.

I'm done fighting. Time to use the gifts my ancestors gave me: running away.

I sprint for the elevator; it's still on our level. I throw myself inside and hit the "close" button. The little guy's running after me with the knife, practically foaming at the mouth. I'm jamming the button but the doors are taking an eternity. Behind him I see Drake breaking the goon's other arm.

The elevator's inches from closing but the little guy's like a human cannonball. He dives forwards, thrusting the knife at me. The doors close around his arm for the briefest of seconds. As they re-open I seize his wrist and force it sideways, slamming it until he drops the blade.

I kick him hard in the chest and he falls into the corridor. Snatching his knife up, I keep it pointed at him as I jam the "close" button again. He's glaring at me, calculating. My gaze moves over his shoulder. There's a six foot-something scientist and semi-pro MMA champion sprinting towards the pair of us with murder in his eyes.

The little guy sees this too and tries joining the elevator, but the flick knife says no. I jab the air until he's forced to back off, and snatch my arm back just as the doors close.

As the elevator descends, the skirmish fades. Drake's wrath is meted out on the little guy who, to be fair, ain't going down without a fight. He's cursing like a champ as Drake tries to beat rapid answers out of him.

I'm getting ready to run when the elevator stops just two levels down. Hiding the blade behind my back, I smile politely as a retired couple step inside, giving me a curious look.

"Are you new to the apartment?"

"Lo siento, no entiendo," I say, curtseying.

The woman's eyes light up and she holds out a "bear with me" finger, while tapping her wrist. A holographic translation interface appears, hovering between us. Dammit. I forgot this was a yuppie neighborhood.

"¿Hablas español? Tenemos amigos de Honduras. ¿De dónde eres?"

She speaks English into her wrist, and the machine spits her words out in real time Spanish, with a floating transcription for good measure.

"Lo siento, no entiendo," I say, again, with a pained smile.

The woman looks perturbed and taps her wrist device hard, then shouts into it.

"I SAID DO YOU SPEAK SPANISH? WE HAVE FRIENDS FROM HONDURAS. HONDURAS? *HOONNNDUUURAAASSSS?*"

The door chimes open revealing the lobby. Sweet mercy. I was starting to wish the little guy *had* stuck me.

I'm running for the exit when the stairwell bursts open. The retired couple scream.

It's Drake, and he's got a sword.

"You're a dead man, Luke!"

As he charges at me, I'm wondering how he managed to

take out all three guys *and* find time to go back to his bedroom and fetch that thing off the wall, but it's definitely not the time to be asking.

We're outside and I'm running across the parking lot towards the highway.

"Drake, I can explain," I yell.

"Shut your mouth and get back here!"

"I think we got off on the wrong foot, it was nothing personal!"

The highway is a cargo artery, meaning nothing but huge trucks roaring between cities. I'm not usually one for jaywalking, especially when it's me versus a juggernaut, but when a guy's running at you with a samurai sword, your perspective on risk changes.

I leap the barrier and freeze as a truck roars past, its horn blaring. I dart into the next lane and wait for a gap. Only six more lanes to the central reservation.

I'm *really* hoping Drake gets hit by a truck right about now. Forty years ago, it might have happened but today's algorithms are too damned good. Three hundred HGVs brake in unison like someone hit slow motion. Now I'm running like hell, because there's nothing slowing Drake down anymore. The walking-pace trucks are stopping automatically as he runs, picking his way through with ease.

A siren approaches above the traffic. Heavens be praised, it's the po-po! Floating above us is a highway patrol drone, keeping pace as we weave between vehicles.

Citizens. You are walking in a non-designated area. Leave the road immediately.

"Drake, I really think we should listen to what it says. I'm gonna go this way, why don't you go back home?"

I'm running directly into the oncoming traffic, darting between lanes, trying to shake him off.

Citizens, you will be charged with trespass if you do not leave immed-

"Get back here, Luke, I'm taking you in!"

"Save yourself the hassle, I'm surrendering to the cops!"

"I'm not talking about the police, you're coming to the lab. You're gonna tell them what you did to me, and what you stole, and I'm gonna get my name cleared. Then I'm gonna tear you apart!"

Citizens, force will be used...

"I'll level with you Drake, that's a sucky line up for me."

"You should've thought of that before you attacked me!"

Force will be used...

The drone's voice has an echo now. It's split in two. One half is coming right for me.

"Who are you working for?" yells Drake. "The Republic? The Russians?"

"Seriously, dude, let's talk when you've had a moment to calm down. I think you're overre-"

Before I can finish my sentence a piercing tone fills the air. It's agonizing; forcing me to my knees, cowering and covering my ears in a futile attempt to shut it out. I know enough about police restraints to know they aren't flooding my ears with actual sound waves; they're targeting me with an infrared pulse to overload my auditory cortex. It's brutally effective.

I'm weeping with the pain of it when the sound vanishes. The drone falls to the tar before me, sparking. There's a throwing star sticking out of its back. A crazed yell sounds from up ahead. I spin around and Drake's charging at me with the sword held vertically beside him. He looks preposterous. But then again, he's about to cleave my arm off, so I shan't raise it.

I scramble to my feet and sprint into the oncoming traffic. I'm starting to outpace him.

"The more you run, the worse it's gonna be, you snake!"

"I think... the technical term... is *mole*," I pant.

Drake abandons the sword completely, instantly doubling his pace. The gap's shrinking as he rockets towards me. I can hear his feet pounding the tar, the tirade of anger from his lungs.

A fresh siren's approaching from the highway. I wave desperately at the flashing lights. A police hover bike approaches like a bullet. At the last second it swings to a dead stop, floating side on, blocking my path.

"Drop your weapons and spread 'em, both of you!"

The officer looks pissed off as he dismounts. I drop the piddly flick knife, which falls to the ground with a tinny clatter. Drake halts a few yards away with his hands raised, unarmed.

"You mind telling me what the hell you two are doing on a superhighway?"

"Yes, Officer. I assaulted this man two days ago, and I need to be arrested," I blurt.

I lay myself prostrate before him, practically kissing his boots.

"Is this true?" says the officer.

"No, Officer, this has all been a big misunderstanding," says Drake, adopting a sycophantic professional tone. "My friend here forgot to take his medication. I'm his caregiver. We often do role play to ease his delusions. I was trying to get him off the road when you arrived."

"Officer, that's a lie. I attacked him, I swear. Nearly killed him, in fact. I was dressed as Beethoven, he's a classical composer, and I handcuffed him to the bed, then gave him cocaine and rose petals, but I had these latex gloves, see-"

"I think I've heard enough," says the officer, raising his hand. He turns to Drake. "What medication should he be on?"

"They've got him on 800mg of fentexadine, but I think it needs to be increased," says Drake.

"Officer, he's lying. You have to take me in or he'll kill me!"

"Aha, a common side effect of withdrawal. *You need to take your meds, Luke,*" says Drake, in a patronizing tone. He snaps out of it and continues talking to the cop. "Sorry, Officer, this hasn't happened for months. I'll check his dose when we're back at the home."

"Officer, don't listen to him, you gotta help me!"

The officer frowns and eyes Drake up, reconsidering. "Can you prove you're a medical practitioner?"

"Absolutely. If you run me through the system, it will confirm my credentials."

Drake holds out his palm, expectantly. The officer taps some controls on the bike and a beam scans his face and hand.

"Dr. Drake Arnold. It says your employer is classified. You're a fed?"

"I'm not at liberty to say, Officer."

"This is horse crap! He's running an illegal laboratory in the middle of the city! They're experimenting on people and turning them into mutants! I saw a guy with gills!"

The officer looks at Drake and raises his eyebrows, then winks. He kneels down before me and adopts a gentle, sympathetic tone.

"Looks like you've had a hell of a day, champ. Why

don't you go back with you friend, and take your meds all right? We don't want you getting hurt out here."

"Hurt? He's the one who's gonna hurt me - he's got a sword!"

"A sword? Goodness, that must have been scary. I'm sure you two will have lots to talk about back at the home."

"You can't just send me back with him! What about the assault? I broke into his apartment and stole his tablet, that's burglary too! And theft! You gotta arrest me for that."

"Relax, Lukey, I'm not pressing charges," says Drake, in a slithering voice.

"If there are no charges being pressed, I have no basis to arrest you other than the jaywalking, Sir. Given that this was a medical incident, I think we can do without the paperwork on this one."

"Nooo!"

"Thank you, Officer, I'll see to it this doesn't happen again," says Drake.

Drake rises to his feet and extends a hand towards me with a cold, simpering smile.

I've got no choice. I leap up and punch the officer square in the jaw.

"Son of a-"

"Ha! Now you *have* to arrest me! And if you don't, I'll hit you again!" I say, triumphantly.

"God *dammit.* I'm arresting both of you. Your caregiver's culpable for your actions while you're under their supervision. Hands behind your back!"

The officer throws a zip cable over my wrists and pulls it tight. I sigh with sweet relief; cuffs have never felt so good. Actually, that's not strictly true, but it's for another time.

The cop leads me to the hover bike, which has

descended to ground level. Passenger pods unfold on each side like wings.

He's about to seat me in the pod when a wet crunch and grunt resonate behind me. The officer's grip vanishes; he's out cold.

Drake's looming over his body, panting, shaking out his fist. He sets his manic gaze on me and grabs me in a headlock.

"I told you already, 'Luke'. You're coming with me."

The police bike lets out a loud warning bleep.

Officer in distress. Suspected hostiles detected. Initiating field defense protocols.

Drake spins us around. A blue beam is charging on the bike. His grip slackens as he realizes what's about to happen.

"Oh cra-"

A flash of light and my world goes black.

CHAPTER TWENTY-NINE

KEALA

There's a slow-spinning ceiling fan above my face, surrounded by stained foam tiles. A machine is wheezing beside me and I can feel straps around my limbs. As the room comes into focus, I raise my groggy head. I'm lying on a raised platform; flat and un-cushioned. I'm wearing the shoes they gave me, but there are no pants covering my bare shins, I'm in a hospital gown.

Spotlights are pointed at my torso. I peer beneath the fabric and discover marker pen lines across my abdomen. At the side of the room is a trolley of surgical tools, and behind that a medical refrigerator. I turn to examine the opposite side of the room and recoil in shock; a battered medical robot is hovering inches from my bedside, frozen, awaiting instruction.

The door to the operating theater is ajar and two voices are coming from the corridor. I recognize the drawl of the biker who picked me up from the freeway, and the cold tones of his "doctor" friend.

"Why d'you call me, some kinda holdup? Y'all should be up to your elbows in spleen and whatnot by now."

"I did a detailed pre-op scan and I don't think she's a viable donor anymore."

"What you talkin' about? She's perfectly healthy. Few scratches here and there, sure, but I seen worse. Bit of oil never hurt nobody."

"I'm not talking about the hydrocarbon poisoning."

"Then what? C'mon, time is money here."

"Her physiology is altered."

"Speak plain."

"She's showing signs of genetic mutations on a scale I've never seen before."

"You're yanking my chain."

"Her circulatory and breathing systems show significant abnormalities. The scan doesn't indicate scar tissue, which suggests these changes weren't surgical."

"Meaning?"

"Either she was born with never-before-seen genetic defects, or she's been bio-engineered. Whatever the cause, her organs won't be compatible with a regular recipient."

"You're tellin' me we wasted all this time on a freak that ain't worth nothin' to nobody?"

"She might have scientific value to a certain subset of researchers, but it would be a different clientele to our usual market."

"And what exactly do you want me to tell our existing customers? 'Sorry, we accidentally caught a freak? Better luck next time?' Them people can't wait! Better to give them something than nothing."

The argument grows more heated and I've no intention of hearing who wins. The residual anesthetic is making me drowsy but I can feel my strength returning. In fact, I feel better than when I'd arrived; my body's rehydrated and reoxygenated. I pull the intravenous drip from my arm and swivel off the table.

No sooner have my feet touched the ground than the medical robot sounds an alarm. I slam the door and throw the machine down in front of it. The man and woman are thundering towards the siren.

I dart to the window and shove my hands under the ledge. I'm heaving upward but it's screwed shut. The man and woman are pounding the door, yelling at me to open up. The bleating robot is edging away from the door with each convulsion.

I grab the drip stand and smash it against the glass. The man cries in fury; all charm has vanished. His only offer is to make my death painless if I surrender quickly. This is followed by graphic details of how, if I defy him, they'll take my organs as planned, then keep me alive on an old life-support machine until I die of sepsis.

The door rattles in its hinges. I catch glimpses of them as the gap widens. The man is throwing his shoulder at it manically, shunting the fallen bot across the vinyl floor. I swing the stand harder but the glass is tough. With a deranged yell, the man forces his leg through the gap and lands it over the twitching robot. He drags his chest through next, busting a gut to get the door open.

I drop the stand and charge. The man's eyes widen, realizing his mistake. He tries to retreat but he's wedged too tightly. I throw myself against the door as hard as I can.

He howls in pain as the vertical edge hammers into his groin, chest, and head. Enraged, he latches onto my arm with a vice-like grip. I try to pull away, but he's strong. The door jolts further as his colleague shoves from the other side.

"You're gonna wish you surrendered when you had the chance. Now I'm gonna make you pay," slurs the man.

With my free hand I drive my fingers into his eyes. He cries out in pain and I wrench my arm free, rushing back to the window. Recalling something I saw online years ago, I grab a scalpel and scratch a cross into the corner of the glass.

The door shunts again. The man looks deranged. I grab the drip stand and blast it against the weakened glass.

There's shouting behind the door. The woman is insisting about something.

The robot's alarm stops all of a sudden. Its eyes power down and a reboot tone sounds. The machine announces a system diagnostic check. With much hissing and cranking, it restores itself to an upright position, then wheels across the room to its charging station. Unimpeded, the door bursts open and the man hurtles towards me, red faced and wild.

I smash the stand against the glass one final time, with everything I have in me.

It shatters spectacularly. I thrust the stand backwards, hitting the man square in the face, then leap out of the window onto the grass. The jagged frame cuts into my hands and legs as I jump through.

"Get the dogs!" yells the man.

I'm running faster than I've run in my entire life. Barren fields stretch either side of me. The only place offering a chance of hiding is the scrap yard.

I sprint headlong towards it.

As I enter the rusted yard I know my oxygen debt is spiraling. There are no humans in sight, just huge machines crushing cars and sifting through piles of metal. I duck and weave between the clattering robots as they crunch scrap down to size. Dotted around are smaller bots stripping mobile devices apart while ant-sized bots ferry the debris away to ultra-refined piles. I leap over the micro colony and race through the yard.

I'm weaving and turning, trying to create an impossible route to follow, when I hear engines approaching. They sound like ancient gas-powered types. Over them, the man's voice carries.

"You're gonna wish you'd never been born!"

I throw myself behind the shell of a burned out automobile and try to breathe but my lungs are failing. The man's quad bike roars into the yard, followed closely by the woman's.

Then come the dogs. Faceless, powerful, and massive; they're like nothing I've ever known, and they're coming for me at speed.

CHAPTER THIRTY

LUKE

This is the first time in years that I've endured a police stun ray, and I can't say I've missed the experience. My head's pounding as I come to.

The holding cell is a design masterpiece, from the dripping ceiling, to the cockroaches festering in the corner, no grimy details are spared.

The skin above my cheeks feels pinched. I massage it but that achieves nothing; in fact it only exacerbates things. Whoever fitted my headset is a master of petty mind games.

Advances in medical diagnostics mean injuries can be precisely time-stamped. As a result, conventional police brutality has been replaced by the art of custodial passive aggression. These minor incursions are always deniable, and never life threatening, but utterly infuriating for anyone stuck in a holding bunk like me.

I did a piece on the technique a few years back with a friend of a friend who worked as a cop. She said they liked to leave people stewing in the chamber for a while with an itch they couldn't scratch. It wasn't brutality, but it was psychological torture of a kind. Some folk would confess within the first hour, just to get the headset removed.

I give my "cell" a thorough inspection. I'm alone, which means I'm safe. Assuming Drake's not looming over my real world body with that freakin' sword. That's a point - I need to get out of here before him. I call out for help.

"Attendant!"

An automated custodial officer pops up in the middle of my cell.

Detainee 114-H. How may I assist?

"I want my phone call."

Who do you wish to call?

Damn, I should've thought of that first. My instinct is to call Lanelle, which is the drill in these situations, but she's not exactly come through for me so far. Could try my ex-wife, I think there's some dregs of love there? Enough to post bail, maybe? No, I don't wanna bring her and the kids into this mess. What about Chang? Sure, I still owe him a stack of money and he's almost certainly blown my cover, but he seems able to pull off most things. Maybe he could wipe the officer's video log where I confess to assaulting Drake?

Ugh. The confession. A desperate maneuver that didn't even work. If Drake decides to press charges, I'm cooked. Assault, poisoning, narcotics, burglary... Maybe I'm gonna need an actual lawyer?

Do you wish to proceed with your call?

"Huh? Oh, yeah. Call my editor. Lanelle Williams."

The individual you have named is not a legal representative. The purpose of this call is to arrange your legal representation.

"She's gonna get me a lawyer."

Connecting.

If she doesn't come good now, it's all over. I stare at the cockroaches, mesmerized by a glitch in the animation. Watching them loop periodically, I snort with satisfaction; the cheapskates couldn't even afford to animate some bugs properly. The dripping ceiling catches my attention, repeating the same pattern every fourteen seconds. Suddenly I'm not gloating as I realize what's happening. Everything in this chamber is deliberate; fine-tuned to drive the occupant insane.

Lanelle appears on-screen looking flustered.

"Boss, thank heavens, it's good to see you."

"Luke, why are you in prison? What happened at your apartment, you sounded hurt? I've been calling you ever since."

"I got jumped by the lab people, then jumped again by a gang, but I took them to Drake, who-"

The purpose of this call is to arrange your legal representation. Please do not stray from the remit or this call will be terminated.

"OK, another time. Can you get me out of here? I don't know what the bail's been set at-"

Your bail has been set at the county default rate of twenty-four thousand crypto.

Yikes. That's a lot.

"I'll do what I can. Sit tight, Luke."

Please name your legal representative or this call will be terminated.

"Do you want legal representation, Luke?"

"Yeah, ideally a baker. They can smuggle me a file between layers of cream frosting. I'd say try the candlestick maker but I don't eat candles, so the feds might twig."

"Luke, be serious!"

"I don't want a lawyer, I want bail! You need to fix this,

Lanelle, you knew I needed the money and you hung me out to dry."

"You spent money without authoriz-"

"I spent what should have been in my account."

"I already told you it's complicated."

"Allow me to make it simpler. If you don't help, I'm going to jail. You know what jail birds do, Lanelle? They sing. I've got a beautiful number about some journalists at a paper, you'd love it. 'Hacking' barely describes the tricks they pull to get a story, you won't believe it. Oh wait, yeah you will, because you're their editor. I wonder what that would mean for you?"

"Shut it, Luke. I'll do what I can."

"You said that last time!"

"I'll take it to the board."

"Right, because a bunch of pompous, overpaid, corporate ghouls are really gonna-"

Call terminated.

"Dammit it robo cop, why'd you go hang up on me like that? I was just getting into my flow."

Your call was terminated by the other caller.

"Rude."

Do you require further assistance?

"Yeah, someone's fitted my VR mask wrong and it's hurting my cheeks. Can it be adjusted?"

Processing. Ticket assigned. You are number thirty-six in the queue.

Terrific.

Think. That's what jail's good for, right? Thinking time. Got plenty of that right now. If I can just ignore the cockroaches and that damned dripping. The lab will know I'm here, which means I need an exit strategy. No doubt they'll bail Drake out, because he'll use intel on me as leverage. Then again, he assaulted a cop, so his bail will be stratospheric.

If Lanelle bails me out I'm going straight to Canada. I've already picked out a nice cabin in the woods where I can lay low, drink cider, and avoid writing my memoirs. That should give Lanelle plenty of time to do her job and blow this story wide open. The lab will be a national scandal, there'll be an inquiry into government methods, yada yada. The point is, once the story's out there I'll be in the clear. No charges, no money problems, no more gangs. Of course, if she *doesn't* do her job, then screw it, I'm still going to Canada. The only difference is that I'll be murdered in my sleep by the lab people. They seem like the type to hold a grudge.

Maybe I should stay in prison?

The cell vanishes from view. Someone's tugging a headset off my face. A young, short-haired cadet is unshackling me from my bunk.

"Dr. Ragazzi, you're being released on bail."

I take it all back. Prison is for roaches, my editor's the best, I'm moving to Canada and getting huskies.

The police holding chamber stretches before me. Hundreds of bunks are piled high, just inches apart. The occupants are shackled and motionless, their eyes covered by VR masks, and their motor neurons suppressed.

The cadet helps me out of my bunk. As I soon as I'm clear, a robotic arm collects the bed and sweeps it upward, slotting it back on the shelf where I was stored, fifty levels up. I follow the cadet to the checkout desk.

"You must remain in Park Morpre until further notice.

You are required to check in with this precinct via geo-tagged video call by eight PM every day, starting today. If you attempt to leave the city, or fail to uphold the conditions of this bail, you will be detained indefinitely pending trial. Do you understand?"

"You got that all memorized, huh, kid?"

The cadet looks at me taken aback. For a moment, her mask slips.

"It, uh, comes up on my AR feed."

"Nice. Wish I'd had one of those for my marriage."

I go to retrieve my belongings from the discharge box then remember all I have is the clothes I'm in which, for record, could smell fresher. As my late grandmother used to say, orange juice and sweat do not make eau de toilette.

I step out of the police station and hope to hell Lanelle's got a new passport for me because I'm intending to fly to Canada. It's a *heck of a* drive to reach the bit I've got in mind. As I survey the bustling sidewalk, something sharp scratches my leg.

"Ouch! Watch it, dude!" I yell, nursing my calf.

The guy doesn't even apologize. Just keeps on walking with his suit and umbrella. Who carries an umbrella in this town? It's the West Coast for God's sake.

That's when it hits me. The dizziness, I mean. The realization that I've just been spiked? That comes in a few seconds time when I hit the deck. Right abouuuuuut... now.

"Oh my God! Are you OK?"

A passing couple rush over, looking concerned. I'm lying on my back, trying to get the words out, but my vocal cords are paralyzed.

"I think he's having a seizure! Call an ambulance!" cries the woman.

Some cops rush out to assist. They're moving my limbs,

checking for a pulse, but I can't feel a thing. I recognize one of their faces, but she looks blurry.

"He's paralyzed," says the cadet. "It makes no sense, he was fine when I checked him out a moment ago."

"God dammit, rookie," grunts her colleague, "I'll get the defib. He's about to go into cardiac."

I can hear an ambulance approaching. With screeching brakes it pulls up by the curb and paramedics rush out. A smart stretcher scoops me up, and before I know it, I'm in the back of the wagon, surrounded by medical paraphernalia.

The doors slam shut and the siren blares. We're speeding away. I'm blinking, gasping, fighting to stay awake, but my vision's getting darker. I try to sit up, but my body won't respond.

The paramedics lean over me and pull off their surgical masks, revealing the faces I dread most. Pierre and the director.

"Good to see you again, Dr. Ragazzi."

CHAPTER THIRTY-ONE

KEALA

The dogs are like nothing I've seen before. Their faces are flat, save for a needle protruding from the front, where the snout should be. Their metallic legs look powerful, and their bodies tough as steel.

"Hunt!" yells the man.

The two dogs vanish into the rusty maze. The man and the woman split up, covering the rest of the yard. They aren't racing on the quad bikes now, they're prowling. She doesn't know it yet, but the woman's coming right at me.

I duck down and press myself flush against the peeling paintwork of the burned out car. As she approaches I keep crawling around the perimeter to stay out of sight. I hold my rattling breath as she rumbles by armed with a pistol.

As she disappears behind a pile of scrap, I hurry down the avenue from which she came. I'm in a clearing with no idea which of the eight paths leads back to the entrance. I can hear the rumbling engines echoing from opposite sides of the yard, like pincers moving in on my position.

I pluck for an alley ahead and run, sprinting between super-stacked walls of cars. The alley twists, merging with a mega lane that's thousands of cars long. The opposite wall is a mound of stripped parts.

An electrical snarl makes my heart freeze. It begins with a tone climbing in pitch, like it's warming up, or acquiring a target lock, until it peaks. Now it's like a real dog, sampled and stretched to create an eerie, never-ending pulse. The effect is disorienting, almost hypnotic.

The dog bounds towards me. Its metallic limbs power through the dirt faster than any natural canine. The syringe is primed right for me.

I throw myself onto the scrap mound and scramble up as fast as I can. Fresh cuts from the rusty metal join those from the smashed surgery window.

The robotic barking is getting closer. It's reached the base of the mound and is staring at me, calculating. It places a paw on top of the loose poles and rusty sheets. Then another paw. Then its hind legs follow.

A beam gives way beneath me and my leg plunges through the gap. The rubble around me is so loose I can't push myself up and the dog is getting closer. The terrain has slowed it only, it's moving one sure-footed limb at a time, testing, calculating, executing.

Fishing blindly, I find a foothold within the cavity. I stretch my fingers wide to try and spread the surface weight - any sudden motion could dislodge the pile above, and bury me in an avalanche of metal.

As loose pieces ripple past my legs, an idea strikes me. I grab a nearby hunk and hurl it at the robot hound. It strikes the dog's shoulder, tipping it off-balance. I throw another down even harder, this time striking the dog's front leg and dislodging some of the metal around it. The dog slides several feet down the pile. Seizing all the loose pieces I can reach, I hurl them behind me and scramble higher. The dog presses itself flush against the mound, waiting for the torrent to cease.

When I look back, it's like the creature has shrunk. Its limbs are shorter, but its paws have become massive. They're thinner, but much wider, like snow boots. The dog stretches its new foot panels out. The material spans several pieces of rubble, and grips the edges of each piece like a set of fingers. The dog looks at me and tilts its head, then starts climbing at speed.

I stagger upwards; the top is nearly in reach.

A black shadow appears above me. The second dog has scaled the other side of the mound. It trains its needle towards me, then pounces.

As the dog leaps, I lunge to the side and thrust a pole into its underbelly. Direct hit! My traditional hunter training finally paid off.

The robot tumbles down the mound. It collapses at the base, seeping battery juice into the soil. The first dog looks from me to its fallen peer and back, recalibrating, then redoubles its attack, quickly closing the gap between us. I grab a pole and swing it hard but the dog ducks and dodges. Changing tact, I suddenly jab it hard like I'm fencing.

I strike the syringe perfectly. The needle snapped off, leaving clear liquid oozing down its metal skin.

Mistake.

The broken syringe retracts inside the dog's skull. Its flat face splits in two, becoming a huge jaw. Metal teeth gnash at me like a bear trap on legs. The electronic bark shifts to a low pitched growl, and it sprints towards me.

I hurl myself over the top of the mound and land on a line of stacked automobiles. The dog appears inches behind me but falters at the apex; its modified paw has become trapped in a shifting pile.

A quadbike skids into the lane. "Give it up, lady, it's over," yells the woman.

I sprint across the stacked cars but she's drawing level. Up here I realize the junk yard stretches for hundreds of acres. Even if I found somewhere to hide, I'd starve in the maze. There, beyond my stack of cars, is my only hope of escape.

"You're only making it worse for yourself," yells the woman.

At the end of the lane is a double-armed crane - like two spider legs. It's rooted to the spot and rotating, grabbing cars from my line and dropping them into a shredding machine. The empty gripper passes over the one way out: a sweeping river.

"This is your last chance. When I shoot you, you're gonna fall, and we're not gonna give you any pain meds."

As I stagger across the metal mountain range, something moves in my periphery. The woman's taking aim. She fires but the bullet ricochets off the car. Whatever it is, it's not a regular bullet. Cursing the quad bike, she tries to reload but the terrain is against her.

Something lands behind me with a clang. The dog has freed its paw and is sprinting towards me.

I'm running with everything I have left, but my lungs are screaming. The crane's empty claw rotates towards the stack and grabs a vehicle. If I don't make this pick up, I'm a dead woman.

A second quad bike skids in front of the crane. The man draws his pistol and fires, narrowly missing my shoulder.

The dog's metal limbs are thundering closer. I prepare to leap with all that I have. If I miss, I'll fall six stories. But as I go to jump, something liquid explodes across my ankle.

"Gotcha!" yells the woman.

My foot goes numb but it's too late. I've committed to the jump with all my momentum. My right foot casts off as planned, but my left leg fails to fire.

Diving face first off the pile of cars, I throw my hands out before me.

I land hard on the hood of the moving car. The crane's motion sends me skidding across the top. I'm grappling for something to hold onto but there's nothing. My legs fall first, then my hips follow, dragging my torso over the edge.

At the last second, my skin latches onto the bumper. I'm dangling, helplessly, as the crane turns towards the shredder. The screech of grinding metal fills my ears.

The dog is darting across the yard onto an adjacent pile, anticipating the crane's arc. It's going to try and intercept me. Shaking my numb foot hard, I dislodge the pellet, then use the crane's motion to my advantage and swing my leg up.

The shredder is fast approaching. I clamber across the hood towards the crane's claw. I have to get a hold of the main arm or I'll be shredded along with this vehicle. As I edge towards the roof, a crunch draws my attention backwards.

A metallic claw smashes onto the hood like a pickaxe. Then another. The robotic dog drags itself up onto the hood, with a hunk of the car's bumper in its mouth. It snaps its jaws shut, shattering the bar, then digs its hind legs into the hood. Shaking itself out, it recalibrates its limbs for an attack on all fours.

Sparks fly as we soar towards the shredder. My numb foot slips across the windshield as I scramble towards the crane's claw. Ready to attack, the dog's razor hooks tear through the hood as it chases after me.

Seizing the crane's claw, I use my good leg to jump

higher. My palms latch onto the crane's arm and my legs follow, grabbing it in a koala grip. But my numb leg slips, dangling below. The dog pounces with its bear-trap jaw. At the same moment, the crane's claw unfurls, dropping the car. The dog freezes in mid-air, defying gravity as it soars towards me for a split second, before plunging into the grinder with a yowl. I shield my eyes as its battery explodes in the machine, spewing fire and smoke from the funnel.

As the crane rotates towards the river I realize I misjudged the landscape. From the line of cars way back, it had looked like the crane's arm passes over the middle of the river. From my position now, clinging to the vertical dangling part, it's clear it skirts the riverbank. *The impact* would shatter me. I need to get higher if I'm going to reach the water.

A pellet strikes the crane and flecks shower my calf. I cower, thinking fast. Jumping from the top will leave me too exposed - they'll get a clear shot, and kill me in the fall. There's only one thing for it.

I shimmy my way up to the highest part of the crane's arc. I'm clinging to the side shielded from the man and woman's shots. Placing my feet flat against the metal, I tuck my knees beneath my chin. My arms are stretched across the top, gripping the far side, where a bombardment of pellet spray dusts my fingertips. I tense my whole body so I'm coiled like a spring. Tilting my head backwards, I quiver as the crane approaches the water.

In one motion I spring, flinging my arms up and over, driving my functional leg out as hard as I can, forcing my body into an arc.

Pellets fly past me as I fall. My stomach's in my mouth, and all I can see is the ground racing towards me.

CHAPTER THIRTY-TWO

LUKE

Water drenches my face, waking me with a cold shock. I'm spluttering and trying to see but the lights are bright, so it takes me a minute to figure where I am. When I do, my heart sinks. I'm at the lab, and my former bosses are standing before me.

The director's holding an empty bottle of water and wearing a malicious smile.

"I thought you guys would've stretched to something a little more high-tech," I splutter.

"Have a towel," says the director, dabbing my face.

"What happened to the paramedic's uniform? We were inches from realizing my ultimate fantasy."

"Men's fantasies often fall a few inches short," she says, dabbing me tenderly.

I'd be lying if I said I wasn't at least thirty percent turned on.

"Cute routine you two had with the whole ambulance thing. Do you guys do other fancy dress together? Sailors? Golfers? Magicians? I can see that for you, Pierre. Definitely a high school magic type."

"Enjoy these words, Dr. Ragazzi. They will soon be your last," he snorts.

We're at a strong fifty percent now. I make a mental note to speak to my counselor about consensual subjugation sometime.

The director approaches carrying a plastic crown.

"You get that at a drive thru?"

"DARPA," she shrugs. "Although, strictly speaking, they don't know we have it. So no telling. Oh wait, that's right, you won't be *able* to tell anyone, silly me. Hold still, naughty boy."

Eighty. Definitely eighty percent.

She taps a few buttons and the device whirs. There's something bright rotating inside the transparent tubing. The bead of light does accelerating laps until it forms a steady halo. The director places the device on my head and fusses over its positioning until it's level. A soft tingling spreads across my skull.

"What does this thing do?"

"Electromagnetic neural stimulation," replies Pierre. "It simulates the effects of being drunk."

"You take that back! I'll fight you both. Hey wanna come back to my place?"

They look at each other concerned until I crack up laughing.

"Gotcha."

The director smiles in a way that lets me know I'll be paying for that. The pair take a seat opposite me.

"We need to know who you work for, and what you stole from us. You're going to tell us everything," says the director.

"Sure, want my bank details too?"

"If we ask, we'll get them. In the next minute your

brain's capacity to inhibit thoughts will be suspended. You'll be an open book."

"Careful what you wish for," I chuckle.

My laugh masks genuine concern. If I spill the beans, they'll find Lanelle, reclaim the tablet, and crush the story. I'll be a dead man, her life will be in danger too, and all this will have been for nothing.

In spite of these fears, I'm giggling like a teenager at a boozy sleepover. Giddiness is taking hold.

"You came close, Dr. Ragazzi," continues the director.

"I'd love to get closer," I reply, chomping my teeth.

"Sweet."

"How dare you, I've never been called sweet in my life. I'm roguishly handsome. Or as many women will tell you, 'not at all like the photo'."

"Years of hard work nearly ruined. You have no idea what we sacrificed to make this project succeed."

"Great, so you guys are gonna kill me in the next half hour, right? Once I've blabbed all the state secrets and admitted I miss my ex-wife's lasagna. You should get drapes in here by the way, they'd brighten the place up."

The director frowns at me and examines the halo's manual. "It doesn't say anything about attention deficit or hyperactivity."

"It's a prototype, don't expect it to work perfectly," mutters Pierre.

"Er, I'm hyperactive because I'm a *fun* drunk! For real. At parties they'd always be like, 'get Luke, get Luke!' Aw dammit, I darn gone told ya my real name."

"Luke is your *fake* name."

"Real name, too!"

"Your real name is the same as your fake name? That's the dumbest thing I've ever heard."

"Is it? Or is it... *genius?* What if we're out for office drinks one night and someone from my real life is in town and they're like, 'Hey Luke, who are these dorks? They look really boring.' Because then you'd all be like, 'Wait, your name's *not* Alfonse von Schmittelberg the third?' And I'd have to be like 'D'aww, ya got me!' Come to think of it, you got me anyway, so maybe I *should've* gone with the fake name. Would've been way cooler."

"I'm turning this thing down," mutters Pierre.

"How come you two didn't already know my real identity? I thought Chang spilled the beans?"

"Drake called us from the police station and told us you're the mole. Who's Chang?"

Oops.

"Uh. No one. A friend. My mom. Christmas."

Nailed it.

The director marches over and snatches the crown off my head.

"He just lied! We need to crank this thing up, not down," says the Director.

She fiddles with the settings and the tingling intensifies, making me giggle a bunch more. Pierre stalks over, stony faced. He gets real close to me, and whispers in this cold, rattling breath.

"When the laughter stops, you will realize why none of your predecessors have ever been seen again. We don't like waste in this facility, we use whatever resources present themselves to us. Rats, guinea pigs... even moles."

CHAPTER THIRTY-THREE

KEALA

By some miracle I hit the water. I'm sinking deep and the river's sweeping me away, far from the biker man and the organ-harvesting woman. But my relief is short lived.

I can't breathe.

My gills won't open and I'm being pinned down by the powerful undercurrent. The last gasp of air I took on the crane is running out fast. I'm trying to kick but the numbness has spread to my entire leg; it's a total deadweight.

The only one way I'll make it to the surface is by climbing. Using my arms, I steer myself to the side, preparing to grab hold of the reeds. But the riverbank is barren, its sides are made of concrete. I paw at the wall, trying to latch on with my skin, but the current is moving me too fast. I spin around so my feet are pointing downstream, then put my working leg against the concrete and use it as a hopping brake. It slows me just enough for my hands to lock onto the stone.

Air bubbles escape my lungs. The surface is several

meters above me. I rip a hand from the wall and reach higher, dragging myself up like a free climber in a cyclone. With a gasp, I break free of the water and suck in the sweet air.

A horn blares across the river; a barge is approaching at speed, laden with scrap metal. It's as wide as the river itself, and motorized wheels line its hull. They're angled into the concrete banks, protecting the barge and providing additional thrust.

The horn sounds again. If I don't move I'll be crushed. I've made it to the surface, only to discover the concrete sides continue beyond the water, forming a five meter high wall either side of the river. There's no way I can scale it in time with a dead leg.

The barge is nearly upon me. I take a gasp of air and dive, but to my horror the vessel is as deep as it is wide, and covered in churning wheels from top to toe.

I'm not diving fast enough; the hull is going to smash me. If it doesn't break my bones, the barge will drag me back to the man and his doctor. I'll either drown en route, or die on their operating table. The only escape is down. I expel all the air from my lungs and sink like an anchor.

I press myself flat against the riverbed and cower as the barge rumbles overhead, inches from my face. It's endlessly long and segmented like a freight train. As my body suffocates, I'm fighting my lungs' instinct to inhale. With a flush and a splutter, my gills break open. Whether it's the water temperature, or the truly desperate state of my body, I don't know, but something forced them to respond.

A huge set of propellers churns the water into a white wash, signaling the end of the floating train, but there's no time to recover. The barge's wash has dislodged me and I'm being swept away at speed. I face upstream and place all fours against the concrete river bed, trying to slow my passage.

There's a tightening around my back. Something has caught hold of my gown. I can't turn; it's clamped to me like a straitjacket. Friction burns my skin as I dig my hands and feet into the concrete. I'm still losing ground; the suction is too strong. There's no way this is the current. I cough and a plume of oil spurts from my gills. The hydrocarbon poisoning is progressing, weakening me further.

My dead leg slips, then the opposite hand dislodges. The force against my chest triples. I clutch on desperately until I'm ripped from the concrete. Flying backwards like a bungee cord, I smash against something hard. My eyes bulge as the crushing intensifies. The last of my strength is being squeezed from me.

CHAPTER THIRTY-FOUR

LUKE

The director puts the experimental "halo" device on my head for a fourth time, on yet a higher setting. Frankly, I don't think she knows how to use it. I feel like a diaper in a tumble dryer; stinky, messy, and the end result of other people's problems. Why are they questioning me in the dark lab of all places? What if this is part of my cunning rouse? For all they know, I could be lulling them into a false sense of security, and now that I'm inside, ka-*blam*, I pounce. Make my move. Oh yeah. All kinds of things could go down. I could be blowing this gasket wide open. Front page news. Luke Remini does it again. Investigative journalist of the year.

The director leans in front of me, frowning. "You realize you've been speaking aloud this entire time?"

Dammit.

"Quite. So, tell me, journalist of the year, which paper put you up to this?"

"I may be brain-drunk, director, but I ain't no snitch. You better find the setting that makes pigs fly. Because *that's* the day I'll-"

"Clearly this isn't working," she says, conferring with Pierre.

"I believe our subject may have insufficient inhibitions for the technique to have its usual effect," he replies.

"Agreed. Bring me the interface."

Pierre brings her a glove which she slips on and flexes. A robotic arm swings down from the ceiling and mirrors her movements. Behind her, I see a figure moving in the mist-filled cubicle. It's the test subject I discovered earlier; the one I tried dragging back in when he got the jump on me. Poor devil's sealed in now.

"Don't worry, 'Dr. Ragzzi', or should I say, *Mr. Remini*, you'll have plenty of time to make it up to him when you're neighbors," says the director.

"I've already got neighbors, thanks. The last thing I need is *more* people to ignore in stairwells."

"This is your new home, Mr. Remini. See that cubicle over their? That will be yours. How exciting! I can't wait to see what we learn from you. It would be such a shame if your body went to waste."

"My body's been wasted for years. Three kids and two marriages do that to a guy."

She smiles at me, then her face tightens, and she reaches forwards with the glove. The robotic fist shoots towards me and grabs my shirt. She raises her hand and I'm lifted from the ground.

"How did you discover this facility?"

"Anonymous email, we get tip-offs all the time. Everyone else ignored it but I was curious so dug a little. When I realized how off-grid this place is, my curiosity became suspicion, and it mushroomed from there. Of course, now that I'm being roughed up in a secret lab where I'll probably die a sad, lonely mutant, I wish I'd marked it as spam. Should've taken the story on speed cameras. That piece was-"

She slams me back down in the seat.

"Ouch! God damn that hurts! Have you ever been made to sit down by a robot? Jeez, a few more cushions next time, please."

Her robotic arm slaps me, then grabs me by the hair.

"Who was the tip off from?"

"I told you already, it was anonymous! Probably my predecessor, if I'm reading the room right. Maybe even that guy in the mist tank? Hey, guy! Did you send me an email like three months ago?"

Fish man vanishes into the mist while the robot hand slaps me again. It's weird, it's not like a regular hand, it's more like a suction cup that can be morphed into any shape depending on the task required. Right now, that task is beating me up. I think the tip's made of silicone, so it feels like I'm being mugged by a pastry chef.

"Drake's tablet. Who's got it?"

"No idea."

I told another lie! Eat it, DARPA. Admittedly, it felt like I was squeezing a gall stone through my brain, but I overcame the halo. The director presses on, irritated.

"You claim no knowledge of the tablet yet you knew Drake was assaulted. How could that be?"

"Ask Beethoven," I say, collapsing in a fit of giggles.

Dammit, cancel the victory parade. My laughter is rewarded by a punch to the gut. I rock out of my seat and onto the floor, winded. Next thing I know I'm being dragged from the floor by my hair and it hurts like hell. I'm on my tiptoes but the arm keeps rising like the director's trying to pull my whole friggin' scalp off. She's staring at me, waiting for me to blab. The machine goes higher still. I climb onto the chair, trying to get ahead of the pain.

She lets go suddenly and I sigh, nursing my tender scalp in sweet release. The robotic arm sweeps down and chops under the chair, splintering the wooden legs, and sending me crashing to the ground.

"Ouch, all right! So I stole Drake's tablet, big deal. There's no point busting my balls about it, it ain't comin' back so I suggest you get over it. My therapist says carrying anger in the heart hurts the angry person above all else."

"Let's test that hypothesis, shall we? I'm getting very angry indeed. But I suspect you're about to get a lot more hurt," says the director.

She curls her glove into a fist. Just as she's about to re-sculpt my face, the lab is plunged into darkness. The director and Pierre are swapping alarmed exclamations. As the seconds mount, their panic increases. The emergency generator should have kicked in by now.

I've got this giddy anticipation rising inside me. I'm picturing a SWAT team storming the lab, arresting those two, and awarding me the Medal of Honor. Then my editor will walk in, say something cool like "case closed," and present me with that journalist of the year award.

"There's no SWAT team coming, and you're never leaving this place!"

Ouch! Someone's grabbed me in a headlock. I think it's Pierre. It sounds like him. Dammit. I have *got* to stop thinking aloud. Argh, they're squeezing real tight. I think these two have had enough of my five star banter. Typically, a person in my position would have specialist combat training for this level of mid-torture smack talk. Luckily, I have my natural talents to fall back on. As my delinquent Aunt Bettina used to say, "Us Reminis are blessed with three things: thick skulls, loose tongues, and a gift for getting punched."

The emergency lighting kicks in. The AC fans are revving up again too.

"Thank god," mutters the director, releasing my head.

An automated message comes over the Tannoy.

Critical system failure detected. Initiating anti-contagion protocol.

"What? No! Override! Computer, override that protocol, director's order!" she yells.

A buzzer sounds.

All samples will be terminated in ninety seconds. Human personnel should vacate the premises immediately. This is not a drill.

"We have to get out of here!" yells Pierre.

"What about him?" says the director.

"Forget him!" cries Pierre. "You want to fight him without the robot arm? He took out our only MMA-trained employee. I'm getting to the panic room."

The director turns to me, looking desperate. "Come with us."

"Are you insane?"

"This chamber is about to self-sterilize. We can protect you, in return for what you know."

Seventy seconds to purge.

I look her in the eye and grit my teeth. "I'd rather be purged."

If I had a cigarette, I would've lit it for effect. The director looks at me with deepest loathing, then flees after Pierre through a side door.

Sixty seconds to purge.

I'm looking around the dark lab and I have no clue where to go. The passage into the animal lab is sealed. I'm stuck with two empty tubes and a box full of mist for company.

A hologram pops up in front of me, around the size of a tablet.

"I thought they never leave," chuckles a familiar voice.

Chang takes a drag on his cigar, then chomps it in his teeth and leans forwards.

"*You* did this? You're sicker than I thought."

"Relax, Lukey boy, I busting you out."

"Why? So you and your boys can finish me off? Maybe I should have gone with those two."

"I was about send your file to lab, then I got interested. I look in their servers. Their security is Pentagon level, it good. But that only make me more curious. Couple hours later, I in, browsing their files. They into some messed up stuff."

Forty seconds to purge.

"Can we talk about this later?"

"You see, I from large family. We looking after each other."

"That is generally how crime syndicates work, yes. How do I get out of here?"

"When they attack part of our community, they attack all of us. So I attack them."

"Wonderful. Pleased to hear it. Seriously though, despite my hard talk earlier I'd really like *not* to get purged, so can we cut to the quick?"

Thirty seconds...

"I help you escape. Then we discuss money you owing me.

"Terrific."

"Service door on right. I opening now."

Emergency lights flicker on, revealing a doorway across

the chamber. I'm about to run over when my eyes fall on the mist box.

"Chang, I need you to get this door open. The box with the light."

"Happy to. I check system for 'box with light'. Aww, no search results."

"Quit goofing! There's someone in there, they're gonna get terminated if we don't get them out!"

I run to the box and pound against the glass.

"Hey! You in there! You need to get out, this place is gonna blow!"

Chang's typing. "Hmm. Box not showing on main schematic. I guess is hidden sample. I try power trace. Got it."

The glass door hisses open, and mist billows out. "Yo, person in the box of mist! Follow my voice, I'm busting you out!"

Twenty seconds to purge.

"You hear that? Come on, hurry!"

A shadow lumbers towards me. The guy with the gills edges out of the container like he's expecting a trap. He looks at me, then remembers my face. He raises his fist and lunges forwards, but he stumbles and collapses onto my chest.

"Woah, easy buddy, I got you! I said I'd bust you out didn't I? This is it, let's go."

I throw his arm over my shoulder and hurry for the side door.

Ten seconds to purge.

A buzzing sound fills the air. It's coming from the ceiling.

I'm aiming for the door, but fish face is dragging me to the side.

"Hey, we don't have time for this!"

Eight seconds...

The buzzing's getting louder.

He slumps to the ground.

"Dude, get up!"

He's reaching for something.

Seven seconds...

A faint glow appears around the ceiling, like a polygonal outline. Yeah, I said polygonal.

Six seconds...

I realize he's looking for the device on the side. I grab the thing, then I grab him.

"Come on!"

Five...

The buzzing's deafening now. We're hobbling towards the side door.

Four...

The ceiling glow intensifies. The room is filled with a neon blue from the crackling beams overhead.

"Guys, what you doing?" yells Chang.

Three...

I'm running now, fully dragging fish face with me.

Two...

The threshold's inches away.

One...

I jump, throwing the both of us over the line.

"Chang, close the door!"

But he's vanished.

The buzzing's stopped.

A split-second of silence.

Commencing purge.

A piercing tone rings out. The glowing blue bars in the

ceiling drop like guillotines. Blinding light cascades down the walls.

"Chaaaaaang!"

The door seals shut with a hiss. We're lying in total darkness, panting. I'm rubbing my eyes, trying to get rid of the glow that's burned into my retinas.

"You cut that fine," says Chang, popping back up on the floating screen.

"Where the hell did you go?"

"I have to switching to service network."

"That was *way too* close for comfort!"

"Not my fault you two go souvenir shopping on way out."

Groaning, I rub my eyes some more. It really is pitch black in here, save for Chang's floating face.

"Chang, how about a little light?"

He taps away. The lights flick on, revealing a vanishingly long, narrow corridor built from steel meshes. There are dozens of levels above and below us. I can't gauge exactly how many because they disappear into the shadows.

"There is staircase to street up ahead," says Chang.

"How far do we have to get down?"

"You mean *up*."

"We're underground? I swear the elevator goes *up* to this level?"

"They trick you. I looking at blueprint. You hundred feet down right now."

An arrow appears on screen above Chang's head, directing us to the stairs. I help fish face through the piping and cabling.

"Quick, system coming back online," says Chang.

"What? But the message said 'critical failure'?"

"Only critical for lab rat. They all dead. But mainframe

computer coming back very soon. I shut down security but is only temporary. They counter-attacking my firewall. You guys need get moving."

Fish face grabs my hand. He's wheezing. He points to the device in my pocket - the one I snatched on his behalf. I hand it over and he fixes it to his gills, then gasps with relief.

"Can you walk now?" I ask.

He nods, panting.

"Then let's get moving. We need to get the hell out of here before the director tracks us."

CHAPTER THIRTY-FIVE

KEALA

Whatever's throttling me has slammed my back against a kind of porthole. A powerful current is sucking me into the cavity, reeling my gown straps in like a lasso. The pressure is curling my spine and crushing my airways. Shrink-wrapped and suffocating, I'm trapped at the bottom of the concrete riverbed with no way of escape.

A plume of white bubbles tears through the water, surrounding a mass of black like an anchor dropping. A scuba diver is swimming towards me, with weighted boots, a utility belt, and an overhead torch.

I don't know what they were expecting, but it sure as hell wasn't me. The diver freaks out majorly. Bubbles gush from their mask as they eek tones of alarm.

They tap their wrist controls and the crushing suction around me fades to nothing. My gown is still pinned back but at least my chest is no longer being compressed to a pulp. The diver swims closer and presses their emergency mouthpiece to my lips. I bat their hand away.

"I don't need it."

The diver's eyes widen as they register my voice in the water; clear as day, without a single bubble leaving my lungs. I tap the gills on the side of my neck. There's no point trying to hide them now.

The diver backs up and pulls a knife from their belt.

"Woah! I can explain!"

They come towards me at speed, with the knife extended.

"Please, no!" I beg.

The diver slips past and cuts my gown loose. Breathing deeply with relief, I clutch the drifting garment to my chest and face my rescuer.

They point to the surface. I peer upwards, nervously, wishing I could see what's waiting on the shore. The last person to "save me" tried to harvest my organs half an hour later.

The diver hands me the huge diving knife, backs away with their hands raised, then kicks their way to the surface. I watch them struggle out of the water until their flippers disappear from the white foam.

I turn, steady-footed, and confront the porthole that nearly killed me. It's an underwater turbine, one of several spanning the river. They continue downstream in a checkerboard layout, although all neutralized for the time being. Clutching the knife, I carve a large "K" into the round, metal casing of the one beside me, then kick my way to the surface.

I tread water and survey my surroundings. There's a van parked on the grassy verge, and a blanket laid out before it, covered in tools, monitors, and diving kit.

The scuba diver is sitting on the side. Her mask and hood are off, and she's tugging at her flippers. She spots me bobbing in the water and freezes, then raises a cautious hand and waves. I wave back.

"I won't hurt you," she calls.

Her voice is soft, earnest, and quavering. She seems more afraid than I am, which really is her own fault. In the space of a minute she's gone from encountering her first mutant human, to encountering her first mutant human *armed with a massive knife*. She may be regretting the noble gesture.

"I won't hurt you either," I croak.

My voice grates as my windpipe reopens. I swim a little upstream and shove the blade into the grass like a flag, then drift level with the woman again and climb out, taking care not to let the gown disappear.

"Here," she says, passing me a towel.

I tie it around my waist, gratefully.

"Thanks. And thanks for cutting me free."

"Don't mention it... What, er, were you doing down there?"

She tries to sound casual, like we've bumped into each other in the chocolate spread aisle of a supermarket.

"You mean how come I can breathe underwater?"

"Yeah."

"Someone did this to me."

"Who?"

"That's what I'm trying to find out."

"You look like you..."

She pauses, trying not to be impolite.

"Just escaped a mental asylum? Yeah, I can see how you'd get that vibe. The gown wasn't my choice either."

I show her the felt tip marks on my abdomen.

"Some couple tried to steal my organs. I'm *really* hoping you're not the same."

"I'm not!" she says, hastily. "Do you want some clothes? I have a dry set in the van."

She stands up with her hands raised, and beckons me in. I follow, but keeping a five meter distance. If she's about to pull a gun, I need to be close to the river. She opens the van door and rummages through stacks of tools and kit. After a moment she throws a gym bag my way.

"It might not fit, sorry, but it's better than nothing," she says, awkwardly.

I unzip the bag. The clothes are soft and inviting, and I don't trust her at all.

"You don't have to wear them, it's just an offer," she adds. "I won't try anything while you're changing. I need to change too, so, you know, whatever works."

Peeling off the wetsuit, she dries herself with a towel, smiling nervously as she wobbles between feet. She turns her back to me and takes off her sports bra, then continues to dress, shielded by the van doors. Not that she needs the privacy; we're in the middle of nowhere.

I dry myself and pull on the clothes as quickly as I can, overtaking her in the process. When she turns around to sit down on the back of the van and pull on her socks, she's startled to find me fully dressed.

"Oh, great! They fit pretty good!" she says.

Her fashion taste is criminal.

"We should go to the police," she adds, pointing at my stomach. Panic flashes across my face, and she reads it quickly. "To tell them about the organ harvesters, I mean. What they tried to do is horrible - and tot*ally* illegal."

"No police," I blurt.

"I really think-"

"I'm here illegally. The only reason those organ people caught me is because I was running from the immigration department."

I show her my arm, and the faded red outline where the drone had branded me.

"Ugh, it's barbaric they still do that. All right, no police."

"What's your deal?" I ask, gesturing to the van.

"I'm a field engineer."

"Was it your people who made the river concrete?"

"God no, that was done before my time. My generation are trying to undo the insane things our predecessors did."

"By putting turbines in the water? On behalf of all marine residents: not cool. Those things are death traps."

I blush a little. Is that how I identify now? Pond life? What the hell.

"Nothing can grow in this channel, they keep it scrubbed for the barges. The turbines actually help control the flow of the water, which is super important. I don't know if you noticed, but rivers move hella fast when you make them like gutters."

"Fun fact: I *did* notice. Right before I got sucked into your power plant down there."

"In my defense, we're making green energy on a brownfield site. Besides, if we're being really honest, you weren't exactly supposed to be down there."

"You think I *wanted* to be down there?"

"Sorry, of course not, that was dumb. What I meant was-"

"It was *exactly* what you meant! It's what all of you mean! We're not supposed to be anywhere. Not down there, not back home. As far as you're all concerned, we don't belong. In fact, it's worse than that. You don't think we *deserve* to belong. Whether it's rivers you're destroying, or islands that have stood for thousands of years, anywhere we go we're just *in your way*."

I'm shouting. My fists are balled up and I'm shaking. My head is pounding with anger. The woman looks worried.

"I'm sorry, your neck is-"

"It's freakish, yeah I know, you people did this to me. To all of us!"

I'm crying now. The pounding sensation is getting worse. The woman edges towards me with her hands outstretched.

"I didn't mean it like-"

"Take a good look at it," I yell. I turn side on and prize my gills apart. "This is the choice your people made!"

"Please stop!"

"The truth hurts, doesn't it? I will never stop. Not until the world knows what you did to our-"

"You're bleeding!" she cries.

I dab my gills. Shiny red and black liquid clings to my fingertips.

"You need a hospital," she insists.

"Tried that and look where it got me."

"The black stuff, is that the color of your blood?"

I laugh, bitterly. "It's poison. *Your* poison."

"What is it?"

"Oil."

"*Oil?* How did you...? That's highly toxic!"

"Don't I know it."

"I've got a friend who might be able to help, her lab's across town. I promise you this isn't a trick. If you've got crude in your system it could cause permanent organ damage. Please, let me help you."

I stare at the woman. She looks so earnest, so concerned. Either she's the second genuine person I've encountered in thousands of desperate miles, or she's the best liar. I can feel my head getting fuzzy from the contamination. If I want to save my people, I need to stay alive, and right now she's my only chance.

"It's a modified bacterium. We've optimized it to break down noxious hydrocarbons. Long chain, short chain, it'll chow down the lot, doesn't even need us to cut it up first. Which is just as well, because the old dispersants-"

"Thanks, Jen, but she doesn't need a chemistry lecture. She just wants the solution."

Jen, the NGO woman, marches away to rummage in a cupboard. I'm sat in the offices of Sea Sprint: Better Oceans for a Better World. I'm sincerely hoping their operations are better than their decor; the place is dank. Either it's staffed by people who don't care what color their walls are, or it's so underfunded they can't afford the paint. The latter possibility hardly fills me with confidence in their medical supplies.

The air feels thick, and my brain is foggy. I'm wearing a towel around my neck to keep my gills hidden. I loosen it a little, hoping the fresh air will remind my gills we're on land, and that my lungs need to work normally again.

On the way here, the scuba diver explained about the NGO. She used to volunteer for them during her engineering degree. Her name is Winona, by the way. "Like the actress?" I said. You should have seen the look she gave me. It was like I'd just slapped her. Apparently it's a name from her ancestral culture, meaning "first daughter". She lightened up when she remembered I'm not from her country. Apparently that gives me a pass on these things. Winona clarified that, although she herself doesn't identify as Native Continental, she reserves the right to take offence on behalf of all Native Continentals when people denigrate their culture with "casual white privilege". Which was a weird thing to say, given that, of the two of us, she's the white one. Not white as in skin color, white as in, you know, being from a rich country. If I hadn't been busy gargling a cocktail of blood and oil for the entire journey, I might have pointed out that her stance is insane.

Looking back, I think she was being ironic. Being foreign gives me an irony pass too.

Jen returns from the cupboard holding a bottle. The label is densely-written, with a bunch of symbols I don't like the look of. She frowns at me and turns to Winona.

"Remind me what your friend needs this for again? And what *is* her name?"

Winona hesitates. "Uhhh...."

"Keala," I say.

I try not to sound too liquidy as I speak. As I extend a hand to Jen, the towel around my neck slips. I'm quick to catch it but her eyes dart to my neck. Did she see?

"Nice to meet you, Keala," says Jen. "How long have you known Winona?"

"About an hour," I croak.

Winona laughs hysterically and nudges me like I've made a big joke. Jen and I stare at her, and she settles down with a defeated sigh.

"It's true."

"Cool," snaps Jen. "I'm gonna skip the fact your friend's wearing your clothes and ask why she's *bleeding from the neck?*"

"Don't be mad-" begins Winona.

"I have a right to be mad! You said you wouldn't pull any more crazy stunts!"

"What stunts?" I ask.

Jen eyes me up warily.

"It's nothing like that, Jen, I promise. She needs our help."

"By 'help' you mean 'biochemical agents'. I've not heard about any major oil spills nearby, so I can only presume there's something else going on here. This is super weird, Winona, even by your standards."

"Please, I just need you to trust me," begs Winona.

"Yeah, that panned out real well last time. How do you like our new digs by the way? They were an absolute steal. *Unlike* the legal fees from your 'maverick' activism!"

"I've apologized so many times for that-"

"And I'm sick of hearing it! I'm waiting for you to fix it."

"I'm trying! But the business is taking a while to get off the-"

By this point the two North Bloc citizens have practically forgotten I'm in the room. My head is still pounding, and my gills are still secreting oil and blood; I don't have time for their quarrels. I lift the towel from my neck and drop it at Jen's feet.

The argument halts as both women stare at me. Jen looks from the bloodied, blackened towel to my neck. Seeing my gills properly, her mouth falls open.

"What are...? How is that...?" she stammers.

"They're gills. It's weird, trust me, I know. I've had them for a few days, I'm still getting used to them. Winona found me underwater because I got caught in one of her turbine traps. Then I started leaking blood and oil, probably because I swallowed a barrel full on my way here."

"By 'here' you mean...?"

"The Northern Bloc."

"And you swallowed oil on the way? Why?"

I fixed Jen with a withering look that demands she raise her impression of me to someone who *doesn't* intentionally knock back gallons of the black stuff for fun.

"Sorry, Keala, I mean *how* did the oil get into your system?"

Better.

"I hitched a ride on a deep sea pipeline drone. Fun fact: the pipe leaks. Not great if you breathe water. So if you don't mind sharing whatever miracle cure you've got in your hands there, *Jen*, I'd really appreciate it."

"Will you tell me how you got gills, if I do?"

"Will you deny me the medicine if I say no?"

Jen shifts, embarrassed, then hands the bottle over.

"Let's be clear," she adds, "This stuff isn't really 'medicine'. It's classified as safe for marine life, but that doesn't mean it was ever intended for direct application in a concentrated dose."

I crack the lid off. It smells awful.

"How much should I take?"

"Maybe two cupfuls now, see how you get on? Keep the bottle. You can top up the dose if needed, but I think it's unlikely; the bacteria should proliferate in your system."

"Proliferate? For how long?"

"A day? They'll pass out naturally, don't worry. They won't hang around forever."

Winona gives me an encouraging nod, but something doesn't feel right. Their faces look so familiar. They're both wearing the same, warm smiles like the man with the painted nails.

I pull the bottle away from my lips and hold it out to Jen.

"You drink first."

Jen looks at me, baffled.

"It's OK," says Winona, intervening. "I'll do it."

She pours a capful and drinks.

"Disgusting, but otherwise harmless," she says, wincing.

I take the bottle back from her. It really does smell awful. Holding my breath, I take a swig. Here's to not getting brain damage.

Two hours later, we're still sat in Jen's office. It turns out she only has one proper colleague, and he's away on a field visit, so the place is ours. The oil-eating bacteria have worked with extreme efficiency. The bleeding has stopped, and my gills are no longer seeping black tears, both of which I find encouraging. Jen's been supplying me with a steady flow of water to cleanse my system of by-products.

With the nausea subsiding, my appetite has returned with a vengeance. I devoured the cereal bars in Jen's drawer, then let it drop that I haven't eaten hot food in days. Both women looked appalled at this news, and clearly felt guilty for not thinking to ask sooner. Winona ordered three large pizzas, two of which I demolished.

As I sit, stuffed like a pig, guilt creeps in. Here I am, feasting, while my kin starve on an island no one even knows the name of.

More confident that neither of these two women are going to harvest my organs, I tell them of my journey and they listen, open-mouthed.

"We have to help your people!" insists Winona.

Jen nods emphatically. "Where do you think the island is?"

We move over to her computer. I had thought everyone in rich countries uses AR screens, but apparently some people are still on the old stuff. Jen's homepage opens on the news channel and my heart freezes.

"Wait! Go back to that page!" I cry.

Breaking News, reads the banner.

A studio reporter is standing beside a video screen, commenting on footage that's making headline news across the nation. I can't believe what I'm seeing. A face I know so well. One I thought I would never see again.

Malo is alive.

CHAPTER THIRTY-SIX

LUKE

It's nighttime. I'm on the street with fish man and we're running for it. The guy I've freed is young, beautiful, and topless. By contrast, I'm old, fat, and ugly, and I look like his customer. I take off my juice-stained jacket and hand it over.

"Put this on, you look like a sex worker."

"What?"

"We need to look inconspicuous."

"Easy for you to say, you don't have gills and a respirator."

"Trust me, kid, that ain't the problem right now. The thing that's gonna turn heads is a sweaty four running from a topless nine."

"Nine?"

"You got small ears."

"Weird thing to say."

"I think this truth thing's still messing with my brain."

"What 'truth thing'?"

"They dosed me with an electromagnetic halo to suppress my inhibitions. It was a prototype though and I'm having delayed onset. Has anyone ever said you have the most amazing eyes?"

"Yes, but none of them were men."

"Sounds like you come from a very repressed culture."

He shoves me against a wall and presses his face inches from mine. His eyes are goggling, like he's ready to pull my head off.

"You know *nothing* about my culture. If you did, you would show more respect."

"Ugh, paging Captain Sensitive, quick reminder that I just saved your ass."

He steps back like he's seen a ghost.

"Who told you I was a Captain?"

His eyes are wrought with worry. Nope - not worry - *anger*. Yup, definitely anger.

"Are you part of it?"

"Buddy, chill, I have no idea what you're talking about."

"Don't lie to me!"

He shoves me against the wall again.

"Firstly, ouch. Secondly, kid, even if I wanted to, I'm biologically incapable of lying right now. Seriously, ask me anything."

"Who are you and how do you know about me?"

"I'm Luke, I'm a journalist, and I infiltrated the lab to find the truth. Apparently that truth is you. I want to help you, and hold this government to account."

"The government? They're behind all this?"

"They're supporting the lab for sure."

"Not just the lab, I mean what happened to my people. The rafts, the evacuation, the trap."

"I have zero idea what you're talking about, kid, but it sounds messed up. We need to get somewhere private, where we can't be overheard by the trillions of devices around us."

"You know somewhere we can hide?"

"I really want ice cream right now."

"What?"

"Sorry, yes, hiding place. Hundred percent. Let's go. Do you have any money by the way?"

He glares at me.

"Plan B then: can you tell a lie?"

Frowning warily, he nods.

"Great, I'm hailing a cab and you're gonna say we'll pay cash. If I start yapping, distract me, ask which flavor I want. FYI, it's cinnamon. *Dammit.* You'll have to act surprised when I reveal that later. Oh, one last question. Are you a good runner?"

We're outside the safe house, panting, having finally shaken off the taxi driver. Apparently all of them give chase in this godforsaken town. The kid's wincing as he fidgets with the respirator on his jaw.

"Your neck thing sounds like a kettle."

He scowls at me as I lead the way into the lobby, where a concierge bot greets us.

Ah, Mr. Remini, welcome. It's wonderful to see you again.

"It's been a while, dear Concierge."

It has been precisely one hundred and sixteen days and nine hours since your last visit.

I lean into the kid's shoulder and whisper, badly. "Ignore the robot. It can be real anally retentive about stuff like that. I think they skimped on its humor algorithm."

Would Sir like to hear a joke? I am programmed with over eight thousand quips and witticisms.

"Do you have any of the old racist ones?"

Yes. Would you like to hear one?

"No! Why would they program that in you?"

I concur, Sir, it is a most inappropriate setting.

"Are you just saying that because you're programmed to side with your guests?"

Yes.

"So you are racist?"

No.

"You just have lots of racist material in your database?"

Yes.

"I think that makes you kinda racist."

The robot's eyes glaze as it buffers for a moment, before refocusing.

Aha. I believe Sir is deliberately oversimplifying my faculties for personal amusement. If Sir enjoys hyperbole, perhaps you would like to hear the one about the astronaut who couldn't moonwalk?

"Is it funny?"

The robot's eyes glaze again.

A fraction of users have enjoyed this joke.

"How many?"

Nine.

"People?"

Percent.

"How many people is that?"

One.

"Is that one person you, Concierge?"

It is, Sir.

"Then I'll pass. Can we get the key to our apartment, please?"

At once, Sir. May I ask the purpose of your visit today? Business or pleasure?

I give fish boy a withering look. "I *told* you to put the jacket on. Even the robot thinks you're on the clock."

He scowls and puts my stinking blazer on.

Sir? presses the robot.

"Oh, business. I'm an undercover fugitive, and he's a mutant on the run."

The robot's eyes glaze again, then it lets out a mechanical laugh.

Excellent humor Sir. You are truly first rate.

"Thanks, Concierge. Is anyone else in our suite at the moment?"

Ms. Williams checked in ten minutes ago.

"Lanelle?"

Indeed.

"She knew we were coming?"

Yes.

"Did she say what *her* reason for coming was?"

The robot's eyes twinkle. *Pleasure.*

I stare at it in amazement for a second, then the robot lets out another mechanical laugh.

A joke, for Sir.

"Very good, Concierge."

The humor derives from the fact Ms. Williams is substantially more attractive and successful than you.

"Hey, no need to spell it out, jeez."

I have three point eight additional jokes pertaining to your sexual prowess. Would you like to hear them?

"No, but I can put you in touch with my ex-wife, I'm sure she'd lap it up. We gotta go - thanks for the key."

See you later, Alligator Sir.

"In a while, you overgrown abacus."

I tap the card against the door but it stays shut; Lanelle's turned on the security filter. A screen pops up showing her face inside the apartment.

"Boss! I'm so pleased to see you. On the way up, I really wasn't, because of how you stiffed me over the whole money thing, and for a while I definitely wished you were dead. Well not dead just mildly disfigured, but now I'm delighted you've ridden to our rescue! I realize what a great friend and colleague you have always been, barring the past seven days."

"That's a little on the nose, Luke, even for you."

"My brain got fried by a truth device. I'll explain inside."

The door buzzes open and Lanelle yanks me into the apartment. The curtains are drawn and we're lit by a bedside lamp.

"Ooh la la! The robot *wasn't* kidding. Pleasure it is! We're filming this, right? Who wants to go first? There are three of us, so maybe one person does comments and requests on the live stream, and we take turns tapping out?"

Lanelle fixes me with a withering look. "If you need to 'tap out' of sex, you're doing it wrong."

"Speak for yourself."

"Get a therapist, Luke, divorce isolation is clearly driving you nuts."

"Pff, please. I am *not* isolated. I made a friend on the way here."

"The concierge robot?"

"Maybe."

"It's a conversational vending machine, not a friend."

"He's gonna be really hurt you said that. Ooh, maybe

we should get him up here too? Would really spice up the video."

"No one is making a porno!"

"Statistically, *somewhere* in the world right now-"

"Enough. What's that smell?"

"Orange juice and sweat. The finest perfume these men can buy. If you want the finest perfume a *robot* can buy, then I must introduce you to my uncle Rami sometime. He set up the first 'robo aroma' store in Abu Dhabi. 'Sensuous senses for the semi-sentient.' Pretty good, huh? I came up with that. Did you know that 'step mom' was the most popular fragrance in the under 25 market? Raises some questions, eh?"

Lanelle points to fish guy.

"Who's this?" If you say 'he's here for the porno' so help me God I will hurt you."

"We haven't done names yet. We were kinda busy escaping the insane genetic engineering lab you sent me to infiltrate. They're legit sociopaths by the way, so thanks for that. This dude's the mystery package I mentioned at dinner."

Lanelle eyes up my ward like he's a schoolboy in trouble.

"What's your name?"

"Malo."

"Where are you from?"

"Nowhere."

"Everyone's from somewhere."

"My country has been erased by the Pacific."

"Where was your home?"

"Makamesia."

Lanelle's eyes narrow. "What the hell were you doing in a laboratory in Park Morpre?"

I chip in at this point. I can see he's getting riled by her tone. She has that effect on people.

"Lanelle, easy with the grand inquisitor act. This guy's a victim, not a suspect."

She used to be a prosecuting attorney. It makes her a phenomenal commissioning editor, but a lousy agony aunt. She purses her lips and paces the room.

"Sit," she says to Malo.

He sits, looking more on trial than before. I take a seat on the bed to make things less weird. The apartment was never properly furnished, so he's got the only chair, and it's a cheap studio one. My former editor blew the paper's budget finding a building with robo concierge. No regrets there though, BFFs for life.

Malo seems groggy. Lanelle passes him some water and an energy bar.

"Are you the FBI?" says Malo, chewing.

"We're journalists. We've been investigating the lab you were held in, looking for evidence of illegal activity. Can you tell us how you got there? And what they did to you? Your testimony could help us bring them down."

"How can I trust you?"

"Because I saved your life, kid," I pipe up, from the bed.

Malo stands abruptly and looms over me. I hadn't appreciated how tall he was until now. I take it back, he's a solid ten.

"Stop calling me 'kid'. I am a chief-in-waiting, a leader of my people. You will speak to me with more respect. I am sick of your kind treating me like filth."

I hold my hands up in surrender.

"No more nicknames, gotcha. For the record, ki-... *Malo*, you could definitely take me in a fight. You've got broad shoulders and you're obviously buff ting. Though if you do come for me, first thing I'll do is rip those things off your chin. I think that'll tip the scales in my favor. Ugh, dammit. Rule one of fighting dirty: never announce your strategy. OK, pretend I didn't say that. I mean, obviously I *did*, and it's one hundred percent true, but you need to forget it. If we wrestle later, act surprised when I tear your breathing blocks off. Damn that halo."

"What *are* those things on your chin?" says Lanelle, peering closer at Malo.

"A device the lab was trialing to stabilize my breathing on land."

"As opposed to...?"

"Underwater."

"You can breathe underwater?" she says, raising an eyebrow.

Malo twists one of the blocks off, revealing his gills.

"Good Lord! They did this to you in the lab?"

"No. It happened when my people were evacuated."

"Wait, there are *more* of you like this?"

Malo frowns at her, baffled. "Of course. They poisoned us all. How do you not know this?"

Lanelle grabs her phone and starts tapping.

"Boss, what are you doing? If you make that call we're busted. They'll get a lock on your position right away."

"I'm calling my contact at the FBI. This is bigger than I ever imagined. They're doing wide scale genetic engineering on live human subjects here *and* overseas. This is major."

"Stop! We don't know that we can trust them!"

"The FBI? I've known this person for years, Luke, they're solid."

"Their superiors might not be. Whoever's behind this operation has ties to the heart of government. We can't risk them quashing the story, our only option is to go public," I insist.

"We only get one shot at breaking this story. If we get it wrong-"

"Wrong is better than waiting until we're silenced. Boss, people need to know about this *now*. The lab will be looking for us and they're extremely well connected in the security world. They could already be on their way here."

Lanelle curses and lowers her phone.

"Malo, move the chair in front of the curtains. Luke, point the lamp at his face. We're doing one take then I'm pushing it across our channel and copying in every free journalist left in the country. You guys better be ready for this because we're about to throw a brick at a hornet's nest."

Malo takes a seat on the chair, placing his hands on his knees. He doesn't look nervous, he looks angry but composed. I hover beside him and shine the light so there are no shadows on his face, and his gills are plainly illuminated for the world to see. Lanelle raises the camera before him.

"OK, Malo of Makamesia. I need you to tell us everything, from the beginning."

CHAPTER THIRTY-SEVEN

My heart stops. He's there, on screen. The room doesn't look military, but it's so nondescript he could be anywhere. We watch his testimony in silence. Someone behind the camera is asking him questions. The video freezes and annotations appear on screen. The network presenter talks through the image of Malo's gills. An identical image of Malo appears beside the frozen video, but this one shows him with normal skin.

"This footage sent to us by the White House shows the interviewee in fine health, supporting the Government's claim that the footage is indeed a hoax."

For a moment, I think I've misheard her.

The screen changes to a map of the Pacific, and highlights several island chains.

"As for his 'testimony' that Makamesia's evacuation was a trap, these are clearly the fantasies of a mentally ill man. Footage just received from the international team leading the resettlement shows islanders settling into life on their new home island of Uku, which was generously donated by the international community."

The news feed cuts to footage I could never have prepared for.

My parents.

"We're settling in really well, the voyage was straightforward, and it's been amazing arriving into a space that's so familiar. It's like home - only, everything's brand new. Thank you, world."

Thank you world? Mum was never simpering or banal, she was a woman of insight.

I feel sick. It's all starting to make sense. The "journalists" who came to interview our island before we left, they weren't reporters at all. They were government agents harvesting data; gathering video footage of our movements and voices, so that they could pump out deep fakes at the drop of a hat, should anyone discover the truth of the mission.

I shake my head in disbelief. Tears of rage are forming in my eyes. "*Liars.*"

"You know them?" asks Winona.

"They're my parents."

"What's the matter with th-?"

"They're dead."

I relay my story to the two women, corroborating all that Malo said on the News, and filling in the details he hadn't witnessed. It's easier for Winona to believe me right away; she's already seen me breathing underwater. But I can see Jen is battling some inner skepticism; some part of her brain is yearning to dismiss me, craving her government's simple lies.

I take Jen's hands and press them to the folds of flesh

under my jaw. Her last semblance of doubt vanishes for good.

"What can we do?" she says, earnestly.

"My people need help."

I point to the map of the Pacific Ocean on the office wall. "The island we got shipwrecked on is somewhere around here."

"That's a big area, Keala," says Jen, nervously.

"My nation had two hundred islands to evacuate. That meant hundreds of rafts, all with a common destination. I promise you, if you search in this area, you will find people."

"It's been several days, if the other rafts sunk in open waters like your parents'..."

"Others must have survived, I'm sure of it. They could have deliberately run aground like Malo? Besides, even if the others rafts sunk, the people on board may still have lived. The mutation didn't work on my parents' raft, but maybe they were given a different dose. If it worked on others, they'll be out there right now, alone in the ocean, with no way of contacting anyone. We *have* to look for them."

Jen pulls up a live satellite feed of the area I had pointed to. The cyclone is covering almost half of it, with a fifty percent chance it will roll through the rest.

"It's too dangerous for ships to search in that area. We're better off using satellites."

"To find them among all that?" I cry.

"One satellite, many eyes," says Jen, tapping away.

She opens a forum on her screen.

"Is that...?" says Winona.

"Ugh, yes, it's dark web, whatever. Don't rat me out to teacher," says Jen.

"After all the grief you gave me for the protest!" says Winona.

"This is different. I only use this to keep our chats private."

"Is the whole group on here? Wow, if I wasn't feeling left out before, I sure am now," says Winona. "Just to be clear, I *was* feeling left out before."

"Yeah, I got that," says Jen, tapping away. "OK, I'm sharing the coordinates with the group. They'll put it out across their international networks too. I reckon we can get at least a hundred sets of incognito eyes searching the area using the geo sat ultra-res feeds. I'll patch in my AI to calculate a roster based on everyone's time zones. We'll get a round-the-clock search going from people's apartments. The government won't even know we're looking."

Jen turns around proudly, with more than a hint of "ta-daaaah" about her. I give her a weak smile, but for all my optimism that people are looking, I can't take my eyes off the giant cyclone swirling across the screen.

Jen's still looking at me. Winona too.

"What?"

I realize I misread Jen's face. She wasn't asking for accolade, she was setting the stage.

"Oh no, you can't be serious," I say, backing away.

Jen sets up a webcam on top of her screen. "It's fine if you don't want to speak, but it would make a-"

"I'm not afraid of speaking, I'm worried about the government finding me and throwing me in a lab!"

Winona places a hand on my arm. "If they're gonna help, they need to see you first."

"Why would they believe a video of me over a video of Malo in the news?"

"Because this one's coming from *me*," says Jen.

OK, *now* she's got a "ta-dah" face on.

"These people trust me, Keala. If I tell them I've met you, they'll believe me. But I have to show them your gills. It's the easiest way to prove the government's counter footage of your friend was fake."

"Fine. You can show my gills, but keep the rest of my face out of shot."

The recording is uncomfortable. Jen touches my gills to show they're real. She doesn't mean to jab them, but she does, regularly, and it's damned painful. I'm having an out-of-body experience, standing there, dumb, while a stranger points to parts of my body and narrates the oddities to a video audience.

I say a few words. All of them sound stupid to me, like I'm a bumbling child, a charity case, going with a begging bowl to digital strangers, relying on the very same countries that lit the fuse on our demise. I feel numb.

"You did great," says Winona, stroking my arm.

"What happens when they find something?" I say.

Jen looks to Winona uncertainly.

"Well, uh, usually in these situations the first step is to corroborate the finding. Other searchers review the flagged footage and verify-"

"No, I mean after that. Let's say twelve hours from now, they've found my people, and it's beyond doubt. How do we rescue them?"

"Twelve hours is ambitious," says Jen.

"We need a deployment plan," I say, firmly.

"The truth is... we don't know how the rescue will work," says Winona, awkwardly. "It's complicated. The Government is trying to cover the whole thing up, which means we can't just put out a regular distress call to ships in the area and expect them to respond. We need to convince them it's real, or charter a rescue mission from scratch, which needs a bunch of resources we don't have."

I listen carefully and mull over her words.

"What you're saying is... the only way we can incite a meaningful rescue mission is by disproving the Government's lies?"

"I guess, yeah," says Winona.

"Then that's what I'll do."

"How?"

"The same way I convinced both of you. I will go to the President in person, in front of the cameras, and prove I am real; that *we* are real, and that we *cannot* be ignored. The government might be able to deny a single video, but they can't cover up something if it happens in front of the world's media. Not in this country, at least."

"I don't want to pick holes in your plan but... how are you going to meet the President?"

"Holy crap, she might just be able to do it," says Jen, piping up. "He's holding a re-election rally tomorrow, but it's in San Dellsza." says Jen.

"That's six hundred miles. We'd have to leave right now," says Winona.

The News feed in the background leaves the fake footage of my community arriving at their new homes, and returns to a loop of Malo's video. A photo of a middle-aged woman appears beside him, above a Newspaper logo.

"In a statement published on the paper's website," continues the presenter, "Commissioning Editor Lanelle Williams writes: 'Malo has not been seen in public since his whistleblowing, and we fear for his safety after the FBI stormed our press conference this morning. The dossiers we've uncovered show this goes to the heart of government and further."

I watch in astonishment as they cut to footage of a news conference. The same women who was pictured beside the newspaper statement, Lanelle, is on a podium, talking to a gathering of reporters. Armed officers burst into the room and order everyone onto the ground. The camera pans around. Journalists are being beaten and tased. The camera falls to the floor. A hand flops down in front of the lens, twitching. The feed blacks out.

I stare at the screen, trembling with anger.

"Take me to the President."

CHAPTER THIRTY-EIGHT

LUKE

I'm standing in the green room, giving Malo a crash course on interview technique. It's his first time giving a press conference, and the last thing we need is for him to be a total rabbit in the headlights. As it happens, he's got the confidence of a natural leader, and the humility of someone with serious amends to make. He's gonna be a star.

"What?" says Malo.

"I'm just saying, once this is all over, you could totally have your own reality series. People will go mad for it. We could do a whole underwater dating thing, set it in a pool with a bar. It's all coming to me. Picture this, you're in a tuxedo, you get out of a swag car, and walk down a set of steps into a pool. There's a dining table at the bottom with a rose, and a hot human girl with a scuba kit ready to meet you. Not that you're not human, of course. You're super human. And *super* eligible. How about this for a working title: *The Aquachelor?*"

Malo looks at me like *I'm* the one who's sprouted gills.

"I said it was a work in progress, Jeez. All right, mull it over."

"I don't want a stupid TV show, I want a better future for my people."

"Oh my god, I *love* it. We can totally use that in the trailer."

"Are you for real? I'm about to go out and tell the world of an atrocity *your* country has committed, and you're already trying to make a spin-off?"

"Er, *duh*. Yesterday I got beaten up by two gangs, a robotic glove, and nearly lasered to death. I'm done with investigative work. I think I've earned the right to plan a retirement based on the fruits of my labor."

"You're a piece of work," says Malo.

"Relax, kid, I'm yanking your chain. Mainly to distract me from my own nerves. No pressure, but this *needs* to work."

"I'm aware of that."

"It's time. You got this."

Out front I hear Lanelle addressing the crowd. She thanks them for coming and asks them to report honestly on everything they're about to witness.

Malo and I embrace in a firm "good luck" hug. We're tight now, he and I. I saved his life, he wore my sweat orange. Stuff like that brings you close. He gives me a solemn nod, and I escort him to the doorway.

The main hotel conference room is packed. We've invited every reporter we know. Lanelle and I have decades of journalism between us, so our network's sizable. It's rare that journalists tip *other* journalists off about a story, let alone hold their own press conference. But today we need our rivals. We've promised them the biggest, most explosive story of the decade. In the emails, we said 9 AM start. In our separate, encrypted chats, however, we've told them 7.30. We know the feds will be monitoring us, tipped-off by the lab, and we need to stay ahead.

Malo enters the conference room and a hush falls across the crowd. Fifty reporters fill the seats, while two dozen more are packed in standing at the back and sides. Above them all floats a small armada of press drones, piloted by journalists from the rest of the country and abroad.

Malo steps up to the podium. A video relay is projecting a giant version of him onto a screen immediately behind the stage. Slowly, and dramatically, he removes his scarf. A gasp sweeps the conference room as people see his gills. He leans towards the microphone.

Before he can speak, the rear doors burst open.

"FBI! Everybody down on the ground!"

Dozens of bomber jackets storm in, armed with batons and stun guns. They cleave their way through the standing journalists. Seats churn as the others try to escape the mayhem.

Notification sounds ring out across the room. Malo shouts at the top of his lungs. "Check your devices! They contain the truth!"

Every journalist we know has just received a copy of all the material we gathered on the lab's operations. From the evidence Lanelle's team found on Drake's tablet, to the footage from my button camera, to the testimonial and close up of Malo himself. Plus all the dirt Chang uncovered when he hacked their mainframe. It's out there. We did it.

Two agents tackle Malo to the ground. Another pair take me and Lanelle down. Cuffs are being thrown around our wrists.

Malo's face falls off.

At this point I can't help but laugh.

The officer kneeling on me seems confused. Other agents howl in frustration as they realize what's happening.

Malo's face has been replaced by someone completely different. A person I've only met once before, and who owes me half a beer. Lying on the stage across from me, where Malo's face once was, is Val; the woman Chang had sent to meet me in the bar days ago. She had graciously worn Chang's face for the meeting, and had kindly volunteered to wear Malo's avatar today. Well, "volunteered" in exchange for money. Chang hired her and two others. I blow her a kiss. She gives me a wink, then my feed vanishes.

The FBI weep as their blunder is broadcast live. Malo's full video testimony is dominating social media, while our dossier is hitting front pages worldwide.

Cards.

Meet table.

The extent of the genetic engineering program goes further than we ever imagined possible. I look forward to the White House trying to suppress *this*.

Oh, I should clarify, the bit about the FBI agents weeping? Yeah that's a smidge of poetic license on my part. My avatar feed cut out so I didn't actually see that bit. But I presume it's what happened. Those nerds *live* for the job. I can only assume they would bawl their eyes out in this sort of situation.

No doubt, you're wondering where the hell Malo, Lanelle and I *actually* are right now? I wish I could tell you, really I do. But I wouldn't want to spoil the feds' next surprise. Let's just say we're going for broke. That's right, it's road trip time.

CHAPTER THIRTY-NINE

KEALA

I'm on my knees, with my head fully submerged in a basin of cold water. The water comes up to my ears, and the faucet's running at a constant rate. I can't open my mouth, or my nose.

It's bliss.

I mean that in relative terms, of course. The past few days have dramatically lowered my benchmark for happiness. If I could wind back time and avoid being mutated altogether, believe me, I would. But for the first time in days I can truly *breathe*. I don't count the river incident, on account of nearly getting my chest compressed to a peanut by that turbine, and having a barrel of crude floating around my system. Right now is different. I'm not running anywhere, or swimming for my life. I'm static, and breathing deeply through what has become my dominant respiratory system. My head feels clear at last.

My knees are sore, but you can't have it all.

My stomach rumbles. Winona should be back any minute with breakfast. I don't know what I'd do without her. She drove us almost six hundred miles yesterday, then paid for us to sleep over in this motel. She kept apologizing, saying something about it not being the *Bellagio*, but truthfully, I couldn't fault it. We each had a bed, the motel didn't break apart in the night, and no one drowned. In my books, that's a five star stay.

I discovered this little basin-breathing system last night at Winona's suggestion. I was feeling fit to black out by the end of the drive here; my windpipe had been shutting down more with each hour that passed. There's no bathtub here, but Winona got me to the basin. She filled it and quickly had my gills submerged. With the plug left open, and the tap always running at max, the pool of water was being continually refreshed, while staying full.

Half an hour of water breathing was enough to soothe my system last night. It cooled me and lowered my heart rate, so that my regular lungs could get me through to morning.

Of course, I woke up with a splitting headache, so it was straight back into the sink for me, while Winona headed out in search of bagels.

The door opens somewhere behind me. My stomach rumbles again, but I keep my head submerged. I want a few precious more minutes of breathing. It's doubtful I'll be able to do this again until after the Presidential rally, and yes, I'm aware today could go badly.

Two firm hands grab my shoulders. I'm being hauled out of the water. I land on the floor, spluttering, as my windpipe rattles half-open. A woman's looming over me looking deeply concerned.

"Senorita, are you OK? You drowning!"

I wipe my eyes clean and look at her properly. She's around fifty, dressed in a house keeping uniform, with a cleaning trolley parked behind her.

"I'm fine, I was just resting," I mutter.

Her face shifts from concern to horror. She's seen my gills.

The woman screams and stumbles backwards. "Diablo! Dios me protege!"

"It's OK, please be quiet," I beg.

I reach out for her but she recoils, terrified.

A voice calls from the doorway.

"What's going on?"

Winona's back, clutching a food bag and two drinks. The house keeper runs for the door. She shoves Winona away and races for the main reception, wailing in rapid Spanish.

"We need to get out of here before she wakes the entire city," says Winona.

She hauls me off the ground, and we hurry for the van. Within seconds, we're gone.

Winona pulls over. We're miles away from the motel, and there's still at least an hour's drive to go, but my breathing's already falling to pieces. I'm burning up, too. We've got the air con on max, yet I feel like I'm in an oven.

She stops on the hard shoulder, staring at me as if I'm dying, which seems like an overreaction until I see my reflection. Maybe I *am* dying.

"Don't move," she says.

I try to say something witty back, but I can't get the words out.

Winona climbs between our seats, into the back of the van, and rummages.

I watch cars speeding past on the highway. The

majority are sleek and autonomous, but there are occasional others like ours. Winona calls them "rusty relics"; human-piloted automobiles, with all the scratches and dents to prove it. I don't think she drives it because she's the romantic type. Though that didn't stop her nicknaming the van "Romita".

Romita the rusty relic.

I murmur something incoherent. I'm feeling drowsy.

"Hey, don't fall asleep!"

Winona's slapping my cheeks. My eyelids flutter open as she straps something to my neck. I hear some clicks, and equipment being adjusted, then a gargling sound.

My eyes flick open properly.

I can breathe.

"What did you do?" I ask, astonished.

Winona beams at me, proudly.

"While you were sleeping I reverse-engineered my scuba kit as a water exchanger. It's rudimentary, but better than nothing."

I feel the suction cups hugging my jawline. I inspect them in the mirror. They're not exactly subtle. I follow the cables down to a gallon-sized water bottle behind my seat, which is bubbling gently with each breath I take.

"You'll need this too," says Winona.

She wraps a thin shawl around my neck so that it covers my jawline. As I draw deep breaths of the water, feeling my faculties swiftly returning, a dreadful realization sweeps over me.

"Winona, I don't think I can survive on land anymore."

It terrifies me just saying it. My body has crossed some invisible line of no return, and now I'm more vulnerable than ever. Winona looks concerned.

"Look, we don't have to do this. There might be other ways we can raise your case?"

I shake my head. "Malo tried that and look what they did to him. No, it has to be this way. I have to get before the President. Only by seeing us together will people believe the truth."

A siren approaches. A police drone appears in front of the van with its lights flashing. A traffic officer's weary face peers at us from the display screen. Her eyelids are droopy and surrounded by lines, and her lips sag in a permanent downturn.

"Good morning, Ma'am. This lane is for emergency break downs only. Our scans show your vehicle is operational, which means you're illegally parked on this freeway. I am obliged to record this offence against your driving record. The points will be automatically added to your license with immediate effect."

The officer's brow furrows.

"Ma'am, I need you to step out of the vehicle."

"Why is that, Officer?" says Winona, calmly.

"You've exceeded the maximum number of points you can carry. Your license is being suspended."

"Woah, hold up, Officer, I have extenuating circumstances. My friend here was taken sick, I was tending to her is all. Now she's better, we'll be on our way."

"Mm-hmm. So why didn't you or your friend file a medical ticket?"

"We were about to, then you found us."

The drone descends closer. The officer piloting it approaches my window, scrutinizing me.

"What's with the cables?"

"They're for her medication."

"Do you have a prescription I can see?"

"It's an herbal remedy."

"Mm-hmm. Get out, both of you."

"She *can't*, I told you already Officer, she's sick."

"Non-compliance recorded. I'm seeking authorization to conduct a search of your persons and your vehicular contents. Please prepare to lower the windows. Any attempt to interfere with this craft during the procedure carries a minimum six month jail term. Do you understand these terms?"

"I respectfully decline to comment until your authorization is confirmed, Officer."

A juggernaut rushes past. Its slipstream drags the drone off course momentarily. I use the moment to pull the shawl higher and bury my neck further in it. When the officer returns, she eyes me up with deep suspicion. She continues to stare at me as she talks to a superior colleague off-screen.

"Yeah, I got a four-two-two, subject refusing voluntary search. Suspected narcotics on board. Vehicle is a manual so I'm unable to quarantine, suggest tox screens for passenger and driver and full interior scan."

A satisfied glint flashes across the Officer's face. She focuses on Winona.

"Search authorized. Step out of the vehicle and place your hands on the hood."

"I've already told you, she's sick, *she can't do that*," fumes Winona.

"Citizen, you have five seconds to comply, or force will be used."

A roaring noise approaches from the distance. It's growing louder by the second.

A car rockets past at such speed the whole van shakes in its wake.

"God dammit! You two stay here, this isn't over!" snaps the officer.

She gives me a filthy look then vanishes through the window and speeds after the car.

Winona waits a few seconds, then starts the engine.

"What are you doing?"

"Getting us out of here before that clown comes back."

"Won't they be able to track your plates?"

"Eventually. But it won't be top of their list today, trust me. We need to get to that rally fast otherwise we'll get caught up in a super long security line. Oh crap, our battery's nearly fried. That damned motel - 'free charging' my ass! Sit tight, we're gonna try slipstream off a juggernaut to the next station. Here's hoping there's no sudden braking."

CHAPTER FORTY

We're waiting in line outside the basketball stadium. No one's tried to samurai-kick-box-tase my ass in nearly twenty-four hours, and it's making me uneasy. The team mascot is dancing for the President's supporters. It's a giant sting ray made of fur. I'm praying it sucker punches me; I'm due an ass-kicking and I want it out the way. Rip the band aid.

Everyone around us is giddy with excitement. They can't wait for their elected leader to chopper in and pump them with happy lies and scapegoat rhetoric, then jet off before anyone can actually scratch beneath the surface.

Not today, he won't. I'm here with Malo, mutant-in-chief, and we're gonna ruffle some feathers.

For this to work, a *lot* of things have to go right. We're counting on Lanelle doing her bit behind the scenes, galvanizing the state's press core once again, but in full secrecy this time. When the President arrives, he'll think he's soaring in the polls, as coverage of the rally doubles. He has no idea what's coming his way.

When we get inside, we'll have front row tickets, which

means we'll need to blend in with President Blowhard's brashest supporters. I've got two flags to wave, and Malo's clutching a massive banner. More importantly, we're both dressed head to toe in campaign stash. That said, my top's about four sizes too small. My pot belly's stretching the President's toothy portrait to terrifying new proportions.

The line shuffles forwards.

"You couldn't get me a better fitting shirt?" I mutter.

Chang pops up on my augmented overlay.

"What was that, Luke? It sound awfully like beggar trying be chooser."

I hold my tongue. He's right. I'm still amazed he's helping us at all, given the colossal amount of money I still owe him.

"Remember, only reason I helping is because you owe me colossal money."

Ah. That solves that one.

"What about your family overseas?" I mutter.

"Them too. It fifty-fifty. Heart and head."

"I didn't have you down as the sentimental type, Chang."

Malo's looking at me weirdly. He obviously doesn't have an AR lens fitted, so I'm the only one who can see Chang sitting in a reclining desk chair, puffing on a cigar. The line shuffles forwards again. We're only three places from the front now and I'm getting nervous. The security bots at Presidential rallies are what you might call *diligent*. Especially when it comes to breaking ribs. I swear they ramp it up for street cred.

It works.

"You sure they're on?" I whisper.

"Yes, it make real improvement," replies Chang.

I fidget anxiously with my baseball cap.

"Don't move it! You *want* them see you for real?"

I curse under my breath. When I get nervous, I sweep my hands across my head. It's a habit I should have stopped when my hair left, but for whatever reason it stuck. I never wear caps, and this sudden barrier is putting my tic into hyper-drive.

"Do *not* touch it again, you hearing me?"

"Got it."

"You might as well plant giant sign above your head say 'hey officers, I here!'"

"I said *I got it*, Chang."

I mutter this a little too loudly. The couple in front glance around uneasily. I give them a huge smile and cheer "Blowhard for President!" then waggle my flags until they shuffle forwards.

Remind me to take a shower when this is done.

Here's the thing about our outfits. Obviously Chang supplied them. Malo and I are broke fugitives, which doesn't really lend itself to a shopping spree. Chang's a criminal gang leader with all kinds of levers at his fingertips, and a weird amount of skin in the game. He got us this stash and front row tickets at extremely short notice. I can only presume that somewhere in the city, there are two Blowhard supporters tied up naked in their kitchens, wondering what kind of burglar is *that* politically motivated?

Our jingoistic outfits provide camouflage, but the baseball caps are the deal-breaker. Chang fitted the peaks with face blockers. They project infra-red light across your face, which is invisible to the human eye, but *very* visible to robots. It means that as we approach this security bot, it's going to scan our faces automatically, and it will detect the infra-red pattern being beamed onto our skin. Most ID systems only use the face; they don't hold a full body profile on file. Which means I could rock up with two chins and a stolen tank top, and the robot won't blink an eye. It'll see a skinny factory worker's face and wave me through.

Or at least, that was the idea. Ah crap.

"Chang, a supervisor's coming over," I whisper.

"What?"

"A human supervisor. She's coming to our lane."

"So?"

"These hats can only fool robots, we're not geared up to get past a human check! She's comparing the robot's scans against people's *actual* faces, she's gonna see the disparity between my fat grill and the infrared projection! What are we gonna do?"

The line moves forward. As we cross the stadium threshold, Chang vanishes from my overlay.

"Chang! Chang, come back!" I hiss.

The couple ahead give me another wary look, then get called forward by the robot. An automated message plays out overhead.

Please have your passes ready and remove any glasses or face coverings before security.

Malo's hand twitches for his giant sunglasses but I intervene. His mug was headline news yesterday, we can't risk him being recognized in public.

"Take them off for the robot only, then straight back on," I whisper.

Malo nods. He scratches at the giant fabric flag which is draped dramatically around his neck, hiding his gills.

Irregularity detected. Supervision required.

The robot's tone is sharp and uncompromising. Malo goes rigid beside me. My stomach is in my mouth.

The couple before us are ushered away by the human

supervisor. They protest, vehemently, but the woman politely orders them into a side room for questioning. I grab Malo's arm, and I'm about to tell him we need to bail A-SAP, when the robot calls us forwards.

Next. Present passes. Remove your glasses. Eyes forward.

Malo looks at me nervously, then removes the glasses from his face.

State the purpose of your visit.

"Er, to see the President," says Malo.

Incorrect. You have two chances remaining.

Every second we're here is another chance for a passing supervisor to discover our digital masks.

I intervene. "What's going on here? We've shown you our passes, let us in, dammit."

Rudeness will get you nowhere. What's magic word?

"Are you for real?"

Magic word?

"Please?" I hiss.

Incorrect. Correct answer is: Chang.

The robot's facial display vanishes and Chang's face appears in its place. For the first time, Malo can see him too.

"*This* is your guy?" he says, incredulously.

No. He my guy, corrects Chang.

"What the hell are you doing in that thing?" I hiss.

They blocking all external avatars inside building. I hack security bot. Now I in with you.

"Does that mean our caps aren't working either?" says Malo.

They work on closed loop, they fine. All processing take place in rim of cap, so you not need cloud connection. Hey, you like my moves?

The security bot begins to do a literal robot dance. People behind us comment in astonishment.

"Chang, are you out of your god damned mind?"

The side door opens and the supervisor exits, ushering the previous couple inside the stadium with an apology. She sees the dancing robot and comes over.

"What the hell's going on here?"

"Good question, Ma'am. The robot checked our passes, then started dancing," I say, unable to think of any other credible explanation.

The supervisor goes over to the machine and taps some buttons. The robot freezes. It repeats in a monotonous voice, *system error*.

"Typical, it always has to be one of *my* stalls. Can I see your passes again, folks? Yup, all fine, in you go. I'll get this hunk of metal switched out," she grumbles.

The supervisor taps on the robot's control panel some more.

System resetting. Replacement unit inbound. Returning to maintenance dock.

Chang's robot glides out of its frozen dance posture and marches off into the stadium, out of sight. Whatever he did to their computer must have worked, because the supervisor's not seeing any mismatch between our actual faces and the robot's scan.

I'm about to usher Malo inside when the supervisor raises her hand.

"One second fellas. No augmentations, sorry."

She's pointing at Malo's chin, which is exposed. The flag scarf has slipped ever so slightly, revealing the two aquifiers covering his gills.

The supervisor holds out a security bucket expectantly. "Robot should've picked it up, useless thing."

"I'll get them," I say quickly.

I step in front of Malo and remove the devices, tossing

them into the security bucket like they're toys, so the supervisor doesn't get too interested. In the same motion, I hastily fluff Malo's flag-scarf up, covering his gills.

"There we go, a patriot through and through!" I declare, patting him on the back heartily. Is that over-doing it? It's hard to know where to draw the line at these events.

In the wide stadium corridor beyond, I can see the replacement robot wheeling towards our station.

"Time to go cheer our man!" I say.

I grab Malo and drag him inside, letting the busy line behind us distract the supervisor. I hold my breath as the new robot approaches, but it passes without incident. Our digital masks are working. So long as we don't get interrogated by any more human-robot combinations, we should be in the clear.

"What happened to Chang?" says Malo.

I'm thinking the same thing, as I cast my eyes around the teeming stadium.

"Forget him, the President's due any minute. You'd better be ready for this."

Malo presses a hand to his gills and winces.

"Ready as I'll ever be."

CHAPTER FORTY-ONE

KEALA

We're parked up at a power station, halfway through a five-minute sprint charge. Winona's in the back of the van, selecting bottles to smuggle into the stadium later. My current water-cooler breathing tank has the disadvantage of being the size and weight of a small child. Not ideal for smuggling.

I'm still getting used to the new device fitted over my gills. I thought breathing was my biggest problem, but it looks like temperature regulation is a close second. Winona's bought a bag of ice from the station store and dumped it in my tank, which is helping, but I'm not sure how we'll replicate all this in the stadium.

A car pulls up beside us and a middle-aged couple get out, arguing.

"I was only speeding because *you* told me to put my foot on it," protests the man.

"I didn't say 'go so fast you drain our battery and get us a ticket'," snaps the woman.

"Maybe you should have been clearer."

"Me? This whole thing is on you."

"How so?"

"Last I checked, the Head of Bio Security is supposed to *stop* a facility from being infiltrated, hacked, and purged."

"I told you six months ago we needed to update the mainframe!"

"And I told *you* we couldn't get the extra funding until *your* department produced a working prototype!"

The man says nothing. His face sours and he marches around to the battery cap. He's got a bulbous nose and a small crown of gray hair encircling his otherwise bald brown head. The woman paces, rubbing her fingers anxiously. She's got thick white hair, snow-pale skin, and dark red lips.

A few seconds pass, then their argument erupts again. Winona leans back into the cockpit, drawing my attention away from the feud.

"I'm going to try switching your respirator to a lower exchange rate. It should save power, and make it a little quieter, but it might feel different. If it's uncomfortable, let me know and we'll change it back, OK?"

She gives my shoulder a squeeze then disappears into the back. There's some tinkering, and I feel a change in the water pressure. I test it with a few deep gasps, prompting Winona to rush back.

"Are you OK?" she says, concerned.

"All good, just testing if I could run with this thing. I reckon so."

As I finish the sentence, I realize I'm panting for real. The reduced diffusion rate has left me short of breath. I inhale slowly and carefully several times to regain the balance.

Note to self: you can probably run about five yards.

There's a rap against the window.

The man from the adjacent charging station is leaning close to the glass. He has a cold, exhausted expression. He gestures for me to lower the window. In the background, the battery cap on his car is open, but the power cord has been abandoned, lying idly beside it.

Winona flicks a switch and my window slides down.

"Can we help you, Sir?" she says, in a tone that makes it clear we're not looking for new friends.

He glances at our navigation display. "You two going to the rally?"

Winona flicks the display off and glares at him, demandingly.

"Forgive the intrusion, Ma'am," he continues, "but I couldn't help but notice you were attending to a breathing apparatus on your passenger's neck. I work in biomedicine myself, but I've not seen this sort of set up before. May I take a look?"

He forces a twisted, simpering smile.

"No, we're good," says Winona.

She flicks the window button up, but the man slams his hands down across the rim, triggering the safety stop.

"Please, I'm just curious. I'm not going to steal your patent, if that's what you're worried about. I'm guessing you designed it?"

Winona stares at him, coldly. "Kindly remove your hands from my car."

The white-haired woman walks over and joins the man in peering in at me. She whispers something into his ear. Her eyes are sharp, and eager. The man tries to maintain a thin air of casualness.

"Tubes are clear, so it's not dialysis. Must be doing some sort of fluid or gaseous exchange. From the bubbling sound,

I'd say someone's scuba diving. But that's impossible, we're on dry land," he chuckles.

His laugh is forced and jarring.

"I won't ask again. Let go of my car, or I'm calling the cops," says Winona.

His smile vanishes and he glares at her. Without warning, he lunges for my neck. I jolt backwards with a cry. Winona leaps out of the car and yells for help. The man's hands are clawing at my shoulder, reaching for the suction cups. I'm batting him away, but my breathing rate has spiked. I'm exceeding the device's capacity. Suddenly I'm dizzy and growing weaker. All I can do is lean away.

Winona rushes past the front of the car and barges against the man. He clings onto my arm painfully. Winona grabs him from behind, but the woman grabs her. All three are locked in a struggle. A drone appears, projecting a hologram. It's a representative from the security firm remotely managing the site. "Hey! Pack it in, all of you, or I'm calling the cops!"

With a grunt the man throws himself back at me. His stomach is balanced over the window sill and he's clawing at me viciously. I try to raise a foot but my legs are stuck. Suddenly his aim shifts. He abandons my jaw, and thrusts my sleeve upwards.

His eyes lock on my upper arm, and an expression of certainty, dread, and urgency sweeps across his face.

"This is your final warning!" yells the hovering security guard.

The white-haired woman pulls rank, forcing the man attacking me to relinquish his grip. Winona shoves him away and hurries around the van. She yanks the power cable out and jumps into the driver's seat. We speed away from the station and back onto the freeway. In the wing mirror, I see the man and woman erupt in another explosive argument, as they realize their vehicle hasn't been charging, and they're unable to chase after us, while the security hologram hovers above them, trying to interrogate the pair.

"Any idea who they were?" says Winona, breathlessly.

"No. But they know something."

"What?"

"About me."

"Are you sure? The guy seemed interested in the mask. He didn't see your gills, did he?"

"No, but he saw the scar from my injection. It's like he recognized it. He knew exactly where to look. Winona, I think those people are part of whatever group did this to me. And they know where we're going."

CHAPTER FORTY-TWO

LUKE

As a kid, I always wanted to get courtside tickets for a basketball game. There's something about being that close to the scuffling shoes, the jostling bodies, the full roar of the crowd behind you. It feels good finally being here.

Oh wait, no it doesn't. I'm not about to see the Legends play, I'm about to whoop and cheer for the most self-serving man in the history of the Northern Bloc. And there has been some *stiff* competition for that particular accolade.

This is our last throw of the die. Either we take down the world's most powerful man, or we fail permanently. Scenario A: Malo's taken back to the lab and I'm jailed for life. Scenario B: we're both thrown in the lab, enabling them to perfect their gene editing on us, which they force upon millions of the world's poorest, most invisible citizens. God damn, that loan shark was right; life is just two bad oranges.

The furry stingray mascot takes to the stage and does some oddly sexualized dance moves, sending the audience wild.

"How you doing, kid?"

"I told you to stop calling me that."

"Sorry, chief."

"I'm not chief yet."

"What should I call you then?"

"Malo."

"Can I shorten it to 'Mal'?"

"No."

"Gotcha. So how you doing, M-Dawg?"

His mouth twitches, irked, but he keeps his eyes locked ahead, scanning the stadium, as if the President might be hiding in the crowd.

"I'm fine. Stop asking."

"I mean how's your breathing?"

"Better."

"Without the device?"

"It seems so. Maybe my body's acclimatizing to land again. When I was being held in that mist box, the moisture in the air kept my gills open and suppressed my lungs. I think they were stress testing me, studying how my body handles environmental transitions."

"So it's lucky they confiscated the aquifiers?"

"It's good for my lungs, but bad for us. My gills are easy to miss when they're closed."

"Will they show up on the cameras? Malo, people need to see them open, that's the whole point of getting you next to the President!"

"I know! I'm working on it."

He unscrews a water bottle and douses it across his flag-scarf.

"If I keep them hydrated, I should be able to flex them. I'll have to hold my breath to do it."

"Mmm, sounds sustainable."

"If I can't do both, you'll have to do the talking for me."

"You don't say."

An announcement comes over the stadium Tannoy.

Ladies, Gentlemen, Enbees, we apologize for the delay but the President is running late. He's having a busy morning making your country work for you.

There's a cheer from the crowd. Malo and I are conspicuously the only ones *not* waving our flags like crazy. A delay is bad news. The longer we're here, the greater the chance we'll get busted.

Chang's lingering near our seats, in his robotic guise. Having an extra set of eyes and a hunk of bullet-proof metal is a welcome boost.

"Chang, how long are these caps good for?"

I say another six months – then this jackass get kicked out of office.

"No, I mean the digital masks. What's the life of the batteries you put *inside* the caps?"

Another thirty minutes?

"Are you kidding me? That's it?"

For longer you would having to wear top hat for carrying battery.

"Any sign of the scientists?"

Chang scans the crowd behind us, covering the part of the stadium hidden from us.

No. But their lab is cutting edge. They will using something more sophisticated than hat masks. Stadium system won't detect them entering. There is chance I won't detecting them either in this thing.

"So you're saying you can't see them, but that doesn't mean they're not here?"

No. I not using so many double negatives.

"I only used one."

My point stand.

Chang's robot waves some people to their seats. He knows he can't risk being reported as malfunctioning again - they would manually deactivate his unit, and it would raise all kinds of security concerns. The last thing we wanna do is spook the President's staff ahead of time. So Chang's gotta keep a low profile and play the part, for now.

A woman approaches his robot.

"Excuse me, my friend needs a wheelchair. Can you bring us one please?"

Chang looks at me for a second. I give him a nod. The woman gives me a wary look, clearly picking up on my pseudo-authority over her robot. She sets off into the tunnels, with Chang in tow. I turn my attention to Malo, who's dousing his flag with water again.

"According to the passes Chang got us, we get to ask a question after his speech. Perk of courtside, I guess."

"When?"

"These kinda speeches usually last a half hour, then they rotate through the folk with question tickets. No idea where we come in the ballot but it could be an hour."

"I can't wait that long. We'll have to interrupt him."

"We'll get throw out. Or taken down. Both, probably."

"Then Chang will have to fix that."

"He can't do everything, Malo, he's just some kid. And for once I mean that literally."

I keep forgetting that about Chang. Every time I remember who my fate's resting on, I feel my life expectancy shrink.

"Figure something out together," insists Malo. "I will find the words and show my mutations, but you two have to create the space. If you can't do that, then I don't know why you're here."

I consider telling him about my childhood basketball dreams, but decide it can wait.

"All right, I'll talk to Chang when he returns."

Malo doesn't respond. He's sitting bolt upright, staring at the tunnel opposite. His mouth slackens. I follow his gaze. Three figures are meeting in the shadows. One of them is closer to the court, her sleek bronzed back catches the stadium lights. The silhouetted figures behind her look familiar somehow.

They step into the light. A sickening feeling spreads across my stomach. I know that trim white hair and those hawkish features. The director is here. Pierre is beside her. They're beckoning the young woman into the tunnel. She glances back at the stadium; her face is stunning but fraught with worry.

Pierre clamps his hand over the young woman's mouth and all three vanish into the shadows.

Malo jumps to his feet.

"Keala!"

I try to stop him but he's gone, sprinting like a rocket towards the darkened tunnel.

CHAPTER FORTY-THREE

KEALA

I'm sweltering, sitting against an interior wall of the stadium, trying to breathe. I need to look about a hundred times healthier than I am. The last thing I want is a stranger or steward stopping to check I'm all right.

We had to dissemble Winona's reverse-scuba device before security, to smuggle the parts in. But relying on my lungs has weakened me. The bottles got emptied too, but we expected that. Winona quickly found more iced water, and we reassembled the device in a toilet cubicle. But when it came time for us to move on, I could barely stand. We made it into the hall before my legs gave way completely.

Winona lowered me into my current position and folded my legs so it looks like a deliberate posture. She told me to stay put and focus on regulating my breathing, then ran off.

The iced, oxygen-rich water flowing into my gills is revitalizing me, lowering my temperature. My eyes are still blurry, but they're starting to clear.

My ears twitch. I could've sworn I heard someone call my name. I listen keenly, but there's no repeat, just the wash of tens of thousands of chattering supporters. As crowds sweep through the bustling corridor, my loneliness hits me. I'm so far from everyone I've ever known. We had our differences, but they're still my people and I miss them bitterly. If this plan fails, I'll never see them again. Even if it works, they could be dead by the time we reach them.

Winona returns and I feel a pang of relief. Part of me feared she might have abandoned me as a lost cause. She wouldn't be the first.

She has a robot with her, which is pushing a wheel chair.

"Apparently they don't have any motorized ones here, which I find *crazy*," she says, glaring at the bot.

Ma'am.

Winona looks at it, unimpressed. "Are you gonna stand there or help her up? God damn, who programmed you?"

This unit is operated by West Coast Networks.

"Mm-hmm? Well I'll have some feedback for them when this is done."

The robot kneels down to scoop me up, then hesitates, like it's afraid.

"Never touched a woman before?" snaps Winona.

It jerks upright, looks from me to Winona, then marches away into the stadium.

"I think you offended it," I say.

"Nonsense, they're programmed not to have feelings. That one's just a li'l glitchy. Here we go."

She heaves me into the wheelchair, gasping as something in her back twinges. Guilt overcomes me; I've brought nothing but difficulty to this poor woman's life. She's doing all she can to help me, for something that's not even her fault, and all I'm doing is costing her money and risking her future.

"I'm so sorry," I say, squeezing her arm.

"Are you kidding me? You just got us front row seats."

Winona points to the *Priority Access* tag hanging from the arm of my new chair.

I've never been inside a stadium before, only seen them online. It's something else to experience it in person. The stands look impossibly steep. The people in the top rows are so far away they're mere specks in the crowd. The whole place is teeming like an ant colony.

Winona steers towards the left-hand courtside seats. There's space for my chair on the edge of the row, but nowhere for her to go. She parks my chair, then politely approaches the man next to me. I'm too distracted by the stadium to notice him, and now her body's shielding him from my line of sight.

"Excuse me, Sir, do you mind moving up into the empty seat beside you? I need to sit by my friend, she's in a wheelchair."

I don't hear his exact reply, but it's curt. He leaps out of his seat and sprints across the court to the dark tunnel opposite. Winona gives me a shrug and takes his place.

There's a flurry of activity on stage and the crowd erupts with cheers. The Tannoy and holographic MC thunder into action. *Good people of the Northern Bloc, give it up for your elected champ, President Blowhard!*

There he is. The most powerful man in the world. And I'm about to try and take him down with nothing but words, a wheelchair, and a failing, mutated body.

Mom, Dad, this is for you.

CHAPTER FORTY-FOUR

LUKE

Malo's across the court and into the tunnel in seconds. If I yell his name, I'm giving away our position. But you could argue he's kinda already done that by running right at the people trying to kill us.

"Excuse me, Sir, do you mind moving up?"

Some woman's appeared beside me, up close in my face. She says something else about a wheelchair. She's smiling, but with one of those intense, threatening, liberal smiles that tells you "say yes right now or I'll publish fifty reasons why you're a racist, homophobic bigot."

I enjoy a good wrestle in the echo chamber as much as the next bleeding heart, but she's a distraction I can't afford. The whole plan's on a knife edge. Either I charge after Malo and get my ass handed to me by Jekyll and Hyde in that tunnel, or I stay here, keep a low profile, and hope he comes back.

Though if he doesn't, then I've got nothing to challenge the President with.

God dammit. I gotta go after him.

To be clear, I do all this thinking in a split second. I'm a very quick thinker.

I sprint for the tunnel opposite, dodging the dancing stingray as I go. The crowd lets out an *oooh* as they enjoy the near-miss. Out of the corner of my eye, I see a security robot twist its head.

Crap.

It's got a lock on me.

I hurry through the archway. The whole area's deserted. My eyes adjust to the darkness.

"Malo?" I call out.

I turn and there he is, lying on the ground. The hot girl is standing over him, with her back to me. I run towards the pair of them. I reach out to touch her shoulder but my hand passes right through.

Something sharp strikes my neck. I spin around and two smug figures step forward from the shadows. The director taps a device in her palm, and the young woman's hologram vanishes.

"Ugh, so the hot one's fake, and I'm stuck with you two mugs?"

My words are slurred, like I'm drunk. Something's bitten me like a tic. I try to pluck it off but my fingers are numb. A similar implant is sticking to the side of Malo's neck. He's not moving. His sunglasses lie broken beside him. If anyone were to see his face now, they'd doubtless recognize him from the news.

"Is he...?"

"He's alive. For now," says the director.

"The girl... How...?"

"Yes, it was quite a conundrum for us. The subject beside you doesn't have an AR implant, so we had to use a prototype hologram. It had the advantage of hooking you in too. It's nice to finally receive something from our defense contacts that isn't *entirely* useless, don't you agree?"

I'm swaying like I'm on a roller coaster.

The crowd cheers in the stands above us. A speaker is announcing the President's arrival.

The director edges closer to me, with an insidious smile across her face.

"What you gonna do, boss, stick me in a tank with him?" I slur.

She laughs, once. "That ship's sailed. You're not worth the effort anymore."

Pierre's marching towards me. He's got a syringe.

I try to call for help, but my voice fades into nothing against the crowd.

Pierre lunges forwards.

I leap out of the way and stumble backwards. My vision is blurring. The director watches with her arms folded. "Make it quick, Pierre," she snaps.

He takes another run at me. I kick out sharply and miraculously strike his hip. But the impact throws me off-balance. I crash to the ground beside Malo and Pierre throws himself upon me. He raises the syringe high above my chest. My arms are like lead; I try to resist but my strength is gone.

He cries triumphantly and plunges the syringe down, then snaps rigid. He's frozen, staring at me with bulging eyes. The needle hovers inches from my sternum. His muscles are quivering. Pierre's face is contorted in rage, and saliva is trickling from his paralyzed mouth.

A robotic foot rises out of the shadows and boots him against the wall.

Miss me?

I'm too weak to reply. Chang senses this and scans my body.

Oh dayyyuum, they hit you with anesthetic insect drone. Those things super illegal, I trying get one for years. Would you recommend them? Be honest. As a friend. I don't want throw money down drain if they no good.

I stare at him incredulously, blinking hard just to keep him semi-focused.

I take that as "yes". Awesome.

He trains a palm at me and recoils like he's fired an invisible bullet. The pinching in my neck disappears and the tic-bot falls onto the concrete like a shell casing. I feel myself coming round quickly.

Localized EMP. Man, these security bots are biz. Now I torn. Should I getting one of these for office instead of flying insect drone?

"Chang, can you focus for a minute? Help Malo!"

Oh yeah.

He targets Malo's tic with an EMP. As soon as it's disabled, Malo leaps up swinging his fists wildly.

"Woah, Malo, take it easy! You're safe!"

His gills are wide open - a lingering side-effect of the tic. Malo settles down as he sees Pierre's crumpled figure.

"Is he dead?"

"Pretty sure. Humans tend not to fare so well when they're tossed against concrete. The concrete usually wins."

"What about her?" says Malo.

My eyes move to the director who's standing rigid, staring at us. There's a device flashing on her shoulder, presumably from whatever Chang fired to paralyze her.

I kick her too? says Chang.

"I've got a better idea," I say.

I grab Pierre's discarded syringe and approach the

director. She's rigid like a statue, but quivering; her muscles are pooling with adrenaline and trying to fight the paralysis. I manipulate her digits until she's gripping the syringe firmly. I move her hand in front of her abdomen so that the needle is inches from her skin. I place her thumb over the plunger. I put her other hand on top.

I step back with Malo and we regard her for a final time. Her eyes are frozen, stuck on the spot Pierre had pinned me.

I give Chang a nod. He deactivates the paralysis.

The director's muscles jerk hard as they expend all the pent up energy. She gasps as she plunges the syringe into her own flesh, and squeezes the trigger, all in a single, split-second motion.

Her eyes move down to the needle embedded in her. She looks at her hands in astonishment, then at me, then collapses.

A voice thunders through the stadium. The President's delivering his manifesto of rousing lies, and it's being met with rapturous applause. I grab Malo's shoulder.

"You have to do this now. This whole rally will be shut down as soon as security find these bodies. It's now or never."

If you want get on stage, President security will take you down. I will over-ride robots and using them against human staff. But not from here. Which is shame, cos this thing rocks. When you hearing tone on Tannoy, that mean all clear. You get thirty seconds so do something awesome. Malo, I will putting sonic spotlight on you, for amplify your voice. Good luck.

Before we can discuss anything he says, Chang's robot powers down.

I snatch Malo's baseball cap from his head, so that his

true face can be read by the world's cameras, which are waiting just yards away.

"You got this, Malo. I'm right behind you."

He nods and clenches his jaw.

A tone sounds across the stadium.

The President stops speaking for a moment, baffled at the interruption. As the leader stalls, Malo strides out into the central court with his arms raised.

"Mr. President, we need to talk!" he yells.

Chang switches the stadium's camera onto Malo's face, projecting him on the massive screens. A gasp of recognition sweeps the auditorium. This is the same face that's been dominating the news for the past twenty-four hours. The face they were told is a "deep fake". It's here, and it's real.

The President's human guards are racing towards Malo, but the stadium bots intervene, seizing them, and clearing a path. The crowd watches in disbelief as Malo continues his advance.

"Do you recognize me, Mr. President? We've never met, but you know my face. You told the world the mutations across my neck weren't real. That I was a hoax. Then what do you call these?"

Malo tilts his neck and points to the open gills under his jaw. The President tries to speak, but his microphone's been muted. Malo continues, his voice growing bolder and angrier.

"I call them the truth. Are you ready to tell the truth, Mr. President? About what your government has done to my people? How you experimented on us? How you condemned us to drown, then released fake footage of a safe arrival to cover up your crimes? It's time for justice! It is time for-"

I hear movement behind me. I turn but it's too late.

The director's taking aim.

I don't know how she got the gun past security, or how she's still alive, but I have to stop her.

I fling myself towards her with a cry.

She squeezes the trigger.

The bullet tears through my chest.

The impact twists me as I fall.

I hit the ground, spluttering.

Malo is staring at me in horror.

Screams around the stadium.

Bang.

A second gunshot rings out.

Malo is down.

CHAPTER FORTY-FIVE

KEALA

I'm gasping and overheating as I wait for the President's speech to end. My gills are making a gross slurping sound as my bottles run dry. A voice of fear is growing louder in my head; I'm not going to make it.

Our tickets entitle us to ask a question of the president after the speech, but I can already feel my body shutting down. If I pass out before the cameras get to me, I'll miss my chance forever. I have to interrupt him. He's surrounded by bots and security personnel. I don't know how I'm going to pull it off, but I've got to try.

I flick the brakes off my wheelchair and prepare to launch myself forwards, but as I move someone rushes out of the tunnels opposite. I can't believe what I'm seeing; Malo is here.

His voice and his body are magnified on the holographic Tannoy; it's like he's filling the whole stadium. A hush of awe sweeps the stands as he approaches the stage.

The president's ordering his personnel to detain the intruder, but a fleet of robot guards is restraining them.

People watch with bated breath, astonished at what they're seeing.

"Do you recognize me, Mr. President?" cries Malo.

Rage flows from his voice. I recognize the anguish in his face and the determination in his strides. My heart soars. He's here. He's really here.

A gunshot rings out.

I flinch and the crowd is screaming.

A second gunshot.

I peer through my arms but I can't process what I'm seeing. This can't be happening, not after all we've been through. I scream Malo's name but it's lost in the noise. People are fleeing the stands. Trampling over each other in their panicked frenzy to escape. The security robots have relinquished the President's staff and are sprinting into the tunnel after the shooter. The President is being bundled off stage by his flustered team, surrounded by a metal wall of other bots hurrying him to safety.

Malo lies there, forgotten, motionless, bleeding.

I leap from my wheelchair, ripping out the cables from my water tanks. Tearing the respirator from my jaw, I run to him. Winona calls after me, imploring me to hide.

I fall by Malo's side and take him in my arms. I'm clinging to his body, weeping, begging him to open his eyes as his blood seeps into my clothes. It's spreading across the polished wooden floor around us. A cloud of reporter drones hovers above, ghoulishly filming every detail.

I press his head to my chest and call his name over and over. My lungs are failing as oxygen drains from me. My voice is growing hoarse and weak, and the world is fading. I clutch him in my arms and croak three final words I wish I'd said years ago.

"I love you."

With no air left to expend, my voice fails.
I fall on him, suffocating.
I can no longer move.
I can no longer see.
The last thing I hear is the screaming crowd, and the flurry of drones.

CHAPTER FORTY-SIX

KEALA

A heart rate monitor bleeps, accompanied by a rhythmic gurgling. As my crusty eyelids open I realize I'm wearing a hospital gown, but everything's blurry.

There's a familiar voice behind me, perhaps coming from a corridor. He's angry, yelling at someone.

"Her organs ain't worth jack. Besides, y'all got no proof!"

It hits me like a bolt. The man from the scrap yard is here. With a sickening feeling, I realize what's happening. I try to jump from the bed but I'm tethered by a mass of drip lines. The machine bleeps as my heart rate spikes, prompting a robotic nurse to glide into the room.

Do you require assistance?

There's a syringe protruding from the end of its wrist. I scream and throw a meal tray at the machine. I'm tugging desperately at my gills, trying to prize off the diffuser that's shackling me to this bed. But my fingers are clumsy and tingling, I can't work the straps.

A woman rushes into the room. "Woah, Keala, take it easy!"

Patient is hostile. Requesting authorization to sedate.

"Back off, robot, she's just confused. Hey, someone cut the TV out there!"

The scrap yard man's voice gets quieter in the background. At the same time, the newcomer is barging past the robot to reach me, repeating my name in a soothing voice. Reaching my bedside, she strokes my hand. I flinch; her skin feels crazy warm.

"Keala, it's me, Winona. Do you remember me?"

"I... I recognize your voice... but there's something wrong with my eyes... I can't see."

The opaque blur of color I'm seeing isn't temporary; I'm broken.

"Deep breaths, calm yourself. The doctors said this could happen."

"Where am I?"

"You're in hospital. Shhh, it's OK, you're safe now, truly. We did it, Keala, we took down the President. They got your organ harvest guy too, based on everything you told me. They're doing a feature on the stadium now. Listen,"

The UN Secretary General has been forced to resign, along with several other heads of state. There's a clip of the former vice president - now acting president - who is announcing that her predecessor will face legal charges over the "Pacific scandal", as it's being called. My last memories of consciousness flood back to me.

The stadium. The shootings. Malo!

"Where is he?"

"Shhh, you need to rest."

"Tell me where Malo is or I'll find him myself."

"It's not a good idea for you to see him, not now. Please, Keala, you're still recovering-"

I swing my legs off the foam mattress, onto the floor. Clutching the rail for stability, I feel my way ahead. There's a frame of light before me, which I'm guessing is the door. As I step forward my legs collapse. Winona catches me and rests me against the bed.

"You've been out for two days solid. Give your body a beat to catch up. Can we get an ophthalmologist in here?"

The robot acknowledges the request. Moments later the doctor arrives. She shines a light into my lenses and asks me to discern various objects in the room.

"Your vision is severely impaired. I'm afraid this is consistent with our predictions."

"Your predictions?"

"We undertook a complete scan of your body while you were comatose. We had to understand your, ah, *unique* physiology so we could treat you properly. You have your friend here to thank for the breathing apparatus you're on now. She's been refining the design since you were admitted. If it wasn't for her, you'd undoubtedly have asphyxiated. For the record, I'm glad that didn't happen. Your people have been through enough already. We're proud to have you here, and to be doing our small part to begin making amends."

"Can you make me see again?"

"Let's find out. Try this. Design credit again goes to Winona."

The woman fits a pair of goggles over my head.

"Press the buttons at the side."

I do as she instructs. To my surprise, fluid fills the goggles, submerging my eyes.

"They're wet!"

"How does it feel?"

"It feels… good. Better, actually. Way better."

The itching sensation eases as the room comes into focus.

"What is it?" I ask.

"Brine, mostly."

"Sea water? Why doesn't it sting?"

The doctor shuffles. I can see the awkwardness in her face now.

"We believe your body is still adapting for a marine environment. You may find, while you're on land, your balance and hearing are impaired, along with temperature regulation. Though the latter is being managed by the respirator."

"Back up, you said *while* I'm on land? What does that mean?"

"Until better treatment is available, we think your body needs to be underwater. I've got some people figuring out accommodation options. Right now we're thinking a pool, but we'll need to switch the chlorinated water for brine before we can move you."

Anger swells inside me. "You wanna keep me in a pool like I'm someone's pet?"

"Nothing like that, Ma'am. We're trying to do what we think is in your best health interests. You are of course free to make your own decisions."

"Good. Then I choose to see Malo. *Now*."

His eyes are closed. There are more tubes going into his body than I can count. In the center of his chest is a huge wound dressing. His vital signs flicker on a dashboard. I'm looking for the familiar double-crested spike of his heart rate but it's nowhere to be seen.

"Why... why doesn't he have a pulse?"

"Keala, he lost a lot of blood," says the attending physician.

"Is he dead?"

"He's in a coma."

"But his heart's not beating?"

"The bullet tore both of his atrial chambers, the damage was irreparable. We had to fit him with an artificial heart. It works like a turbine, rather than a compression pump, so instead of having a pulse, he has a continuous circulation of pressurized blood. In some ways it's better."

"Then why isn't he awake?"

"Your friend's physiology-"

"He's not my 'friend!'"

"Sorry, I thought-"

"He's my... we're close."

"I understand. Malo's in a different state to you. We believe he's experiencing a reversal of the mutation process. While you've both got new organs, his have shrunk and seem to be defunct. It's like his body is rejecting the genetic alterations and reverting to a baseline."

"Will he survive the change?"

"We don't know. We induced a coma for the surgery but we've not been able to revive him. This is a long way from what we usually deal with at this hospital, Ma'am. To be honest, anything beyond keeping him stable would be classified as an experimental procedure, given what limited information we have about the genetic engineering you and he underwent. The NSA raided the lab your, uh, *companion* was held in, after his intervention at the rally. We've requested access to their findings, but it's complicated. Given what's happened, the last thing they want now is a bioengineering dossier leaking online. From what little they *have* shared, it seems the lab themselves didn't fully understand the treatment. I'm doubtful reversal is something they'd even considered, which makes what's happening to his body all the more remarkable. I find it deeply curious the exact opposite is happening to you. Sorry, that was crass. I simply meant... Uh... perhaps I should give you two a moment alone."

The doctor leaves. Winona gives my shoulder a squeeze then steps out too. I nudge my wheelchair closer to Malo's bed and take his hand in mine. I press my cheek to his limp palm and squeeze with the ferocity of a full body embrace.

Nothing. Tears spill from my eyes, leaking into my fluid-filled goggles. This powerful, proud soul, dismantled. He led us with conviction, convincing us he was naturally brave while battling fear in private. If only I'd been the one to confront the President, instead of waiting in line like a fool, maybe Malo would be OK.

I weep, as the guilt and exhaustion of the past week engulfs me. I feel Winona's arms around me. I didn't ask her to come back in, but I'm glad she did. Not that I have the strength to acknowledge it. It's all I can do to bawl against Malo's static body.

Winona's watch jingles. The details hover above her wrist.

INCOMING CALL - JEN @ SEA SPRINT.

Winona dismisses it. "I'll talk to her later, sorry about that."

Her watch rings again.

"Take it, I'm fine. Really," I croak.

I gently push her away. She hurries out of the room, leaving me alone with Malo's body. I clutch his hand, serenaded by the gurgling respirator under my wheelchair, and occasional bleeps from his dashboard.

The door slides open and Winona bursts in. Her face is lit up.

"They found them! The satellite searchers! They've found the atoll you described! There's activity on the shore. There are still people alive down there."

My head's spinning. "How many?"

"They're not sure, because the community's moving between the land and the water, but it's at least a dozen survivors. And there's more - they think they've found where the other rafts sank."

"How many?"

"Eleven wreckages so far and they're expecting more."

"Any survivors?"

"They're sending dive drones to explore. All the sites are submerged but some look shallow enough to be in the temperate zone. If those passengers have adapted like you, they might be alive."

"What if they're like Malo?"

Winona's face falters. "Hopefully the search teams will reach them soon."

"But Jen said it was too dangerous for ships to-"

"The cyclone threat has passed. Our government's scrambling a fleet to rescue the survivors now. The Southern Bloc are sending aid too."

I stare at the floor. The world has finally seen us. I thought I'd feel relief, but I'm conflicted; I don't know how to process what I'm hearing. On the one hand, countless survivors may now be saved. But on the other hand, the discovery of more sunken rafts means so many have already perished.

Our nation was tens of thousands of souls. In

desperation and under false promises, we abandoned our homes, taking to the oceans in hundreds of rafts. These watery tombs were built by rich nations, secretly intended to seal us in as we mutated like lab rats. How many of my people have survived this betrayal, and in what form, I can't bear to contemplate.

"Whatever happens next, things will only get better, I promise," soothes Winona. "Without you, all would be lost. But you did it, Keala, you saved your people."

I nod, too upset to meet her kindly gaze. But the invisible vice around my chest is easing. The burden of an entire nation is no longer mine to bear; the baton has been passed onto the rescue fleets sailing to my people.

As Winona's words sink in, relief swells inside me. After risking everything to cross thousands of miles of ocean, enduring unimaginable fear and pain, the world finally knows our truth.

Our islands may be submerged, our people forced into the sea, but we are no longer invisible. We will be reunited, we will adapt, and we will survive. I feel an irrepressible sense of something I've not dared to entertain in years. I have hope.

My attention returns to the hospital room, where I focus on the one precious life hanging in the balance before me. I hold Malo's hand, running my thumb over his fingers and pressing my head against his body.

"Stay strong, chief-in-waiting," I whisper. "We did it."

Malo's hand twitches in mine, snapping me out of my ruminations. It twitches again; it wasn't my imagination!

I jolt up, squeezing his palm tighter, "Malo?" I gasp.

His eyelids flutter.

"Keala?"

CHAPTER FORTY-SEVEN

LUKE

I know, I know, I should've checked in with you sooner. In my defense, I did just get shot. I mean, I *literally* took a bullet for a guy. Plus, I've been busy getting through packs of chocolate cereal for dinner.

Journalist of the year? I think we can all agree so. I'd say I'm looking forward to collecting my award, but I'm kinda stuck in bed right now. Doctor's orders. I'm to stay put, watch TV, and do nothing strenuous for at least two weeks.

Fine. By. Me.

I'm *due* a holiday, you know? Months undercover, living off scraps, fighting for the underdog in an unrelenting search for the truth. I think I deserve a little "me" time.

You can use that on my epitaph, by the way. Which won't be needed for many, many years, because as of this moment, I am a man of leisure. My life of jeopardy is a thing of the past.

Hang on a sec, I got a video call coming in.

LANELLE - BOSS - PUT ON CLOTHES BEFORE ANSWERING

I like to use the "name" field in my address book to

remind me of key details. Really comes in handy when someone calls and the prefix "ex-" flashes up by their name.

I select the *voice only* option and pick up.

"Lanelle, thanks for the basket of fruit. It's very... healthy of you."

"A pleasure. I'm not saying all single men of your age eat like crap, but I heard a rumor that the more divorces you have, the less fruit you eat."

I toast her with my chocolate milkshake. "Vitamins are overrated. I'm all about the calcium."

"Luke, I've got another assignment for you."

"What part of 'I quit' didn't you hear?"

"Oh I heard it, I just know you better than to believe it."

"Well this time I'm serious. That whole lab thing was a nightmare. If I'd have known getting shot was so expensive, I wouldn't have done it. Have you *seen* my medical bills?"

"Yes. We're paying them. On that note, stop trying to claim for chocolate cereal. It's not a 'medical expense'."

"No. It's a human right."

A notification pops up on my inbox.

"Open it," says Lanelle.

"What am I looking at here? I see a rocket launching. So what?"

"Where's it going?"

"I dunno, the Moon, probably. So?"

"It's an undocumented launch. The second this week."

"Impossible. There are like a zillion satellites up there, they would've picked up a gigantic lump of metal blasting by."

"One of them did, but only just. A PhD student at an observational laboratory spotted the anomalies among the noise. They combed the data and found another launch three days prior. FYI these are passenger rockets, so whoever's managed to hide them from the rest of the world has some serious skill."

"OK, so it's obviously a military mission. Big deal?"

"The data says it's non-military. Come on, don't pretend you're not curious."

"Sure. I'm as curious as the next retiree."

"Cut the geriatric act. I want you on board the next launch."

At this point I inhale a spoonful of cereal down the wrong tube.

Much spluttering ensues.

"You're kidding, right? This is a big joke. Like, 'Luke just got shot in the line of duty, wouldn't it be funny if we blasted him into space?'"

"It's not a joke."

"You're aware I'm scared of heights?"

"You'll be in outer space. No heights, no problem."

"Never gonna happen."

"At least mull it over, will you?"

"I don't need to mull. It's a no. Never in a million years. I have zero desire to leave this mattress, let alone this planet."

"It'd be a hell of a way to follow up on the gene editing piece. Journalist of the year two years running? Would be pretty neat."

"You know what else would be neat? *Not* getting shot *ever* again. Hence, I. Am. Done. Thanking you kindly."

"It's the perfect moment, Luke. The whole world's distracted by the Pacific scandal because of your great work, and someone's taking the opportunity. Everyone's eyes are on the ocean, and they're launching an undeclared space fleet."

"Lanelle, for the last time, I'm out."

"Luke, I appreciate you've had a lot on your plate lately, but have you bothered to keep up with the news *at all* since you went undercover?"

"I read the sports section, does that count?"

"It counts neither as news nor as reading."

"In that case, no, no I have not."

"Clearly. Because if you *had* bothered, you would know that our government is due to sign a historic peace treaty with the Southern Bloc in a matter of days."

"Wait, for real? You're telling me the cold war's over? Holy crap, how *did* I miss that?"

"It's not over yet, and that's why this story matters," urges Lanelle. "The treaty rests on both sides agreeing a supply and demand deal for clean nuclear fusion power. The Northern Bloc is supposed to be providing all the fuel via its mining bases on the Moon."

"I'm sensing there's been a hitch in that plan?"

"The Lunar Inspector."

"What about her?"

"She's dead."

"Oof, that's gotta suck. How'd she go?"

"Natural causes, allegedly. But the timing's deeply suspicious. She died earlier this week, just two days after returning from her last inspection of the international lunar bases."

"That's crazy! Why isn't this front page news? Oh, wait, my bad. Continue."

"As soon as we get to the bottom of this, it will be. Since the inspector's 'natural' death, her unpublished report has mysteriously gone 'missing'."

"And you think it's linked to the unregistered lunar shuttles?"

"Something's going on, Luke, and I think whoever's

behind all this is using the peace treaty as a diversion for something bigger."

"Like what?"

"That's what I need you to find out. Come on, Remini, I *know* you're curious. Take the job – I'll even fly you up there first class."

"It's tempting, boss, I'll give you that, but I'll have to decline. Only because I hate literally everything you've described about the mission. Heights, murders, potential to accidentally trigger a nuclear war... no thanks. I am a retired gentleman now, Lanelle. I'm off the clock."

"Ugh, so much for that second journalism award. Enjoy squandering your golden years on chocolate milk and bad TV, Remini. Let me know if you change your mind."

"Don't hold your breath."

"Yah. *Bye.*"

"Oh, wait, Boss, can you order me some more cream soda?"

"I'd love to Luke, but expenses are for current employees only. Last I heard, you're retired?"

She hangs up.

Touché, Lanelle, touché. It's exactly that sort of fiscal prudence that kept our journal alive all these years. That, and our new douche bag owners.

I shouldn't complain too much. She's letting me crash in the safe house until I'm recovered. It's got a mini fridge and a huge TV. I take back everything I said before about it being sparsely furnished. They got the essentials. It's perfection.

My phone rings again.

UNKNOWN NUMBER.

Huh. Weird. I don't give this number out to anyone but my family and my boss.

"Hello?"

"Lukey boy, is Chang here. How your recovering?"

He's got that genial, older-than-his-years tone on.

"Sorry Chang, I'm about to go into a meeting."

My video flicks on - without me pressing any buttons. Chang appears, leaning into the camera, waggling his finger at the screen.

"Lying bring bad luck, Lukey."

"What do you want, Chang?"

"Pick up where we leave off."

"We left off with you disabling all the stadium's security robots, which resulted in me and Malo both getting shot by that psycho lab director."

"Hey let's not forget who save your ass few minutes before. Not my fault you not kill her properly. I did offer."

Damn. He did as well.

"I hate talk shop while you recovering, Lukey, but you still owing me colossal money."

"I think you getting me shot makes us even."

Chang laughs, heartily. "I would *love* if it working like that, I really would. But in my world, there are rules. If rules getting broken, then *people* getting broken. I loan you money. You not pay it back. If word get out that people can easy taking money from me with no consequences, it mean serious problem for Chang. No more business. I can't looking weak, you see?"

"Then why in hell's name did you go to all that effort to help me and Malo?"

"I told you, I from big family, many cousins in Pacific. I helping them and using you to doing it. Now it over, time you repaying me."

"I thought we bonded!"

"That's cute. I like that about you, Lukey. But I don't need washed up father figure in my life, I need money."

For the record, he clearly *does* need some sort of positive parental role model, but that's for another time.

"I'm broke, Chang."

"Then you better get un-broke quickly. Otherwise I sending my people for brokering *you*."

"I think that's technically an insurance term, but sure, I understand the gist."

"You got forty-eight hour, Luke. I being generous because you still recovering. Do not let me down again. It bad for my business, which mean it bad for you."

He hangs up.

I'm staring at my cereal, and suddenly I'm not feeling so chocolaty. Plus it's gone all mushy in the milk. Two days to get a colossal sum of money together, as a broke, unemployed, divorcee? I wouldn't bet on those odds. I tap my phone and dial one of a few numbers in the book.

"Lanelle, it's me again. When's the launch?"

FIND OUT WHAT HAPPENS
IN LUKE'S NEXT ADVENTURE:

PEOPLE OF DUST

OUT NOW

DEAR READER,

It's Marcus here. Thanks so much for reading this copy of *People of Water*, I truly hope it resonated with you. I'm an independent author, which means I publish all my work myself, and bear all the associated costs. The traditional publishing industry is incredibly tough for new authors to break into. After my first series *Convulsive* was rejected by fifty different agents, I realized that to achieve my dream of becoming a writer, I would have to strike out by myself. So I did.

It's terrifying, but I know I can do it; I have wonderful readers like you, who send me encouraging emails out of the blue which always brighten my day. It's my sincere hope that you may be kind enough to sponsor my next book by donating at marcusmartinauthor.com/support. On the next page you'll find out why, and what a massive impact your support will have.

It took five years to write and self-publish the *Convulsive* series alongside stressful day jobs, often working seven days a week. But within six months of completion, the series hit number one in the international Amazon bestseller charts for its genre. That was the single greatest moment of affirmation I could've wished for. I quite literally danced around the room with joy. It didn't come with a windfall of cash like you might think - book margins aren't big - but it was enough for me to finish recouping the editing costs and fund an audiobook version. In fact, since starting out, I've reinvested every cent I've ever earned from my books straight back into my writing - because I know it's the only way I'll grow.

It's still early days for me as a writer, which makes each new book a white knuckle ride. In 2020 I took a leap of faith and left my job to become a full-time author, knowing I would be living off savings and reinvesting any profits to make it work. In that year I gave it my all, and wrote four new books, one of which you've just finished.

I want to continue. My aim is to write four books a year, and keep bringing bold sci-fi ideas to readers like you. I know I can do it, but I'll be honest: there's still no guarantee it'll work out. Mainly because I don't get advances on book deals like conventional authors do.

I love creating new worlds, and I'm a damned hard worker. If you believe my writing deserves a future, and would like to see more books from me each year, I would be so hugely grateful if you would support me with a donation of your choosing. It only takes a moment, just visit **marcusmartinauthor.com/support**

With the support of readers like you, I can produce more groundbreaking sci-fi. I would be humbled to offer you an acknowledgement in one of my future books, and you will have my heartfelt thanks forever.

In gratitude - Marcus.

Cambridge, England, 2021

Convulsive

International #1 bestselling series

A pandemic like no other

Completed five-part epic.

Binge your way through the apocalypse.

Finality

Eerie. Familiar. Radical.

A metaphysical sci-fi novel

"We are unburdened. May we use it wisely."

Available now

Don't miss Marcus Martin's next book.

Join the email list for:

Free advanced copies.

Exclusive content.

Quarterly emails.

Zero spam.

marcusmartinauthor.com/email

*To all the brave souls committed to reversing climate change.
To those on the front line through no fault of their own. To
those taking a stand, to demand the change we need.
Together, we can do this.*

ACKNOWLEDGMENTS

People of Water was made possible by these noble champions.

To my gracious and insightful advanced reader team, thank you all for your encouragement and advice: Heather Binder-Pollard, Jess Donnithorne, Chris Powell, Pete Wills, Marie Thorpe, Chris Hutchings, and Martin White.

To my friends pushing for a better future for our planet and all life on it. Thank you for your dedication, kindness, and tenacity. Mike and Emily Dunning-Price, Issy Barber, Rob Taylor. Karina, James, Brad, Shawn, Gemma and the whole team at Thrive Cambridge. Emma, Johanna, Paul, and the team at Full Circle Cambridge. And to the countless others who are striving to make a positive impact on a local and global level. You have dreamed of a better future for our world, and are making it happen. Keep fighting the good fight, with open hearts and boundless energy. You inspire me, and you'll inspire others to take positive action.

To my whole family, from Scotland to Australia, you're

all legends, and with your humor, love, and encouragement, you have enriched my life more than you'll ever know.

ABOUT THE AUTHOR

Marcus Martin is a British author based in Cambridge, UK. He originally trained as a composer and classical pianist at King's College London & the Royal Academy of Music, before taking a meandering route into a Master's degree in the psychology of music at the University of Cambridge, followed by a postgraduate diploma in religion and politics.

Marcus has performed at the Edinburgh Fringe Festival a number of times as both a stand-up comedian and actor. After living and working in the US and Germany for six months he returned to Cambridge where he wrote and staged his first three plays, before embarking on a career in authorship.

He's worked as a barista, a decorator, a builder's assistant, a teaching assistant, a data entry clerk, a marketing executive, a compliance officer, a pianist, a choral assistant, a musical director, a script editor for BBC Radio 4, a voice actor, and a jingle writer, to name but a few.

Alongside books and voice acting, he's host of the cult sci-fi podcast *Make It Soon*, which brings scientists and comedians together to discuss iconic sci-fi inventions that are becoming a reality. Listen for free at makeitsoon.com

Marcus is currently working on a new book series, as well as several standalone novels. He loves receiving emails from readers, and replies to each one. You can reach him at: marcus@marcusmartinauthor.com

For a sneak peak of Marcus's upcoming releases, join the email list at: marcusmartinauthor.com/email

You can also follow him on social:
facebook.com/MarcusMartinAuthor
goodreads.com/author/show/17601586
bookbub.com/authors/marcus-martin